WHERE LOVE MEANS NOTHING

HOWARD GIMPLE

FIRST SET

1

Brigid Quinlan hoped that the guy she was about to interview wouldn't turn out to be just another douchebag, out to sell a book, a product, a philosophy, a candidate or some other bullshit thing. Russell Townsend was selling the end of the nuclear arms race, so maybe he wasn't a complete asshole. Kelleher thought he was okay, which was a point in his favor. The man was even more cynical than she was.

Townsend was the former assistant director of the U.S. Nuclear Command, turned outspoken anti-nuclear crusader. Tall and gangly, with a permanent 'aw shucks' expression and a nest of wavy black hair, the Harvard-educated physicist from Augusta, Kentucky, was charming, articulate and controversial; in short, the answer to journalists' prayers during a slow news season.

He had just climaxed a rousing speech to the United Nations' General Assembly that received a standing ovation. The ambassadors from North Korea, Iran, Russia and the United States were the only representatives who remained seated.

Brigid was standing in the courtyard of the United Nations.

Behind her was the 39-story chunk of marble, glass and aluminum that was the main U.N. building. What a waste of time, money and real estate, she thought. Like the Boy Scouts, Facebook and the Catholic Church, among hundreds of others, it began with noble intentions and wound up screwing the people it was created to help. The U.N.'s main purpose now was to stay relevant and profitable while wars raged, children starved and corruption ran rampant in many of the countries whose puffed-up delegates bloviated and pontificated in the building behind her.

She'd keep that opinion to herself. Speaking her mind on air is what got her fired from her job as midday anchor at WPIX when she said that she hoped that some gun-toting maniac would barge into the offices of the NRA and shoot Wayne LaPierre and the rest of those bloodsucking vampires the way Adam Lanza killed 20 first graders and 6 adults at the Sandy Hook School. That's why she was now doing puff pieces and human interest stories for a fledgling Brooklyn TV station. The only reason she got this exclusive interview was that she was the only journalist Townsend would agree to speak to.

To her right, behind a police barricade, were about two dozen pro-nuke demonstrators, all white, mostly grizzled geezers and out-of-work bozos with bad teeth, holding signs that said, 'America First,' 'Keep US Strong,' and 'Townsend is a Traiter'—not the most literate crowd.

On the other side, facing them, was a younger, more diverse and probably better educated group, chanting and holding anti-nuke signs. Some reporters and TV journalists mingled with the demonstrators, trying to get a couple of usable sound-bites. From time to time they would glare at Brigid, wondering how she was able to land the exclusive.

She smiled sardonically at her former colleagues and mouthed a little too loudly, "Fuck you all."

Townsend, standing next to her, said, "Excuse me, Miss Quinlan, what did you say?"

"I said, 'Thank you, Lord,' for giving me this opportunity."

Townsend smiled. "The Lord had nothing to do with it. It was your husband, Colonel Kelleher."

"Oh. I was wondering why you called me out of the blue."

"He never mentioned it?"

"Actually, we don't talk that much. We don't have what you might call a conventional marriage."

"The colonel pulled my butt out of a very nasty situation over in the Gulf. I always told him that if there was ever anything I could do for him, it would be a privilege. When he called and asked if I could give you an exclusive interview after my talk at the U.N., I was more than happy to oblige"

Townsend was the chief nuclear inspector in Baghdad in the run-up to the second Iraq War. He was taken hostage by a gang of Jordanian jihadist militants who would eventually become Al Qaeda in Iraq. At that time, Colonel James Kelleher was the head of the Ghost Commandos, an elite military NGO comprised of Delta Force and Special Tactics veterans. Kelleher was tasked with finding and freeing him. He completed the mission in 48 hours.

Before beginning her interview, Brigid positioned Townsend so that the U.N. building would be the backdrop of the shot. She gave the thumbs-up sign to her cameraman.

"This is Brigid Quinlan of Kings County News, at United Nations headquarters. I'm with Russell Townsend, the founder of the Nuke Zero Foundation." She turned to face him. "That was quite an ovation you just received, Dr. Townsend. What do you plan to do for an encore?"

"It wasn't me they were applauding, it was my message. Right now, there's enough nuclear material in America's silos to destroy every living thing on this planet five hundred times over, yet the United States is one of the few countries who refuses to sign a pledge to eliminate or even reduce its stockpile.

"My former bosses at the Nuclear Command don't like it that I'm speaking out. I've been called a turncoat, a traitor and a lot of other names I can't say on TV. And I've stopped counting the death threats. But if trying to stop the Military Industrial Complex from spending millions of dollars, taxpayer dollars, on something that only has one use—to annihilate every man, woman and child, every plant, every animal, every bug and every slug on this planet. If that makes me a traitor, I'll wear that mantle proudly, as did Moses to the Egyptians, Jesus to the Romans and George Washington to the British."

A bicyclist pedaled around the police barricades and headed toward them. He looked like a black panther on wheels. Black teardrop helmet and dark, wraparound goggles, long-sleeve form fitting black shirt, pants and gloves. He swerved around the barricade and skidded to a stop in front of them, blocking the camera.

Brigid gave the 'cut' sign to her cameraman. "What the hell do you think you're doing! Get the hell out of my shot!"

The messenger reached behind his back and produced a large pistol. Gripping the gun in both hands, legs astride the bike, he fired four shots in quick succession. Townsend fell, his blue Oxford shirt soaked scarlet. Women screamed. Men gasped. Most ran wildly, aimlessly, in every direction, some crashing into each other. Seconds later, a fifth shot rang out, hitting Brigid in the chest.

The police drew their weapons but held fire as terrified bystanders, demonstrators and reporters stampeded in front of them, making a clear shot impossible.

2

The shooter wheeled his bicycle around and pedaled furiously through the frenzied crowd, down First Avenue, then west across 41st Street. He weaved in and out of traffic, riding the wrong way down one-way streets, changing direction every few blocks. When he was sure he wasn't being followed, he turned down an alley between a gyro place and a ramen shop on 33rd Street off Fifth Avenue. It smelled of garbage and rancid food. There was a 40-yard dumpster in back of the eateries. He got off the bike and leaned against the wall.

As he gulped air he tried to make sense of what just happened. Who fired the fifth shot? And why her? She was a small time reporter at a half-assed local station. No one besides Goldbarr, Glynn and Stryker knew about the excision. Could one of them be behind this? But why? As far as he knew, none of them had any connection to the reporter. And if it wasn't any of them, then who? Did someone infiltrate the organization? Does he know my true identity?

He checked his watch. Can't think about any of that now. Gotta hurry. He tossed the bike into a dumpster, along with the gun, goggles and helmet. He walked around the corner to a white-brick office building on Fifth Avenue. It was one of the few in the area without a security guard or a doorman. He stepped through the revolving doors and headed for the men's room in the rear of the lobby. He walked to the end stall and pulled the handle.

The door held firm. "Occupied," a raspy voice from the other side growled.

He went over to the sink and slowly washed his hands. Police sirens blared as they rushed past the building. He grabbed a handful of paper towels and methodically went through the motions of drying. A few minutes later the stall door opened and an elderly man wearing what was once an expensive suit walked out without washing his hands. Disgusting. He locked himself in the vacated stall and peeled off his jersey and tights. Balancing himself on the toilet seat, he removed one of the ceiling tiles. He reached up through the hole. After a few furtive seconds he grabbed a black garbage bag, pulled it down and dropped it on the floor next to the toilet. He lifted a powder blue warm-up suit and matching baseball cap out of the bag, along with a pair of tennis shoes and dark aviator glasses. He changed into them and stuffed his black bicycle clothes in the bag.

He walked calmly out of the building, down 32nd Street, heading west, dropping the black bag into a garbage can. As he got closer to 7th Avenue, the street filled with men, women, teens and children, all headed toward Madison Square Garden. The marquee atop the entrance read 'Tennis Champions Show-down Semi-finals Today.'

In the middle of a mob of frenzied tennis fans, he found himself being swept toward the ticket takers. He squeezed, pushed and jostled his way to a side entrance. The steel door said, 'Garden Staff and Authorized Personnel Only.' He slipped through and darted down a stairwell that ended after two flights at a dimly lit landing. He walked through the door, then down a corridor to another door marked 'Players Only.' A beefy security guard stood menacingly in front of it, his massive arms folded, his scarred face creased with a hostile scowl. Twenty years earlier he fought upstairs in the main arena as a light heavyweight contender. In the intervening years he had added some poundage, he couldn't lift his arm over his shoulder and one eye was permanently shut, but he was still someone you wouldn't want to mess with. Now his job was to stop overeager fans from sneaking in through the back door of the locker room and annoying the athletes.

"Players only, buddy. Can't ya read," he growled. "Go buy a ticket."

The shooter took off his hat and removed his glasses. "Hi, Lenny, how are you?"

"Mr. Marks, I didn't recognize you. Better hurry, they were looking for you a couple of minutes ago. Your match is next. You're usually early, what happened?"

"Some kind of trouble over on the east side. Traffic was a nightmare. Police cars, ambulances. My cab got stuck and I had to jog the last few blocks. Glad I left my racquets in my locker. I might not have made it."

"Good luck."

He fist-bumped the guard and walked quickly into the locker room .

3

———

Colonel James B. Kelleher, U.S. Army, Retired, walked up the concrete steps to the second-floor apartment of the red brick two-family house. It had been a couple of years since he saw his older sister. But when he heard her quivering voicemail asking him to come as soon as he could, he feared for the worst. Dotty and her husband Joe were not in the best of shape. She had heart trouble and he had some kind of back issue.

A well worn corn husk welcome mat and a threadbare beach chair greeted him as he stepped onto the landing. Thirty seconds after he rang the bell, a gaunt woman in a faded yellow housedress with short bleached-blond hair opened the door.

"Dottie, I came as soon as I got your message. What's wrong? Is everything okay?"

She stared at him blankly for a few seconds, jerked her head towards the inside of the apartment and shuffled back in.

Kelleher followed. The door opened to the living room. To his left, seated on a cream colored couch with plastic slipcovers, was a man about the same age as the woman. His thick, wavy deep brown hair had not one strand of gray, courtesy of bi-weekly trips to MasterCuts on Rockaway

Parkway. He had big shoulders and thick arms from a lifetime in construction, and a large burn scar that covered most of the right side of his face, a souvenir from his year in Vietnam.

A tall, thin, pockmarked man in his twenties paced back and forth in front of them holding an AK-47. His navy blue, double breasted, pencil-striped suit and brown fedora made him look like a grade B movie gangster out of the thirties. A Soviet era Makarov pistol hung halfway out of his pocket. Kelleher would have laughed except that the AK-47 was pointed directly at his chest.

"Twenty years ago I coulda taken him out," Joe Ryan said. "Now with this goddamn sciatica, I can't do shit no more. I feel like an old fuckin' woman."

"Watch your mouth, Joseph," Dorothy scolded.

The man with the gun said, "Are you Kelleher?" He pronounced it Kay-loo-whore.

With his accent and Soviet-era weapons, Kelleher was pretty sure he was Russian.

"What the hell do you want?" Kelleher asked disdainfully, never taking his eyes off the weapon.

"I am bring you to my boss."

"What are you bothering my sister for?"

"This is address they give me. Let's go." He waved the gun at Kelleher.

"I ain't going anywhere with you, you fuckin' grease-face piece-a-shit."

The Russian looked confused. Either he didn't know what it meant or he wasn't sure what to do next.

"You come or I shoot," he finally said, then stepped forward and thrust the gun up towards Kelleher's head. Kelleher grabbed the barrel with both hands and twisted the gun out of the Russian's grasp. Twirling it around like a baton, he jabbed the barrel into the Russian's midsection, doubling him over.

Then he grabbed a handful of hair and brought his knee up into the Russian's jaw.

While the Russian was moaning and writhing on the floor, Kelleher grabbed the Makarov out of the Russian's pocket and put in on the coffee table next to Joe.

He turned to his sister. "Are you guys all right?"

"We're okay," Dottie answered, her voice a little shaky. "But you could have been killed if he pulled the trigger. My heart's still in my throat."

"Put your heart back where it belongs. The safety was up. The trigger was locked. This clown wasn't shooting anybody."

Kelleher grabbed the Russian's shirt and yanked him upright. He slapped him hard on his bony cheekbone.

"Who sent you?"

"I cannot say."

Kelleher handed the AK-47 to Joe. "Hang onto this for a minute." The older man beamed with glee as he pointed the assault rifle at his former captor. Kelleher slapped him again on the other the side of his face. "The only reason I don't kill you right now is I don't want to get blood all over my sister's furniture." He wedged his hand up into the Russian's throat, his thumb pressing into his protruding Adam's apple. "Gimmee your wallet."

"What?" the Russian choked as the color drained from his face.

"Your wallet."

He reached slowly into his back pocket with trembling fingers and gave his wallet to Kelleher. He shuffled through it until he found the driver's license. "Gennadiy Rogovskiy, Brighton Beach Avenue. What are you doing this far from Little Odessa?"

The Russian was silent.

Kelleher jammed his thumb deeper. "Who the hell sent you, Gennadiy?"

Still no response.

"I'm not gonna ask you again." He pressed harder. "In ten seconds you'll be sucking applesauce from what used to be your Adam's apple."

The Russian choked, gasped for air, then spat out the words, "Gorski. Nikolai Gorski."

Kelleher grinned wryly. "Gorski, huh?"

Kelleher took the assault rifle back from Joe and jammed the tip of the barrel under the Russian's chin. "Okay, let's go see what my old friend Nikki wants."

Rogovskiy, shoulders slumped, walked dejectedly towards the door.

Joe shouted, "What about that gun?" He pointed to the pistol on the table.

"Keep it as a souvenir."

Dottie shook her head. "Please take it, Jimmy. I don't want that thing in my house."

"Sure." Kelleher shoved the pistol into the back of his waistband. He opened the Russian's wallet and pulled out a handful of twenties and fifties and handed them to Joe. "Take yourselves to the best restaurant in Canarsie on Gennadiy. It's the least he can do after all the aggravation he put you guys through. Isn't that right Comrade?"

The Russian shrugged. Kelleher shoved him out the door.

Rogovskiy folded himself into the front seat of a black Lincoln Town Car. Kelleher climbed in the back. There was a Lexan partition in between the two seats. In a sleeve was a limousine driver's license with Rogovskiy's picture on it.

"A limo driver? You're a fuckin' limo driver. What's Gorski doing sending you after me? He run out of real gangsters?"

"I work for Colonel Gorski. He say drive car, I drive car. He say shoot, I shoot."

"Stick to driving. You might live to see your face clear up."

4

After a ten-minute drive on the Belt Parkway, they were parked under the elevated subway tracks that ran along Brighton Beach Avenue. They were in the heart of the neighborhood that used to be known as Brighton Beach before thirty thousand Soviet refugees swarmed in. The oldtimers still call it that. Everyone else now refers to it as Little Odessa.

"Where's your boss?" Kelleher said.

"Across street."

On the other side of the street was a small restaurant that had occupied that corner in various incarnations for over fifty years. It had been a pizza parlor, Chinese restaurant, a knish joint and a falafel stand. Now it was the Volga Cafe, a cross between Starbucks and the Russian Tea Room. From the car, Kelleher could see that the restaurant was about half full of customers, none of whom looked especially threatening.

"What's Gorski doing, waiting on tables?"

"He owns the place." The Russian's voice quivered. It was obvious that he wasn't eager to see his boss with Kelleher prodding him with his own gun.

"Take off your jacket."

"I don't understand."

"Your jacket. Take it off and hand it back here."

The Russian did as instructed and handed his size thirty-eight, extra long jacket back through the slot in the partition. Kelleher wrapped the jacket around the gun and cradled it in his arms. It looked nothing like a baby but it was better than walking down the street holding an assault weapon.

"Okay. Let's go pay Comrade Gorski a visit. You lead the way."

Kelleher followed him across Brighton Beach Avenue to Gorski's place. The subway tracks above threw shadowy stripes across the ground of this perpetually dark and eerie street. They walked through a side door, then up a flight of stairs to another door.

Kelleher tossed the jacket back to the Russian and leveled the gun at his back.

"Open the door and walk in. Slowly."

He didn't move for a few seconds. Kelleher poked him in the spine. He plodded inside. Kelleher followed. He found himself in a large space, a combination storage room and makeshift office. A few wooden chairs were haphazardly scattered around the room. A battered roll-top desk and a small round table were the only significant pieces of furniture. Boxes of papers, file folders and manila envelopes took up most of the unoccupied floor space and table surfaces.

"Hey, Kelleher, you shit-eating son of a bitch. How the fuck are you?" The voice was loud, deep and hoarse from half-a-century of sucking on harsh Soviet cigarettes. Nikolai Gorski sauntered towards Kelleher, extending his hand. He was a little younger than Kelleher, a little shorter and a littler broader, with close-cropped salt and pepper hair and ice blue eyes that stayed frigid even when he smiled. A thick, unlit cigar jutted Bogey-style from his mouth.

Kelleher kept the AK-47 leveled at the Russian's chest. "How've you been, Major Gorski?"

"Why do you point a gun at your old friend?" He put a finger on the side of the barrel and moved it off to the side.

"Why did you send a gunman after me?"

"Gunman? What gunman?" he chuckled. "Gennadiy? He is my driver." Gorski sneered disdainfully at the tall, skinny kid cowering in the corner.

Kelleher looked down at the gun. "Then what the hell was he doing with this?"

"I keep the Kalashnikov in the car in case any trouble happens. I am sure he has no idea how to use it."

"He doesn't. That's why I have it now. The next time it gets shoved up his ass."

"There will be no next time." Gorski pointed to the door. "Go." The kid trudged out the door.

"My friend, I swear. I told him to pick you up, that's all. I didn't tell him to threaten you. He was overzealous."

"You haven't lost your gift for bullshit, Gorski. You got me here. Tell me why." He put the gun down on a table.

Gorski parked himself in a wooden chair. "Sit. Relax. You'll live longer."

Kelleher sat across the table from him. "Okay, what's going on?"

"Some friends of mine, they heard we at one time were...uh...acquaintances."

"Not acquaintances. Not friends. Try associates, and that's stretching it. And that was a long time ago."

"What you will. My friends, they are Uzbeks, they want to hire you. They need your, what is the word? Expertise."

"I'm retired."

"They have money. They are willing to pay two hundred thousand up front. Another three hundred at completion. It should not take more than two months."

Kelleher shook his head. "Not interested. Tell your friends to call someone else."

Gorski smiled through stained teeth. "Turning down half-a-million U.S. You are not a good American. I think maybe you are really a Bolshevik at heart."

"Yeah, whatever." Kelleher stood. "Nicky, It's been swell."

Gorski jumped up, grabbed the Kalashnikov off the table and pointed it at Kelleher. "Don't move."

"What the fuck are you doing?"

"Business. Maybe you don't like money. I do. Fifty thousand dollars for your skin."

"Who's paying you?"

"Americans. I don't ask names. They pay cash. Twenty-five up front. Twenty-five when I deliver you. Dead or alive."

Kelleher still had Gennadiy's pistol in his waistband. He stepped to the side and kicked the gun out of Gorski's hands. Then he dropped to his knees, pulled the Makarov out of his waistband and put two rounds in Gorski's chest. The Russian went down in a lump, blood flowing from his torso.

"You're out of business, scumbag."

A rush of heavy footfalls came stomping up the steps. Gorski's men!

Kelleher climbed through the window to the fire escape.

The old, rusted grated metal platform shook a bit but held. It took him three tries to unhook the rickety ladder and send it clanging to the alley behind the restaurant. As he climbed down he could hear shouts coming from Gorski's apartment. He made his way past the piles of black garbage bags, side-stepping the lemon peels, fishbones, tin cans and other detritus that the cats, rats and squirrels left behind.

The Brighton Beach boardwalk was a block away. It was milling with young couples, families and old-timers, all out for a pleasant evening. It was calmer and less frenetic than its boisterous Coney Island brother, a half-mile to the west. Kelleher fired two shots into the air. Women screamed, babies cried, elderly couples clutched each other. As people scattered frenetically in all directions, Kelleher ran towards Coney Island. Three of Gorski's men ran after him. After about half-a-mile Kelleher's legs were leaden and his lungs were screaming. He was in great shape for a guy his age, but the men chasing him were thirty years younger. In a few minutes they'd be on him. About two hundred yards away he could see Nathan's, the legendary wiener wonderland. Ignoring the pain, he started sprinting.

The hot dog emporium was mobbed. Kelleher got in line behind a seedy derelict wearing a greasy blue wool cap and a tattered gray windbreaker that smelled like week-old fish wrapped in used toilet paper.

"My jacket for yours, even up."

The guy backed off, staring nervously at the gun in Kelleher's hand.

"Your jacket and cap, right now, for mine." He looked at his watch. "You got five seconds."

The bum shrugged. "Anything you say, buddy." He shoved his cap and coat at Kelleher.

Kelleher handed him his leather jacket. "Put it on."

The bum complied.

Kelleher turned and quick-stepped away, throwing on the putrid clothing as he ran. Two minutes later he glanced back to see Gorski's men confront the guy wearing his jacket. Two gripped his arms while a third slapped his face and yelled at him.

After a few blocks, Kelleher was in front of the Cyclone, the granddaddy of American roller coasters. It was there, more than forty years earlier, that he proved himself worthy of joining the Brooklyn Lords, the toughest white gang in Flatbush. His initiation task was to spray-paint the gang's name on the Cyclone sign, 80 feet above the Coney Island surf.

"It's just like climbing the monkey bars," his pal Frankie told him. "My uncle works there. He told me there's a little stand at the top where guys go up to change the lights and shit. You can do it easy. Just don't look down."

Fifteen-year-old Jimmy Kelleher looked up at the skeletal steel girders. His head spun. His mouth filled with bile. He was sure he was going to die. He swallowed hard and started to climb. Slowly. Carefully. A can of red Krylon spray paint, wedged in back of his jeans, jabbed his spine with every move. After what seemed like hours but was only ten minutes, he found the platform and climbed over the railing. Steadying himself, he spray-painted 'BKLN LORDS LAMF' and made his way down. That's how Jimmy 'the Kid' Kelleher became a made-member of the Lords.

Kelleher was roused from his reverie when he saw the Russian thugs lumbering towards him, a few hundred yards away. There was a line of twenty people waiting to ride. He ran to the front, leveled the gun at the pudgy operator and yelled, "This is a hijack."

"You gotta be kidding, mister. It don't go nowheres but here."

Kelleher shoved the barrel under the kid's chin. "How about I make you go to the fuckin' cemetery?"

The kid gestured at the empty cars. "It's all yours, friend. Enjoy the ride."

The line-standers were huddled together, praying that this maniac wouldn't kill them. Kelleher turned to them. "Everybody get in. This ride's on me."

They scrambled nervously into the seats. There were three cars, each with four rows of double seats. Kelleher got into the third seat of the first car next to a couple of middle-aged Japanese tourists.

He glared at the operator. "Let's go. I want you to stop it for ten seconds at the top of the first rise. Got it?"

"No problem. It stops up there anyways."

"I want you to count to ten before you start it up again. That clear?"

"Sure. Anything you say, boss."

There was a metallic groan and the 100-year-old roller coaster started up the wooden tracks. As the red and yellow cars struggled slowly up the 85-foot incline, Kelleher could see his pursuers converge on the entrance. The operator pointed frantically up at him. Then he pointed down the block, where the ride would end. They ran to meet it, guns drawn.

At the top of the first rise, the car creaked to a complete stop. Kelleher gave a silent prayer that the platform he stood on forty years before would still be there. It was. He hopped onto it.

A teenager sitting in the second group of cars shouted, "Hey man, hope you make it," as the cars plunged down its first harrowing dive.

Kelleher watched as the ride finished. The gunmen stood, arms folded, as the riders filed out. When he didn't emerge they climbed into the empty cars and looked under every seat. He could see them gesturing angrily at the operator, who shrugged and shook his head. After several minutes of talking animatedly with each other, they trudged off.

He stayed on the platform until he was sure it was safe, then stepped down onto the Cyclone's steel skeleton. The girders were a lot farther apart than he remembered. He had climbed and rappelled down cliffs and abandoned buildings in the course of his work, both in the army and as a military consultant. But not in many years. And he felt every one of those years in every muscle, tendon and ligament.

He slowly and methodically inched his way down the eight-story structure, ignoring the searing pain in his knee. Back on the street, he leaned against the wall and took a deep breath.

"I'm too fuckin' old for this shit," he said to the ghosts of Coney Island past.

5

Marcus Glynn eased his black Hummer to a stop in front of a police barricade at the corner of Thirty-Second Street and Third Avenue. A ruddy-faced patrolman was directing rush hour drivers uptown, away from the Midtown Tunnel and the F.D.R. Drive. Cabbies and truck drivers leaned on their horns and shouted curses at the cops in a dozen languages.

"Crime scene, pal, can't ya read?" the cop shouted at his open window. "You think this detour's for everyone but you?"

"Yeah," Glynn said, with a smirk. "That's exactly what I think." He flashed a small laminated photo I.D. "Homeland Security Anti-Terror Strike Force."

The policeman looked quizzically at him. "Never heard of it."

"That's right. And after I leave, you'll forget you heard it now. Got that Officer..." He looked at the cop's name tag. "Goldring. Or we could go down to my office on Varick Street, sort this out and lose any chance of finding whoever did this."

He shrugged, turned to his partner and yelled, "Hey, Vinny, let him in."

The Anti-Terror Strike Force was mandated by one of the

more obscure sections of the Patriot Act to be activated only in the event of a national emergency. Glynn, a Major in the Army Rangers and a counter-terrorism specialist, was appointed to be the commander of the unit by Tom Ridge, the first head of the Department of Homeland Security. The unit was disbanded a few years later and replaced by the Joint Terrorism Task Force, a partnership of the FBI and local law enforcement. But Glynn didn't let that stop him from using his lapsed credentials to gain access to secure locations.

A half dozen New York City policemen, two detectives, a medical examiner and two crime scene investigators were milling about the U.N. courtyard. Most of them stopped what they were doing and gaped at him. At six-six, two hundred eighty pounds of mostly muscle, Marcus Glynn, with his black, close-cropped hair and pointy goatee, looked like the devil on steroids. He identified himself to the police captain in command. After a brief conversation, he handed Glynn a hand-written sheet with the names and phone numbers of everyone who claimed to witness the shooting.

Glynn walked over to the blood-soaked body of Russell Townsend laying on the pavement. The forensics team was busy collecting bullets and shell casings, lifting bicycle tracks off the pavement, photographing the bodies and anything else that might be used as evidence.

"Hey!" He shouted at them. "Who's the lead here?"

One of the detectives walked over to him with his hand extended.

"Detective Jon Jamekis, Manhattan South."

Glynn handed him a card. "This is officially a terrorist crime scene. Everything goes to my office."

"Roger that. Anything else?"

"Did they find any unspent bullets?"

"Only one."

"Did you notice anything out of the ordinary about it?"

"As a matter of fact, yeah. It was silver."

"What else can you tell me?"

"The shooter was dressed as a bicycle messenger, helmet and goggles. About half the witnesses are reporters, supposedly they're trained to observe, and we couldn't even get full agreement on whether he was white or black."

"Forget about the shooter for now. What can you tell me about the woman?"

"Her name's Brigid Quinlan. She's a reporter for one of the local cable news stations. No known connection to Townsend except that she was interviewing him for the ten o'clock news. She has one grown daughter who lives in Brooklyn. They're trying to get in touch with her now."

6

This is Barney Bobbins, the Racquet Raconteur. It was billed as the match we've all been waiting for and I, for one, couldn't wait for it to be over. It was supposed to be a classic blood feud between two players who clearly and openly despise each other. One, a back-alley knife-fighter who claws and slashes his way to victory, against a master chef who deftly slices, dices and skewers his opponents. As opposed to a contest for the ages, we witnessed what can only be described as an old fashioned ass-whooping. The gangster made mincemeat out of the gourmet. Tommy Riemer bashed, bullied and bludgeoned Jake Marks in a 6-2, 6-1 drubbing that wasn't even as close as that lopsided score indicates. While Riemer played like a man possessed, Marks sleepwalked his way through two excruciatingly boring sets.

And the Garden faithful were not pleased. Marks, a perennial fan favorite, was greeted with a chorus of boos and catcalls as he walked dejectedly off the court. Even the announcement that he was donating his entire appearance fee, rumored to be close to half-a-million dollars, to the Boys and Girls Clubs of New York, didn't appease the boisterous bastions of the blue seats. In the meantime,

Riemer, tennis's reigning bad boy, reveled in adulation as the assembled multitude gave him a thunderous ovation.

The animosity between these two goes back to their roots when they were the New York area's top two juniors. Riemer cut his tennis teeth on the hardscrabble New York City public courts while Marks honed his skills at Long Island's posh country clubs. They haven't faced each other as pros for over five years. That's why this exhibition match was circled on every New York tennis fan's calendar.

Riemer the Screamer has been telling anyone who'll listen that Gentleman Jake Marks has been ducking him. That he's a spineless coward and an overrated loser who quits when the going gets tough and doesn't have the guts to play any of the top players, especially his truly. Until now everyone thought it was just another Riemer rant, but it looks like the bombastic basher from Bay Ridge might have a point. In fact, I hope someone in the audience knows the Heimlich Maneuver because we just had a major case of choking here at Madison Square Garden.

7

Bunny Fields sat in the driver's seat of his refurbished London taxi, glaring at his iPad. Jake Marks opened the door, slumped into the back seat and tossed his racquet bag next to him.

"Let's go."

"Any particular destination?"

"It doesn't matter. As long as it's away from here."

Bunny headed north, to the Henry Hudson Parkway, then east on the Cross Bronx towards Long Island. After five excruciatingly silent minutes, Bunny said, "I saw the match on the iPad direct feed, and heard about the shooting on the radio. What happened?"

"Are you talking about the match or the other thing?"

"Both. I'm assuming one was a result of the other."

Marks grunted and nodded.

"I gather the woman was not part of the assignment."

"Of course not." Marks emitted something between a sigh and a groan. "Townsend was the target. The woman, Brigid Quinlan, that was her name, should still be alive."

"Everyone makes mistakes."

"There was no mistake!" Marks yelled. "I fired four times.

They all hit Townsend. Then there was another shot and she went down. It came from somewhere behind me. When the ballistics report comes out, it'll show that the bullet that hit her was from a different gun."

"Why would someone want to shoot this Quinlan woman?"

"No reason that I can think of. She was a reporter for a local cable station."

"That makes no sense."

"A lot of things don't make sense."

"What are you going to do?"

"Something I should have done awhile ago. And thanks, Bunny."

"For what?"

"For listening. And for being my friend."

8

Ronald Goldbarr lay drowsily in his antique, hand-carved Louis XVI king-size bed. It was after midnight and he was alone in the penthouse of the Millennium Spire, which occupied the top floor of the 27-story tower on 88th Street off Madison Avenue. On the floor below were the offices of Goldbarr Enterprises.

The national headquarters of the Millennium Society, a supposed think tank that Goldbarr created when he decided to dabble in politics, took up the first two floors. The intervening floors were divided up by offices on the lower floors and residential condominiums, which spent most of the year unoccupied by their billionaire foreign owners, on the upper stories.

His wife, Zlatina, was back on their Bedford, NY estate taking care of their fourteen-year-old daughter Eliana, as well as three Siberian Huskies, five Himalayan cats and four Friesian horses that Eliana rode in equestrian competitions. Goldbarr's head was slightly fuzzy from drinking too much bourbon a few hours earlier at dinner with the junior senator from North Dakota and a former three-star general.

The phone next to his bed rang, startling him. Very few

people had his direct number and of those who did, even fewer dared to call him this late. He checked the Caller ID but it was unknown. Whoever it was, it had better be important.

He grabbed the phone. "Yeah?"

"Mr. Goldbarr."

"You've got some fucking nerve calling here after the way you screwed up today."

"Don't worry. This is the last time you'll hear from me. The Lone Ranger has fired his last silver bullet."

"What?"

"I'm done. I won't do it anymore."

"What the fuck are you talking about?!"

"We were supposed to be the good guys, fighting for freedom. What did you call it, a public-private partnership, doing the dirty work that has to be done that the government can't or won't do? Now I realize it was all bullshit."

"Calm down, Marks. If you're upset about that Quinlan bitch, don't be. I'm glad you killed her, even though it was a mistake. She was a loudmouth, left-wing, anti-American pain in the ass."

"But I didn't kill her. I fired four times and they all hit Townsend."

"So who the hell shot Brigid Quinlan?"

"I don't know. You tell me."

"What, you think I had something to do with it?"

"Nobody else knew I was going to be there. It had to be someone connected to Millennium."

"I get it. You're in denial. You screwed up and you can't face it. I'll tell you what, take some time off. Clear your head. In a week or two you'll come around."

"My head has never been clearer and it's telling me that Russell Townsend was campaigning for a safer world. There's no way his death keeps America more secure."

"You don't know what the hell you're talking about.

Townsend was working with our enemies. He was under-mining our weapons programs and betraying our missile defense systems."

"I don't believe you."

"I have proof."

"Your proof means nothing. Your people can manufacture 'proofs' for anything: torture, assassinations, invasions."

"Listen, I'm gonna make believe we never had this conversation. It's your frustration talking. Call me in a week or two when you come to your senses."

"I have come to my senses."

"Yeah, okay, whatever." Goldbarr hung up.

9

The Millennium Society media room seemed crowded, even though there were only three men in it. Marcus Glynn took up most of the leather sofa that was built to seat three adults. Mendel Stryker was a half-foot shorter than Glynn and 20 pounds lighter but no less imposing. He was a five-time New York City Golden Gloves light heavyweight champion. Then he turned pro and went undefeated in 28 fights. He was in line for a championship match when he was blinded in one eye. The official version was a training accident but it was actually the result of a broken beer bottle smashed into his face during a brawl with a half-dozen Hell's Angels.

The third occupant, Ronald Goldbarr at 74 years old, was a little under six feet tall and carried around 265 pounds of loose flab. Though he was physically no match for the other two, his will, his personality and his billions made him the dominant presence in the room.

Their eyes were riveted on the 95-inch monitor on the wall in front of them, watching video clips of the shooting of Russell Townsend and Brigid Quinlan, culled from the cell phone videos of reporters and bystanders. The images were shaky, hazy and out of focus. On most of them, the three seconds in which the shooting actually happened were barely visible. The network feed, blocked by the shooter, was useless.

"Marks says he didn't shoot the Quinlan woman," Ronald Goldbarr said from behind his huge antique desk.

Stryker gripped the arms of his chair so tightly he left an imprint in the burnished mahogany armrest. "He's a lying sonuvabitch! Of course he shot her." His high high-pitched lispy voice was totally at odds with his hulking presence. "Today he wants to quit. Maybe tomorrow he'll decide to go to the press. Then we're all fucked. I say we excise his ass."

"Okay, Mendel." He turned to Glynn. "What do you think?"

Marcus Glynn was sprawled across the plush turquoise cushions as if he were discussing an upcoming softball game as opposed to the assassination of a colleague.

"I think we should give him some time to come around. You don't grow operatives like Marks on trees. He has access to places most agents can't even get close to. He's a world-class athlete, an international celebrity and a quick study. He can travel anywhere in the world without scrutiny. Until this Quinlan thing, he's never made a mistake. Of course he's rattled. Anyone would be. Eliminating him now makes no sense."

Goldbarr closed his eyes and pressed his fingers together. "I'm with Glynn. Marks could still be valuable."

The big man exhaled slowly, a contented smile meandered slowly across his face like a small crack expanding in a windshield. He couldn't help gloating about winning this round of his departmental sibling rivalry with Stryker, who glared malevolently into space.

He turned to Goldbarr. "Any thoughts on how we should deal with Kelleher, now that the Russians fucked it up?"

Stryker bolted upright. "I told you not to use Gorski. We shoulda taken care of him ourselves."

Goldbarr wagged a finger at Stryker. "Like it or not, Kelleher's an American war hero. His murder would draw intense scrutiny from the press and law enforcement. We can't risk having that connected with us no matter how remote the possibility."

"You know our boy Mendel," Glynn said. "He never met a man he didn't wanna whack."

Stryker said nothing. He glowered at Glynn. The veins on his buffalo neck looked ready to burst.

Goldbarr said, "Good. Marks will get over his hissy fit and he'll continue to be useful. Maybe we'll use him to deal with Kelleher."

10

———————

Kelleher ambled into the detective squad room of the 17th Precinct on East 51st Street and Lexington Avenue. Most of the desks in the large, ill-lit space were unoccupied. Their tenants were out making the streets of New York safer for the good citizens of Gotham. Kelleher walked over to a detective sprawled on his chair, official looking documents spread over his desk, ear buds in his ears, eyes half-closed. His hair was starting to thin and his body starting to fat.

Kelleher leaned over the desk. "I'm looking for Marcus Glynn."

The detective didn't move.

"Marcus Glynn," Kelleher said again, a little louder.

Still no response.

The skin under Kelleher's cheekbones tightened, his nostrils flared and his eyes narrowed. His meaty hands balled into fists. He brought one of them down on the desk.

The detective jerked up abruptly and pulled the headphones out of his ears.

"What the hell!"

Kelleher glowered at him, daring him to be confrontational. "Marcus Glynn. Where can I find him?"

"Who the fuck are you?"

"Someone with information he wants."

The detective glared at Kelleher, opened his mouth ready to snarl, thought better of it, breathed deeply and said, "There's no Glynn in this squad."

"I got information on the U.N. killings. I heard he was the one to see."

"He could be. But he's not here."

"So who's here that I can talk to?"

"About what happened at the U.N.? Nobody. Not our jurisdiction."

Kelleher's lip started to curl. He took a breath and forced himself to stay calm, smile even. No sense getting the police pissed off if it wasn't necessary. "Can you tell me whose jurisdiction it is?"

The detective shrugged. "Don't know. Don't care."

Kelleher scowled. "Thanks for nuthin, detective…" He looked at the nameplate on the desk. "Powderly. Sorry I woke you."

He looked up, ready to tell Kelleher off when his eyes narrowed on Kelleher's face. "You look familiar to me. Were you ever on the job?"

"No."

"Wait a minute, I remember. You're that colonel from the Army Rangers. The one on TV. Jungle Jim, right? You told all those assholes running the show in Iraq that they didn't have a fucking clue. That their incompetence was costing billions of dollars and thousands of American lives and Iraqi lives."

"That was a long time ago."

Powderly jumped up. "My brother was there."

Kelleher tensed.

"He said you were the only guy who had the guts to say what everybody else was thinking." He thrust out his hand. "Sorry I gave you a hard time, Colonel. Can I shake your hand?"

Kelleher gave it a quick pump. The pudgy detective smiled contentedly, then in a stage whisper he said, "They told us not to say anything, but Glynn was in here the other day. Massive son of a bitch. I think he moved to somewhere on Varick Street."

"The federal building?"

"Maybe. I don't know for sure. He didn't really talk to us."

"Thanks." Kelleher walked out.

He climbed into a taxi that was parked in front of the building. Before he said a word, the driver headed downtown.

"Hey!" he shouted at the plastic partition. "I didn't say where."

"Varick Street."

"What are you, a fuckin' mindreader?"

"Glynn's waiting for you."

"You've been following me?"

"Didn't have to. Your phone told us where you were."

Fifteen minutes later, Kelleher walked into the lobby of an austere 12-story limestone building. When the security guard at the front desk asked what office, he answered, "Resiliency," just like the driver instructed.

"Twelfth floor. Room 1210."

Kelleher walked through the unmarked door.

The big man was slouched in an oversized chair with his size 15's plopped on the desk. "Jungle Jim Kelleher, the world's most famous soldier of misfortune. What brings you to my humble corner of the world?"

"Cut the crap, Glynn, you fuckin' brought me here."

"Tell me anyway."

"I want the guy who shot Townsend and my wife."

"So does the FBI, the CIA, MI6, Interpol and about five other international law enforcement agencies."

"What are you talking about? Townsend wasn't that big a deal. And Brigid certainly wasn't."

"It wasn't them. It was who killed them."

"Who?"

"You really don't know? I thought you were more hooked in."

"If I knew who it was, I wouldn't be wasting my time with you."

"You've heard of the Lone Ranger, haven't you? Not the cowboy, the terrorist hit man."

"Yeah, I've heard of him. Carlos the Jackal meets Robin Hood. He's made half a dozen hits that I know of. Crooked cops, dirty politicians, terrorist honchos, weapons dealers. Assholes nobody's gonna cry for. All in broad daylight in front of witnesses. Killing Townsend and Brigid doesn't fit his M.O."

"Maybe, maybe not. But we know he did it."

"How?"

"He leaves a calling card. Your wife was killed with a silver bullet."

"I could take a bullet and paint it silver, that doesn't make me the Lone Ranger."

"It's him all right. The silver bullet's only one indicator. We have others. The shooter was tall and thin. From what we know, so is the Lone Ranger."

"So are a million other guys, but let's say it is the Lone Ranger. Bring me in. I'll deliver him to you on a fuckin' slab."

"We don't need your help."

"You sure as shit need somebody's help. You and all those agencies you rattled off have been chasing this guy all over the world for more than two years and all you came up with was a handful of bullets in one hand and a handful of shit in the other. Give me two weeks, that's all I need."

"So you find this guy, the sonuvabitch who killed the woman you once loved…"

"Not once. Still!"

"Even better. You're telling me you'll bring me the bastard who murdered the love of your life?"

"Right."

"Alive?"

"Yes."

"Bullshit! You'll deliver him all right. In pieces."

"What the fuck are you talking about?"

"There was a story going around about the legendary Jungle Jim. One of many that I heard. In this one you were in country and your interpreter turned out to be working for the enemy. The way I heard it, you did a lot more than apprehend him. Something about stuffing a certain body part down his throat and dumping his mutilated corpse in the town square."

"We were at war. He was one of us. Then he sold us out for money. A half a dozen good men lost their lives because of that bastard. This is different."

"You're right. You weren't in love with them. Some people I work with don't like the way you do business. They say you're a loose cannon, that you couldn't be trusted in the field and you can't be trusted here."

"Who said that?"

"It doesn't matter. You and me, we play in the same sandbox. Except we have rules, standards, a purpose. Your purpose is to get as much money as you can from the highest bidder, no matter who gets fucked in the process. You made us look bad more than once."

"You don't need me to make you look bad. You do a good job all by yourself."

Glynn stood and scowled down at Kelleher. "Stay away from this one. We'll get the guy who killed your wife."

"Fuck you. I'm going after the sonuvabitch. And if you or one of your flunkies get in my way, I'll deal with that too."

"Don't fuck with me, Kelleher. I can throw your ass in jail right now."

"What's the charge?"

"I don't need a goddamn charge. I got the Patriot Act. All I have to do is mumble the magic word 'terrorist' and they'll throw away the key."

Kelleher knew that Glynn worked for Goldbarr, not the government. He also knew that Goldbarr had plenty of high powered connections in Homeland Security. So even though he was sure that Glynn was blowing smoke, he decided to play nice.

"Come on. Don't be such a dick. You want the Lone Ranger. I'll get him for you."

Glynn made a show of thinking about it. He closed his eyes for a few seconds and stroked his goatee.

"I have to talk to my people."

"Who?"

"Mendel Stryker, for one."

"Stryker! He's a psycho sonuvabitch. He should be locked in a high security padded cell."

"Looks like you're familiar with my esteemed colleague. How do you know him?"

"I fought him once a long time ago."

"What do you mean, you fought him?"

"In the ring, the Golden Gloves."

"Who won?"

"He did. Almost broke my fuckin' jaw. But he didn't knock me out. Won a unanimous decision. That was the semi-finals. He put the guy in the finals in the hospital. A Puerto Rican. Stryker propped him up on the ropes and hit him until he was pulp. Turned his brain into goat cheese. I bet that guy still slurs his words, if he's alive."

"Stryker did it on purpose?'

"Absolutely."

"How can you be so sure?"

"The guy called him a maricón, Spanish for faggot. It hit a nerve."

"Have you seen him since then?"

"We've bumped asses a couple of times. Let's just say we don't send each other Christmas cards."

"And you still want to work with him?"

"I'll work with Attila the Hun if it gets me a crack at the bastard that killed my wife."

"Tonight at nine. The Millennium Society, 88th Street and Madison Avenue."

Kelleher raised his eyebrows. "Millennium Society? Sounds fancy. I had you pegged more as a strip club kinda guy."

"Just show up at nine o'clock and we'll see if we can work something out."

"I'll be there."

11

An hour and a half later, Kelleher found himself on a stoop in Park Slope, Brooklyn, staring through the six-inch crack between the door and the jamb into the most intense blue-green eyes he'd ever seen.

"I've already talked to the police," the young woman said, irritation in her voice.

"I'm not a cop."

"No reporters."

"Not one of those either."

"Okay, I give up. What do you want?"

"I just want to talk to you. It's important."

"Not now." She slowly pushed the door.

Right before it closed Kelleher said, "I'm your father."

"My father's dead!" Maggie slammed the door but Kelleher jammed his foot in the doorway propelling it back at her. The chain stopped it from hitting her in the head.

Kelleher leaned on the door. "I know what you're feeling. Just hear me out. I loved Brigid too."

"I don't know who you are, mister, but you're not my father. My father was killed fighting the British in Northern Ireland."

Maggie's eyes probed Kelleher's face through the crack. "You better leave right now or I'm calling the police."

"Listen to me. Your birthday's October 7. Your favorite color is yellow. When you were little you collected little ceramic and glass penguins. Your favorite cartoon character is Tweety. Your mother bought you a kitten for your tenth birthday, you named her Daisy but you were allergic and had to give it up. You were the New York City high school gymnastics champ at fifteen. You made the Olympic team but blew out your knee in an exhibition match a couple of weeks before the games. Should I go on?"

He could see her shaking her head.

"All that information is online. It only proves that you have access to a computer."

"When you were four years old a stray dog bit you in Prospect Park, I'm pretty sure it was some kind of Doberman mix. I'm guessing you still have the scar on your left thigh." Kelleher smirked. "I bet that information isn't available online."

A look of bewildered astonishment washed over Maggie's face. "How do you know that?"

"I was there with you and Brigid. I chased that damn mutt down and had him tested for rabies. He bit me on the wrist for my trouble." He held up his arm. There was a three-inch zipper under the heel of his hand. "Lucky for both of us he was clean."

"For all I know, it was your dog that bit me. It still doesn't prove you're my father."

"Listen, I'm not looking to hurt you and I'm not out to scam you. All I want to do is talk."

"All right," she said, still skeptical. "Come in." She held up her phone and snapped his picture. "I can send the police your photo with one click, so don't try anything." She unchained the door and walked slowly into the living room, limping slightly. She kept her eyes riveted on Kelleher. She pointed the phone at him like a pistol. She gestured with it at one of the upholstered chairs in front of a big bay window. "Sit there."

Kelleher took a slow step towards the chair, then spun around and snatched the phone out of Maggie's hand. She screamed and tried to grab it back. Then she took a swing at him. He caught her fist like a baseball and held it fast as she struggled to break free. "Let go of me!" she screamed.

To her surprise, he did. Then he tossed her the phone and began to yell at her.

"Don't ever let a strange man into your house again. Especially when you're alone. Someone with bad intentions could have found out about all that stuff. Even the dog bite. Your mother was just murdered. You could be next. It's a good thing for you I really am your father." He sat. "Still don't believe me? Ask me a question, about Brigid, about me. I'll tell you anything you want to know."

Maggie eased herself into a rocking chair facing him. She winced as she sat, a remnant of her injury. "I can't think of anything."

"All right, I'll ask you a question. Whose house is this?"

"It's ours...mine."

"How do you know?"

"I've lived here my whole life."

"Did you ever see the deed?"

She shook her head.

"That's because I own this house."

"No way!"

Kelleher reached into his pocket and handed her a folded up piece of paper. "Brigid rented the ground floor apartment here when you were still in diapers. She loved this place. Loved that it was a half-a-block from Prospect Park. She took you there every day. Your favorite spot was the carousel. There was a white horse with a gold mane that you loved. You called him Goldilocks."

Maggie's eyes widened. Her mouth dropped. "Goldilocks. I remember Goldilocks." For the first time since she heard about Brigid's murder a small smile etched across her face.

"An old Italian guy owned this place and rented Brigid the lower level apartment. That was when Park Slope was still a sketchy neighborhood. Then it became what they called a neighborhood in transition. Rich young white couples were moving in, fixing up the dilapidated brownstones and pushing the old-timers out. House prices quadrupled in a few years. A lot of people thought prices would drop just as fast as they rose. Brigid's landlord decided to cash in and sell. He gave Brigid two months to find a new place. There was nothing, not even in the dicier parts of Park Slope. She didn't know what to do. There was nowhere for her to move but she couldn't stay. She was hysterical when she called me." Kelleher paused. He studied Maggie's face. She was coming around. "I get paid a lot of money for what I do. The old ginzo wanted two hundred thousand for the place. I offered him two-fifty. In cash. He grabbed it like it was the brass ring on the carousel. Take a look at that deed. See where it says Brigid Quinlan: Life Estate. That means she could stay here as long as she lived. I wanna do the same for you."

"That's a very generous offer, Mr. Uh..."

"Kelleher. Jim Kelleher."

"All right Mr. Kelleher, let's say you are my father, how come my mother never told me?"

"It's a long story."

"I have time."

"All right." He closed his eyes and took a deep breath. "I'm a military contractor. A soldier for hire. I met Brigid the summer before you were born. We fell in love. We even talked about getting married, but my work takes me all over the world, sometimes for months. Not a good recipe for a successful marriage. I told her I would get out of the mercenary business but she said no, being a soldier is who I am and if I quit because of her I'd be miserable and come to resent her. So we ended it, cold turkey. We decided it would be better if we never spoke to each other again. She never even told me she was pregnant. Then, about two years later, she called. She told me she had a young child, you, and that I was the father."

"And you believed her?"

"Of course. The timing made sense and Brigid wouldn't lie about something like that. She was the most independent person I ever met. Also the most honest. I did ask her why she decided to tell me when she did. Then she told me about getting thrown out of this place. I said I would buy the house for her but only if we got married. We got blood tests and a license and said our vows downtown in Borough Hall.

"The only job I ever had was being a soldier, either for the U.S. Army or for hire. I was still trying to figure out what to do when I got a call to go to Ireland to work with the IRA. I didn't want to leave you and your mother, but the money was amazing and I had a new wife and kid to support." He gave her a little nod. "I was only supposed to be there for a couple of weeks. Then I got arrested for a murder I didn't commit. It was a member of the royal family, a huge deal. The State Department was no help, they were happy to be rid of me. That's another long story that I'll tell you another time. The Brits put me in solitary for life without a trial, but to the Irish underground I was a superhero. Your mom figured it would be better if you thought your father was a martyr of the Irish revolution instead of a murderer rotting in an English prison."

"How did you get out?"

"There was no daring escape. It was ego, stupidity and dumb luck. As time went by, the sonuvabitch who did it and framed me was getting more and more pissed off that I was getting the credit for his kill. He wanted to be a bigshot so he started bragging about it to all his IRA pals, telling them he killed the guy and I had nothing to do with it. He said that I even tried to stop them when I found out what they intended to do, which was true. One of the guys he bragged to was a British spy. Next thing I know he's in prison and I'm on a US Army transport back to the States.

"Why didn't you come back to us after you got out?"

"I wanted to. I met with Brigid a few times but she thought it would be safer if we kept it secret."

"I don't understand."

"I'm a soldier, a damn good one. When I was in Iraq I couldn't stand seeing good men die because shitheads in Washington who didn't know a battlefield from a baseball field were calling the shots. So I quit and went public with what was going on over there, pissing off a lot of bigwigs in the process. Now I fight other people's battles and get paid real well to do it.

"Over the years I made a lot of enemies. Terrorists, jihadists, Albanian mobsters. The worst of the worst. The kind that when they want revenge, they don't just go after you, they wipe out your family. Brigid was fearless, she wasn't afraid for herself, but she didn't want to risk anything happening to you. And neither did I."

Kelleher was trained to read faces. He could see belief in Maggie's eyes as they lost their laserlike intensity. Then, in an instant, acceptance turned to anger. She glared at him and screamed, "Don't you think I had the right to know I had a father! You should've told me."

"I wanted to...a hundred times. When you won the City Championship. When you made the Olympic team. After your accident I flew to Boulder, went to the hospital. But Brigid wouldn't let me see you. She said that after losing your Olympic dream you weren't ready for any more life shattering news."

"So why now, now that she's dead?"

"I wasn't there to protect Brigid. I'm damn sure not gonna let anything happen to you."

"I survived my whole life without your protection. I don't need it now."

"The hell you don't! I don't know why Brigid was shot or if you're also in danger. But until I do, I'm your protector whether you like it or not."

"If you really are my father, I guess I should say thank you."

"I am your father. You want to know more, call Eamon Doyle and ask him about me."

"Uncle Eamon?" Maggie said, taken aback yet again.

"He introduced your mother and me...sort of. It's a pretty funny story." He handed her a card. "If you need to get in touch with me call this number, they'll know where to find me." He leaned forward, kissed Maggie gently on the forehead, then left.

12

———

A few blocks east of Madison Square Garden on thirty-second street, O'Reilly's Pub was nestled between a Korean jewelry store and a Pakistani card shop. In fact, the smoky old tavern was the only non-foreign-owned business on the block. It had been in the same spot since before the Second World War. Some of the hockey and basketball writers hung out there after the games, but the Knicks and Rangers were out of the playoffs so the place was pretty much empty, just a couple of Penn Station commuters killing time until the next train.

It had a long gnarled oak bar and a peat fire going in the stone fireplace summer and winter, which added a smoky haze to its already dusky ambience. Jake Marks sat at a table in a dark corner at the back of the room, sipping a Perrier with lime. Marcus Glynn walked in, surveyed the bar, walked over to Jake and sat down.

Jake said, "Haven't you heard? I quit."

"Yeah, I heard. You mind telling me why?"

"Because I didn't sign up to kill random people. We're supposed to be the good guys, remember? How did Goldbarr put it, 'That the job of keeping the world safe was too important to leave to the assholes in Washington.' It wasn't too safe for Brigid Quinlan, was it?"

"I know you feel bad about that. It was a mistake. We all make them. It's what they call collateral damage."

"I didn't make a mistake. There's no way I hit that woman."

"She wasn't dead when you started firing and she was when you stopped. You got another explanation?"

"I fired four shots and they all hit Townsend. The shot came from somewhere behind me."

"I saw the autopsy report. She was killed with one of your bullets. There's no doubt."

"Reports can be doctored. I know I didn't shoot Brigid Quinlan. I'd bet my life on it."

"Maybe you already did." Glynn put a manila envelope on the table and shoved it towards Jake.

He opened it. "What's this?"

"Have you ever heard of Jungle Jim Kelleher?"

Jake thought for a moment. "Maybe. The name rings a slight bell but I can't seem to place it."

"He's a soldier for hire, one of the best operating today. He's not with any of the big military contractors. Works on his own or with a couple of guys who were with him in the Rangers." He opened the folder and handed Jake a photo of Kelleher. "He fought in Northern Ireland, Sri Lanka, Kosovo and the Persian Gulf. He's one tough sonuvabitch."

Jake pushed the envelope back at Glynn. "Like I said, I'm out of it. Give this excision to someone else."

Glynn grinned sardonically and slowly moved the envelope back towards him. "He's not the target. You are."

Jake jerked upright.

"What the hell are you talking about?" he said more loudly than he planned. The tipsy commuters glanced over at him, then looked away.

"You know that woman, Brigid Quinlan, the one you say you didn't shoot?"

"Yeah."

"That was Kelleher's wife."

"So why am I getting a packet on him?"

"He's going after the person who shot her."

"Does he know who it was?"

"He knows that it was the Lone Ranger."

"There are a lot of people after the Lone Ranger. What's so special about this guy?" Jake pulled Kelleher's photo out of the packet and examined it. "He's old."

"He's pushing sixty, but don't let that fool you. He's smart, ruthless and tougher than one of his old army boots. He can still kick the shit out of most men half his age. I wouldn't want to tangle with him and I outweigh him by a hundred pounds."

"Okay, I'm impressed, but nobody knows who the Lone Ranger is."

Glynn shook his head. "I know. Goldbarr knows. Stryker too, and he's been acting a little strange lately. Paranoid."

"He's always been like that. But he's more loyal than a dog. I can't believe he'd turn on us."

"Not us. You. He never wanted you on the team. He thinks you're a Socialist. That you'll sell us out to our enemies."

"You mean like Russia or China?"

"No. He's sure you're going to go to the *New York Times* or CNN or the Democrats."

"That's insane. Even if I did, they'd never believe me unless I told them I was the Lone Ranger. They still probably wouldn't believe me. But if they did there's no place on earth I'd be safe. The Lone Ranger is on every 'Most Wanted' list in the world. East and West."

"I didn't say he was rational. Stryker took a couple of thousand hits to the head in the ring. Who the hell knows what's going on in that scrambled brain of his."

"What do you think?"

"I think he's a fucking lunatic. But if he got it in his head that you were the enemy and needed killing, there's not much I or anyone else could do to stop him."

A young, plump waitress came to the table and asked Glynn what he was drinking. Her accent was right out of County Kilkenny. He ordered a bourbon, straight up. Marks asked for another Perrier. Glynn eyed the waitress as she walked away from the table.

"You know, Kelleher has a daughter about her age. Almost made the Olympics but she had an accident and messed up her leg. Now she coaches girls' gymnastics in a Brooklyn high school. I think her team won the city championship last year." He nodded at the packet. "It's all in there."

"That's pretty impressive, but what does it have to do with Kelleher finding the Lone Ranger?"

"Maybe nothing, maybe a lot. You might want to find out if she's a tennis fan." Glynn winked, downed his drink and walked out of the bar.

13

____

If there was a bigger doorman in New York, Kelleher had never seen him. He was about six-six and well over 300 pounds. His arms and shoulders strained the seams of his double-breasted blue blazer. He had caramel skin and almond eyes. His head was the size of a basketball from taking too many steroids. 'Millennium Society' was embroidered in gold over his left breast pocket. His plastic name tag said 'Herman.' His bulk filled most of the front door with his arms folded across his chest and a scowl on his face.

Kelleher said, "I'm here to see Marcus Glynn."

Herman grunted, "Name."

"Kelleher."

Herman pulled a sheet of paper out of his pocket and squinted at it. He nodded and said, "Yeah. Go head." He opened the door and stepped aside.

Kelleher found himself in what could have been the lobby of a five-star hotel or the grand ballroom of a billionaires' social club. The large, lavish space was paneled in dark wood. Burgundy leather chairs and sofas were situated near mahogany coffee tables and end tables. Golden crystal chandeliers hung from the high ceiling and Persian rugs covered the polished oak floors. Kelleher was taking in his surroundings when Glynn appeared through a side door.

"Jungle Jim, I wasn't sure you would come." He gestured at a chair. "Park it."

Kelleher sank down into the plush cushion then shot himself up and sat stiffly on the edge. He didn't want to get too comfortable.

Glynn sat on a sofa diagonally across from him.

Kelleher scanned the room.

He shook his head slowly.

"I guess I was wrong about you. I figured you for a beer and brats kinda guy. I never had you pegged for a place like this. Looks like one of those clubs where rich assholes hang out, sipping martinis with their pinkie stuck in the air and their head up their ass."

"This is a different kind of club. The members are all former top men in Washington. I'm talking Defense, Homeland Security, Pentagon."

"Then I guess I won't be getting an invitation to join anytime soon. Most of those Washington dickheads hate my guts."

"Does Ronald Goldbarr hate your guts?"

"I'm sure he does. He's one of the biggest dickheads of them all. Inherited his father's mattress business, made billions, bought some radio and TV stations and now he thinks he's a politician."

"You're wrong. Goldbarr's on the same page as you. He has no use for those Washington empty suits either. He's no politician. He's a patriotic American who loves this country but is fed up with the bureaucracy."

"If he's not a politician, why the hell is he doing all this political bullshit? Rumor is he wants to run for President."

"He's gonna run. And he's gonna win. Then you'll see some shit hit the fan."

"I have more chance to be President than Goldbarr. The man's a fucking clown."

"You're wrong. Goldbarr knows how to get things done. His father gave him 20 stores. He built it into 2,000. Then he bought two dipshit radio stations. Within two years Millennium Media was in every market in America. His sports network was giving ESPN a run for its money."

"So why'd he quit?"

"Cause he was tired of running editorials about what's wrong with the country and decided to do something about it. That's why he started the Millennium Society. He's got some of the smartest guys on the planet here. It's a think tank on steroids."

"I know all about think tanks. A lot of overpaid windbags with fancy degrees and three-thousand dollar suits sitting around in rooms like this one, making a lot of noise, wasting a lot of dead trees with their reports, analyses and white papers that nobody reads."

"This one's different."

"Yeah, how?"

"The Millennium Society's got what they call a tactical wing."

A puzzled frown contorted Kelleher's face. "What the hell does that mean?"

"It means that they don't just sit around coming up with long-range strategic analyses that get filed in some asshole bureaucrat's drawer. They figure out what needs to be done, not next month, next year or in five years." Glynn slammed his ham hock of a fist against the table. "Right fucking now!"

"Then what?"

"Then we fucking do it."

Kelleher sat up. "We?"

"Right now there are two sections. I run one. Your old sparring partner Stryker is in charge of the other one."

"That's just two guys. You ain't gonna change the world with that."

"I can have twenty men here in 24 hours. Warriors. Ex-military, ex-law enforcement. They're all ready to fight and die for their country whenever they get the call."

"I read something about Goldbarr hooking up with those militia fuckups. That's your elite fighting force? Give me a fucking break."

"Don't sell them short. Those guys are tough."

"Yeah, when they're going up against unarmed college kids at a demonstration or half-starved Mexicans at the border."

"We also have access to elite operatives with specialized skills for specific assignments, like eliminating high profile targets."

"You mean like Russell Townsend?"

Glynn nodded.

"So what are you telling me? That the Long Ranger is on your payroll?"

Glynn paused for a few seconds. "Yes and no. He worked with us once or twice."

"What's his name?"

"I don't know."

Kelleher jumped to his feel and yelled, "Bullshit!"

"Calm down and listen," Glynn said softly. "The Lone Ranger's an independent contractor. Never works with a team. We use him for jobs that no one else can do."

Kelleher sat. "How do you contact him?"

"Encrypted message boards, websites, burn phones. I don't understand most of it. We let our tech guys handle it."

"You still never answered my question. You coulda told me all this downtown. Why am I here?"

"Mr. Goldbarr wants to meet you."

"So why isn't he here?"

"I AM here," Ronald Goldbarr announced as he strode through the door, a drink in one hand, a small leather portfolio case in the other and his trademark arrogant smirk across his face.

Kelleher didn't know if Goldbarr heard the dickhead crack or not. And he didn't care. He seemed like the same loudmouth blowhard that's been all over TV, except he was shorter and fatter in the flesh. His jowls were thicker and his face more lined. His bleach blonde pompadour looked glued on. But his voice and presence had the same power and authority that convinced millions of people to buy his crappy mail-order mattresses and millions more to tune into his radio and TV stations.

Goldbarr leveled his steely gaze at Kelleher. "So you wanna get the Lone Ranger?"

"I want the sonuvabitch who killed my wife, if that's the Lone Ranger, then yeah."

Mendel Stryker padded silently into the room. He stood, scowling, against the back wall, arms folded like a muscle-bound Buddha hewn out of black granite. Goldbarr glanced quickly at him then turned his attention back to Kelleher. "Some of my advisors tell me that you can't be trusted to bring in the Lone Ranger or anything else."

"From what Glynn just told me, the Lone Ranger's on your payroll. Maybe I should just shoot you."

Glynn and Stryker both jumped up, guns out.

Kelleher grinned. "Pretty jumpy, ain't you, boys? Sit down, I was kidding. Anyway, for all I know, the Lone Ranger had nothing to do with my wife's murder."

Goldbarr put the portfolio on the table. "Here's the proof. Read it and decide for yourself."

"Let's say he did do it, why do I need you?"

"Because we have resources you could never get on your own."

"I have my own resources."

Glynn turned to him, "C'mon Kelleher, don't be such a hardass prick. If things work out on this it could be very profitable for everyone. There's a million dollar price on his head."

"I'll think about it."

Stryker glared at him. "Thanks for proving me right. I didn't want you anywhere near this operation but I was overruled." He sneered over at Glynn, then back at Kelleher. "I'll be watching you. You screw us on this, I'll beat you a lot worse than the last time."

"Why wait?" Kelleher sprung up, knees bent, fists up. "Let's do it now."

Stryker rose slowly and inched towards him, fists curled at his sides. A big cat stalking his prey.

Goldbarr cowered as Glynn jumped in-between them, arms outstretched. Like a father separating his feuding sons.

"You wanna mix it up after this is done, fine," he shouted. "Find an alley somewhere and bash each other's brains out." He turned to Kelleher. "Right now we got business to attend to."

He handed Kelleher the portfolio. "Read this and let us know what you wanna do. If you want to work with us, fine. But if you go it alone and the Lone Ranger winds up dead, it won't be good for you."

Kelleher snatched the portfolio off the table and stormed out of the room.

Goldbarr smiled at both men. "Good job. If we're really lucky, Marks and Kelleher will kill each other. If not, we'll only have one to deal with."

Glynn said, "You never said why Kelleher's on the x-list."

Goldbarr grinned. "I made a little deal with the Saudis. When I run, they'll cut oil output. That should drive up costs and drive down votes for the asshole in the White House. In exchange, they want Kelleher dead."

"How come?"

"Their biggest threat is a pro-democracy rebel group called Arabs Arise. Kelleher worked with them before. They don't want him back there again."

Stryker said. "Why are we wasting time hoping they'll take each other out? Let me take care of them both. Case closed."

Goldbarr said, "C'mon Mendel, we went over this before. We can't do anything that might lead back to us. Not now."

14

———————

Jake Marks stood at a podium in the middle of the stage at the main auditorium of John Jay High School on Seventh Avenue in Park Slope, Brooklyn. He wore a beige polo shirt and khaki slacks. His long, wavy blonde hair reached almost to his shoulders. Seated next to him on a straight-backed folding chair was the principal. The athletic director was on his other side, smiling broadly at his good luck. Usually the end-of-year awards assembly was a dull, long-winded affair, sparsely attended except by the athletes and their families. Then Jake Marks called and asked if the school was interested in having him visit sometime and talk to some of the players. When the A.D. told him that the awards assembly was the next day, Jake said he'd be happy to come.

For the first time in recent memory, the auditorium was filled to capacity, not only with coaches, athletes and their families, but with teachers and students, mostly girls, who didn't care at all about sports, but wanted to get a glimpse of the dreamy tennis superstar.

"To excel at something, whether it's sports, your studies or a job, takes commitment, dedication and sacrifice. All of us would rather hang out with friends, watch TV, play video games or spend time on social media, as opposed to putting in countless hours of practicing or studying. But a few are willing to make that sacrifice to be the best that they can be. They're the young men and women being honored here tonight. They worked long and hard, and competed to the best of their ability. They didn't win every time they played, but they played every game with everything they had." A few of the teachers applauded politely and most of the boys gazed blankly at the ceiling. Many of the girls stared longingly at Jake.

He continued in this vein for another few minutes. Then the athletic director introduced the coaches, one at a time, who presented members of their teams with various awards, including Most Valuable Player, Most Improved Player and Rookie of the Year. The ceremony went on for over an hour, culminating in the athletic director presenting the Athlete of the Year trophy to one of Maggie's gymnasts.

After some announcements by the principal about student discount tickets to the New York City Ballet, which was received with groans and yawns, a reminder about appropriate skirt lengths, which was greeted with a chorus of boos, and yet another 'thank you' to Jake Marks for coming, the assembly was over.

The principal asked Jake if he would like to join some of the staff for refreshments in the teachers' lounge. Once there, Jake got buttonholed by two spinsterish English teachers who seemed to know every detail of every match he ever played. After what seemed like hours, but was only about five minutes, Jake excused himself and walked over to Maggie.

"Maggie Quinlan?"

Maggie stiffened, her green eyes saucerlike, her mouth agape. "Uh, yes."

"I might have a proposition for you."

"I beg your pardon."

"Not that kind of proposition, though I'm sure you get your share of those." Jake smiled his killer smile. "I've been told that you're one of the best gymnastics coaches in the city."

"I'm okay, I guess."

"Your modesty is admirable, but winning the City Championships two out of the past three years is a lot better than okay. Anyway, since I got back on the tour after being away for awhile, my movements haven't been as fluid as I'd like. I thought maybe I'd try something a little different, like gymnastics training."

"You want me to train you? I teach high school girls to do summersaults and balance on a four-inch beam. I'm flattered Mr. Marks, but I've never worked with a professional athlete and I don't know anything about tennis."

"First of all, no more Mr. Marks. It's Jake. Secondly, it doesn't matter that you don't know tennis. I know tennis. You know about making bodies supple and flexible, which is exactly what I need. And thirdly, if I'm not mistaken, you learned gymnastics from the great Illya Phillipi, himself."

"Well, I don't know," she said. "I still have my work here. And my mother recently passed away."

"Oh, I'm very sorry about your mother. But as far as your work here is concerned, I already cleared it with the principal and the athletic director."

"Can I have some time to think about it?"

"Of course. But while you're making up your mind, factor in that you'll be paid five thousand dollars a week for six weeks."

"Thirty thousand dollars for six weeks? That's insane."

"If it helps me to win one extra match, it's a bargain. Think it over, but not too long. Wimbledon's on the horizon."

"I'll let you know in a couple of days."

"Thank you." Jake thrust out his hand. "It was a pleasure meeting you, Maggie."

15

It didn't take Maggie long to make up her mind. She never followed tennis. She had heard the name Jake Marks and knew he was on the tour, but that was about it. After some online research she found out that he was ranked number eighteen in the world and was once the only American in the top ten, ranked as high as six. The only blips on Jake's otherwise spotless record were mysterious absences when he dropped completely off the radar for weeks, sometimes months, at a time. Rumors abounded, from illness to injury to a nervous breakdown. She double-checked with the principal and was assured that it was okay.

Two days later, at eight-thirty in the morning, a vintage London taxi pulled up in front of Maggie's Park Slope brownstone. Bunny Fields, five feet six inches, with pale blue eyes, an aquiline twice-broken nose, in a tweed cap, white shirt, red tie and blue blazer, hopped out of the black cab, walked smartly up the steps and pressed the bell.

When Maggie opened the door a crack, Bunny lifted his hat, placed it over his heart and intoned, "Mr. Jake Marks requests the pleasure of Miss Maggie Quinlan's company for breakfast."

She opened the door and couldn't help smiling at the funny little man. "You mean right now?"

"Yes, mum, if it's convenient."

"Well, uh...okay. Give me five minutes."

Maggie had just gotten out of the shower. There was no time to deal with her thick, wavy red hair so she grabbed a scrunchy and put it in a fluffy ponytail. She dabbed her face with a little powder, put on her white Ralph Lauren warm-up suit, the one she was given at the Olympic trials, and was ready to go.

Bunny stood at attention by the taxi door like a guard at Buckingham Palace. He held it open for Maggie. "Allow me, Miss."

He closed the door, then got behind the wheel.

"Excuse me, uh sir, what's your name?"

"Elroy Hopper, Miss. But my friends call me Bunny. I would be honored if you would as well."

"Well, Bunny, where are we going?"

"The Waldorf Astoria. Mr. Marks owns an apartment there."

"And you work for Mr. Marks?"

"Oh no," he said proudly. "I'm self-employed."

He turned and handed her a business card. It read, *Britannia Transport, Elroy Hopper, President.*

"I have provided transportation for diplomats, corporate executives and theatrical luminaries. I drive for Mr. Marks whenever he is in town."

When they arrived at the Waldorf, Bunny nodded to the doorman and escorted Maggie to Peacock Alley, one the hotel's premier restaurants. The maître d'hotel escorted them to a table near one of the huge arched windows, with a carafe of coffee and a tray of rolls and pastries in its center. Jake Marks put down his *New York Times* and stood. Bunny pulled out the chair to Jake's left. Maggie sat, then Jake.

"Is there anything else, sir?"

"I think I can handle it from here, Bunny."

"If you need me for any reason, ring my mobile." He tapped the black leather phone holster hooked to his belt, then he made a small bow, turned sharply and walked briskly out of the dining room. A waiter, standing nearby, poured coffee.

"That Bunny's quite a character," Maggie said as her eyes followed the diminutive driver out the side door.

"He's great. He served in the British Army. Used to drive British officers around Northern Ireland."

The color drained from Maggie's face. "So Bunny was a British soldier in Northern Ireland," she said glumly, her eyes downcast. "Too bad, I was just starting to like him."

"I didn't realize you were a supporter of the IRA."

"My godfather was Eamon Doyle. He published The *Gaelic Guardian*. His office was the unofficial New York headquarters of the IRA."

"I think I read something about him. He's supposed to be a pretty colorful character."

"Oh yeah. He was wonderfully kind to my mother and me when I was growing up."

"What about your father?"

"There's another weird story."

"How so?"

"If you would have asked me that a week ago, I would have told you he was dead, killed by the British in Northern Ireland."

"And now?"

"I just found out that my father is very much alive. His name's Jim Kelleher."

Jake's mouth dropped open. "Jungle Jim Kelleher? Didn't I read somewhere that he's the second most decorated living American soldier? I had no idea he was your father."

"Actually, neither did I. I only found out a few days ago, right after my mother was murdered."

Jake's face contorted in sympathetic grief. "Your mother was murdered? Oh my God, how awful!" he said much too loudly. The Waldorf brunchers near them turned to stare. He lowered his voice to a near-whisper. "When?"

"I'm sorry, I thought you knew. About a week ago Russell Townsend, the anti-nuclear activist, was assassinated while being interviewed in front of the U.N. It was on the news."

"Yes, of course. I remember it."

"My mother was interviewing him. She was killed too."

"I did read about a journalist being shot. I had no idea that she was your mother. I'm so sorry."

"Thank you," she said, wiping a little moisture from her eye with a napkin. "Now Kelleher is going after my mother's murderer."

"He knows who did it? The last thing I read was that the police were still baffled."

"He says he knows."

"What's his plan?"

She shrugged. "No clue. I hardly know him."

"I had no idea all this was going on in your life. Maybe this isn't a good time for you to work with me. If you'd rather not, I understand."

"No, actually it's the perfect time. Whatever Kelleher is doing has nothing to do with me. And to tell you the truth, I'm happy to have something to take my mind off my mother's murder."

"Good. I'm skipping the clay court season and it's six weeks to Wimbledon. Do you think you can work with me until then?"

"I'm totally free until the school year starts in September."

"Now about your fee, is thirty thousand enough?"

Her face lit up. "Are you kidding, that's half-a-year's salary?"

"Then the money's all set and the time commitment's no problem. Have you given any thought to the training program?"

"Just a little," she said. Her demeanor subtly changed from a young woman in awe of the man she's with to a professional presenting a work schedule. "Gymnastics is about strength, flexibility, balance, and stamina. I would imagine that those qualities are important in tennis too."

Jake nodded. "Extremely."

"There are preliminary drills and exercises we can do to work on each of those categories."

"That sounds terrific, when can we start?"

"Today's Thursday, how about this Monday?"

"Perfect."

"Where?"

"I train at the Vanderbilt Tennis Club. It's on the fourth floor of Grand Central Station. Would you like me to send Bunny for you?"

She shook her head. "It's not necessary. I know how to get to Grand Central. What time?"

"Eleven a.m."

"I'll be there."

Jake smiled. contentedly. "I think this is going to turn out exactly as I had hoped."

16

———

Nestled on the fourth floor of the legendary Grand Central terminal, the Vanderbilt Tennis Club's full-size court looked out on Park Avenue and Forty-Second Street. Jake loved the idea of playing tennis in the heart of New York City, tapping into the energy of the early morning hordes as they bounded out of the station.

He had just finished some intense two-on-one hitting with Columbia University's nationally ranked doubles team and was about to begin his serving drill, a hopper full of balls at his side, when he saw the door to the court slowly open. He glanced up at the clock over the big bay window, 10:15. Maggie wasn't supposed to show up until eleven. Now he'll have to cut his session short. He hated deviating from his schedule and wanted to shower and change before meeting her, but what the hell, if she really does become his trainer, she'll be spending a lot of time with him dripping in sweat. Why not start now?

Daria, the young receptionist at the front desk, walked onto the court. Though only a sophomore, the stocky 5'7" brunette was second singles on the NYU varsity tennis team. Sometimes Jake would hit with her. The front of her pink t-shirt proclaimed, 'Never love a tennis player' and on the back was written, 'Cause in tennis love means nothing.'

"Excuse me, Mr. Marks. You have a visitor."

"Thanks, send her in."

"Her?" she mumbled, giving him a curious look. Then she ambled back to the front office. A few seconds later the door opened again, but instead of the lithe former gymnastics champion with flaming red hair, the hulking Marcus Glynn lumbered across the court and parked himself on a bench next to the net. He clutched a manila envelope in his giant paw.

Jake walked over to him and said, "What the hell are you doing here?"

"I got you a deal with Goldbarr. We need you to do one more excision. If you do this job you can retire the Lone Ranger for good."

"I already did."

Glynn shook his head and said, "Uh-uh. You don't retire from Millennium until the boss says you're retired. It's like the mob. You can't just walk away. What's in your head could take down the organization. Hell, it could take down the government. You've got to prove you're not a threat. The last thing you want is to be on Goldbarr's shit list."

"Shit list or hit list?"

Glynn smirked. "Yeah."

Jake jumped back, eyes wide. "Goldbarr put an excision order out on me?!"

"Not yet."

"What the hell does that mean?"

Jake was glad he was drenched in perspiration. That way Glynn wouldn't see the beads of stress sweat that were forming on his forehead.

"It means right now you're okay. But you know how it is. Options get discussed."

"I know who wanted that option."

Glynn smiled deviously. "I'm not saying who it was. It was discussed and the boss rejected it. For now."

"And how does the situation change if I complete this excision?"

Glynn leaned in and lowered his voice even though there was no one else in the room. "I convinced him that you're still one hundred percent with us but you're burnt out, you need a rest, a long one. That's why you screwed up and shot the Quinlan woman."

Jake shook his head vehemently. "I didn't shoot her."

"Yeah, whatever. It doesn't matter," Glynn said dismissively. "Goldbarr needs to know you're still loyal."

"And he thinks one more job will do that?"

Glynn shrugged. "I gave up trying to figure out how his mind works." He handed the manila envelope to Jake.

Jake opened it and removed three photos of a man around forty with long salt-and-pepper hair pulled back in a ponytail. "Who is he?"

"Mohammed Levi."

Jake stared at the picture. "I heard of him. Isn't he some kind of singer or something?"

"He's the Middle Eastern Bob Dylan. Half Palestinian, half Israeli. The kids there love him, the Jews and the Arabs. Adults too. He's huge all over the Middle East and lately he's become very popular in Europe."

"Is Goldbarr going crazy? First you target an anti-nuclear peace activist, now a folk singer. Who's next, the Pope?"

"Goldbarr believes this guy's a major threat. He's been connected to Russia and Iran. And there's some noise about him running for office. Right now he would probably be elected in both Israel and Palestine."

"Isn't that what we want, someone who can bring the Israelis and Palestinians together?"

"He'll bring 'em together all right. Together with our

enemies. The Millennium strategists think that if he becomes a power broker in the Middle East, it'll be a big problem for us."

"Suppose the strategists are wrong?"

Glynn snapped at him, "When the smartest guys in the country think it's a problem, it's a fucking problem."

"Like all those weapons of mass destruction that were supposed to be in Saddam Hussein's basement?"

Glynn ignored him. "Listen, this guy needs to be taken out publicly so that the world knows not to fuck with us. That's why it needs the special talents of the Lone Ranger. Are you in or not?"

"When does this have to happen?"

"Soon, in the next two weeks."

"I'll be in England then, prepping for Wimbledon."

"I know. He'll be there at the same time. He's doing a concert in London right around Wimbledon. He's a big tennis fan. He tries to time his concerts to coincide with the Grand Slams."

"Give me the packet."

Glynn handed it to him. "So you're in?"

"I want to read it before I decide."

"You better decide fast. Kelleher can't wait to put a bullet in your brain. And Stryker's no fan of yours either. If Goldbarr sics them on you, there's nowhere in the world you can hide."

Glynn stood and marched out of the gym.

Jake lifted a document out of the envelope. It looked like a press release.

Mohammed Levi is thirty-seven years old. His mother is an Israeli Jew, his father a Sunni Muslim from the West Bank. Trained as a nurse, he was a medic in the Israeli army, then worked for several years in Southern Hebron as a volunteer in free clinics. Everywhere he went, his guitar was his constant companion. Most evenings he would entertain and enchant his patients and colleagues with song-stories he composed in the troubadouric tradition. Tales of the poor and the pitiful, the despised and the downtrodden, the sweepings of society. His reputation grew by word of mouth and soon he began performing throughout Israel and Palestine, always donating half his earnings to local health care agencies. As his fame increased he toured the Middle East, Europe and Asia, amassing a huge fan base.

It went on to talk about his sold-out concerts and record-breaking CD sales. It mentioned that he met with the heads of Russia and China, but also with the leaders of Germany, France, Japan and the UK.

Jake felt physically ill. His guts churned. He sat with his head in his hands, his brain spinning like an out-of-control slot machine.

Could this folk singer really be a global threat?

Has Goldbarr lost his mind? Is he a paranoid sociopath?

If he is, how many innocent people have I already executed?

Am I already in the Millennium excision protocol?

He needed time to think. But there was one thing he was sure of, he wouldn't kill this singer. He'll go to London and let them believe he'll carry out the assignment. That will give him some time to figure out what to do after that.

"Mr. Marks." A female voice jarred him out of his mind-storm. "Are you ready to start training?"

After everything that Glynn just dumped on him, he forgot all about Maggie.

"Uh, no. Sorry Maggie, there's been a change in plan."

Her face sagged. "You don't want me to work with you? I knew it was too good to be true."

Jake smiled. "Of course I want to train with you. More than ever. Just not here."

She perked back up. "As long as we have some room to work out in and I can bring in a few pieces of equipment, it can be anywhere."

"How about London?"

"London?" She flinched. "I don't know."

"I did say we were training for Wimbledon, didn't I?"

"Yes, but I guess I didn't really think it through. I didn't realize I'd be going there with you."

"Have you ever been there?"

"No."

"It's a great city. You'll love it."

"Okay, yeah. I'll go. When do we leave?"

"Actually tonight. The flight takes off around seven."

"Tonight? Whoa! I don't know about that."

"It's only 11 a.m. now. Think it over. If you decide to come, I'll have Bunny drive you to JFK."

"I can't just pick up and fly off to London at a moment's notice. I need time to get ready, to pack."

"Do you have a passport?"

"Yes."

"That's all you need. I'll cover your plane fare, hotel and food, of course. Just pack your essentials. Whatever else you need you can get there. It'll be part of your compensation package."

"Really?"

"Absolutely. You can go to the best shops in London. Money is no object. It's a tax write-off for me."

"It's all happening so fast. I'm just not sure."

"Think of it as a paid vacation, a shopping spree and a great job all at the same time. We'll only work for a couple of hours a day. Then you can see the sights. Also, how about a ten thousand dollar travel bonus as an extra incentive?"

After fifteen seconds she said, "Okay. Let's do it."

17

———

Kelleher walked along 21st Street on the way back to his condo on Gramercy Park East, a gift from the half-brother of the Sheikh of Abu Dhabi after he and his team extricated the playboy potentate from an ISIS prison compound.

Lately he'd been spending a lot of time thinking about Brigid. The first time he saw her was in O'Malley's, an Irish dive bar in the East Village that was also the unofficial New York headquarters of the IRA. The owner, Eammon Doyle, asked Kelleher to talk to some of the eager young toughs who thought fighting the British in Northern Ireland would be a great adventure.

There were about twenty would-be revolutionaries in various stages of shitfacedness glaring up at him.

Kelleher spoke in a low voice. "Hello men. I'm not here to sign you up, just the opposite. I'm here to tell you that if you got any romantic notions about battling the British for fame and glory, forget it. The Brits are well-trained and well-equipped. The IRA is an unruly mob. Training is minimal, discipline is lax and the equipment is either ancient, broken, or homemade."

One of the boys stood up. "So what are you telling us, that we haven't got a chance?"

"No, I think your side can win. But it'll be a long, slow, war of attrition. The Brits don't want to be there and you've got to punish them for staying. It may be a noble cause, but it won't be a noble fight. You will never see real combat, only assassinations, kidnappings, bombings, and murder. Innocent people will be killed. You'll be hated and vilified, branded as criminals and cowards, even by some of your own people. If you're not killed, there's a better than even chance you'll spend the rest of your life rotting in a British prison." He looked out at the sullen crowd. "Now, if any of you are still interested, give your name to Mr. Doyle."

A voice from the back of the bar shouted, "So if it's so bloody awful, why do you do it, Mr. Jungle Fuckin' Jim Kelleher?"

"I don't do it because I'm Irish or because I believe in a free Ireland, though I am and I do. I do it because the IRA Central Committee pays me handsomely for my work." Kelleher glared at the kid. "And I wouldn't advise talking to me in that tone again. Next time I might take offense."

Doyle stood. "Don't be givin' Colonel Kelleher a hard time. What he's tellin' you is true. I thank him for sayin' it, and you lads for hearin' it. Now everybody in the house gets a drink on me."

Brigid Quinlan walked over to Kelleher. She was petite and perky with auburn hair and sky blue eyes. The green apron she wore did little to hide her tight, curvy figure. "What can I get for you Colonel?"

"Double Jack Daniels, no ice," he mumbled, unable to take his eyes off her.

As soon as she left, a young headbanger walked over to him. He wore a black t-shirt, black jeans and motorcycle boots

"You think yer sho tough," he slurred.

Kelleher glowered down at him. "Go home boy, you've had enough."

"Washa matter, too chickenshit to fight me?"

The kid launched a slow roundhouse right. Kelleher caught the flailing fist like a shortstop snagging a hot line drive and bent it all the way back. There was an audible crack. The kid yelped then cried, "You broke my wrist, you fuckin' bastard."

Kelleher let go. The young punk fell backwards onto the floor. Kelleher looked down at him. "Remember what just happened the next time you decide to take a swing at somebody."

The kid rocked back and forth, holding his wrist, wailing, "Fuckin' bastard! Fuckin' bastard! Fuckin' bastard!"

As soon as Kelleher turned his back, three of the kid's buddies jumped him. Kelleher tried to shove them off, but his arms were pinned at his sides. They flailed away, fists and feet coming from all different angles. It was like fighting a drunken octopus. He grabbed a finger, twisted it and heard a muffled yelp, but whoever was attached to it was too sloshed to feel much pain.

Brigid tried to get to Kelleher but Doyle held her back. "Don't worry darlin', the Colonel is fully capable of takin' care of himself."

After a minute, she broke free, grabbed a half-full bottle of Jameson's Irish Whisky and bashed it over the head of the one holding Kelleher. The kid fell awkwardly to the floor.

Kelleher quickly subdued the remaining two, cracking two ribs on one, then breaking the nose of the other with a head-butt.

After things settled down, Doyle ambled over to Brigid. "That was a terrible thing you just did."

She glared at him. "You have a problem with women in bar fights?"

"Not at all." He grinned. "I thought you acquitted yourself

well, save for one thing. The next time you want to knock someone on the head, grab a water bottle, a soda bottle, even a baby's bottle fer Chrissakes—but please, keep your mitts off the John Jameson." With that he gave her a quick kiss on the forehead.

After the fracas, Kelleher insisted on walking Brigid home, in case any pals of the goon she conked on the head were lying in wait. She invited him in for a drink. He stayed three days.

The screech of tires snapped Kelleher back to the present. A late model black Cadillac Escalade stopped in front of him. Two men in blue jeans and hoodies jumped out. One was black, the other Asian. The Asian hoodie stood in front of him. The black guy circled behind fluidly, like they'd done this many times before. Size-wise they were middleweights not heavyweights.

It was almost midnight. The street was empty except for an old guy walking a small dog with a pushed-in face. He scooped it up and shuffled as fast as he could toward the park, a half block away.

Kelleher smirked. "Nice entrance. Did you mooks practice that or was it an ad lib?"

"Get in, old man," the Asian said, his voice even.

"And if I don't?"

"You ever been tased?"

"Not lately."

"You won't like it."

Kelleher sized up the situation. These guys knew what they were doing. Even if he took the front guy out, the one behind him would have a clean shot with a Taser or something worse. He liked his chances better in the car.

"Okay. Let's go for a ride," Kelleher said.

The Asian sat next to him in the back seat. The other one drove.

"Where we goin'?" Kelleher said to no one in particular.

"You'll see," came the gruff reply.

They drove up Madison Avenue for about fifteen minutes, turned down 128th Street and parked in front of a four story brownstone townhouse.

Kelleher tried to think who in Harlem would want to grab him. He drew a blank.

"Last stop."

This would be the time to make his move. He could take out the guy next to him with a quick elbow to the neck, then deal with the other one. Instead he followed the Asian onto the street. He was curious to see what was coming. If they were out to mess him up they would have done it already.

They went into a large, dark room on the ground floor. A video screen took up most of the front wall. Three rows of plush movie-style seats faced it. Marcus Glynn sat in the last row, one seat in.

He turned and said, "Thanks, Carl. He give you any trouble?"

The Asian said, "Nah. Just some lip."

Then he walked out.

Kelleher said, "Why the hell am I here?"

"I want you to see something."

"So why send those two bozos to drag me up here? You coulda just called."

"I did call. About fives times. You never called me back."

"Maybe I didn't get the message."

"Or maybe you're just an asshole."

"Why'd you drag me up to Harlem? What's wrong with the building on Madison Avenue?"

"We don't trust you. If you decided to make some kinda scene, nobody around here gives a shit. Downtown, it could cause some embarrassment."

"What kind of place is this?"

"It's one of Goldbarr's video production studios."

"If we're gonna see a movie, don't I at least get a bag of popcorn?"

"Just sit down and watch. We'll talk after."

Kelleher sat down next to Glynn. The big man hit a remote and the lights dimmed. An image filled the screen. Maggie and Jake Marks sitting at a table at the Waldorf Astoria. Then it cut to footage of them boarding a jet at the British Air terminal at JFK.

"So my daughter's going out with some guy. Looks like they're taking a trip. Good for her."

"That's not just any guy, that's Jake Marks. Ever heard of him?"

"No. Who is he?"

"He's a top tennis pro. Was once number six in the world. Still in the top twenty."

Glynn pressed a button and played several clips of Jake playing and accepting trophies in several tournaments.

"Even better. She's going out with a big-time pro tennis player. Probably rolling in dough. Is this why you dragged me up here, to tell me about my daughter's love life?"

"Jake Marks isn't just a tennis player. He has another job." Glynn paused for effect. "He's the Lone Ranger."

"You're fulla shit."

"I got one more video to show you."

Glynn hit the remote and it was a close-up of Jake, dripping with sweat, on a bench at the Vanderbilt Tennis Club. The other guy wasn't on the screen but from the voice Kelleher knew it was Glynn.

"Listen, this guy needs to be taken out publicly so that the world knows not to fuck with us. That's why it needs the special talents of the Lone Ranger. Are you in or not?"

"When does this have to happen?"

"Soon, in the next two weeks."

"I'll be in England then, getting ready for Wimbledon."

"I know. He'll be there at the same time.

The screen goes dark.

Kelleher screamed, "You knew the whole time that this scumbag killed my wife, you fuckin' son of a bitch. Then you hand him my daughter. I should kill you right now."

"Calm down, Kelleher," Glynn said. "I didn't tell him Maggie was your daughter. I didn't have to. Once he found out about you and Brigid, he looked her up."

"You're a fuckin' liar!"

"I don't give s shit if you believe me or not. You want the man who put a bullet in your wife, go get him. He's on a plane to London right now with your daughter. They're staying at Brown's Hotel. His target's a singer, Mohammad Levi. Levi's doing a concert at London's Royal Festival Hall. Look up the date. He's only there for one day. That's when Marks will make his move. He likes to operate in crowded places and lose himself in the chaos. So far it's worked."

Kelleher glared at Glynn. "This better not be another one of your bullshit stunts."

"This is legit. You got everything you need to take this guy out. But you better make it count. He's the best. If you miss the first time there won't be a second. For you or Maggie."

Kelleher stood and walked toward the door. "I won't miss."

He turned back to Glynn. "So how come you're helping me out all of a sudden?"

Glynn smirked. "Goldbarr thinks Marks lost his nerve. Shooting your wife wasn't part of the plan. It was a big fuck-up. Marks is making noise about hanging it up. Goldbarr doesn't want to take a chance of him going to the papers and screwing up his shot at the White House."

"That doesn't explain why he wants me to take him out."

"Taking Marks out won't be easy. The boss didn't want to risk one of our key men to do it. You're expendable. If you get him, fine. If he gets you, we're okay with that too."

"Fuck you, Glynn." He walked out.

SECOND SET

18

———

Maggie and Jake stood outside the Terminal 5 Arrivals Gate for twenty minutes while well dressed businessmen and women hustled into limousines, goggle-eyed tourists studied guide books and maps, and families ran into each other's arms and hugged.

Jake assured Maggie that Bunny had arranged for their transportation.

After twenty minutes he said, "I'm sorry to keep you standing here. You must be exhausted. Bunny's usually very organized about things like this."

"I'm fine," Maggie said, stifling a yawn. "What time is it?"

Jake looked at his watch. "It's almost nine o'clock."

He flagged a taxi and told the driver to take them to Brown's Hotel.

The doorman out front greeted patrons emerging from Jaguars, Daimlers and Bentleys. When he saw Jake and Maggie get out of the cab, he bowed, tipped his hat and said, "It's a pleasure to have you with us again, Mr. Marks."

"Great to be here," Jake said. "I'll try to get some grounds passes for you for the first week, if you're free."

"You are very kind, sir."

"This is where we're staying?" Maggie said, awed by alabaster facade with the pink Doric columns.

She was even more dazzled when they entered the lobby, bedecked with Louis XVI furniture, gilt-edged beveled mirrors, floor-to-ceiling windows and crystal chandeliers.

"Wow! It seems more like a grand estate than a hotel."

"That's why I love staying here. It's the oldest hotel in London. It was built during the reign of Queen Victoria. I think at one time it was some Duke's home. You can't get more British than that."

Jake had reserved a suite for himself and a single room across the hall for Maggie. The rooms weren't as fancy as the lobby but still quite posh.

After showering and changing, Jake knocked on Maggie's door.

"All settled in?"

"Not much to settle. I took hardly any clothes, remember?"

He smiled. "We're gonna fix that right now, if you're up for a shopping spree."

"I'm always up for shopping. Where are we going?"

"Not we, you. I hate to shop. Five minutes in a store and I become a terrible person. I start pacing and snarling. Growling at sweet little old ladies. Trust me, you'll do a lot better without me."

"I don't know anything about London. I wouldn't even know how to start figuring out where to shop."

"No worries. I arranged it all with the concierge. There's a personal shopper waiting for you at Harvey Nichols. They have everything you need, clothes, toiletries, whatever. There's a taxi out front ready to take you there. "

"What's my budget?"

"Unlimited."

Her eyes widened. "Really?"

"Absolutely. Go crazy. Don't worry about the cost."

"In the meantime, I'm gonna check out a gym I think might work for us. I'll meet you back here in a couple of hours."

In the lobby, Jake introduced Maggie to Alex, the assistant head concierge, who assured them that everything was taken care of. A car was waiting for Maggie to take her to Harvey Nichols and another to drive Jake to the Castlehaven Sports Center, twenty minutes away.

Jake had known the manager of Castlehaven, Nick Pashim, for several years. A licensed massage therapist and personal trainer, he tended to many of the players during the Wimbledon fortnight. He once told Jake that if he ever needed a place to train in London, he could arrange it. Jake texted Nick before he left to ask if the gym was still available. Nick texted back with the address of the gym and said he'd wait for him there the next morning.

When Jake got to the gym, the door was locked. He banged on it a couple of times and was about to leave when someone he never saw before opened the door. About twenty-five with a shaved head and both arms full of tattoos, he was dressed in black jeans and a skin-tight black t-shirt. A cigarette dangled from his lips. He looked more like a roadie for the Sex Pistols than someone who would be working for the fastidious Nick.

"You Jake Marks?" he said.

"Where's Nick?"

"He had an emergency. He left word for me to let you in."

"Maybe I should come back later. I wanted to talk with him about renting the gym for a couple of weeks."

"That's okay. He said to tell you to have a look round. The lockers are in back. He'll ring you later."

Something didn't feel right. If Nick couldn't be here, why didn't he text me?

Jake walked gingerly into the gym. He looked around, hyper alert for any sound, smell or feeling of malevolence. But the room was still. No one jumped out at him. Getting paranoid in my old age, he thought. He relaxed and checked out facilities. Basketball hoops at each end, ropes snaking down from the high ceiling, stacks of mats in one corner, a chinning bar and pommel horse in the other. It smelled of sweat and sneakers. He walked into the men's locker room. It was clean and well maintained. As was the shower. Then he inspected the women's lockers. All good. He'd tell Maggie they could start as soon as he cleared it with Nick.

As he walked back into the gym he heard a noise behind him. He turned to see a knife thrusting at his chest. As he swerved awkwardly out of the way, the blade cut his arm.

The skinhead stood flat-footed, waving the knife in front of him. His eyes were wary. His hand quivered. He had his chance and he whiffed. Jake took a quick step forward, feinted with his right hand and delivered a roundhouse kick into his attacker's right arm. Yelping in pain, he dropped the knife and grabbed his dangling arm with his other hand.

Jake was about to make the kid tell him who sent him when a shout came from the other end of the gym.

"Hey!"

Jake turned to see a black guy with dreadlocks running towards him.

"Shit!" Jake said out loud.

With Jake's back turned, the skinhead ran out the back door.

The dreadlocks guy was almost on him.

He stopped a few feet in front of him and smiled. "Jake Marks?"

"Who are you?"

"Name's Deke. I'm a mate of Bunny's." He extended his hand.

Jake shook it hesitantly.

"He asked me to fetch you at the airport and look after you

while you're here. Sorry I missed you. I had to leave town for a family emergency and I didn't know how to contact you. I went over to Brown's and they told me you'd be here."

"How do you know Bunny?"

"We served together. The Special Reconnaissance Unit. We met in Ulster back in 2001, during the Belfast riots. My sister moved to New York a few years back and Bunny helped her out. I owe him."

He looked down at Jake's bloody arm. "Looks like he sliced you pretty good."

"Just a scratch. I'm fine."

Deke got a towel from Jake's tennis bag, folded it in half, then into quarters.

Deke said, "Hold this on it for now. I'll see if they have a first aid kit around here somewhere."

He left to find it.

Two minutes later he was back, his face creased with distress. "Bad news."

"Don't worry about the first aid kit. The bleeding's pretty much stopped."

"Not that. You're not the only one that kid carved up. There's a body stuffed in the supply closet. Throat slit."

"Oh my God!" Jake screamed in anguish. "It's Nick. Nick Pashim. He runs this gym. He's a friend of mine. Where is he? I need to see him."

Jake took a step towards the door. Deke grabbed his arm.

"That's the last thing you need to do. You're playing at Wimbledon in a few weeks. You can't be messin' with any dead bodies."

"But..."

"No buts. We gotta get you outta here."

"What? Why?"

"Too many people know you were coming here. The people

at the hotel. The cab driver. Maybe more. Once you're gone, I'll take care of your friend."

"Are you sure?"

"Don't worry, I'll handle it."

Jake was confused, disoriented. He had been in tense, dangerous situations many times, but somehow this felt different. He tried to regain control. He took several deep breaths.

"I guess you're right. I'll cover the cost whatever it is." He pulled out his wallet.

Deke held up his hands. "No money. This is brothers looking out for brothers. Bunny'd do the same for me." He gestured over to the door. "Now get your arse out of here."

Jake decided to walk the three miles back to the hotel. He needed time to think about who over here wanted him dead. There's a long list of people who would happily put a bullet into the skull of the Lone Ranger, but none of them knew his true identity. Tommy Riemer hated him with a fierce intensity, but he didn't have the wherewithal to hire a hit man in London. Stryker was a vicious animal, but he would do the job himself, face to face, not hire some two-bit punk to stab him in the back. The only one who made sense was Kelleher. Somehow he must have figured out that Jake was the Lone Ranger. Or maybe somebody told him.

Back at Brown's, Jake went straight to Maggie's room. When she opened the door he could see Harvey Nichols shopping bags of all sizes and shapes scattered around the room. Jeans, trousers, workout pants, t-shirts, and polo shirts were folded neatly in separate piles on the queen size bed. Pairs of running shoes, tennis shoes, dress shoes and flip-flops were lined up on the floor next to the bed. A black dress hung in the closet.

Jake gestured at the clothing. "Looks like you did all right. Did you have fun?"

"It was amazing," she squealed. "Everyone at Harvey

Nichols was wonderful. They treated me like I was part of the royal family."

"That's what I was hoping for," Jake said. "The manager is a huge tennis fan. They sponsor one of the pre-tournament events. I met him a couple of times. He said if I ever needed anything to give him a call, so that's what I did. I told him you were a special friend of mine."

She threw her arms around Jake. "Thank you so much."

They were in the middle of putting the rest of Maggie's new wardrobe away when there was a knock on the door. Jake opened it to see a bellman holding a package. It was about the size of a shoe box and wrapped in plain brown paper

"This came for Ms. Quinlan."

Jake handed him a five pound note and took the package.

"What is it?" Maggie said.

"I don't know. It looks like a shoe box. Are you missing any shoes?"

Maggie shook her head. "All the shoes I bought are here. I have no idea what it could be."

"Only one way to find out," Jake said, handing her the box.

She tore off the paper and opened the box. Whatever was inside was covered in bubble wrap. When she ripped it away her face contorted in horror.

"Oh my God. It's a gun," she shrieked. And threw the box away from her like it held a dead rat. A small pistol fell out.

Jake picked up the gun gingerly, holding it by the barrel with his thumb and a couple of fingers. It was matte black and not much bigger than a cell phone.

"Was this some kind of a sick joke? That looks like a toy."

"It does, but it's a real gun," he said, examining it. "Why would someone send you a gun?"

"I have no idea."

"Maybe there's a note." He poked around in the box and

found a small card folded in half. He opened it and read. "It's from your father."

"What does it say?"

Jake read, "You are in danger. Use this to protect yourself. I'll be there as soon as I can. Kelleher."

"What's going on?" She was now shaking. "Why would my father think I'm in danger. Maybe the Lone Ranger thinks I know something. I could be next on his hit list."

"I don't think so. There's no reason for the Lone Ranger to target you."

"If not that, then what?"

"I don't know." He indicated the small pistol still in his hand. "Meanwhile, what would you like me to do with this?"

She recoiled. "Please, take it away."

"Where?"

"I don't care. Throw it in the river. Hand it in to the police. Bake it in a cake for all I care. I hate guns. Just get rid of it."

"Okay, you'll never see it again." He went across the hall to his room and put the little pistol in the drawer on the bedside table.

19

____

"We've been to Stonehenge, the ancient city of Bath, Westminster Abbey, Kensington Palace, the Tower of London and Big Ben. We've seen *King Lear* and *Phantom of the Opera* in the West End and eaten in some five-star restaurants. What we haven't done yet is any training," Maggie said as they ate breakfast at Charlie's, one of Brown's elegant eateries. "I thought I was supposed to be helping you get ready for Wimbledon."

It was their fourth morning in London.

"I thought you'd like to see a little bit of Britain before we started."

"I'm not complaining. It's just that I'm feeling a little guilty about not earning the money you're paying me."

"Oh believe me, you're earning it. Usually before a Grand Slam I'm a nervous wreck. Having you here has done wonders for my mental and emotional well-being. More players lose big matches because of nerves than because they were out of shape. If it makes you feel better, we can have a workout this afternoon, but there's one more thing I want you to see. And it's only a short walk from here."

They ambled over to Hyde Park. It was Sunday morning

and that meant Speakers' Corner would be in full swing. Men and women of all ages and ethnicities dressed in suits or uniforms or jeans or kooky costumes, standing on orange crates, step ladders or park benches, bellowing out their opinions on everything from religion to politics to vegetarianism. Each speaker had an audience, ranging from a few friends and relatives to several dozen listeners to hundreds, if the speaker was especially compelling. People in the crowd would heckle and taunt the orator, who would answer back in kind.

"Are these people for real?" Maggie asked. "Or are they actors here for our amusement?"

"They're totally real," Jake replied. "People have been coming to Hyde Park Speakers' Corner to say what's on their mind for over a hundred years. I read somewhere that there's a law recognizing this place as a haven for free speech."

"Really? That's pretty cool. How do you know so much about it?"

"Being on the tennis tour means spending a lot of lonely nights in hotel rooms, especially if you don't have a coach or a manager or a girlfriend or wife. When you run out of books and magazines and there's nothing on TV, the only thing left to read are the Bible and the city guides. Since I'm not religious, that leaves only one option. I've read them all from cover to cover at least twice. I probably know more about London, Paris, Rome and Melbourne than most of the people who live there."

They walked over to an excited throng listening to a young woman standing on an apple box. Her head was wrapped in a Muslim headscarf. A large Star of David hung around her neck. She wore black jeans and a black t-shirt with huge white block letters emblazoned across the front that said 'FUCK WAR.' Underneath, in smaller letters, was 'Mohammed Levi's Peace Warriors.' A poster on an easel next to her advertised Levi's concert for the next day.

"The Israeli government, Hamas, Hezbollah, the Americans, the Russians, none of them want Middle East peace. War made them rich. War made them famous. War puts dollars in their pockets and filet mignon on their tables. Peace, to these people, means poverty and obscurity. Leave it up to them and there will be war in the Middle East for the next thousand years.

"The Saudis, Egyptians, Iranians, they're all scared to death of a tranquil Palestine," she lectured. "They're afraid that if the world averted their eyes from the West Bank and Gaza, maybe everyone would see how their own countries are systematically robbing and abusing their people, feeding them hate while denying them food. Teaching them to kill but not to read. The only people who want peace are the men, women and children who are suffering every day because a few selfish, murderous old bastards can't stop playing chess with their lives."

The crowd broke into thunderous applause. Even Maggie, who never thought about politics, was moved. Jake, though, seemed unaffected. He stared, transfixed, at the speaker, as if she were an exotic museum exhibit.

While a couple of other Mohammed Levi acolytes distributed flyers about his upcoming concert at the Royal Festival Hall, a tall, husky, fortyish woman in a blue velour warmup jacket, black stretch pants and a wide-brimmed floppy straw sun hat pushed her way through the crowd towards Jake. She was holding an oversized blue tote bag with a round purple and green Wimbledon Championships patch.

"Jake Marks, is it really you? My husband and I are your biggest fans. We saw you at the U.S. Open last year. We booked our vacation for London this year just so we could see you at Wimbledon. We have tickets for the quarterfinals. I'll be cheering for you."

"Thank you," Jake said. "I hope I make it that far."

"Oh, I'm sure you will." She reached into her bag and pulled out a copy of the Tournament Directory. She turned to the page with Jake's bio and photo. "Do you think you can sign this for me?"

"It'll be my pleasure."

"I have a pen," she said as she began digging through her bag. "I know it's in here somewhere."

Out of the corner of his eye, Jake saw a jogger heading toward them. He was a big guy in a black jogging suit, a black baseball cap, black fingerless gloves, dark sunglasses and a black N95 mask covering his nose and mouth. He pushed Jake out of the way and crashed into the woman, knocking her to the ground. He mumbled something then took off into the park.

Someone in the crowd screamed, "There's a knife. Oh my God. She's been stabbed."

The hilt of a dagger protruded from under the Nike logo of her jacket. A red stain formed around it .

Jake looked up at the frantic crowd. "Please, somebody call an ambulance!"

Most of the onlookers gaped at Jake in terrified silence. A few people screamed. Some ran. Others began snapping pictures on their phones.

A husky guy in a rugby shirt made his way through the manic mob. "Let me through, I'm a nurse."

He kneeled beside the lifeless body, felt for a pulse, then sadly shook his head. He reached into the bag laying next to her, pulled out a strange looking little pistol that looked like it belonged in a Star Wars movie. It was light gray with a weird barrel shaped like a whiskey flask. Shielding it with his body, he furtively dropped the gun in the messenger bag hanging from his shoulder. Jake, who was huddled next to him, looked on in astonishment.

The nurse whispered, "This guy was going to kill you."

"Guy?"

The nurse nodded, whispered, "He's a hired killer. Poses as

a woman to get close to his targets, usually in crowded places. Shoots them point blank, then fades into the crowd. That crazy gun has a built-in suppressor."

Jake said, "Who the hell are you?"

"Special Reconnaissance. Didn't you recognize Deke? He was the jogger. Regards to Bunny."

He winked, then he stood and blended in among the onlookers.

A moment later an officer on a motor scooter pulled up. He hopped off and took out a black spiral notebook. "What happened here, sir?"

"This, uh, person's been stabbed," Jake answered.

"Did you know her?"

"No, sir. I'm Jake Marks, the tennis player. I'm here for Wimbledon. She came over to ask for an autograph."

"Mr. Marks, of course. I should have recognized you. Can you tell me exactly what happened?"

"It all happened very fast. A jogger bumped into us."

"Is he the one who stabbed her?"

"Could be. I can't be sure."

"What did he look like?"

"Well, he was a big guy."

"What else?"

"Hard to tell. He was all covered up. Wore a hat, a mask and sunglasses."

"Well, if you remember anything else." The policeman looked down at the body. "Aye, what's this?" He picked up something next to the body. "My God, it's a bullet." He stared at it as if he was examining a fine piece of jewelry. "It's silver."

Jake recoiled as if slapped in the face. "That's impossible. Are you sure?"

"Excuse me, but I think I know a bleedin' bullet when I see one."

The crowd, which had grown, gave a great communal gasp.

"Unless I miss my guess, isn't that the calling card of the terrorist they call the Lone Ranger?" the policeman said. He puffed out his chest, proud that he was involved in what was sure to be a celebrated crime of international importance.

"Oh God, I can't believe it!" Maggie shrieked and covered her face with her hands.

The policeman turned to her. "Excuse me, miss, do you know something about this?"

Tears streamed down her cheeks, but she made no sound except for a muffled whimper.

"This is my personal trainer, Miss Maggie Quinlan," Jake said while putting his arm around her. "Her mother was murdered in New York a few weeks ago. The New York City police think that the Lone Ranger was the perpetrator."

The policeman glared at Maggie, his brow furrowed. "Being involved in two Lone Ranger murders in the space of just a couple of weeks. What are the odds of that, I ask you?"

Jake stepped in front of Maggie. "If you're implying that this young lady has anything to do with what just happened, you're way out of line, officer."

"I'm not implying anything sir. I'm just stating a fact. This is a murder case. Until we know what happened and who's involved, everyone's fair game, including the Queen Mother."

"Well then I suggest you go talk to her, because you're not saying another word to Maggie. She's been through enough." Jake grabbed her arm and strode away through the crowd.

A big, black van drove slowly past them. Probably the coroner, Jake thought.

20

———

Neither Jake or Maggie spoke as they made their way out of Hyde Park. The long, snake-shaped lake, aptly named the Serpentine, with its rowboats and paddleboats, ducks and gulls, was a much needed tranquil distraction as they walked towards the exit.

Just as they were leaving the park, she turned her head and said, "Why would the Lone Ranger want to kill that woman?"

Jake shook his head. "It doesn't make sense. Since you told me about your mom, I've done some research. The Lone Ranger only goes after high profile targets."

"My mother wasn't high profile."

"That's what's bothering me. Why is he suddenly targeting random innocent people, like your mother and that poor woman just now? One accident I can buy, even though he's supposed to be super methodical. But two? It doesn't add up."

"What do you think is going on?"

"I think there's a good chance that it wasn't the Lone Ranger at all. Anyone can paint bullets silver. If the police are spending their time looking for the Lone Ranger, whoever really did kill your mother and that other lady is home free."

"But they have nothing to do with each other. That doesn't add up either."

"I know."

"Unless that guy today was really after me," she said nervously.

"You?" He tilted his head and looked at her incredulously. "Absolutely not."

"Maybe it was the Lone Ranger and he was trying to tie up loose ends. You know, first my mother, then me."

"Whether it was the Lone Ranger or a copycat, the target at the U.N. was Townsend, not your mother." Jake said emphatically. "Her death was an unfortunate, tragic, terrible accident. That's what the police told you and I agree."

She took a deep breath, fighting to remain calm. "If that's true, how do you explain what just happened?"

Jake shook his head. "I can't."

Back in Maggie's room, Jake sat next to her on the bed.

She gazed at him dolefully. "I'm so, so sorry. I'm supposed to be over here training you, instead I've been nothing but a huge distraction. You're concentrating on me and my problems when you should be concentrating on your tennis." She began to cry. "I'm sorry I'm such a coward."

"You're not a coward!" He kneeled down next to her and took both her hands in his. "Your mother was brutally murdered and you're in a foreign country and someone gets killed right in front of you. No one could be okay after that. I remember how I felt when my coach, Alex, was murdered."

Maggie sat bolt upright.

"Really? What happened?"

"I'll tell you about it sometime, but right now you need to try to rest. And me being in here isn't helping."

Jake went to his room, sat down on the sofa and closed his eyes. His mind went immediately to the day when everything in his life went sideways.

It was the day after he won the NCAA Men's Singles Tennis Championship as a Columbia University sophomore. His coach, Alex Espinosa, told him it was time for the next step in his development.

"You mean turn pro?"

Alex nodded.

"Do you think I'm ready?"

"Your game is ready. Whether your head and heart are ready, I don't know. There is only one way to find out."

A few weeks later, Jake and Alex were in Guayaquil, Ecuador, where Jake was scheduled to play in his first professional tournament, the Guayaquil Challenger.

Most young players start in the Futures, the lower minor leagues of professional tennis, played mostly in backwater towns of Europe, Asia, and South America. The Challengers tour is a step up. The equivalent of Triple A baseball, it was where young pros earned their reputation, some money and, most importantly, ATP points, which count toward players' rankings and helps them qualify for big-money tournaments and, eventually, Grand Slams.

Guayaquil always had one of the best fields on the Challenger tour. Novice players like Jake never get invited to tournaments of this caliber, but Alex was one of Guayaquil's 'Four Horsemen of Ecuadorian Tennis,' along with Pancho Segura, Andres Gomez and and Nick Lapentti, so when Alex called the president of the Ecuador Tennis Federation to see if he could give Jake a special invitation, he was happy to oblige.

"Now we will see what kind of a player you really are," Alex said the morning of his first match. "Up to now you have beaten boys who play tennis for fun and glory. These are men who play for their supper. They are older, stronger, and more experienced than you. Every point you win is money out of their pocket and they'll hate you for it, especially because you are a gringo."

Jake said, "I know that a pro tournament is going to have strong players. I'm just going to go out there and play as well as I can. If I win, great. If I lose, I'll know what I need to work on."

"I hear the right words on your lips. I hope they are also in your heart."

The next day, they arrived at the Guayaquil Tennis Club two hours before the match. Jake hit with Alex for an hour to warm up. His opponent, Fernando Rios, was a member of the Peruvian Davis Cup team. He had solid ground strokes but a mediocre serve. Tall and reed thin, he wore his jet black hair in a long pony tail and had a tattoo of a coiled snake on his forearm. There were about five hundred people scattered around the bleachers. Some waved Peruvian flags. All of them cheered for the South American and booed Jake mercilessly.

Jake and Rios began the match tentatively, like two boxers feeling each other out in the first round. As the match wore on, Jake picked up the pace on his ground strokes. He realized that the Peruvian couldn't match his power. He knew then that his opponent didn't have a weapon that could hurt him. If he could avoid making too many unforced errors he'd have a good chance of winning.

After being tied at three games apiece in the first set, Jake reeled off eight games in a row and was getting ready to serve out the match. Two drunken hooligans started throwing bottles on the court as Jake was about to serve. One landed a few of feet away from him in an explosion of glass shards. Jake stopped in mid toss and glared up at the stands. They responded by giving him the finger and chucking a few more bottles his way. Jake gestured toward the chair, looking for some help. The referee shrugged and commanded him to continue.

Alex jumped out of his courtside seat and marched over to Jake's tormentors. He told them in no uncertain terms that if they didn't cut it out, he would take a couple of those beer bottles and shove it up their asses. They sized him up. Tall, slim, fifty-plus years old, they must have figured they could take him easily. So they attacked. Unfortunately for them, the same powerful left hand, amazing reflexes and dazzling footwork that took Ecuador to within two points of beating the United States in the Davis Cup finals some twenty-five years earlier, was still formidable enough to break the jaw of one of them and leave the other one doubled over in agony.

Play was stopped while the fight was taking place. The Guayaquil police came within minutes and the combatants were carted off. The thugs to the hospital, Alex to jail. Jake was more than a little shocked to see his coach being ushered out of the stadium in handcuffs, walking proudly erect, head held high, like a victorious matador exiting the bullring.

Visibly shaken, Jake lost the next three games but was able to summon the concentration he needed to finally hold his serve and win the match.

As soon as it was over, Jake ran out the arena and hailed a cab to the police station. When he got there, he found Alex playing cards with the police chief.

The coach turned to his protégé and said nonchalantly, "Did you win?"

"As a matter of fact, I did. But I lost a couple of games I shouldn't have because I was worried about you. The whole way over here I've been trying to figure out how to bail you out of jail."

Before Alex could answer, the police chief stood. He was about sixty. You could see that at one time he was powerfully built, but whatever muscles he had turned to flab.

"Let me assure you, Señor Marks, throwing rocks and bottles is not the way we treat our honored guests. Please accept my apology and my assurance that the scum that caused the disturbance today will be punished severely."

"Thank you," Jake said, slightly bewildered.

"If we had known that the famous Alex Espinosa was your coach, we would have given you a police escort to the arena."

Alex stood and bowed slightly. "Thank you for your kind words and your help. I must now take my leave, as my young charge is scheduled to play another match soon and needs his rest."

"Of course," said the chief. "Perhaps you will allow me to take you to one of Guayaquil's fine restaurants before you return to the States."

"I think we will like that," Alex said as he shook the chief's hand and headed for the door.

Back at the hotel, Jake said, "How'd you go from getting arrested to being an honored guest?"

"In Guayaquil, everything has a price. In this case, it was two hundred dollars American for each of the officers and five hundred for the chief."

"Unbelievable."

At six the next morning, while Jake was still asleep, Alex dressed for his morning run. He usually finished five miles in less than forty minutes, plenty of time to shower, have breakfast and get to the stadium for Jake's ten o'clock practice session. He stretched for five minutes, walked down three flights of stairs and out of the Hilton's lobby before he broke into a warm-up trot. After two blocks he was at full speed and headed toward the waterfront. Like everything else in his life, Alex planned his route carefully. It was a little less than a half mile to the harbor. He would then run two miles along the river and two miles back, finishing off with a cool-down jog back to the hotel.

The streets were empty. One of the few cars on the road, a beat-up, blue Ford Bronco, slowly followed Alex from the hotel. Two blocks from the harbor, the Bronco charged at him from behind. At the last minute, he heard the roar of the engine and leaped out of the way, landing hard on his right side. With his knee throbbing and his elbow bleeding, Alex struggled to stand. The car u-turned and sped at him again, like a crazed metallic bull. Limping badly, he managed to squeeze himself between two parked cars as the Bronco went by him. He hobbled towards the harbor and safety. The driver jumped out of the car and ran after him. He caught him less than a block from the harbor, pulled out a snubnose revolver and shot Alex four times in the back.

Twenty minutes later the phone rang in Jake's hotel room.

"Señor Marks?" The voice said in heavily accented English.

"Yes."

"I'm afraid I have some very unfortunate news."

"What is it?" Jake's first thought was that he would have to forfeit because of yesterday's brawl.

"I am sorry to tell you that we have found the body of your coach, Alex Espinosa."

"Found the body? Are you telling me that Alex is dead?" Jake's legs wobbled. His stomach turned. "That's not possible," he screamed. "No way. It's a mistake."

"I am very afraid so, sir. We found the body around six-thirty this morning. We will need you to identify it." He gave Jake the address of the hospital morgue where Alex was taken.

A half-hour later, Jake walked into the morgue. He told the policeman there that it was indeed his coach, Alex Espinosa.

"I'll kill whoever did this!" Jake screamed. "I swear I'll kill him!"

The cop put a hand on his shoulder. "Do not fear, señor. We will find the scum who did this and see that justice is done."

"Sure you will," Jake said and stormed out.

21

The piercing double-ring of the phone startled Jake awake. Between what happened at Speakers' Corner and reliving Alex's murder, he got barely two hours of sleep.

"Hullo," he said, stifling a yawn. He had scheduled a wake-up call for eight. The clock next to the bed said six-thirty. "Who is this?"

"It's Glynn. We have to talk. NOW!" His voice was sharp and loud.

"Can't it wait?"

"No."

"Okay, what is it?"

"Not on the phone."

"Where are you?"

"I'm here."

"You're in London?"

"I'm in your hotel. In the lobby."

"Oh. What are you...never mind, I'll be right down."

Jake tried to focus. Glynn never showed up at his assignments, why now? Could it have something to do with Speakers'

Corner? Or his friend Nick's murder? What else could it be? He put on some clothes and went downstairs.

Glynn was the only person in the lobby, taking up most of a two-person settee.

Jake said, "When did you get in?"

"Last night."

"What's so damn important that you had to come to London to tell me?"

In a low monotone, Glynn said, "Kelleher knows."

"Knows what?"

"He knows who you are."

"You mean…"

"Yeah."

"What !? How? How could he possibly know?"

Glynn shrugged.

"Stryker. It was Stryker. Has to be."

"You don't know that."

"Who else could it be?"

"Kelleher's very resourceful. He has ways of finding out things."

That didn't make sense. A lot of people with a lot more resources than Kelleher couldn't crack his identity, how could he? It had to be someone in Millennium. If it wasn't Stryker, maybe it was Glynn.

"All right, thanks for the heads-up."

"One more thing," Glynn said calmly, as he played with the fronds of the palm in the pot next to him. "He's here in London."

"Since when?"

"I don't know. But if I were you I'd ditch that little bitch daughter of his."

"You're the one who told me to get close to her."

"That was before we knew Kelleher figured out your identity."

"But I can use my relationship with her to my advantage."

"Absolutely not. Too many potential problems."

"Like what?"

"How about because she'll slow you down. Or maybe because the press will find out whose daughter she is and we don't need that kind of publicity. But the main reason is there's a good chance he told her that you're the one who killed her mother. She could be in touch with him right now."

"She hardly knows Kelleher."

"How do you know?"

"She told me."

Glynn stood and glared down at Jake. "Use your fucking mind!" he growled. "Of course she would tell you that if she wanted make you trust her."

"She's not lying. I'm sure of it."

A look somewhere between disappointment and disgust washed over Glynn's face. "You're starting to have feelings for this girl."

"You're wrong. I'm using her to leverage Kelleher. That's all."

"Prove it. Get rid of her one way or another."

"I will."

"Do it soon." Glynn stood up abruptly and walked out of the lobby.

22

———

Jake opened Maggie's door to see her pacing frantically back and forth across the room, tears running down her cheek. He was holding a tray with a carafe of coffee and assorted mini scones, croissants and pastries, along with plates, cups and silverware. He put in on the nightstand.

"I called your room and there was no answer. I was so scared. Where were you?"

"I couldn't sleep so I went down to the lobby to get us some breakfast. I figured that with everything that happened yesterday we could use a day to just chill."

"I'm sorry for being so weird. You shouldn't have to check with me every time to go out. I'm just still really freaked out."

"Don't be silly. You're not weird at all. What you've been through would freak anybody out."

"What about you? You seem okay."

"Believe me, I'm far from okay. I was up all night reliving what happened, trying to think if there's anything I could have done to save her."

"What about your tennis training? It's been almost a week and we haven't done a thing."

Jake smiled. "Actually, I think I found another gym we can use. I know the head of the American School in London. I've given a couple of tennis clinics there. It's summer break. The students are gone. I'm pretty sure they'll let us use their gym for a couple of hours a day."

Maggie perked up. "Great. When do we start?"

"Not today. We're both emotionally drained. That plus zero sleep makes this a bad day to start serious training. Let's take it easy today and get a fresh start tomorrow."

Maggie nodded. She looked relieved. "Thank you."

"Good. Now let's have some of this breakfast before the coffee gets cold."

They spent the day walking around London, checking out some sites. Sherlock Holmes' apartment at 221B Baker Street, Madam Taussauds Wax Museum, Shakespeare's Globe and the crosswalk at Abbey Road.

That night at dinner, Jake said, "There's one more thing I'd like to do before we begin serious training tomorrow. If you're up to it."

THE ROYAL FESTIVAL HALL'S 2,900 seats were filled will a dizzying cross-section of humanity. Affluent young men and women, still dressed for business. Students, some wearing polo shirts and pressed jeans, others with rainbow hair and pierced nostrils. Muslim women covered head to toe in veils and robes. Many held signs and banners calling for peace and an end to bloodshed in the Middle East. Journalists, some with tape recorders, others with small notebooks, lined the back of the room.

Every entrance was guarded by a uniformed security officer standing in front of a metal detector. The assistant manager met Jake and Maggie outside and ushered them through a private entrance, past a line of security guards and into a special VIP seating area to the left side of the stage. After dusting off their seats, the manager shook Jake's hand and said, "Enjoy the show. And best of luck in the matches."

Maggie asked, "How on earth did you manage this?"

Jake grinned. "I traded VIP seats for tonight for VIP seats to the finals."

After a few minutes, muffled conversations in English, French, Arabic, Hebrew, and several other languages came to a stop as the house lights dimmed and a solitary blue beam lit the center of the stage. The room burst into deafening applause as a slim man in his early forties walked slowly towards it. His close-cropped, salt-and-pepper hair was beginning to thin. His skin was the color of maple syrup. He wore round, wire-rim glasses, a black t-shirt and faded jeans.

"A lasting peace is impossible," Mohammed Levi said matter-of-factly into the microphone.

Everyone in the auditorium stopped their murmuring and stared at him. This is not what they had come to hear.

"The human race is not capable of it," he continued. "The earliest recorded documents tell of war, of battles, of one group of people conquering and subjugating another. Because of race, because of religion, because of land, because of property, because of greed, power and ego.

"Why should anyone think that this generation can do what thousands of generations before us have failed to do? You might answer, 'If we don't we'll all die.' That is true, but the prospect of death has never deterred men from going to war. In fact, nothing has ever deterred that basic human instinct.

"So what should we do? Give up? Throw our arms in the air and say we have no choice, we're addicted to war?" He paused for a second, then shouted, "No! We fight our addiction. Just like an alcoholic or drug abuser fights his. One day at a time. We admit that we're all bloodthirsty barbarians and collectively decide that we won't make war today. Then tomorrow we decide the same thing. And the next day, and the next. We can't eliminate war, but maybe we can put it on hold for a long, long time. Won't that be a kick in the ass to the bastards in Washington, Jerusalem, Teheran, China, and Moscow who make a fortune every day war goes on. Sure the warmongers will yell and scream about spreading democracy, or God's glory, or national pride, but that's just to make the poor suckers like you and me lay down our lives so that they can cash in just one more time. They've been fucking us for years, no, for centuries, no, make that millennia. It's time we fucked them back. Let's say 'fuck you' to the war profiteers and 'fuck you' to war."

Mohammed Levi's band, a guitarist, bassist, and drummer, who had quietly taken their places upstage while he was speaking, started playing loud, pulsating, primitive Afro-Celtic-Arabian rhythms. He began shouting to the beat, "Fuck war, fuck war, we won't take it anymore. Fuck war, fuck war, war's a bastard, war's a whore."

Some people in the auditorium rose to their feet and began stomping and shouting, "Fuck War. Fuck War. Fuck War!!"

The hall shook with excitement as more and more people stood up, stamped their feet, banged their fists against the chairs in front of them, and screamed the Fuck War chant in time with the music. They hollered until they were hoarse. Levi ran from one side of the stage to the other, exhorting them to a fever pitch. He went down the steps and waded into the audience, not far from where Jake and Maggie were sitting.

Suddenly, a spectral figure ran towards the singer wearing white flowing robes and a white turban.

Levi turned and smiled at who he thought was an ardent fan. His smile turned into a mask of horror as he saw his attacker charging him with a scimitar knife poised to strike him in the chest.

"No!" Levi yelled as the madman was now upon him.

Two shots rang out. The back of the attacker's robe oozed

blood. He stumbled and staggered into Levi. Both he and his weapon fell awkwardly to the floor next to the terror-stricken singer.

Most of the people in the room had no idea what was happening. They were still stomping, chanting and cursing war. A half-dozen security guards appeared instantaneously and surrounded Mohammed Levi. Shouts of solidarity morphed into terrified screams.

Maggie turned to Jake, "What's going on?"

"Somebody just tried to kill Mohammed Levi."

"Oh God!"

"It's all right. Looks like he was shot before he could do any damage."

The arena erupted in chaos and confusion. A policewoman hustled Levi backstage as security guards, reporters and photographers converged on the scene of the attack. The would-be assassin lay prostrate just feet from where Jake and Maggie were sitting. When Jake saw who it was lying on the floor, he gasped. It was the custodian who tried to stab him at the gym the other day.

A noisy confrontation was going on behind them. Jake and Maggie turned to see three policemen wrestling with a stocky, older man dressed in military fatigues. One of the cops held a gun by the barrel, while the other two were struggling to subdue him.

"Get your fuckin' hands off me. I got a license for that," Jungle Jim Kelleher shouted.

"I'm afraid that your license isn't valid here, sir," the officer replied, trying to remain civil. "You'll have to come with us." They started urging him slowly towards the exit at the front of the auditorium.

"I saved that guy's life while you mooks were sitting around with your thumbs up your assholes," Kelleher screamed. "You should be giving me a fuckin' medal."

Kelleher's eyes locked on Maggie. His defiant attitude melted away as soon as he saw her.

Then he saw Jake standing next to her.

"What the hell..." he mumbled as the uniformed men dragged him out of the auditorium.

Maggie burst into tears. "What's going on?" she shrieked. "I don't understand any of this. Why is Kelleher here?"

Jake shrugged. "I don't know."

23

———

Maggie felt like she was drowning. She struggled for breath. Her vision blurred. A clammy mist oozed from her pores. She desperately needed to escape but felt paralyzed in her seat.

She turned to Jake. "I can't breathe. I think I'm having a heart attack."

"Can you stand?"

"I don't know."

Jake grasped her arms and gently lifted her up. They were in the middle of a crush of people still in shock and confusion, heading haphazardly to the exits.

"Please," she urged, "we have to get out of here. Now!" She was gulping air.

"Okay, hang on. Try not to breathe so hard."

Jake held Maggie with one hand, and pushed, shoved and elbowed through the crowd with the other. They made it to the exit, leaving a trail of curses and reprimands in their wake.

"Want me to get an Uber?" Jake said, holding his phone.

Maggie was still gasping and quivering. "Let's just walk."

"Are you sure?"

"I don't think I could handle being cooped up in the back of a car right now."

"You feeling better?"

"Maybe a little."

They walked the mile-and-a-half back to Brown's, mostly in silence. Every couple of minutes Jake asked Maggie how she was doing. She would nod and say, "Okay."

By the time they got to the hotel, her head had stopped throbbing, her breathing was steady and she wasn't shaking. They went to her room. She sat on the bed. Jake sat down next to her.

"I don't understand," she said.

"What?"

"Any of it. What was my father doing there? How did he know there was going to be an assassination attempt? Was he working for Mohammed Levi? Why did they arrest him? And what was going on with me? I really thought I was dying. Was it a heart attack?"

Jake stood and faced her.

"I have no idea why your father was there or why he shot that guy. I do know that if he didn't, Mohammed Levi would be dead right now, so that would make your father a hero, at least to some people. I'm pretty sure I know what happened to you."

"What?"

"You had a panic attack."

"No. This wasn't all in my head. I couldn't breathe. I was dizzy. My heart was racing. I don't know if it was asthma, bronchitis, a mini stroke or something else. I really thought I was gonna die. Whatever it was, it wasn't my imagination. I'm not crazy."

Jake threw his hands in the air.

"Whoa. No one said you were crazy. Panic attacks are real. Very real. I had my first one when I was fifteen."

"What?! You had one of these?"

"More than one. The first time was at the 14-and-under finals at the Orange Bowl International. It was my first big tournament. I was in the locker room going over the game plan with Alex, my coach. Next thing I knew my chest was throbbing, I was gasping for breath and soaked with sweat. I could hardly move. There was no way I could go on with the match. I was sure I was gonna drop dead right then and there."

"What happened?"

"My coach called an ambulance and they took me to the ER. The doctors checked me out and told me there was nothing wrong with me. That physically, I was fine. They said I had probably had something called a panic attack. I didn't believe them. I was sure I'd get a different diagnosis when I got back to New York. My regular doctor looked at all the test results from Florida, then gave me a really thorough examination. He told me the same thing. I didn't know whether to be happy that I didn't have anything serious or freaked out that I lost my mind."

"Oh my God, that's exactly how I feel."

"Don't worry, you're not crazy. The doctor told me that more than six million people suffer from panic attacks in the U.S. every year. I still didn't believe it, so I googled it. It's true."

"But this never happened to me before. Why now?"

Jake rolled his eyes. "Gee, I don't know. In the last couple of weeks your mother was murdered, possibly by a notorious international assassin. You find out you have a father that you never knew about. You wind up here in London with a guy you just met. A random woman gets stabbed to death right in front of you. Then you witness your newly discovered father shooting some crazy assassin in the middle of a concert. If you're not a prime candidate for a panic attack, I don't know who is."

"I never thought of it that way. Am I going to have these

attacks for the rest of my life? Is there some kind of medication for it?"

"My doctor gave me some anti-anxiety meds, but I hated the way they made me feel."

"What do you mean?"

"It was like somebody hit me in the head with a baseball bat. I was out of focus. Dull."

"You said the one in Florida was your first time. That means you've gotten more. If you don't take medication, what do you do?"

"I learned how to talk myself down. I concentrate on my breathing and tell myself that I'm okay."

"That works?"

"Most of the time. The good thing is that most panic attacks don't last very long, so if can settle myself down for ten to fifteen minutes that's usually enough."

"Usually isn't always. What if it's not enough?"

"I still have my meds. I haven't had to take any yet, but it's my safety net. Do you want to take one now to see how you feel?"

Maggie shook her head.

"I think what I need right now is for you to hold me."

Jake smiled tenderly. "That will be my pleasure."

He wrapped his arms around her, her head resting on his shoulder. He felt stirrings that he'd never felt before. Not lust or libido, something else. It couldn't be love. Not possible. Men like him didn't feel love. He cleared his head and tried not to think about it. After five minutes she was asleep. He covered her with a blanket and went back to his room.

24

———————

"How did you get the gun into the concert hall, Mr. Kelleher? We had metal detectors at every entrance."

The British inspector wore a pressed white Oxford shirt with a blue silk tie. He spoke slowly and easily. He held a pair of tortoiseshell glasses and chewed at the arm of the frame as he spoke.

Kelleher didn't look quite as dapper as his interrogator. His clothes were bedraggled from a night in the cells. He was in desperate need of a shave and a cup of coffee. His voice was even more gravelly than usual.

"It's an experimental model that was developed by the Israeli army to be undetectable by enemy sensors. The gun and the bullets are a zinc and titanium alloy," Kelleher replied.

"How were you able to obtain one?"

"I did some favors for the Israelis."

They were in a small room on the third floor of New Scotland Yard, sitting on either side of a spotless glass table. A metal pitcher filled with ice water and a tape recorder were the only items on it.

"Tell me again, if you don't mind, why you attended that

particular event and why you felt it necessary to bring a loaded pistol into the hall with you."

"I had information that Mohammed Levi would be the target of an assassination attempt by the terrorist hitman known as the Lone Ranger."

"And where did you get that information?"

"You know better than to ask me a question like that. Confidential informants are the most valuable tool men like you and me have."

"Mr. Kelleher, please try to be a little more cooperative. You are currently not in the employ of any police or military organization in our computer database."

"Maybe your database needs an upgrade. Or maybe the organization I'm working with doesn't want you to know about it."

"Let's put that aside for now. There are many people in Britain who appreciate the work you did in Kosovo and the stand you took against your own government during the Iraq War. But that does not give you license to parade around London, shooting people, even people you may believe to be murderous terrorists."

"What about saving that guy's life, what's his name?"

"Mohammed Levi."

"Yeah, Levi. If it wasn't for me he'd be dead right now. Where the hell were your people when I took out the shooter?"

"Speaking of the shooter, did you know him?"

"Never saw him before."

"But you thought he was the Lone Ranger."

"Not after I saw his face."

"What made you think he might be the Lone Ranger?"

"My information was that the Lone Ranger would be at that concert, and sometime before it was over, he would try to kill Levi."

"And you trust your source?"

"Why shouldn't I? It all went down just the way he said it would, didn't it? Except that it was some shithead punk and not the Lone Ranger."

"You don't believe that the man you shot was the Lone Ranger?"

"No."

"We found a handful of silver bullets in his pocket."

"I don't care if you found them up his ass. He ain't the guy."

"You know the identity of the Lone Ranger?"

"Not exactly."

"Then how do you know it wasn't him?"

"I just know."

"If he isn't the Lone Ranger, who is?"

"I'll let you know after I'm done with him," he said with a smirk.

"Perhaps you'll find all this less amusing when you're in the dock facing life in prison."

The door opened and a young officer walked in and handed the inspector a folded piece of paper. He read it quickly, then crushed it and flung it violently into the wastebasket next to his desk.

He glared at Kelleher. "It appears that I underestimated your influence, Colonel." He spit the words out. "It seems that you suddenly have diplomatic immunity. You are free to go."

Kelleher was just as surprised as the inspector. There was no reason for him to have diplomatic immunity, but he wasn't going to argue.

"Please rest assured that we here at the Metropolitan Police do not take kindly to being made fools of. Be very careful during the rest of your stay in London."

"Yeah, sure," Kelleher said as he left the room.

Waiting for him outside, looking like a grizzly bear in a J.C. Penney suit, was Marcus Glynn.

"Fuck you Glynn. You set me up."

"What are you talking about? I just got you out. You should be thanking me."

"For what, landing my ass in jail? It was supposed to be Marks, not some random punk, trying to take out Levi."

"Our information was that Marks was going to excise Levi during the concert. Maybe this guy beat him to the punch. Or maybe Marks couldn't get there for some reason."

"He was there. I saw him. Sitting in the VIP section with Maggie. I thought you were supposed to know what you were doing. For all I know Marks has nothing to do with the Lone Ranger."

"He is the Lone Ranger. You saw the tape."

"Tapes can be doctored. But even if you're right, after last night the cops will be all over me like a fucking rash."

"Just sit tight. I'll let you know what the new plan is."

"Fuck that. You can shove your plan up Goldbarr's ass. Marks is still with Maggie and I was arrested. From now on, I'll make my own plans."

Glynn didn't say anything for a couple of seconds.

"All right. Let me know what you're planning to do."

"Why? So you can fuck it up again?"

"You really are a prick, you know that, Kelleher? We can provide some backup or create an alibi if we know what you're doing." He handed him a slip of paper. "Call me at this number when you figure it out."

25

The phone on Jake's nightstand chirped. He reached out a woozy hand and grabbed it. It was five a.m. The caller was unknown.

"Who is this?" Jake whispered.

"Get your ass to the London Eye." It was Stryker's distinctive falsetto. "New mandate on Levi."

"Now?"

"Right now.

The line went dead.

Jake sat up, fully awake. He was trying to decide what was going on. Is it a trap? Is Stryker setting him up? Is he in cahoots with Kelleher? Is Glynn in on it? Only one way to find out.

He put on his warm-up suit, running shoes, baseball cap and running gloves. London mornings can be chilly, even in summer. He grabbed the pistol out of his nightstand, the one Kelleher sent to Maggie, and shoved it into his waistband. On the way out he stuck a sticky note on Maggie's door, 'Going for a Run.'

The sun was already up. The air was breezy and brisk. The streets were empty, save for a couple of dogwalkers.

The London Eye was about a mile and a half away, on the other side of the Thames in an area known as the South Bank. To reach it he had to cross one of two pedestrian spans that hugged either side of a century-old railroad bridge. Built in 2002, they were named the Golden Jubilee Footbridges to commemorate the Queen's fiftieth year on the throne, another fact Jake gleaned from the guidebook.

As he jogged over the bridge he was still trying to figure out why Stryker wanted to meet him, why so early and why at the London Eye? What's wrong with the hotel lobby or a coffee shop?

As per the guide book, 'The London Eye is a colossal Ferris wheel built by British Airways to welcome the new millennium. Rising as tall as a twenty-five-story skyscraper, its egg-shaped capsules of steel and glass are bolted to the outside of the wheel. The ride creeps along at a snail's pace, making a complete rotation in exactly half an hour. At its apex it rises more than 430 feet over London, giving it the distinction of being the city's tallest structure. Located next to the Thames, its spectacular panoramic views of the city make it one of London's busiest tourist attractions.' But not at five-thirty in the morning.

As he walked towards the Eye on the riverfront promenade, a black Lincoln Town Car pulled up in front of it. Mendel Stryker stomped out. He wore a gray tweed sport coat with charcoal slacks. He was met by a bright young man in a crisp white shirt, red vest and blue blazer. 'London Eye' was embroidered on the upper left-hand pocket.

Jake ducked behind a sidewalk sign advertising a new Asian Fusion restaurant. He was close enough to hear their conversation.

"Good morning, Mr. Stryker," the young man said, standing at attention. "Collins. Nick Collins. I'm the daytime duty manager here at the London Eye." He thrust out his hand.

Stryker ignored it. "You were contacted yesterday, right?"

"Yes, sir."

"Have all the cameras been disabled?"

"Yes, sir. But I'm not sure why…"

"You don't need to know why," Stryker barked. "You just need to know that what we're doing is top secret. If any pictures or videos of this meeting wind up on the internet, your ass will wind up in prison for a long time."

"Understood."

"Is the area blocked off? We need a hundred-foot perimeter. Absolutely no one is to breach it for any reason."

"Barriers are being put up as we speak. As per your instructions, signs have been posted reading, 'Closed for Maintenance.' You'll be quite isolated."

"Good. One of my men will let you know when we're finished." Stryker nodded toward the Town Car where two men were having what looked to be a casual conversation. "Now get out of here."

Collins turned and marched away, shaking his head.

Nothing about the conversation he just heard made Jake feel any more comfortable. He waited until the attendant was gone and walked over to the capsule. Ten feet long, five feet wide and eight feet high, it looked like an egg-shaped subway car. An oval wooden bench in the center was bolted to the floor with bulletproof glass panels all around.

Stryker walked inside and motioned for Jake to follow him.

The door shut as the wheel began to move, making its slow ascent.

Jake said, "What's this all about?"

"Calm down. Take in the view. We got plenty of time."

Stryker stood for quite awhile, arms folded, gazing out at the expanse of London as it unfolded before him. Then, as if remembering Jake's presence, he said, "I didn't think you'd show up."

"What the hell's going on? Where's Glynn?" Jake stood uneasily on the other side of the capsule, the bench between them.

"He couldn't make it."

"Why?"

"He had to take care of something."

"What?"

"He's cleaning up last night's mess."

"You mean with Kelleher?"

"Yeah."

"Why was Kelleher there at all?"

"Cause we didn't trust you. You lost your guts after Kelleher's wife went down on your last job."

"I told you I never shot her," Jake shouted "I fired four times and they all hit Townsend. I don't know who killed Brigid Quinlan but it wasn't me."

"I know you didn't shoot the bitch," Stryker replied, pursing his lips as if he were about to spit. His cold, soulless eyes bore into Jake's. "I did."

The revelation hit Jake like a knee to the groin. He rocked backward, grabbing one of the capsule's support bars to steady himself. "Why?"

"To get rid of your ass once and for all. Now Goldbarr don't trust you and Kelleher's out to kill you."

"You're insane!" Jake screamed. "You sacrificed an innocent woman's life for nothing. Even if Kelleher knows I'm the Lone Ranger, he won't touch me as long as I'm with Maggie."

"I know. That was a bad break. That's why I finally realized I have to do it myself."

Stryker reached into a shoulder holster and pulled out a huge, sinister looking monster of a handgun. It had a bronze barrel that had what looked like shark's teeth on top. Jake recognized it as a Desert Eagle. It was more of a showpiece than a combat weapon. A favorite of action movie heroes but disdained by professionals. At almost five pounds, it was too heavy to keep steady and had a kick like a brahma bull. Jake guessed Stryker, whose main weapons were his fists and his intimidating demeanor, might never have fired it. Just showing that gun strapped to his side would be enough to make most people cower. If Jake could somehow make Stryker miss the first shot he would have a chance. He slowly moved his hand toward the small gun in back of his waistband.

"You're going to shoot me here? Not smart. How are you going to explain away a dead body to the attendants?"

Stryker smirked malevolently. "No attendants. Just my men. By the time the attendants get here, you'll be long gone and the capsule will be cleaned up."

Jake inched backward. "You know, I'm fairly well-known. Don't you think people will look into my disappearance?"

"You were kidnapped by terrorists. A ransom will be paid, but the bastards killed you anyway." The smile twisted into a vicious sneer. "End of conversation, Marks." He leveled the heavy gun, one-handed, at Jake's chest.

Jake knew that the longer he held it, the shakier it would be.

"Wait! What about Glynn? He's okay with this?"

"I don't answer to Glynn or anybody else. Offing the Quinlan bitch was all me. Goldbarr doesn't even know."

Jake saw Stryker's hand quiver as his wrist tightened. He had a fraction of a second to react. He dove behind the wooden bench as Stryker fired. The 50 caliber bullet put a big gash in the bench inches from his head. The tremendous recoil sent Stryker's arm flying in the air. The noise in the capsule was like a thunderclap inside a church bell.

Still huddled behind the bench, Jake fired three shots. One hit Stryker in the shoulder. The other two missed. Stryker dropped the Desert Eagle as blood trickled down his shirtfront. He stood motionless, a bewildered look on his face. Jake sprung to his feet, steadied the gun and fired twice more into Stryker's barrel chest. He staggered backward but didn't fall. His legs wobbled as he tried to steady himself. Jake fired again. He hit Stryker's throat, piercing the carotid artery. Blood gushed. Stryker crumpled to the floor.

The capsule was on its downward rotation. In about fifteen minutes he would be back on the ground, trapped in a locked steel-and-glass bubble with Stryker's bullet riddled corpse laying in a pool of blood at his feet and a couple of his henchmen waiting for the door to automatically open.

Jake figured his best chance would be to get out of the capsule before it landed. He yanked the door with all his strength but it held fast. He dropped the little pistol, picked up the Desert Eagle by the barrel and hammered at the window. Nothing. He spent the next few minutes frantically looking for some kind of emergency exit. There was none. The Eye was now ten feet from ground zero.

Stryker's phone buzzed inside his jacket. Probably the two goons awaiting instructions. Jake saw them on the platform ready for the capsule to touch down. One was short and lean, with olive skin, thinning brown hair and a goatee. He wore a blue blazer and gray slacks. The driver. The other was taller with thick tattooed arms, a barrel chest and shaved head. He wore jeans and a sleeveless t-shirt. The muscle.

Jake held Stryker's body propped up in front of him. As the door opened he thrust the blood-splotched corpse at the stunned driver, who grabbed at it instinctively, uttering a guttural "ugh." Over the driver's shoulder Jake could see the muscle guy reaching for his waistband. Jake held the Desert Eagle with both hands, steadied himself and fired. The 50 caliber bullet hit like a howitzer, knocking muscle-boy five feet back. He was dead by the time he hit the ground, a bloody hole in the middle of his chest.

Jake turned his attention back to the driver, who had shed

the husk that was formerly Stryker and was now frantically trying to unholster his gun. Jake put a bullet in his gut.

No one had yet breached the barricade. Jake, his hearing gone (he hoped temporarily) from the ear-piercing blasts of the Desert Eagle, shoved the gun into his waistband, ducked under the stanchions, blended in with the crowd on the walkway and headed back towards the Golden Jubilee Bridge. At about mid-span, with no one near, he leaned over and dropped the huge hand cannon into the Thames. At that moment he realized that in the chaos he left Maggie's pistol on the floor of the capsule. He thanked his luck and London's morning chill that he was wearing gloves.

26

———————

"What room is Jake Marks in?" Kelleher barked at the startled concierge.

At six in the morning, Brown's Hotel lobby was almost empty and the young management trainee was the only staff member behind the front desk. Brown's clientele usually favored dark suits or a blazer and slacks. The last person he expected to see standing in front of him was a grizzled, buzz-cut, scary looking senior citizen in full camo with two days of whiskers and the glare of a demon beast.

"I'm afraid I can't give out that kind of information."

"You got three seconds to change your mind," Kelleher said menacingly. He leaned in over the desk. His shark eyes bored holes in the terrified clerk's retinas. Kelleher opened his over-shirt just wide enough to reveal the Glock 23 hanging loosely in his shoulder holster.

The clerk gaped at the handgun. He looked around frantically for a manager or security guard, anyone to help him deal with the madman in front of him. But no one was anywhere in sight.

"There are two rooms registered to him," the petrified clerk gasped out.

"Gimmee both."

"Two-oh-three and two-oh-four."

"Touch that phone in the next ten minutes and it'll be the last thing you ever touch. I got people watching," Kelleher growled as he headed for the stairwell.

He used a universal hotel key card to unlock Marks's door. It was empty. He went across the hall. As he opened the door he could hear muffled snoring. He walked in silently, gripping the Glock with two hands in front of him. Someone was asleep in the bed, buried under the covers.

Kelleher leveled the gun at his sleeping target.

"Get the fuck up!" Kelleher yelled. "I want you to look in my eyes when I shoot you."

Maggie jerked up. She was about to scream. Then she realized who was pointing the gun at her.

"Kelleher?"

"Maggie? What the..."

"What...what's going on? What are you doing here?"

"Me?! What are YOU doing here?" Kelleher said. He eased his gun back in the holster. His hand shook slightly with the realization that he was a half-second away from blowing away his daughter.

"This is my room."

"What the hell are you talking about? It's registered to Marks."

"I'm working for him. The room's in his name."

"Are you screwing him?"

She glowered at him. "That's none of your goddamn business. Who the hell do you think you are?"

"I'm your father."

"Yeah, for about ten minutes. You left me and my mother in the lurch a long time ago. That cancels any rights you have as my father. And what the hell were you doing waving that cannon at me? Were you gonna shoot me?"

"No. Never."

"Then why?" As she spoke a grimace of horror washed over her face. In a quivering monotone she said, "You wanted to shoot Jake?"

"Damn right."

"Why?"

"He murdered your mother."

"What!" she screamed. "You don't know what you're talking about. The Lone Ranger killed my mother."

"Exactly."

She recoiled. "Now you're telling me that you think Jake is the Lone Ranger?"

"I know he is."

"You're either deluded or delusional. Maybe both. I seriously believe that you need psychological help. Jake Marks is generous, kind and understanding. He's one of the best people I've ever known."

"You've only known him for a couple of weeks."

"I know him long enough to know that there's no way he could be the Lone Ranger. I've been with him day and night since we got here. I might not have known him before, but I sure know him now." She stared up at Kelleher. "And, for your information, our relationship is purely professional."

"I don't believe you."

"I don't care if you believe it or not. And I'll tell you something else. If our relationship did become something more, that would be fine with me."

"I'm sorry, but you're the one who's deluded. Marks doesn't give a shit about you. He's using you to get to me."

"You're insane. That doesn't even begin to make sense."

"It makes a lot of sense. He knows you're my daughter. And

he knows that I know he killed Brigid. He probably intends to use you as a human shield."

Her mouth gaped open. Her eyes bulged in horror.

"You're crazy. I'm sure you're wrong about Jake. Please promise me you won't go after him."

"I can't promise that."

"Then give me some time to prove you're wrong."

"How?"

"I don't know. But I will."

"All right. You got a week."

"Can't you wait until he's out of Wimbledon? I'll be training him full time until it starts, then I'll get you your proof."

"I can't make any promises."

She put her palms together in the prayer hands gesture. "Please."

His scowl softened. "Okay. You got till after the tournament." He took a folded piece of paper out of his pocket and handed it to her.

"This is the number of my burner phone. Call me if you need me."

He lumbered out of the room.

27

When Maggie heard Jake open the door to his room, she followed him in.

"That was some run, you were gone almost three hours."

Jake had trained himself to always have a cover story ready. He concocted this one on his way back.

"I went over to a park a couple of blocks from here that has a three-mile loop. A lot of early morning runners use it before work. One of them was the tennis reporter for the *Guardian*. I've known him for a couple of years. When he asked me if he could run with me, I couldn't say no. Then he offered to buy me a cup of coffee and we wound up doing an interview."

"How did it go?"

"Pretty well for most of it. He knows his tennis and he's fair."

"Most of it?"

"Towards the end he started asking me about my absences from the game."

"Like the mysterious lost year," she said with a sly grin. "I read about that. It was shortly after you turned pro, right? You were off the grid for a long time and you never talk about it.

What's the big mystery?" She paused for a few seconds, then said, "I'm sorry. It's none of my business. I should never have brought it up."

"It's not a big deal, just something I'm not comfortable talking about with most people, but you're not most people."

"Are you sure?"

"Yeah. I know I can trust you." He took a deep breath. "Okay here goes. Since I was four years old my whole life was tennis. It started with my grandfather. He was a great athlete, a top minor league shortstop in the Cubs organization. An injury kept him out of the majors. After he was out of baseball, he took up tennis and before long he started winning local tournaments. For my fourth birthday he bought me a racquet. When I showed an aptitude for it, he became obsessed with turning me into a tennis phenom. He would drill me for hours every day but I didn't mind. I liked playing tennis and I loved him. I was about ten when I started beating him. That's when he hired Alex Espinosa to be my full-time coach.

Soon I was going to junior tournaments with Alex and my grandfather. First up and down the east coast, then all over the country. Tennis was my whole life. I had no friends, only training, practice and tournaments ."

"What about school?"

"I was home schooled."

"Oh."

"At sixteen I was the number one junior in the country. A year later, I got a scholarship to Columbia and won the NCAA Singles as a freshman. That summer I entered my first pro tournament. A Challenger in Ecuador. I won my first match. The next day, my coach was murdered.

"Oh my God! What did you do?"

"Truthfully, I'm not sure. Those days are a blur."

That was a lie. Every minute of that day—the day his life

turned inside out, upside down and sideways—is laser-etched in his brain.

He's in his hotel lobby, consumed by rage and grief, waiting for a cab to take him to the airport when a pudgy man in a wrinkled black suit runs, more like waddles, over to him.

"Uno momento, señor, I have something I think you'll be interested in."

Jake shouts, "Get the hell away from me."

"I have the name and address of the one who killed your coach."

Jake glares at him. "How do you know anything about it?"

"Señor, I am a newspaperman, it is my business to know. Alex Espinosa is a hero in this country. When he was in the semifinals at the U.S. Open, the entire nation watched and cheered. So when I see him running out of a hotel early in the morning, I follow. Who knows, there may be a story."

"Okay."

"As you can see." He pats his belly. "My jogging days are over, so I walked. When I finally caught up with him he was dead, shot in the back."

"And you saw who did it?"

"As clearly as I see you now."

"So tell me who it was."

"Señor Marks, this is Guayaquil. Everything has a price."

Jake shakes his head in disgust. "Okay, how much?"

"One thousand American dollars."

Alex once told him that Ecuadorians didn't respect you if you didn't bargain.

"Sorry, I don't have that kind of money."

"How about five hundred?"

"Still don't have it."

"Three hundred and not a penny less."

"Okay, let me see the name."

"First I must see the money."

Jake pulls two hundreds and two fifties out of his wallet and hands it to the reporter, who writes something on the back of a business card and hands it to Jake.

Ramon Huaracho. The name means nothing to him.

"How do I know that this is the guy?"

"It's him."

"Where can I find him?"

"Tombstone. It's a topless bar. He's there most nights." He opens his briefcase and takes out something wrapped in a brown paper bag and hands it to Jake. "When you find the man who killed Alex Espinosa, use this."

Jake looks in the bag. It's a gun, a Smith and Wesson .38 with a two-inch barrel.

"How much for this?"

"No charge. Señor Espinosa has many friends here. This is from them."

Tombstone Taverna is in the Garzota, the neighborhood the guide books tell tourists to avoid at all costs. The dive bar/whore house was built to look like a wild west saloon, complete with swinging doors and a long wooden bar. Johnny Cash's 'Folsom Prison' blares out of two loudspeakers as Jake walks in, oblivious to the glares of the pimps, hustlers and hookers. He orders a Bud Light. He's three sips into it when a young woman sits down next to him. Her close-cropped hair is jet black. Her tight, white tank top stops just short of her midsection, revealing a gold belly-button ring. She smiles at him through thick, red lips and asks him in heavily accented English if he wants to buy her a drink.

Jake says, "Sure," and nods to the waiter.

"They say you are with the tennis."

"How did you know?"

She shrugs. "You do Wimbledon, U.S. Open?"

"Not yet. Someday. What's your name?"

"Elena."

"Elena, could you do me a favor? I was supposed to meet a friend here, Ramon Huaracho, do you know him?"

"Ramon is upstairs. Do you want me to get him?"

"Just tell me what room he's in. I'll surprise him."

"Ramon is with one of the ladies of the house. Maybe he think not so funny."

"Trust me, he'll die laughing. What room?"

"Vente y seis, twenty-six."

He walks upstairs.

Room 26 is the last door in the corridor.

Jake reaches around his back to grab the gun that was in his waistband. His hand is shaking. He flings the door open and points his gun at the naked man and woman on the bed.

The woman screams.

He shouts at her, "Get out of here." She gathers her top, shorts, and sandals, and scrambles out the door.

Jake glowers at the naked man on the bed. "You killed Alex Espinsoa."

"I don't know no Alex Espinosa, why should I kill him?"

"I know you did it. One of your friends ratted you out," Jake lied.

"Which one?"

Jake is now positive this is the man who murdered Alex.

"Who paid you?"

Ramon Huaracho curls his upper lip and sneers at Jake.

"No one paid me. I killed him because he's an old man and he lived long enough. I killed him because he hit me when I wasn't looking. I killed him because nobody fucks with Huaracho and lives."

He slowly reaches over to the end table, grabs a lamp and throws it at Jake. In an instant, Huaracho is on him, grabbing at the gun. Huaracho is big and powerful, but he's drunk and spent from sex. Jake is in top condition and buoyed by rage. They grapple. Jake manages to turn the gun into the other man's stomach. He fires. Huaracho staggers. Blood trickles down his side. Jake yanks the gun out of his grasp and shoots him three more times in the chest.

People at the bar run upstairs at the sound of gunfire, filling the corridor. They scatter when they see Jake lurch, zombielike, toward them, gun in hand. Only Elena holds her ground. She takes Jake by the arm and leads him to the fire exit. She guides him down a flimsy metal stairway to a back alley. They walk for a block until they come to an old Toyota Corolla.

Once in the car, Jake begins to regain his composure.

"Thanks for your help. I could have never made it out of there without you."

"Don't mention it," she says.

"You know I shot him."

"Of course."

She starts the car.

"Where are we going?"

"My place."

It's a one-room studio on the top floor of a four-story walk-up.

Elena opens the door and says, "All right, Jake Marks. We need to talk."

At that moment he realizes he never told her his name and her accent is gone.

28

———————

Maggie said, "Jake, what happened? You zoned out for awhile."

"Sorry. I flashed on the day Alex was murdered."

"I'm sorry I brought it up. It must still be very painful. Let's talk about something else."

Jake paused and looked intently into her eyes. "No. I don't like talking about it with random people or reporters. I want to talk about it with you."

Like the best cover stories, a lot of what he was about to tell her was true.

"I had a nervous breakdown. Anxiety, depression, PTSD. I seriously thought about suicide. I was in and out of mental health facilities for the better part of a year. Mostly in."

Maggie walked over to him. She gently took his hand in both of hers. "Look how good you're doing now. If you told your story it could help others suffering from the same things."

"I know. I've thought about it. I'm just not ready to be the poster boy for mental illness. That's enough about my sordid past. I'm going to take a quick shower."

Five minutes later Jake walked out of the shower wrapped in a white terrycloth bathrobe.

Maggie said, "By the way, you'll never guess who dropped by to visit early this morning."

"Girl or boy?"

"Boy. Sort of."

"Good looking?"

"Maybe in an older, rugged sort of way."

"Should I be jealous?"

She giggled. "Absolutely not."

"Okay. I give up."

"Kelleher."

Jake stiffened. That couldn't be a good thing. Once he saw Kelleher get taken away in handcuffs, he stopped worrying about him.

"I thought he was in police custody."

"They must have let him go."

"That doesn't make any sense. He shot someone in front of a dozen policemen. I saw the police arrest him."

"He saved Mohammed Levi's life. Maybe they ruled it self defense."

"He didn't defend himself, he defended someone else."

She shrugged. "Maybe he was working as Levi's bodyguard, I don't know. He was here and he wasn't in handcuffs." Maggie rolled her eyes. "But he should be in a straight jacket. I really think he's losing his mind."

"What did he do this time?"

"It's not what he did, it's what he said."

"Oh, what's that?"

"He said that you were the Lone Ranger."

"What!" Jake was stunned. He wasn't ready to have Maggie suspect that he was the Lone Ranger, even for a minute.

"What did you tell him?"

"I said it was ridiculous. That he was way off base."

"Did he believe you?"

"Not exactly."

"I know he's your father, but he's also a killer. A killer who seems to be able to shoot someone right in front of the police and not pay any consequences. If he really believes I'm the one who murdered your mother, what's to stop him from killing me?"

"I'll stop him. I told him I'd prove to him that you weren't the Lone Ranger."

"I love you Maggie, but I can't see how you can definitively prove that."

Maggie's eyes bulged. Her mouth gaped. "Wait a minute. Did you just say you love me?"

"Yeah, I guess that's what I said."

"Do you mean it?"

Jake pondered for a few seconds. "I think I do." He reached over and held her hand.

She looked up at him, tiny tears forming at the corners of her eyes. "I think I love you too."

"That's what I was hoping for."

She looked into his eyes. "I want the bastard who killed my mother dead too. I hope Kelleher finds him and beats him to death with a dull rock, once we show him it's not you."

"How do we do that?"

She smiled. "We just have to get you both together. Once he meets you, he'll know you couldn't possibly be the Lone Ranger."

"That's not proof. And I'll probably be so nervous that I'll convince him the exact opposite."

"What's there to be nervous about?"

"Besides being number one on Jungle Jim Kelleher's hit list, there's this little tournament coming up soon that I'm nowhere near ready to seriously compete in."

She slapped her head with her hand. "Oh my God. Of course. We're supposed to start training today. Are you still up for it?"

"Absolutely. We both need to take our minds off everything that's happened. A day of hard training should be just what we need."

"Do you think it'll work now that we're a couple?."

"Sure. There are plenty of players who have relationships with someone on their team. It happens all the time."

After a day of intense training, Jake used his tennis connections to reserve a table at Zēphyr, reputed to be one of London's most romantic restaurants. They ended their evening in Jake's suite, enjoying their first night as lovers.

Maggie's phone chirped. She grabbed it off the nightstand. The time was 8:45. Kelleher's name showed on the screen. Why would he be calling her first thing in the morning?

"Kelleher?"

"To whom am I speaking?" The British-accented voice was stiff, unfriendly, middle aged and male.

"This is Maggie Quinlan. Who the hell are you?"

"This is Inspector Nigel Parker of the London Metropolitan Police."

"Why are you calling on my father's phone?"

"James Kelleher is your father?"

"Yes. What happened? Is he all right?"

"Mr. Kelleher has been arrested for murder. You were his phone's only contact."

"What!" she screamed. "I thought you people already settled that. That guy was trying to kill Mohammed Levi. Kelleher saved his life."

"Sorry for the confusion. We're holding Colonel Kelleher for the murder of Mendel Stryker."

"Never heard of him."

The inspector said, "The late Mr. Stryker is listed as a security consultant attached to the U.S. Embassy."

"When was this supposed to have happened?"

"Early this morning. I'd say around seven o'clock."

"You've got the wrong man. Kelleher couldn't have done it."

"Why do you say that?"

"Because he was here with me in my hotel room at seven o'clock this morning."

"Where are you?"

"Brown's Hotel."

"In Mayfair?"

"Yes."

"Perhaps you'd better come in and have a word with us."

"Yes, I think I'd better. Where?"

"Come to the Kensington police station. Do you know where it is?"

"I'll find it," she said and hung up. "Holy crap, I can't believe it!"

Jake sat up and said, "What did Kelleher do now?"

"He's been arrested for murder."

"I knew he couldn't just shoot that guy at the concert and get away with it."

"He didn't get arrested for that."

"What? He killed someone else?" Jake said incredulously. "Who?"

"Someone named Streaker or Striker, something like that."

"Mendel Stryker?"

"Yes, I think so. The detective said he was some kind of security consultant for the embassy here. Do you know him?"

"I met him at an embassy party for American tennis players. Where are they holding Kelleher?"

"At the Kensington Police Station. We've got to go down there and get him out."

"Hang on. Maybe we shouldn't. I'm feeling a lot safer knowing your father's under lock and key."

"But he didn't do it."

"How can you be so sure?"

"Because he was here when the guy got killed. The cop said that it happened around 7:00. While I was talking with Kelleher I heard Big Ben strike seven. Even Jungle Jim Kelleher can't be in two places at one time. Now do you want to come with me or should I go myself?"

"Of course I'm coming with you."

They were at the Kensington police station in fifteen minutes.

Maggie walked purposefully to the front desk.

"I'm Maggie Quinlan. An Officer Parker wanted to see me."

"You must mean Detective Inspector Parker, Miss." The young policeman behind the desk smiled warmly. "I'll ring him right up."

Jake walked over and stood behind her. After the desk officer made his call he looked up. "You're Jake Marks, the tennis genius, are you not?"

"Well, I don't know about the genius part, but yes, I'm Jake Marks."

"Oh...major fan," the policeman stammered slightly. "I already have my seats for the finals. I'm sure I'll be seeing you play."

"I hope so."

The cop handed Jake a small pad and a ballpoint pen. "Would you mind?"

"It would be my pleasure." He signed it.

"Excuse me, officer," Maggie shouted. "But my father's sitting in a cell right now accused of a murder he didn't commit. If you don't mind, I'd like to see him. Or at least the moron who put him there."

"I believe that would be me, young lady," a deep, booming

voice said from in back of her. She turned to see a tall, slender, balding man in his forties striding towards them. "And you are?"

"Maggie Quinlan, Colonel Kelleher's daughter."

"A pleasure to meet you, Miss Quinlan. Detective Inspector Parker."

He thrust out his hand. Maggie ignored it.

"I'm sure you want to help your father in every way, but I must tell you, we have some very strong evidence against him."

"I don't care what evidence you think you have. You're wrong."

"Come with me to my office." He turned and walked through a door into a long corridor. Jake and Maggie followed. Parker stopped walking a few strides later and turned to face Jake.

"Are you a solicitor?"

"Are you kidding?" Maggie said. "This is Jake Marks, the tennis player."

"Sorry. I don't follow tennis. I'm afraid the name means nothing to me."

"That's okay," Jake said.

"So you understand that I have to see Miss Quinlan alone?"

"Of course." He turned to Maggie. "I'll wait in the lobby for you."

"No, go back to the hotel. I have no idea how long this'll take. I'll be fine." She followed Parker into the elevator.

His desk was clear except for one file folder. He sat down behind it. There was a computer off to one side, a pen and small pad of paper next to it. Nothing else. The walls were covered with antique maps of London and environs. Maggie sat at the other side of the desk.

"Now Miss, tell me why are you so sure that your father didn't kill Mr. Stryker."

"Because he was with me at the time that you say the murder was committed."

Parker started writing on the pad on his desk.

"I think you may be mistaken, Miss Quinlan. Either that or you're lying to protect him."

"I'm not lying!" she shouted.

"Maybe lying was a bit too harsh." He smiled and nodded slightly. "Maybe you're just slightly enthusiastic in your zeal to prevent your father from spending many years in jail."

"Don't patronize me! My father was in my hotel room in Brown's Hotel from 6:30 to 7:30 this morning, and I have witnesses."

"Oh?" His voice was quizzical, almost amused. "Please continue."

"Well, he spoke to a desk clerk on his way up to see me."

"And you have a record of this?"

"I imagine that there are video surveillance cameras in the lobby. I'm sure he'll be on them. But even if he isn't, the hotel manager let me know that my father made a lasting impression. So much so that he's not welcome at Brown's Hotel anymore. I'm sure the desk clerk who he threatened will remember him vividly."

"Let's say you're correct, how do you explain the fact that his gun was found at the murder scene?"

"I have no idea. Maybe someone stole it. Or it isn't his gun and whoever told you that it is made a mistake. Or maybe they were bribed to say that." She took a deep breath to calm herself down. "Anyhow, I don't have to explain it. That's your job. I just want you to let my father out right now."

"I'm afraid I can't do that yet."

"Why the hell not?" she yelled.

"Please Ms. Quinlan, there's no need to shout. First we will have to examine your evidence to see if it's...uh, credible. Then we'll have to explain, to my satisfaction, not yours, how a twenty-two caliber Beretta registered to James Kelleher of New York City killed Mendel Stryker in London."

Maggie's eyes opened so wide they practically popped out of the sockets. "Did you say twenty-two?"

"That's correct."

"Then it's definitely not my father's gun." She stared blankly at Parker as a flood of emotions cascaded through her. "It's mine. My father gave it to me."

"You took a pistol with you to London?"

"No. My father had the gun delivered to my hotel room. My mother was murdered by the terrorist they call the Lone Ranger. Kelleher sent it to me to protect myself if somebody attacked me."

"Did anyone know you had it in your possession?"

"Nobody."

"You told no one about it?"

"Who would I tell? It's not like I have a whole bunch of friends in London. Besides, I hate guns. I put it away as soon as it arrived and haven't seen it since."

"How about your tennis playing friend?"

She didn't want to say that she gave the gun to Jake to get rid of. Being in the middle of a police investigation was the last thing he needed right before Wimbledon.

"Jake? I might have told him, I'm not sure."

"Try to remember. Your father's freedom could depend on it."

"So now you're telling me that Jake Marks is a murderer? That's even more ridiculous than saying it was Kelleher."

Parker stood and glared at her. "I'm telling you that a man was shot and killed this morning with a gun registered to James Kelleher that you claim is yours. If it is, in fact, the gun that was delivered to you, and we will verify that, that leaves only you or someone who had access to it as possible suspects. I sincerely doubt that you shot Mr. Stryker, which means your father and Mr. Marks seem to be the only two people who could have done it."

"Maybe someone stole it from the room. Someone who works in the hotel and knew the gun was there. Or someone at the messenger service who delivered it."

"Perhaps. We'll check all of that out, but I need to talk to you about where your father was at seven o'clock."

"He was in my hotel room, I'm sure of it. I heard Big Ben chime while he was there. That's why I remember the time so well."

"And was Mr. Marks in the room as well?"

"Uh...no. He was out for an early morning jog."

Parker nodded his head slowly. He wrote on the notepad. "We might need to speak with him. How long will you and Mr. Marks be in London?"

"Hopefully, until the end of Wimbledon."

"Excuse me?"

"You have heard of Wimbledon, the tennis tournament?"

"Yes, of course."

"Jake is playing in it."

"Oh, I see."

"Can I see my father now?"

"I'll have someone take you to him." He picked up the phone. "Can you send Miss Shankar in. I need an escort for Miss Quinlan up to the holding area." He smiled at Maggie. "Miss Quinlan, your father is very lucky to have a daughter like you. You might just have saved his life. Or, at least, his freedom."

The policewoman was younger than Maggie and taller. She marched, rather than walked, into the room, ramrod straight, chin out. Her silky black hair was pulled back in a tight bun.

"Miss Shankar, please take Miss Quinlan to see Colonel Kelleher. He's in custody room number two."

"Certainly, sir."

Constable Shankar led Maggie down the hall and around a corner.

Both women walked down a corridor until they came to door number two. To Maggie's surprise, it looked more like an office cubicle than a jail cell.

Officer Shankar knocked on the door. "Colonel Kelleher, you have a visitor."

She unlocked the door and stepped to the side to let Maggie enter. Kelleher was doing pushups. He turned. "Maggie." Kelleher jumped to his feet. "I didn't expect to see you here."

She smiled. "This isn't where I thought I'd be seeing you either."

"Are you all right?"

"I'm fine. What about you?"

"I'll be a lot better once I'm out of here."

"They think you killed some guy. You didn't, did you?"

"Of course not. I couldn't have," he said emphatically. "I was with you when they say it happened. Didn't they tell you that? The only evidence they have is a gun they say belongs to me. A twenty-two. I've never owned a twenty-two caliber gun in my life."

"Sorry, it is your gun, technically. It's the one you sent me."

"Your gun? How did they get that gun? Marks! Did he know you had a gun?"

"I might have mentioned it."

"Well did you?" He stood up, glowering.

"I think so."

"I can't believe it! That son of a bitch, he shot Stryker with that gun knowing I'd get blamed."

"You're wrong!" she cried. "It must have happened some

other way. Jake's no killer. He loves me. He would never do anything to hurt me."

"Don't be stupid, Maggie. He's a stone cold murderer. He killed your mother, he killed Russell Townsend, he killed Stryker and he'll kill you if he has to, to get to me."

Kelleher paced up and down the small room while Maggie sat in the center.

"Jake Marks is not a murderer," she screamed. "I don't care what you say. I don't care what anybody says." Maggie's eyes were streaked with tears. She spun around and stormed out of the room. Miss Shankar, the policewoman, hurried to intercept her.

"All done, Miss?"

"Yes, I'm finished," she sniffled.

She left the police station in a fog. Her head was spinning. Could Jake really be the Lone Ranger? Could he have murdered her mother and all those other people? She refused to believe it. But if he didn't do it, how did her gun wind up shooting that man? Jake was the only person who knew it existed, besides her and Kelleher.

Her eyes were blurry with tears when she reached the street. A misty drizzle was falling with few people walking about. She had no idea how to get back to her hotel or how to get a cab. She felt disoriented, confused, lost.

A taxi appeared, almost magically, out of the haze.

The driver opened the window. "Can I be of assistance, Miss?"

"Oh, thank God you came," she gasped. "I didn't think I'd ever find a taxi down here. Can you take me to Brown's Hotel in Mayfair?"

"Of course." He stepped out of the cab to open her door. He was a giant of a man but he moved with the grace of a dancer. Once he was behind her, he jabbed her shoulder with a hypodermic needle.

"Oww," she yelped, turned around and screamed "What the hell do you…" Suddenly her eyelids grew sandbags and the mist turned black.

Marcus Glynn picked her up effortlessly and positioned her limp body on the back seat of the cab.

30

Jake Marks strained to lift his head off the carpet. Feet flat on the floor, knees pointed towards the ceiling, veins popping from his neck, he was well into his third set of 300 twisting crunches after doing 100 pushups.

Whenever he was tense, anxious or didn't know what to do with himself, he exercised. At the moment he was all three. He wanted to make sure he was in the room when Maggie came back from talking to her father, but he had no idea when that would be. Or how she would feel about him. Kelleher would certainly tell her that Jake murdered Stryker as well as her mother. Would Maggie believe her father, then despise him and never want to see him again? Or would she figure that Kelleher was crazy and didn't know what he was talking about?

Then the phone rang.

Jake knew Maggie would be at the other end of the phone. In a few seconds he would find out if she still believed in him or hated him with a passion. He was prepared to hear either one. What he wasn't prepared for was Marcus Glynn's snarly voice.

"All right Marks. Listen to me and listen good."

"Glynn, what the hell do you want?"

"Just shut up and listen."

There was some rustling noise in the background. Then Maggie's voice. "Jake, is that you?" She sounded weak, drugged. "They told me to tell you that if you don't do what they say, they'll kill me."

Jake's hand shook. Bile rose from his gut. "Maggie, are you okay?"

"I think so. I'm still a little groggy."

"Where are you?"

"I don't know."

"They didn't hurt you, did they?"

"No."

"Don't worry, I'll get you out of there soon. I promise."

The phone went silent for a few seconds.

"Do I have your attention now, asshole?" Glynn barked.

"What the hell is going on?"

"You want your girlfriend to live, you'll do what you're told."

"Why are you doing this? I'm not your enemy."

"After you killed Stryker, the boss ordered you excised."

"You know damn well that Stryker tried to kill me. He lured me to the London Eye. Made sure no one was around. And started shooting. I was lucky. He missed. I didn't."

"It doesn't matter. Listen to what I'm saying and maybe you'll get lucky again and you get to see your girlfriend alive."

"All right. I'm listening."

"I talked him out of it. Again. Do one more job for us and we wipe the slate."

"I don't believe you."

"Believe this. If you don't, she's dead."

"All right. Who, Levi?"

"Forget about Levi. Your new target is Kelleher."

"Kelleher? I thought he was with you guys."

"You thought wrong. We want him out of the picture."

"He's in jail. How am I supposed to get to him?"

"Don't worry about that. He'll come to you. You got 48 hours. If he's still alive after that, your girlfriend won't be."

He hung up.

31

———————

At eleven the next morning, an African American woman in a gray suit and short blunt bobbed hair walked into the Kensington Police Station, introduced herself as the Assistant U.S. Consul for Public Affairs, and presented the officer at the front desk with her credentials and a piece of paper proclaiming that James Kelleher was to be immediately released. After some heated back and forth with Detective Inspector Parker, Kelleher and the Consul walked out the door and onto the street. She told him brusquely that this would be the last time the embassy would intervene for him, then got into the back of a waiting Mercedes limousine.

As Kelleher started walking, a Cadillac Escalade pulled up next to him.

"Jim Kelleher?" the driver asked through the open window.

"Yeah."

"The person who arranged your release would like to speak with you."

"Who's that?"

"You'll find out if you get in the car."

Kelleher tried to figure out who it was. He was pretty sure it wasn't Glynn this time. The only other person who even knew he was in London was Maggie, and she didn't have the juice to make it happen.

They rode in silence the rest of the way.

The car pulled in front of Brown's Hotel.

"Thanks for the ride," Kelleher said as he left the car.

So it was Maggie. How the hell was she able to pull this off? A few minutes later, he knocked on Maggie's door .

The door flew open, but Maggie wasn't on the other side. Jake was. He took two steps back and leveled an impressive looking pistol at Kelleher's chest. "I hear you've been looking for me."

"What the fuck!" Kelleher said. "Where's Maggie?"

Jake backed into the room, never getting within five feet of Kelleher. He gestured at a green wing chair on the other side of the bed. "Just walk in slowly and sit down over there."

Kelleher did as he was told. His eyes darted around the room, analyzing every feature for a possible tactical advantage. "If you did anything to her..."

"Shut up and listen." Jake paced back and forth on the other side of the room, keeping the king size bed between himself and Kelleher.

"Maggie was kidnapped from in front of the Kensington Police Station right after she saw you."

Kelleher glared at Jake with undisguised rage and hatred. "Why would anyone want to kidnap my daughter?"

"To use her to make me do something I don't want to do."

Kelleher's muscles tensed. He stood. "So you admit that you're the Lone Ranger?"

Jake nodded.

"That means you shot Brigid."

Jake shook his head. "I didn't. Stryker did."

"That's bullshit. Why the hell would Stryker want to kill Brigid?"

"To get you to come after me."

"You're full of shit. I saw the police report. It said all the bullets came from the same gun."

"You never saw the real report. You saw Marcus Glynn's doctored report."

Kelleher shook his head skeptically. "It doesn't wash."

"It didn't make sense to me either...until yesterday."

"What happened yesterday?"

"Stryker arranged for me to meet him. That's when he told me he shot Brigid. The plan was for you to kill me and they arrest you or vice versa. Best case for them is we kill each other. No matter how it turns out, it's a win-win for them. Goldbarr wants us both out of action. He's convinced I'm gonna rat out his secret hit squad. I don't know why he wants you dead."

"I do. I screwed up one of his deals with the Arabs. I didn't know he was involved with the warlord I helped take down. Turns out he lost billions on some kinda oil deal. He's a vindictive son of a bitch."

"Are you starting to believe me?"

"The jury's still out. Even if everything you're saying is true, why would Stryker tell you all this?"

"Because he had a gun pointed at my chest and he was about to pull the trigger. He wanted to gloat a little before he shot me."

Kelleher nodded. "Yeah, that sounds like him, fuckin' asshole. So how did he get dead and I get blamed?"

"After you killed the wrong guy at the Levi concert, Stryker decided to take me out himself. I guess it's been a long time since he fired a Desert Eagle, if ever. My bet is he wears it cause it's the most badass looking gun around. His shot was off, probably because that gun weighs almost five pounds. I was able to dive out of the way and get a shot at him. The only gun I had access to is the one you gave to Maggie. It didn't even occur to me that they would trace it back to you."

"That's a nice story. It might even be true. But right now I don't give a rat's ass either way. I just want Maggie back healthy. If they want you to take someone out, just do it. I don't care if it's the folksinger or someone else."

Jake shook his head. "I'm out of the assassination business."

"Fine. But this is for Maggie, not for Goldbarr. If you love her like you say you do, you'll do this one last job."

"You don't understand. It was one thing when I thought I was doing something good. Taking out scumbags. Protecting America. I thought I was a soldier on the front line in the war for freedom. Killing innocent people, even to save the woman I love, I could never do that."

"If you don't, Maggie's dead. And it'll be on you. I'll tell you what, tell me who it is and I'll do it."

"I can't."

"Why the hell not?"

"Because the target is you."

Kelleher froze. His face showed no emotion. The skin around his hands and face grew taut. He stared directly into Jake's eyes.

"Go ahead, shoot. I never thought I'd live this long anyway. At least my death will do something good." He stood up, hands clasped behind his head. "Make it clean."

Jake steadied himself, took a deep breath, leveled the gun at the older man's chest. Tiny dewdrops of sweat dotted his forehead. He concentrated on his breathing. He knew what he was about to do could easily cost him his life and maybe Maggie's too. But he also knew that it was the only way he could save her.

He handed the gun to Kelleher. "You wanted to kill me. Here's your chance. Either use it on me or use it with me."

Kelleher was so stunned he could hardly hold the gun.

"You're fuckin' crazy!"

"No, I'm finally fuckin' sane."

Kelleher leveled the gun at Jake. He stared into the younger man's eyes for several seconds. Jake's gaze was steadfast.

"Either you're telling the truth or you're the best fuckin' poker player who ever lived." Kelleher handed the pistol back to Jake.

"You'll help me get Maggie?"

Kelleher nodded. "Yeah. But don't get any ideas. We're not partners. We're not friends. We'll work together this one time because we both care about Maggie. After that, all bets are off. Understood?"

"Understood."

32

———————

Kelleher shouted into the phone, "Glynn, it's Kelleher."

"Kelleher?" Glynn sounded surprised. "Where are you?"

"Don't worry about where I am. We gotta meet."

"Okay, yeah, sure. Tonight. I'll tell you where and when."

"No, now. This can't wait."

"Okay, tell me. What's so important?"

"Not on the phone. There's probably half-a-dozen British cops listening to us right now. They were pissed off when they thought they had me nailed. Twice. I bet they got half the force tailing me and the other half recording me."

"Get over yourself, Kelleher. You're not that important. But you're right, it's better we don't talk on the phone. Give me ten minutes. Where?"

Kelleher looked at his watch. "It's a little after eleven. Meet me at the Marble Arch at 11:30. Come alone."

"Wassamatter, Kelleher, don't you trust me?"

"Yeah, as much as you trust me."

"Look for me. I'll be in a black Suburban."

Twenty minutes later a gargantuan SUV double parked across the street from the Arch. The windows were black. As

Kelleher walked over, Glynn cracked open the driver's side window. "Get in."

Kelleher shook his head. "No. You get out."

The big man snorted, stepped out of the car and leaned his bulk against the front fender. Kelleher walked around the car, peering through the windows.

"What the hell are you doing?"

"Just making sure there's no surprises. I wouldn't want any of your friends jumping out and dragging me somewhere."

"You're getting paranoid in your old age. You said come alone, I'm alone. What the hell is so important?"

"Hold your fuckin' horses, I'm almost done," Kelleher said from the other side of the vehicle.

When he was sure he was out of Glynn's line of sight, he stuck a magnetized GPS tracker inside the wheel well on the rear passenger's side.

Kelleher walked around the car. "They're gone."

Glynn looked confused. "Who's gone?"

"Marks and my daughter."

"What the hell are you talking about? Where did they go?"

"How the fuck should I know. I texted Maggie this morning. Nothing. I called her. No answer. So I went up to their room and let myself in. No trace of Marks or Maggie. No suitcases. No tennis stuff. Nothing."

Glynn's brow furrowed. He chewed on a knuckle. If Jake really did leave town that would mean he doesn't care what happens to Maggie. Suddenly all his leverage would be gone.

He recomposed his face. "We'll find them. They can't have gotten too far."

"Are you kidding? They could be anywhere. Paris. Rome. Fuckin' Timbuktu."

Glynn shook his head vehemently. "No. They're still in London."

"How do you know?"

"Number one, Wimbledon starts soon. If he withdrew, it would be all over the newspapers. They take their tennis very seriously around here. Number two, we have all the airports, trains and bus stations monitored. We would have picked up something."

"I don't buy it. We're not talking about some random douchebag. Marks is a pro. He's the fuckin' Lone Ranger for Chrissakes. He slips in and out of countries like most people slip out of their skivvies. There's a dozen ways he can smuggle himself and Maggie out of the country."

"I'm telling you, Marks is in London somewhere and we'll find him."

"What am I supposed to do in the meantime?"

"Just sit tight and try to stay out of jail for a couple of days."

"Fuck you Glynn. The only reason I was in jail was because I listened to you. If I did things my way, Marks would be dead and Maggie would be safe."

"I tell you what. Give me 24 hours to find them. After that you can do whatever the hell you want."

Kelleher smirked. "All right. You got one day."

As Glynn sped away, Kelleher unwrapped a new burner phone and dialed Jake's number.

"How'd it go?"

"Fine. He bought it."

"You sure? Glynn's no dope."

"He was rattled. I could see it in his face. He was trying to figure out his next move."

"What about the tracker?"

"Yeah. It's in."

"Good."

"Did you get to the safe house?"

"I'm going there now."

"What about Brown's?"

"I cleaned out both rooms. If Glynn checks he won't find anything."

"All right. Unless there's a problem, we'll go tonight."

"Yeah."

Jake hung up.

Kelleher tossed the burner into a trash can.

33

———————

The safe house was a bed and breakfast on Rosary Gardens in South Kensington. Kelleher rapped on the door at 11:53. He was dressed all in black from his wool cap to his combat boots. Even his mission bag was black.

As Jake opened the door, Kelleher said, "You got the location?"

"Yeah. A boarded-up bar in Peckham."

"What the hell is a Peckham?"

"It's London's version of the South Bronx: dirty, decrepit and dangerous."

"Good, that works for us. Anybody spots us, we're just another couple of hoods."

Kelleher dumped the contents of the bag on the bed. Two large guns with suppressors, two small pistols, two pairs each of night vision goggles and tactical gloves.

Jake said, "What the hell is all that?"

"Materiel."

"I guess you never heard of traveling light."

Kelleher growled, "We're not going on a fucking boys night

out. We're on a mission to save my daughter, the woman you supposedly love."

Jake winced but said nothing.

Kelleher continued, "We gotta be ready for whatever the hell is over there, including the possibility that Glynn coulda found the GPS and is sending us on some wild goose chase or into a trap."

"Don't worry, it's the right location."

"How do you know?"

"I have a guy watching the house. Glynn's been in and out a few times. Once with a couple of takeout bags."

Kelleher threw up his hands. "Whoa, wait a minute. What do you mean you got a guy? What guy?"

"He's a local. A good man. I trust him."

Kelleher shook his head. "You trusting him doesn't mean shit to me. I never work with people I don't know."

"Neither do I, usually. But this is different. Neither one of us have any idea about how things work in London. Deke's lived here all his life. He knows the streets, he knows the people. We need him."

"You ever work with him before?"

"Not exactly. He served in the British Army with a friend of mine."

"How good a friend?"

"A guy I trust with my life."

"And he vouched for this guy?"

"I texted my friend and he wrote back that he was a good soldier but didn't say much else. But I can vouch for him myself."

"You just said you never worked with him. Make up your mind."

"We never did a job together, but I had two attempts on my life last week and he helped me out both times."

"You mean besides Stryker on the ferris wheel?"

Jake told him about the attack at the gym and the incident in Hyde Park.

"So twice this guy appears out of nowhere and saves your ass. I don't like it. It a classic setup. Gain trust and you got a man on the inside."

"You think he could be working for Glynn?"

"I'd bet on it. Glynn told me he could mobilize a dozen men in a day. My guess is your friend is one of them."

"No way."

"Did you ever hear from the cops about what happened in Hyde Park?"

"Not yet."

"That's because that cop was a fake. Like the woman and the nurse."

"What about my friend at the gym? You think he was on Goldbarr's payroll too?"

"I don't know. I still don't like it."

"I think you're way out of line about this."

"I don't give a rat's ass what you think. I'm not putting my life on the line, or Maggie's, for some random jerkoff. Give me a day to check him out."

"We don't have a day. If we don't go tonight Maggie might not be there tomorrow."

"She'll be there. Glynn wants us dead. She's no use to him except as bait. As long as he thinks he has a shot at us, she's safe. But if this guy is a plant, we're fucked."

"You're wrong. My guy is no plant. I'd bet my life on it."

"That's just what you're doing."

"I'm going tonight, with or without you."

"Fine. Good luck." Kelleher started gathering up the equipment on the bed and putting it back in the bag. He handed Jake the gun with the suppressor. "Take this. You'll need it."

Jake shook his head. "I don't want that. It'll weigh me down. How about the Sig 365?"

"Yeah, sure." He tossed him the small handgun. Jake tucked it in his waistband. The cold steel of the barrel against his spine sent a shiver down his leg.

Kelleher grabbed his bag and lumbered out of the room.

Jake texted Deke, who texted back that there was no sign of Glynn. Then he hit the Uber app on his phone. Twenty minutes later he was at Blenheim Grove, a dark, sinister street with train tracks on one side and disconsolate storefronts on the other, all with bars on their windows, most with steel security grills covering the doors. Some vans, trucks and an abandoned car that had been worked over pretty well were parked next to the tracks. One of the vans blinked its lights.

Deke opened the window as Jake slowly approached.

"Where's your mate?"

"He's not coming."

"What happened?"

Jake didn't want to tell him that Kelleher didn't trust him, so he just said, "Just said he couldn't make it."

"The old guy lost his nerve. Doesn't matter. This should be a snap. Glynn never came back. The place is an old pub, closed more than a year. Store room's downstairs. Your girl's there."

"Are you sure?"

"Every time Glynn comes by, he goes downstairs for a few minutes, then leaves. What do you think?"

"Yeah. Makes sense. Stay here and keep watch. If Glynn comes back, buzz my phone."

"Roger that."

"This shouldn't take long. If we're not out in five minutes, it means something's wrong. Call the police. Tell them you heard gunshots."

Deke shot him a thumbs-up.

Jake crossed the street to the remnants of the Brickhouse Pub. The lock on the front door was broken. The room was dark and musty. The stench of stale beer and spent cigarettes hung in the air. He unclipped a small tactical flashlight from his belt and looked around. All of the furniture, tables, chairs, barstools, even the light fixtures, were gone. The long, lonely bar was covered with dust, the ceiling with spider webs. The basement door was behind the bar. The wooden stairs creaked as Jake made his way slowly down to the concrete cellar floor. The fetid air was dank with must, mold and other foul smells that he couldn't name and didn't want to think about. He clicked the light switch. A bare bulb revealed more spider webs on the ceiling and rat droppings covering the floor. Maggie was seated in the middle of the room on an old metal bar stool with a high slatted back. Thick black tape lashed her wrists and ankles to the chair. Two layers of tape covered her mouth.

"Maggie, it's Jake," he shouted.

She began shaking her head frenziedly and rocked the stool from side to side, yelping guttural noises through her covered mouth.

"Don't worry honey, it'll be over soon."

"Yeah, you're right, Marks," came a voice from behind him. "But not the way you figured."

Jake turned to see Glynn, smirking as he leveled a gun at his chest. Jake's mind raced. Deke said Glynn left. How did he get back in without Deke seeing him? Could he have come in another entrance? Was he here all the time? At this point it didn't matter. The only thing that mattered was Maggie.

34

"All right Marks, turn out your pockets."

Jake did as instructed.

"Pull your shirt up and turn around."

After Jake turned, Glynn smiled.

"Take that peashooter, drop it on the floor and kick it away."

So much for the remote chance that Jake could somehow get a shot off.

"Lift your pants."

After Glynn saw that Jake had no other weapons, he said, "Now go stand next to your girlfriend."

"All right. You have me. Let her go."

Glynn shook his head. "We still need her for Kelleher. But we don't need you for anything."

His only hope was that Deke would come to see what was taking so long. He needed to stall for as long as possible, so he said the first thing that came into his mind.

"You really think you can get away with this?"

Lame, but he had no time to be creative.

Glynn nodded smugly. "You're a dangerous terrorist. Wanted all over the world. I might get a medal for killing you."

"That's fine. But Maggie's no terrorist. She's an innocent woman. Nobody's giving you a medal for murdering her. And what about Kelleher? He's a retired Army colonel with two Silver Stars and a Purple Heart. Besides being an American war hero, he's a former Army Ranger and a vindictive sonuvabitch. When he finds out you killed his daughter, nothing will stop him from coming after you."

"That's what we're banking on. When the police get here, it'll look like you kidnapped Kelleher's daughter. He tracked you here. There was a shootout and you killed each other. Too bad your girlfriend got hit in the crossfire. Open and shut. It was supposed to happen today. Guess we'll have to wait another day or two for Kelleher to play his part."

"Kelleher spent his whole life doing raids like this. He won't be as easy to trap as me."

Glynn snickered. "He's an old man, way past his prime. Maybe ten years ago he would have been a problem. Not anymore."

Jake didn't know why the usually taciturn Glynn was being so chatty, but the longer he could keep him talking the better the chances for Deke or the police to show up.

"You have one more problem. I have a friend outside watching the place. If I don't come out of here with Maggie, he'll call the police."

Glynn snickered. "You're sure about that, huh?"

He took out his phone. A self-satisfied grin washed over his face. "Hey Deke, come down here. Your pal Marks wants to say good bye."

Jake sagged. "How the..."

"It wasn't hard. Once we knew you were headed to London, we did some digging. We came up with your driver Bunny's pals in Special Reconnaissance. Turns out Deke Wiltshire has a gambling problem. He owes about $50,000 to bookies all over London. We showed him proof that you were the notorious terrorist they call the Lone Ranger with a huge price on your head. The reward will clear out his debts and leave him with a nice chunk of change left over. But he has to be the one to pull the trigger or the deal's off. We need him to have some skin in the game."

There went Jake's last hope for an eleventh-hour rescue. No wonder Glynn was in no hurry.

"Just tell me one thing. We were the good guys, going after drug dealers, terrorists, dictators, human traffickers. The worst of the worst. Enemies of the United States and a threat to freedom. Guys who killed and tortured innocent people for money or power. All of a sudden we're going after people like Townsend and Levi. What changed?"

"America changed. We're getting weak, soft. Inching more towards socialism every day. Guys like that are a lot more dangerous than gangsters and terrorists. They're the real threat to America, not these petty crooks and despots. If we become a pacifist nation, China and Russia will eat our lunch."

"Sounds like Goldbarr's political bullshit. You can't really believe that."

"Of course I believe it. If you don't, you're not paying attention."

"Even if it's true, it doesn't explain why you had Nick Pashim killed. He operated a gym. What kind of danger was he to the American way of life?"

Glynn smirked. "Your friend Pashim is alive and well. Turns out he had a really bad bout of food poisoning the night before he was supposed to meet you. Almost killed him it was so bad. He was in intensive care for two days."

Jake looked bewildered. Then he realized he never saw a body. Deke told him there was a dead body in the closet and he had no reason to doubt him. If Jake wasn't facing imminent death, he'd be impressed at the way the operation was conducted.

"What about Brigid Quinlan? Stryker killed her in cold blood. Was she a threat to America?"

Glynn stiffened. "Stryker was a psycho. A wild animal. Killing the Quinlan woman was totally unauthorized. I didn't know about it until after it was done. Neither did Goldbarr. You did us a favor when you took him out."

"Did Goldbarr think so too?"

"Goldbarr had a soft spot for Stryker, like he was his pet pit bull. Fierce and loyal but hard to control."

The sound of footfalls coming down the steps echoed in the basement.

"Here comes your friend Deke now. Just for the record, Marks, I thought you were okay. Too bad you lost your nerve." Glynn turned towards the staircase.

This was Jake's chance. He was ready to spring, but before he could make his move, the room went dark.

"Hey!" Glynn shouted. "What the hell are you doing? Turn those lights back on. I got everything under control."

"I don't think so," a gruff voice said.

It was Kelleher.

Glynn spun around and shot blindly. Jake lunged at him in the darkness. Glynn staggered but stayed on his feet. They grappled like a couple of blind mud wrestlers. Jake grabbed for the gun. Glynn bent Jake's wrist all the way back. Jake screamed in pain, then sunk his teeth into Glynn's hand. The big man bellowed and let go of the gun. As it clattered to the floor, he smashed his fist into Jake's face. Jake fell to the ground, semi conscious, drooling blood.

With Jake out of the line of fire, Kelleher emptied his gun into Glynn. He took off his night vision goggles and turned on the light. Glynn was prostrate on the floor, a crimson puddle forming under him. Kelleher put two fingers on his neck, feeling for a pulse. There was none. He turned to Maggie.

"You okay?"

She nodded, still bound and gagged.

Kelleher glared down at Jake with a look of contempt and disgust. He stepped over him and gently removed the tape covering his daughter's mouth. Tears streamed down her cheeks. He took a black folding knife out of his pocket and cut the binding on her hands and feet.

Jake slowly got to his feet and went over to Maggie. "It's over."

She wrapped her arms around him. "I was sure he was gonna kill us," her voice cracked as she spoke.

Jake glanced over his shoulder at Kelleher, who was standing a few feet away, his arms folded in front of him, an indelible scowl etched on his face. "I'm sorry. I really fucked up. You said not to trust Deke and I didn't listen."

Maggie walked slowly toward her father on wobbly legs, numb from being strapped to the chair. She hugged him and said, "Thanks for saving our lives, dad." It was the first time she called him 'dad.'

"Don't worry about it," he mumbled, looking uncomfortable.

Jake said, "I owe you big-time, Kelleher."

"Yeah, whatever."

"By the way, what happened to Deke?"

"Don't worry about him. Just get Maggie out of here. I'll clean up."

Maggie said, "We can stay and help you."

"No, just go."

Jake Marks stood at a podium in the media center of the All England Lawn Tennis and Croquet Club. His wrist was bandaged and there was a band-aid across the side of his forehead. A throng of reporters and photographers crowded around him in a semicircle, their phones and cameras thrust in the air. A few old-timers who still used ink and paper stood in the rear and took notes.

"I'm afraid I'm going to have to withdraw from the Championships. I was involved in a traffic accident last night and sustained a level two concussion and a sprained wrist."

A reporter stood up. "You don't look so bad, are you sure you can't play?"

"Right now I can't even hold a racquet, much less swing it. The doctors told me that with treatment it should start to get better in three or four weeks. They said if I rushed it, especially while recovering from a concussion, I could do permanent damage that would end my career."

"What is your response to some people who say you are afraid to face Tommy Riemer and have fabricated your injury to avoid him?" blurted a young female. She had tattoos covering both arms and a ring through her nose.

"By 'some people' you mean Tommy Riemer. If you like, you, Riemer or anyone else can have a look at my MRI and see that I'm not faking anything."

The door in the back of the room flung open and Riemer stormed in.

"Why don't you tell the truth, you chickenshit bastard? You're scared shitless of me," he screamed. "Admit it, Marks, you're just a fucking coward."

Patrick Calabrian, the All England Club's media relations director, jumped up from his chair next to the podium. Short and slim with wavy brown hair, the one-time tennis columnist for the Daily Telegraph wore a well tailored gray pinstriped suit and affected a David Niven mustache. His rumored affair with a Danish doubles player was never confirmed, but the rakish Calabrian never denied it either. "Please Mr. Riemer," he shouted. "That kind of language will not be tolerated here. I must insist that you leave at once."

Riemer folded his arms over his chest and glared defiantly at him. As two security guards approached from either side of the room, Riemer spit on the carpet and darted out the door.

Most of the reporters ran after him, hoping to get a quote that they could actually print in a family newspaper.

One of the remaining writers asked Jake to respond to Riemer's attack.

"Tommy Riemer is a gifted tennis player but a very disturbed young man. I hope he gets some help before he ruins his career and his life."

"Are you afraid to play him?" came a shout from the back of the room.

"I won't even justify that question with an answer."

Calabrian walked to the podium. "I'm afraid that's all for now."

As the tennis media ambled out of the room, Calabrian whispered, "Between you and I, what is it between you and that punk Riemer? He's an arsehole under the best of circumstances, but he seems to have a special reserve of venom for you."

"It started a long time ago when we were both highly ranked juniors from New York. I was the number one 16-and-under player and he was number two in the 14s. He was an obnoxious brat even then. The one time I played him in a match I was beating him pretty easily when he had a hissy fit and we never finished. Afterwards, I told him what I thought of his behavior and that I'd never play with him again. That's when his hero worship turned into seething hatred."

"It seems like he hates everyone he plays."

"That's true. He's just been hating me longer."

"Now he'll be shouting it from the rooftops."

"I'm sure you're right. The only way to shut him up will be to kick his butt at the U.S. Open."

The next day's tabloid headlines screamed, Bloodbath in Peckham. It went on to talk about a shootout between an American policeman and a low-level British gangster that neither survived. At the bottom of the page a banner blared, 'Marks Out at Wimbledon.'

THIRD SET

36

───────

Jake Marks sat in a cramped booth in the middle of the Ball and Glove, a trendy New York City sports bar under the watchful eyes of two cameras and two hundred customers, talking to Gary 'Taz' Pirelli, the host of SportsBreath, New York's highest rated sports talk radio show that was also simulcast on the MSG TV Network.

Painfully thin, with a long, pointy nose and thick black glasses, Pirelli was always the last kid chosen in the schoolyard and the first one to get bullied by the jocks. He was getting even by bullying them on the air and making a small fortune doing it.

Greg Filiano, the publicist for the U.S. Open and a longtime friend, begged Jake to do the interview. TV ratings for the Open had been lagging and Filiano thought that it might give them a bump.

"I'm here with New York's own Jake Marks, who a lot of people who pay attention to tennis said would follow in the footsteps of Connors, McEnroe, Sampras, Agassi and Roddick, and bring America back to the top tier of the sport. He's just back from London where he had to withdraw from Wimbledon for, what was it, a boo-boo on your pinkie?"

Jake knew Pirelli's combative, in-your-face style and decided that the best way to deal with him would be to ignore the jabs and put-downs.

"Actually, it was a sprained wrist." He held up his hand to show his wrist in a soft cast from the middle of his forearm to the first knuckle of his fingertips.

"So tell me Jake Marks, is it my imagination or do you seem to have a hard time finishing tournaments? According to my records, you've dropped out of five ATP 1000 tournaments in the last five years. No other tour player has dropped out of more than one. How do you explain that?" Pirelli asked, staring intently into Jake's eyes.

"Bad luck? Bad karma? The evil eye? I wish I knew, then I would fix it."

"Yeah, okay. But what about all those unexplained absences from the tour?" Pirelli leaned forward and glared at Jake from across the table. "There are rumors that you had a mental breakdown and were locked up in some high priced psychiatric hospital. So, were you locked up in the loony bin?"

"Do I look crazy to you?"

"How the heck should I know? I'm no shrink. I bet there are a lot of lunatics out there who look as normal as I do."

Jake rolled his eyes. "If I say no, do you think that will put an end to the rumors?"

"I doubt it."

"So what's the point?"

"To get it on the record."

"Okay, for the record, no. I've never been locked up in an insane asylum."

"What about Tommy Riemer?"

"Whether or not he's mentally ill? I think that the jury's still out on that one."

"I meant your supposed feud with Riemer. Weren't you two once buddies?"

"We were never friends, but for a short while we got along."

"What happened?"

"You'll have to ask him. He's the one who decided we were enemies."

"I did. He said the only time you played as juniors you quit then too."

"Did he tell you that I was ahead 6-1, 5-2, when he started yelling, screaming, throwing his racquet and accusing me of cheating on the line calls? I told him to shut up and play and he started cursing me out, then slammed a ball at me when I wasn't looking. I walked off the court and he got disqualified."

"That's not the way he tells it."

"Well, there were a couple of hundred people watching the match. Instead of listening to rumors, why don't you try to do some real journalism for a change and find one of them to see who's right?"

"What about the beating you took in Madison Square Garden?"

Before Jake could answer, a shout came from the other side of the room. "That's right. I kicked his ass in the Garden and I'm gonna do it again right here." It was Riemer, drunkenly lumbering across the restaurant, spewing curses and bumping into tables. "You're a liar and a coward and a mental patient," he screamed, his face turning redder and redder with every word.

Jake turned to Pirelli. "You set this up, didn't you?"

"No. I swear," his hand twitched as he pulled reflexively at his chin. "This is a restaurant. We can't control who goes in and out." Meanwhile, he was motioning behind his back to his cameraman to keep rolling

Riemer was now at the table. He leaned over and put his face nose-to-nose with Jake's. "What's the matter, faggot, you afraid to hear the truth?" he shouted.

"You wouldn't know the truth if it spit in your eye." Jake yelled back.

"How about if I spit in your eye?" Riemer screamed. Then he spit a beer-smelling glob of saliva into Jake's face.

Jake jumped from his seat and lunged at Riemer, clubbing him hard in the left ear with his bandaged right hand. Riemer lost his balance and fell into another table. Though a gifted athlete, he had no clue how to defend himself. He got into a lot of fights because of his obnoxious mouth and won a majority of them because he was stronger, quicker and in better shape than most of his victims. He had none of those advantages over Jake. And Jake was trained in several of the martial arts.

They were now both standing in the middle of the floor, facing each other. Jake was in his Krav Maga stance. Riemer stood with his fists balled in front of him like a bare-knuckle boxer for the 19th century. Most of the patrons of the Ball and Glove rose from their seats and backed away from the combatants

Pirelli stood next to them, waving his mike like a cheerleader's baton. "It looks like these two long-time enemies aren't going to wait to get on the court to settle their differences. Oh baby, this is gonna be something!"

"Why don't you just walk away, Tommy? Don't make me hurt you."

"Hurt me, you son of a bitch. I'm gonna fuckin' kill you right here."

Riemer lowered his head and charged at Jake like an enraged buffalo. He swung a long roundhouse right at Jake's head, which Jake ducked easily. Jake connected with a solid punch to Riemer's midsection with his left. He followed it with a clubbing right hand to the jaw as Riemer doubled over in pain from the first shot.

"Keep it rolling. Keep those cameras rolling," Pirelli shouted to the studio crew. Both cameramen were veterans of hundreds of sporting events and they immediately went from interview mode to game mode. One camera stayed on the action, while the other scanned the crowd for reaction shots. The young director in the production truck, parked right outside the restaurant, spit out his gum, sat bolt upright and started working the controls, shouting rapid-fire instructions to the cameramen.

Riemer fell to the ground. When he got up his mouth was gushing blood. He took a few wobbly steps towards Jake and launched a slow-motion overhand right. Jake grabbed Riemer's arm at the top of its arc. He snapped the arm down and around. With Riemer's back to him, Jake kicked him in the middle of the butt, and sent him flying towards the door.

Riemer steadied himself on the doorknob. He turned and shook both fists at Jake. "I'll kill you! I'll fuckin' kill you, you bastard!" he screamed through a bloody mouth. "You're a dead man, Marks. Do you hear me? Dead!" Then he staggered out of the restaurant.

Pirelli was panting with excitement. "Did you see that?" he shouted into the camera. Un-freaking-believable. Who said tennis was for sissies? These guys took a page right out of Mike Tyson's handbook. I'm surprised Riemer didn't take a bite out of Marks's ear. The winner of the first round of the heavyweight tennis season is Mr. Jake Marks by a TKO. But I have a feeling that Tommy Riemer still has some fight left in him. That's all for tonight from The Ball and Glove. This is Gary 'The Taz' Pirelli. And you've got SportsBreath."

Pirelli walked over and shook Jake's hand. "Thanks man, that was great television. Where'd you learn to fight like that?"

"The insane asylum," Jake said matter-of-factly.

Without another word he walked out of the restaurant.

37

———————

"What the hell happened?" Maggie said as she stood at the door of her brownstone as Jake walked in.

"I was ambushed."

"That's no excuse," she scolded. "The U.S. Open is less than two months away. You said you wanted to play in one or two tournaments before that. Your wrist is almost better. We were gonna start serious training in a few days. You probably set that back a couple of weeks."

"What did you want me to do, let him punch me in the mouth? That might have set us back even more."

"You could have walked away like most civilized men would have done instead of getting into a schoolyard brawl with that jerk." Her scowl broke into a wry smile. "The little prick did have it coming, though."

"For a second, I thought you were really pissed off at me."

"As your trainer, I was. As your girlfriend, I thought it was great. And sexy." She wrapped her arms around him and kissed him deeply and passionately.

They'd been back in New York less than two weeks. Jake explained everything to Maggie during the plane ride home.

From his recruitment by Goldbarr's operatives in Ecuador to his confrontation with Stryker on the London Eye. It was a lot to take in, especially after everything she'd been through in London. He kept waiting for her to have a reaction but she seemed okay. Maybe she was getting battle-tested.

She asked him if they should still be worried about Goldbarr. Jake told her that with Glynn and Stryker out of the picture, Goldbarr didn't have the manpower to keep going after them. He was almost starting to believe it himself.

At breakfast the next morning, Maggie said, "Since we're not training today, I thought we'd do something special."

Jake raised an eyebrow. "Oh?"

"I want to take you to the Botanical Gardens. It's my favorite place in the world. I've always gone there alone, but I want to share it with you."

The Brooklyn Botanic Garden was Maggie's fortress of solitude. It's where she came when she needed to relax, or think, or turn off her brain and lose herself in nature's beauty. It's where she came the day before she won her first New York City High School gymnastics championship. And after the accident that ended her Olympic dreams.

Over the years, Maggie had become friendly with many of the attendants. Sometimes they would let her in before the official ten o'clock opening so she could enjoy the garden all by herself. After all, what good is a fortress of solitude without the solitude?

They were at the main entrance at 9:15, hoping someone would let them in. The gate was open and unattended. Strange. She grabbed Jake's hand and walked in.

She loved every lush inch of the 52-acre floral paradise. The Fragrance Garden, with its extraordinary scents and textures. The Shakespeare Garden, which housed every tree, plant, flower, and shrub mentioned in the Bard's plays and poems. The Rose Garden, with more than 12,000 varieties.

Her favorite spot was the Japanese Hill and Pond Garden, an island of tranquility amid the sea of chaos that was the rest of the city and the rest of her life. The only sound they heard as they walked over the small teakwood bridge to the miniature Shinto shrine was the whoosh of the rushing water through the narrow stream below. A profusion of willows, dogwoods and cherry trees made a natural canopy overhead.

"Thanks for coming here with me today," Maggie said. "I wanted to share this place with you."

"I'm thrilled you did. It's absolutely breathtaking. Now I have a surprise for you. I've been carrying this around in my pocket since the day we got back, but I've been waiting for the right time and the right place. I think this is it."

Jake squatted down on one knee. Seconds later, he heard a muffled, metallic cough and saw splinters fly off the wood column above him.

"What was that?" Maggie cried.

"Somebody's shooting at us," Jake screamed. "Get down!"

Jake pulled her to the ground and dragged her behind an ancient Japanese maple just as a bullet hit the tree. Jake grabbed the small 32 caliber revolver that was holstered around his ankle and fired at the shooter, who was standing on the wooden bridge they crossed moments earlier.

"I'll never reach him with this but at least he won't come any closer."

Jake grabbed his phone and called Bunny, who was sitting in his taxi in the Botanical Gardens parking lot, reading a Dick Francis novel while he waited for them.

"Hello sir. Finished already?"

"Bunny, I need your help," Jake shouted into the phone. "Somebody's shooting at us."

"My God! Are you all right?"

"Yeah, but I don't know for how long. I need you to call 911. Tell them you heard gunshots in the Botanical Gardens."

"Immediately, sir. Where are you now?"

"We're in the Japanese Garden. The shooter's about 100 yards to our east on a small footbridge. I have a pistol and can hold him off for a little while."

"Don't worry. I'll do what's needed."

Bunny made the 911 call. Then he pulled open the tailgate of his cab and grabbed an impressive bow and a handful of arrows from the boot. The bow was almost as tall as he was and it was a thing of beauty, made of exotic hardwoods in rich browns and tans, inlaid in intricate patterns and polished to a high sheen. It had the classic shape of a longbow, the kind Robin Hood used, at least in the movies.

As he walked through the front gate past the Visitors Center, he heard muffled cries. He opened the door and saw three park attendants squirming on the floor. Their hands were bound behind their backs with zip ties. A strip of duct tape covered their mouths. They wiggled and writhed and tried to say something but only muffled squawks came out.

Bunny said, "I'm urgently needed elsewhere at the moment, but don't fear, help is on the way."

He continued up the path until he spotted the sniper, who was resting his rifle on the handrail. Bunny stood behind a thick oak tree. He was about forty yards from the gunman. The uneven footing and overhanging branches made the shot much more difficult than on the archery range. Taking three slow, deep breaths, he placed an arrow on the bow and sighted. He mouthed a quick prayer and let it fly. It sailed over the sniper's head, plunging into the branch of a sycamore tree ten feet behind him.

Startled by the whoosh of the arrow, the sniper looked around, searching for the source of the noise. It took him a few seconds to spot the arrow. That was enough time for Bunny to get off a second shot. This one was true. It hit the sniper in the back of the neck and emerged out his throat, along with a trickle of blood. He clutched at his throat and fell to the ground.

Jake and Maggie saw the sniper go down, but they didn't know why. Then they saw Bunny standing next to the fallen gunman. They ran over to him.

Maggie's eyes filled with tears. "You saved our lives." She kissed him on the forehead.

Jake gave his friend a quick pat on the back, knowing how uncomfortable he was with public displays of affection or even appreciation.

"That was terrific shooting."

Bunny shook his head. "Actually. it was a poor shot. I was aiming at his back. And I missed the first shot completely. Nerves."

"You still get a gold medal in my book," Jake said, grinning broadly.

Maggie collapsed on a nearby bench and buried her head in her hands. She was nauseated and hyperventilating. This latest brush with death finally broke the dam.

Two minutes later, a couple of New York City cops ran towards them, guns in hand. Just before they got there, Jake snatched the bow out of Bunny's hands.

"All right, what happened here?" said the first cop. Jake guessed he was around forty. He was short and a little rumpled, Columbo's nasty twin. His name tag said 'Sarica'. The other cop, Officer Serrano according to his tag, was tall and lanky and in his mid-twenties.

Jake said, "This guy tried to kill us."

"Who is he?"

Jake shook his head. "Never saw him before."

"Why would someone you don't know want to kill you?"

"I have no idea."

Sarica shook his head, a look of disgust on his face. "So your story is you're taking a nice romantic stroll through the

Gardens with your girlfriend. This guy, he gestured at Bunny, is riding shotgun. All of a sudden a complete stranger with a rifle is shooting at you. And just by coincidence, you just happen to be carrying a bow and arrow."

"Well, you know," Jake said sheepishly. "It worked for cupid."

"I guess you think homicide is a joke," the cop growled.

Before Jake could retort, Bunny said, "Excuse me, officer, but he's obviously lying in an attempt to shield me."

"Who the hell are you?"

"I'm Bunny Fields, Mr. Marks's driver. I was waiting for him and Ms. Quinlan in the parking lot. When I saw that man shooting at them, I intervened. That's my longbow. It has my initials laminated on the grip. I'm a member of the New York City Traditional Archery Association. I've won the club championship twice and placed second three other times. I keep the bow in my trunk."

"That's a lie," Jake shouted. "It was me."

Sarica snorted and wiped his forehead in exasperation.

A slender African American woman and an even thinner Asian male walked over to them.

"I'm Detective Walsh," the female said, "What happened here?"

"One deceased." Sarica pointed at the body with the arrow still in its neck. "Both these jokers claim to have shot him."

"All right." She turned to her partner. "Gary, take these two down to the precinct. I'll meet you there as soon as I talk to her."

She walked over to the bench where Maggie was still sitting as the other detective and the two police officers escorted Jake and Bunny to the exit.

38

———

It was evening by the time Jake and Bunny walked out of the 78th Precinct. A horde of reporters from the crime beat and the sports pages shouted questions at them. When a famous athlete is involved in a suspicious death it's big news. Even in blasé New York.

Bunny tried to hide behind Jake, who was used to dealing with media scrums. Jake put his arm around Bunny and regaled the cream of New York journalism with his friend's heroics, turning the diminutive driver into a combination of Sir Galahad, Robin Hood and James Bond. After awhile Bunny overcame his shyness and answered all their questions.

When they got back to Bunny's taxi, the sun was setting. Jake opened the back door and held it.

"Get in the back, tonight I'm driving."

"I don't understand."

"You saved our lives. You're a hero. And tonight you're going to be treated like a hero." He had already texted Maggie about his plan and invited her to join them. She texted back saying that she would pass. She could do with a quiet evening.

"I feel extraordinarily uncomfortable with this," Bunny said nervously from the back seat. "Are you sure you wouldn't like me to drive? I really wouldn't mind."

"Not tonight."

Jake drove leisurely up Flatbush Avenue and over the Manhattan Bridge to the Lower East Side. "We're almost there."

"Pardon me, sir." Bunny looked nervously at the tenements, flop houses and seedy hotels along Chyristie Street. "Are you sure you know where you are going? I'm beginning to get a bit concerned about our surroundings."

Jake turned and winked. "That's no way for New York's latest hero to talk."

Suddenly they came upon dozens of gleaming luxury cars. Jaguars, Benzes, Town Cars and limos double- and triple-parked outside what looked like a dive of a restaurant. The sign above the front entrance said "Benny's Litvakian Steak Palace."

Jake drove past it, turned down a side street and parked Bunny's taxi in front of a stoop where two Latino kids were playing dominoes and drinking Bud Lights from long-neck bottles. One was no more than fifteen, the other a couple of years older. They both wore blue hoodies with a smiling devil in profile. Jake was surprised that these two ghetto kids would be Duke Blue Devils fans.

As he walked towards them, they stiffened. Jake took a fifty-dollar bill from his pocket and handed it to the older one. "Could you guys do me a favor and keep an eye on my car for a couple of hours? If you're still here and the car's in one piece when I come back, there will be another fifty for you."

"What kinda car is that? Never saw one like it. The steering wheel's on the wrong side," the older one said.

"It's a London taxi."

The kid looked at the bill in his hand, looked at the black cab, grinned and said, "You wanna give me the keys in case I gotta move it?"

Jake smiled. "I don't think that'll be necessary, but thanks for the offer."

Two minutes later, Jake and Bunny walked down three steps into a boisterous maelstrom. Through the din they could hear a piano playing something that sounded like it should have been from Fiddler on the Roof, except the words, some in English, some in Yiddish and some in a language Jake couldn't recognize, were about a woman with gigantic breasts who suffocated her diminutive husband between them. They were met by a tall, skinny guy in his early forties. He wore a shiny black suit with a white shirt open almost to the navel. His thinning hair was slicked back and his neck was covered with gold chains.

"Jake, Jake Marks, my favorite tennis knocker (he pronounced it 'kuh-nocker'). Come in, come in," he beamed. We haven't seen you since...well since your grandfather passed away. How have you been?" He thrust a sweaty hand out at Jake.

Jake grabbed it with both of his. "Pretty good, Lenny. How about you?"

"Can't complain, it's a little quieter than usual, but it's the summer, everyone's outta town."

Bunny's face was a picture of surprise and incredulity. This was the noisiest place he had ever set foot in.

"So what brings you to our little corner of paradise?"

"My friend Bunny did something really awesome today and I'm taking him here to celebrate."

Lenny squinted down at Bunny through his Buddy Holly glasses. "Hey, you look familiar. Didn't I just see your picture in the paper?" He ran his hand through what was left of his thinning hair. "I got it. You're that bow and arrow guy. The one that saved those people in Brooklyn."

"Yes, that was me," Bunny said, sheepishly.

"And it was me who he saved," Jake said.

Lenny turned around and shouted into the restaurant. "Hey

everybody, we got a genuine (he pronounced it 'jen-you-wine') hero here. The bow and arrow guy from the news."

Everyone in the restaurant broke into a sustained applause while the pianist played 'The Theme from Rocky' as Jake and Bunny walked in.

"Your money's no good in here tonight, neither one of youse," Lenny said as he escorted Jake and Bunny to a table.

Bunny, who hated being the center of attention, slunk into his chair. His usually pale cheeks were crimson with embarrassment. Soon a series of waiters brought plate after plate of exotic appetizers, each one screaming "Food for the hero!" as they banged dishes on the table in front of Bunny with a flourish. Roasted pickled peppers, chopped liver, kishka, chicken fricassee, kasha varnishkes, potato latkes. It was like a dozen Jewish bubbehs were cooking in the kitchen.

"Better leave room for the steak, Bunny. That was just the first course," Jake said, through a mouthful of stuffed cabbage.

"First course?" Bunny yelped. "We've had six or seven courses already."

Lenny, himself, brought the steak. The marinated tenderloin slabs were served on huge plates, yet still dangled over both sides. Welts of garlic dotted the glistening meat.

"This is more food than I usually eat in a week," Bunny said as he chewed.

"You need an egg cream to wash it down," Jake said.

"Egg cream? Is it some kind of breakfast food?"

"It's a famous New York libation, the poor man's cappuccino. Would you like to try one?"

"Why not? I've tried everything else," he said, stifling a burp.

At Jake's signal, the waiters brought a couple of clean soda fountain glasses, two long-handled teaspoons, a seltzer syphon, a quart of milk and a bottle of Fox's U-bet chocolate syrup.

Jake poured an inch of chocolate into the bottom of each

glass. Then a quarter-inch of milk. He lowered a spoon into the glass and shot the seltzer into it to diffuse some of the carbonation. Then he stirred briskly from the bottom until the liquid turned the color of creamed coffee and a foamy head formed at the top. "My grandfather taught me how to make egg creams when I was about ten years old. What do you think?"

Bunny gingerly picked up his glass and had a taste. "Quite delicious," he proclaimed. "But when do you add the egg and the cream?"

"There are no eggs or cream in an egg cream."

"Then why is it called that?"

"That's one of the mysteries of New York," Jake said, grinning.

Bunny laughed and took a big gulp. "Suddenly it makes perfect sense to me," he said, a dollop of foam sitting on his nose.

After more than three hours of eating, drinking, joking, singing and talking, Jake and Bunny ambled back to the car. The two Latino boys were still on the stoop, though now they were playing cards instead of dominos. A dozen empty long-necks were lined up in three rows behind them like bowling pins. Bunny's London taxi looked none the worse for wear, so Jake walked toward them with the other fifty dollars.

He was halfway there when two large men jumped out of a car that was parked down the block. One was about six-four, the other a little shorter. Both were thick, not fat. They wore leather vests, black wool caps and motorcycle boots. The taller one had some kind of pipe in his hand.

"Bunny, run. Go back to Benny's and call the police," Jake yelled.

"Absolutely not!" Bunny cried. "I won't desert you, sir. New York has proclaimed me a hero and a hero I shall be."

Before Jake could stop him, the plucky little Brit ran directly at the one with the pipe and launched himself knees-first into his chest. He wrapped his legs around the thug's waist and pummeled his head with his fists. The stunned thug groaned at the impact, doubled over and lurched back a few steps. He regained his composure, steadied himself and smashed Bunny's ribs several times with the pipe and threw him down on the sidewalk, leaving him semi-conscious and groaning in agony.

Both men turned their attention to Jake, whose only escape route was blocked by a dozen garbage cans set out for the next morning's pickup.

Jake faced his attackers, who were stalking him methodically from either side. He took a few quick steps towards the one who just finished with Bunny, figuring he'd be more winded. The thug swung the pipe at Jake's head. Jake ducked and deflected the blow with his left forearm. Then he hit him in the gut with a side kick followed with a quick strike to the throat and a blast to the temple, knocking him out cold.

Before Jake could turn around, the other goon jumped him from behind. He lifted Jake off the ground and squeezed him in a bear hug. The man's grip was a vise. Jake's arms were pinned to his sides. He struggled to break free, but his strength had ebbed from his fight with the first guy. His chest tightened and his head throbbed. He was on the verge of blacking out when he heard a dull clunk behind him and felt the grip loosen. A second thud and he was free. His eyes regained focus enough to see blood pouring down the thug's face as he fell to the ground. The older kid stood over them with a beer bottle in each hand. His friend was a few steps behind him.

"Uh, thanks," Jake said, still groggy. "Thanks a lot."

"If it's worth a hundred bucks to watch your car," he said, smiling, "how much to save your ass?"

Jake pulled out his wallet. He counted out ten hundred dollar bills and handed them to his rescuer. "Will this do?"

"Yeah, that's good. By the way, bro, that was nice work the

way you took out that first guy. What's that, some kind of kung fu or something?"

"Krav Maga," Jake said, still gulping air. "Israeli martial arts."

"I might check that out."

"You did a pretty good job with a couple of bottles of Bud."

Jake reached out his hand. The kid made a fist and bumped it lightly.

"This wasn't your fight. Why'd you help me out?"

"This is Diablo territory, man," the kid said, pointing to the devil emblazoned on his jacket. "Nobody takes anybody out down here except us. You know, bad for our cred. Right, Hector?" He turned and winked at his friend.

The first attacker started stirring.

"Could I borrow one of those bottles?" Jake asked the elder Diablo.

"Sure." He handed him a bottle.

Jake grasped the bottle by the neck and pounded it on the sidewalk producing a ring of razor sharp shards. He grabbed a handful of the still-groggy thug's hair, bending his neck back. He pressed a point just under the thug's Adam's apple.

"You tell Goldbarr I'm coming for him."

The thug sneered. "Goldbarr? Who the hell is Goldbarr?"

"Don't fuck with me, asshole, you know who Goldbarr is." He pushed the tip in a little farther.

"You mean that guy on TV?" he said with a stammer. All his bravado had dissipated.

"Yeah."

"I don't know him."

"Stop lying." Jake sliced a line very lightly across his throat. Just enough to draw a little blood."

"I ain't lying, I swear on my mother. Don't cut me no more." His face was bleached white.

"If it wasn't Goldbarr, who sent you?"

"I didn't talk to the contact. I don't know no names. It was some tennis player," he cried, somewhere between a shriek and a croak. "That's all I know."

Jake smashed the guy's head into the sidewalk, knocking him out again.

"Hey, that's pretty severe for an old white dude," the Diablo said.

"Can I ask you to do me one more favor?" Jake said, inwardly grimacing at the 'old white dude' remark.

"Like what?"

"Help me carry my friend back to the car?"

"No sweat, man." He grinned. "For another grand I'll carry him home for you."

They carried Bunny to the cab and gently laid him down on the back seat.

As Jake got into the car, the kid said, "Whenever you're in the neighborhood, I'm your boy. Just ask for Spider."

39

Jake texted Maggie that he was on the way to the E.R. with Bunny.

What hospital?

Mount Sinai in Brooklyn Heights.

What happened?

We were attacked.

I'll meet you there.

Fifteen minutes later she stormed into the E.R. looking frantic and frazzled. She ran to Jake, who was sitting in a far corner of the crowded waiting room.

"Are you okay? Where's Bunny?"

"Whoa! One thing at a time."

"All right," Maggie said, calming down. "The last time I spoke to you, you said you were taking Bunny to your grandfather's favorite restaurant to celebrate. Somewhere down on the Lower East Side, I think. How'd you wind up in the E.R.? Did you get mugged?"

"Actually, we got ambushed."

"Ambushed?"

Jake gave her a blow-by-blow of the evening's events, from

Bunny's being regaled as a hero by everyone at Benny's to their being jumped by the two thugs and finally, how Spider saved the day.

"My God! Are you okay?"

"I'm fine."

She looked Jake up and down and shook her head.

"You sure don't look fine. Your face is all red and swollen. Your shirt's torn." She pointed to a red stain on his sleeve. "And that looks like blood."

"It's not mine. Trust me, I'm okay."

She shook her head skeptically. "If you say so. What about Bunny?"

"They took him to x-ray his ribs. They said they might want to check his lungs and heart too."

"Don't tell me he had a heart attack."

"No, nothing like that. The doctor said a broken rib could puncture a lung or nick an artery."

"Oh." She looked around the room. "By the way. How'd you get him treated so fast? I had to come here a couple of times and never waited less than an hour-and-a-half."

"It turns out the triage nurse is a big tennis fan. As soon as he saw me in the waiting room, he ran right over. Usually I decline preferential treatment, but not this time. Bunny was in pretty bad shape. I was happy they took him right away."

"Why is this happening?" Maggie said, anxiously. "You said with Glynn and Stryker both gone, we didn't have to worry about Goldbarr anymore. Then yesterday we were almost killed. And today you and Bunny get jumped. Looks like Goldbarr is still a huge worry."

"I'm pretty sure the guys who jumped us tonight weren't Goldbarr's men. One of them said they were hired by a tennis player."

"How do you know he wasn't lying?"

"That blood on my shirt, that's his blood. When I asked him

who hired him, I had the sharp edge of a broken bottle pressed against his throat. My guess is Riemer hired them after what happened at the Ball and Glove."

"Great. Now there's two different gangs of killers after us."

"Not us, me. Everyone close to me winds up hurt or killed. Alex, Danny and now Bunny. And you had two close calls, one in London and yesterday. That's it. It ends here."

"What are you gonna do?"

"I'm leaving."

"You're leaving me?"

"No way. I love you. I'm just leaving town."

"Where are you going?"

"I called the director of the Montreal Open. It starts in a week. I talked him into giving me a wild card slot in doubles. I'll be teamed up with Eugene Petkovic. He's my one friend on the tour. Once I'm gone you'll be safe."

"You can't be sure of that."

"There's no reason for Goldbarr or Riemer to target you."

"You're really convinced?"

"One hundred percent."

"Then I'm going with you."

"Absolutely not. The whole idea of my leaving is to keep you out of danger. The two times you were almost killed, I was the target, and you were with me and I couldn't protect you. If it wasn't for Kelleher, neither one of us would be here. Speaking of Kelleher, have you heard from him?"

"Actually, I just did."

Jake looked slightly taken aback. "Really? When?"

"Last night, while you were out with Bunny. He read about what happened at the Botanical Gardens and called to see if I was okay."

"Did you tell him we're still together?"

"It came up."

"I bet that pissed him off."

"Why?"

"'Cause I'm sure he hates my guts."

"He doesn't hate you."

"Of course he does and rightfully so. I really screwed up in London. He warned me about Deke and I didn't listen. That almost got you killed. And part of me thinks he still blames me for your mother's death."

She shook her head. "He knows you didn't do it."

"Really? He told you that?"

"He has friends high up in the NYPD. They let him see a copy of the real ballistics report. My mother was shot with a sniper bullet. It couldn't have come from your gun. That convinced him you were telling the truth. He also said that we should't worry about Goldbarr. That he would take care of it. Now can I come with you?"

"Kelleher's one of the best. If anyone can neutralize Goldbarr, he can. But until I know for sure, I don't want you anywhere near me. And Riemer's crazy. He still might try something."

"Do you really think he would try again, now that he knows you're onto him?"

"How would he know?"

"You said one of the guys who attacked you ratted him out. I'm sure he told Riemer that you know."

"Maybe. I'll tell you what, if nothing happens in Montreal and Kelleher can handle Goldbarr, we'll meet in Cincinnati. There's a tournament there the week after Montreal."

"Okay." She smiled and kissed him.

"Why don't you go home. I'm gonna wait for Bunny."

A half-hour later, a young doctor walked into the waiting room. He was tall, slender and Asian."

"Are you Mr. Marks?"

"Yes."

"I'm Dr. Lin."

"How's Bunny?"

"He's a lucky man. If you didn't bring him in he could have died."

"From broken ribs?"

He shook his head. "His rib injury was serious but not life threatening."

"I don't understand."

"We did some preliminary imaging. That's what saved him. Your friend had a two centimeter aortic aneurism. Anything more than one-and-a-half is a rupture waiting to happen."

"Sounds bad."

"It is. That's why we're doing emergency surgery."

"When?"

"Now."

"My God. You guys don't waste time."

"There was no time to waste. It could have ruptured tomorrow. And the survival rate once that happens is minimal."

"But now he'll be okay?"

"He should be. Those muggers probably saved his life. But between his ribs and the surgery, it'll be at least six weeks until he's on his feet. Probably more."

40

Jake was a little rusty when he stepped on the court in Montreal for his first match. Maybe a lot more than a little. Hitting with a couple of fairly competent teaching pros is one thing. Facing top players with 130 mph serves, jackhammer groundstrokes and lightning volleys is a stratospheric leap.

When he took the court for his first match with his friend, Eugene Petkovic, he was met with tepid cheers from the sparse morning crowd. He was grateful for the early start time on a far court, as he struggled to find some semblance of his old form. His footwork was leaden and his reaction time was slow. He sprayed his groundstrokes ten feet off the court on numerous occasions and clanked the ball off the frame several times. They lost the first set 6-4, but it wouldn't have been that close if Eugene hadn't played out of his mind.

Jake's game started coming back to him around the middle of the second set. Out-of-control forehands were now finding the lines. He began to hit his one-hand backhand, which a commentator had once called 'a thing of beauty and grace,' with more precision and velocity. His loose volleys were suddenly crisp and decisive. He even cracked a couple of aces.

They won the second set 7-5 and managed to eek out a victory by winning the third in a tiebreaker.

Jake ached all over. He trudged to his chair and sat with a towel draped over his shoulders. Eugene was his usual buoyant self, greeting the few fans in the stands and signing autographs.

He bounced back over to Jake. "Great match."

"Yeah, for you. I sucked. You dragged my ass over the finish line."

"Not true. In the first set you needed to get your sea feet."

Jake chuckled. "You mean sea legs."

"Yes. But you were better in the next sets. Soon you will be back to old Jake."

"Right now I'm feeling like very old Jake."

Jake spent the next couple of hours getting treatment from one of the tournament trainers. Then he vegged out in his room at the Fairmont Hotel in downtown Montreal, where most of the pros stayed. He called Maggie, then met Eugene for dinner at the hotel restaurant. They were about to order when Eugene's newly minted agent, Gregg Little, sat down with them.

Most of the players on tour traveled with a big entourage. Their teams could include any number of supporters, helpers and hangers-on, including, but not limited to, coaches, trainers, therapists, nutritionists, sports psychologists, agents, managers, wives, girlfriends, best friends, siblings, parents and children.

Jake was one of the few players to go it alone. Eugene also travelled light. He had just parted ways with his coach, and his wife was at home back in Croatia with his daughters, so his agent was his only traveling companion. Young and eager, the short, skinny Little had been a college intern with Apex Sports Management during his senior year at Syracuse and was offered a job with them when he graduated. Eugene was his first client, and they told him that if he did well with him, they'd give him some real stars to work with. Selling Eugene to sponsors proved to be harder than Little anticipated. An ankle injury that took longer than expected to heal plunged his ranking from a high of seventeen to the mid-forties. His English was good, but his Eastern European accent was thick, which only worked as a pitchman if you were Arnold Schwarzenegger. And his short, stocky physique and long stringy brown hair were not what tenniswear companies looked for in a mannequin for their overpriced merchandise.

Jake, on the other hand, was a sponsor's dream. Tall and lean with a thick shock of blonde curls, he was a GQ spread waiting to happen. And though his lack of play moved him down in the rankings, he was recently a top-five player and could easily get back there again. The problem was that Jake steadfastly refused any and all sponsorship offers.

"I'm so glad I found you guys," Little gushed. "Eugene, I finally got you the deal we've been waiting for. Half-a-million dollars for a one-year commitment. It's from a new company, Sustennis. They make tennis clothes that are 100% organic and totally sustainable."

Eugene's face lit up. "This is some very great news!"

He had confided to Jake that he desperately missed his wife and two-year-old twin girls and was thinking seriously of leaving the tour. His dream was to open a tennis academy in his hometown of Pula, on the Adriatic Sea. This money would go a long way to making that dream a reality.

"There's one small issue that we have to iron out first."

Eugene's smile melted into a scowl. "Oh yeah? What?"

"They want you and Jake together. They won't do it without both of you. Some knucklehead in their marketing department came up with a gimmick, the 'Sustennis Twins.' You guys'll wear the same clothes and use the same bags. Their stuff of course. You'll do a photo shoot or two, then you pocket 500K." He grinned at Eugene. "Pretty sweet, huh?"

The Croat was crestfallen. He knew Jake had an aversion to sponsorships. They spoke about it once and Jake told him he didn't think it was right to coerce fans into buying stuff that they didn't need at prices they couldn't afford. Jake never mentioned that his side gig as a global assassin might make any sponsorship appearances and commercial shoots tough to fulfill. Eugene was about to ask Little to see if he could arrange a deal without Jake, even if it were for less money.

Suddenly Jake said, "Sounds like fun. I'm in."

Eugene almost did a spit-take with his Coke. He looked incredulously at his friend.

"Really? No joke?"

Jake put his arm around Eugene. "I'm all for saving the planet and I need some new duds, anyway. The stuff I'm wearing is five years old. It's getting pretty raggedy."

Little stood, grinning from ear to ear, probably thinking about his first big commission.

"That's great. I got some work to do to get the ball rolling. Why don't you guys meet me in my room tomorrow morning, around eleven. The owner of the company will be there. If all goes well, and there's no reason why it shouldn't, we can finalize the deal and sign the contracts right there." He looked at Jake. "I hope you like green. That's a big color for them, being earth friendly and all."

Jake said, "Green's fine."

Eugene grinned. "It's a good color."

Little patted his client on the shoulder. "It's the color of money."

After Little was gone, Eugene hugged Jake. "Thank you, my friend."

"Are you kidding? I should be thanking you. First you carry me in today's match and now you just made me a big chunk of money."

"But you never do sponsorships."

"People can change. This seems like a good product. And I get to do it with my buddy."

"We must have a toast," Eugene said, joyfully. "I know we're still playing in the tournament, but one small glass won't hurt."

Eugene ordered a bottle of Dom Pérignon and insisted on paying.

He raised his glass. "To us!"

Jake tapped Eugene's glass with his and drank the two fingers of bubbly.

There was a young couple a few tables away and Eugene told the waiter to give the almost-full bottle to them.

Jake said, "You're pissing your money away before you even get it."

"Oh no," Eugene said with a grin. "After this, all my pennies are pinched."

Jake woke the next morning still stiff and achy. After a quick breakfast of fruit, yogurt and orange juice, he spent a couple of hours in the hotel spa. Then he called Maggie. By the time he was done it was a little after eleven. He hustled to Little's hotel room for the meeting. The door was half open so he walked in and closed the door behind him.

"Sorry I'm late."

"No worries." Little ushered him inside.

Eugene was already there, pacing anxiously back and forth. As soon as he saw Jake, he relaxed.

The bed looked like the bargain table at Macy's. Shorts, sweatpants, polo shirts and t-shirts were scattered from one end to the other. The shirts, in vibrant neon green, featured a wavy blue horizontal line across the chest. Instead of the Lacoste alligator or the Ralph Lauren polo player, the logo was a light green tennis ball with a darker green leaf at the top. The matching pants and shorts were the same color as the shirt, with the blue squiggle going up the leg. The huge tennis duffle bags repeated the design. The blue squiggle underlined the word 'Sustennis' over the front of the bag.

Little said, "Jake Marks, I'd like you to meet Natasha Ferris, the president and CEO of Sustennis."

Six feet tall with long blonde hair and ice blue eyes, she was a highly ranked tennis player at Stanford a decade earlier and still looked to be in playing shape. Jake was pretty sure he had seen her before, but he couldn't remember where or when.

Jake thrust out his hand. "It's a pleasure to meet you, Ms. Ferris."

"Please call me Natasha," she said, shaking it. "I've been a fan of yours for a long time." She gestured toward the bed. "We've been making clothes for women for a few years. We're now branching out into men's gear and we think you two will be our ideal brand ambassadors. What do you think of our planet-friendly designs? The solid green represents the earth and the blue wave is the ocean."

Before Jake could open his mouth, Eugene blurted, "They're super. We love them."

"I'm so happy you like them." She looked soulfully at Jake. "And I'm thrilled you agreed to represent us. I know how particular you are with endorsements."

Jake put his arm around Eugene. "We're both big supporters of conservation and protecting the earth's natural resources. We're proud to represent a company whose values are the same as ours."

"Wow," she said. "I think you just wrote our first ad."

After they signed the contracts and picked out their outfits for the next day's match, Little invited everyone out for a celebratory lunch.

Jake declined, saying he was tired. Eugene had a Zoom call scheduled with his family back in Croatia. And Natasha Ferris also gave her regrets. She needed to get in touch with her marketing team to jump-start the new campaign.

The next morning, resplendent in their colorful new tennis togs, Jake and Eugene won in straight sets. Jake's game, which had been blurry the first match, came into focus. His serve was crisp and accurate, his groundstrokes deep and penetrating and his volleys precise.

As they packed their racquets into their new matching Sustennis bags, Eugene said, "Now you are the Jake I know. I think maybe these new clothes bring you back to life."

"Whatever it is, we're gonna need it. Tomorrow we play the top seeds."

"Nobody thought we would get this far. We're playing with what is it, home money."

Jake chuckled. "It's house money, but you're right. Let's just go have fun tomorrow."

Jake turned to see Natasha Ferris running towards them.

"You guys were fantastic," she gushed. "And you both look so handsome in your Sustennis gear."

She was wearing a green and yellow tennis outfit.

Jake said, "You look pretty nice yourself."

"That's one of the perks. I get to sample the newest fashions before they hit the shelves."

Eugene said, "Yes, you should be a model."

"Why, thank you." She smiled. "I can see it's going to be a pleasure working with you two charming gentlemen. Not every player on the tour has your manners." She pulled out her iPhone and snapped a few pictures.

"Is that for the ads?" Eugene said.

She smiled. "Oh no. We have professional photographers for that. I write a little column for our social media sites. My next one is about you two." She checked the time on her phone. "Oops, I have to run. There's a factory in Mexico City that we're considering working with. I'm due at the airport in an hour. Sorry I won't be here for your next match."

She gave Eugene's hand a quick shake but took Jake's hand in both of hers and held it tenderly for several beats longer than usual.

"Good luck tomorrow," she said, as she turned and walked away.

Eugene winked at Jake. "I think she likes you."

"I know her type. The only thing she likes is the money she thinks we can make for her."

"I don't know. I've never seen a woman look at money the way she looked at you."

"Even if that's true it doesn't matter."

"Why? You don't want to mix business with pleasure?"

"No. It's because for the first time in my life I'm in a serious relationship. I don't want to jeopardize that."

Astonishment swept over Eugene's face. "You? I don't believe it. I had you for a whole-life bachelor. Who is she?"

"Maggie Quinlan. I met her a couple of months ago. She was a world class gymnast. She probably would have won an Olympic medal but she ripped up her knee right before the trials. Tore her ACL and MCL."

Eugene made a face. "Ouch."

"Ouch is right. But she didn't let it stop her. She went on to become a super successful high school coach. Won the New York City championship."

"I didn't know you were a gymnastics fan."

"I'm not. I hired her to be my flexibility coach. Then I fell in love with her."

He gave Jake a huge hug.

"That's wonderful. Congratulations, my friend. And you get your coach for free. That's a win-win."

"We better get some rest. We play tomorrow at noon in the Grandstand. No more hiding in the boondocks."

Eugene looked puzzled. "Boondocks? What is boondocks?"

Jake smiled. "It's a place in the middle of nowhere. Like those out-of-the-way courts that we've been on for the last two matches."

"Yes. We're big time now. Big matches. Big sponsor. No more boondocks. I love it!"

"Okay, my friend. I'll see you tomorrow."

When they walked onto Centre Court the next day, they were greeted by boisterous if not thunderous applause. The stands were three-quarters full, which for a quarter-final doubles match was a huge crowd.

Seated on the other side were Jari Danilovic and Karl Kull, the number one seed and the number two ranked doubles team in the world. Kull, a big, stocky Dane, had a hard serve and vicious forehand. Danilovic, from Serbia, had a fluid, all-court game. Eugene glowered at the Serb.

"What's up?" Jake said. "We said we were going to play this one for fun. You look like Mike Tyson before a fight."

"I hate that bastard. He thinks he's hot shit. I know him since juniors. He was an asshole then. A bigger one now."

Jake clapped him on the shoulder. "Don't let him get inside your head. He's a doubles specialist. You've been a world top 20 singles player. And you just landed a big sponsorship. Who's hot shit now?"

"You're right. Let's go."

But Danilovic did get into Eugene's head. When he was at net Eugene hit every ball as hard as he could right at him. The Serbian doubles wiz was able to volley most of Eugene's bombs deftly into the open court for clean winners. Eugene and Jake lost the first set 6-2 and were down a break in the second.

On the changeover Jake said to his partner, "I have an idea. We're probably gonna lose this match anyway, so let's mess them up. We'll make the points as long as possible and tire them out so they lose in the semis."

Eugene smiled. "Yes. Great idea. We win even if we lose."

They began hitting lobs and safe, deep shots to the base-line. As the points lengthened, Danilovic and Kull started pressing, trying for second-serve aces, aiming for the lines on every shot. They hit several showstopping winners but wound up with a boatload of unforced errors. Eugene and Jake broke back in the seventh game. The set went to a seven-point tiebreak. Neither team could break the other's serve. They were tied at seven, then again at eight. Danilovic and Kull finally won two points in a row and won the tiebreak and the match.

The stadium, which had been pretty quiet during most of the match (Canadian fans tend to be more polite than their American counterparts) erupted in thunderous applause.

As they walked, exhausted, to their seats, Danilovic said something to Eugene in Serbian. Eugene bristled and screamed at Danilovic in his native Croatian. They started toward each other, fists clenched. Jake grabbed Eugene and led him back to their seats with Eugene shouting at Danilovic, who walked calmly to his chair, a wry smile on his face.

After his friend calmed down a little, Jake asked, "What did he say?"

"In his Serbian gutter language he said that I look like a faggot in these clothes and I played like a faggot."

"And you said..."

"I called him a motherfucker in Croatian, and told him I'm man enough to kick his ass."

"If Serbian and Croatian are two different languages, how did you guys understand what the other one was saying?"

"Is like American English and British English. The same language but different."

Jake smiled. "How about this? We'll kick his ass on the court in Cincinnati. That'll hurt him a lot more than beating him up and getting a big fine and possibly suspended. And as far as clothes, he's jealous that you got a big endorsement deal and he's still buying his stuff off the rack. And now, since we're not playing anymore this week, let's go have a couple of drinks."

After more than a couple of Molsons, Jake went to his room and called Maggie.

"You played great!" she said.

"You saw the match?"

"I signed up for Tennis Channel. They didn't show your first couple of matches, but your last one made it. Sorry you lost."

"Are you kidding? We made it to the quarter-finals and lost to the top seed in a tiebreaker. I thought we'd be one and done. I played like crap in the first match, but Eugene was terrific. He basically won it single-handedly."

"You looked pretty good when I saw you."

"Thanks. My game's starting to come around."

"By the way, what the hell were you guys wearing out there?"

Jake told her about the sponsorship deal and how much it means for Eugene.

She said, "You're a good friend. Speaking of friends. I went to see Bunny yesterday. Looks like he's gonna be okay, but between the ribs and the aneurism, he has to go through a lot of rehab. He apologized for not being able to go to your matches at the Open."

"Next time you see him, tell him I'm dedicating the Open to him."

"I will." Then she lowered her voice. "Seen any of Goldbarr's men around?"

"No. How about with you? Any issues?"

"None. Do you think it's okay?"

"I'm not sure. I hope so."

"Do you still want me to come to Cincinnati?"

"Oh yes. I really miss you."

"I miss you too. I can't wait to see you."

"Eugene and I are leaving for Cincinnati tomorrow. We'll be at the Marriott Northeast."

"I'm having dinner with Kelleher on Saturday. I'll see you on Sunday."

41

———

Jake had just finished unpacking when there was a knock at his hotel room door. Who the hell could it be? It was after ten on a Thursday night. Maggie wasn't supposed to be in Cincinnati until Sunday. Eugene told him he was going to be FaceTiming with his wife and kids back in Croatia. Natasha Ferris should still be in Mexico. He couldn't think of anyone else who would be visiting him at this hour. All he could think of was it was one of Goldbarr's men coming to finish what they started in New York.

Jake didn't have a weapon. No gun, not even a knife. He crouched into a Krav Maga fighting stance. Chin down, hands up and flexed, knees bent with feet apart, the left slightly in front. Then he threw open the door ready to spring with feet and hands flying at whoever was on the other side.

A tall, lean guy with thinning blonde hair jumped back.

"Whoa, easy there pal."

He was wearing a blue polo shirt with the FILA logo on the left side and the Cincinnati Open logo on the right. It was Edgar Schultz, a recently retired veteran of the tour who had just been named as the Cincinnati Open tournament director.

He threw up his arms in a sign of mock surrender. "I come in peace."

"Hey Edgar, sorry about that," Jake said sheepishly. "The dust-up that Eugene had with Danilovic made it onto YouTube. He's gotten some nasty threats. I even got one or two. I thought maybe one of those crazy Serbs wanted to do more than intimidate us."

"No worries. I've already doubled our security staff and there are cameras on every floor. I had them put extra cameras facing Eugene's room and yours. No one is getting close to here who doesn't belong."

"That's good to know. I'll sleep easier. So what's up? Don't tell me you personally welcome all the players."

He smiled. "No, just the ones who kicked my ass on the tour. All kidding aside, I wonder if you could do me a huge favor. Two of our top players have dropped out, our second and fifth seeds. We need a star like you in the main draw to drum up some excitement, create some buzz."

"I don't know if I'm a star. I sure don't feel like one. But anyway, I'm already in the doubles draw."

"Nobody gives a shit about doubles. I need you in singles. Can you do it?"

"I don't know. I'm a little rusty."

"Rusty my ass. I saw you last week in Montreal. You looked pretty damn good to me."

"If you were watching closely, you know that Eugene carried me."

"That's not what I saw." He paused for a second. "I'll tell you what. I'll give you a bye in the first round and you'll face a qualifier in the second. It'll give you time to get rid of the rust. And you'll be in the quarter-finals without breaking a sweat. After that, whatever you do is a bonus. Whaddaya say, it would really help me out."

After a couple of seconds, Jake said, "Yeah, why not. I'm

planning on playing singles at the Open, might as well take my lumps here."

"Terrific. I owe you." He held up his hand for a high-five.

"Let's just hope I don't embarrass both of us," Jake said as they slapped palms.

He was out early the next morning on a practice court, hitting with Eugene, both decked out in their colorful new Sustennis tennis clothes when Kull and Danilovic walked past them to practice on a nearby court. The Serb yelled something at Eugene. Jake had no idea what was said, but it compelled Eugene to throw down his racquet and start shouting curses as he stomped menacingly toward Danilovic. The two were soon bellowing indiscernible epithets at each other. Then they started pushing and shoving. Jake and Karl Kull, Danilovic's doubles partner, pulled the combatants apart.

"That's enough practice for today," Jake said as he walked away with his friend. "C'mon, I'll buy you a cup of coffee."

As they walked away, Eugene was contrite. "I'm so sorry. I know I shouldn't let that Serbian cocksucker get to me. I lost some friends in the conflict. His old man was some kind of officer in the Serbian army and every time I see him my blood steams."

"The best thing we can do is to beat the hell out of him and his partner next time we battle them on the court. That'll hurt more than a few punches."

"He's not on our side of the draw."

"Then we'll have to make it to the finals and do it there."

Eugene's face lit up. "Okay. I like it."

Their first doubles match was scheduled for ten the next morning. When they arrived at the courts at eight they were besieged by a horde of reporters, shouting questions at Eugene about his confrontation with Danilovic. A tall, husky middle-aged woman dressed in a business suit hustled out of the players entrance and ushered them into the facility.

Once safely inside, Jake said, "Thanks for rescuing us."

"No problem. That's my job." She thrust out her hand. "Leslie Sherman, I'm head of security."

"What the hell was that all about?" Eugene said.

"I'm surprised you don't know. Your little scuffle the other day went viral." She showed them a phone video of his clash with Danilovic. "This got 200,000 views."

"Wow," Jake said.

Eugene shrugged.

"Well, thanks again," Jake said, and they walked into the men's lockers.

While they were changing, Schultz walked over to them.

Eugene said, "Sorry about losing my cool, Edgar. It won't happen again."

Schultz broke into a broad grin. "Are you kidding? That was the best thing to ever happen to this tournament. Look at the stands, three-quarters full. We usually lose money on early doubles matches. Today we'll at least break even, maybe even come out a little ahead." He looked over at Jake. "Remember I told you nobody gives a shit about doubles? I was wrong. Looks like every Croat in Ohio is in the stands. A couple of buses came all the way from Cleveland. We're gonna have to move you guys to Center Court if this keeps up."

Jake and Eugene won their match six-three, six-four. The other team was totally unnerved by the wild roars of the crowd every time Eugene hit a winner. Jake had almost completely regained the form that made him a top-five player. His first serve and forehand had more power and pop. His backhand was fluid and precise and his footwork, like Jack in the nursery rhyme, was nimble and quick. He felt ready for his first foray into singles competition, which was scheduled for two the following afternoon on Center Court.

The stands were packed when Jake walked out to raucous applause. He was surprised to see Maggie in the players row, ground level, right next to the court. The Croatian contingent filled the top five rows on the opposite side. Eugene joined his compatriots at the beginning of the first set, which elicited the loudest cheer of the day. Natasha Ferris was also in the stands, probably to make sure Jake was wearing his new tennis togs.

Facing Jake on the other side of the court was Gonçalo Coelho, a young Portuguese player, ranked in the 120's, who was a 'lucky loser.' He lost in the qualifying round but was randomly selected to play when a high seed dropped out, opening up a slot in the main draw. Tall and gangly, he had an awkward but effective game. He was cat quick and hit with a lot of spins and slices.

It took Jake several games to get his singles mojo working and solve Coelho, but once he found his rhythm he cruised, winning 7-5, 6-2. After the match, he jogged over to the Players Row and gave Maggie a big hug and kiss.

"It's so great to see you. I wasn't sure you'd get here in time for the match."

"I wasn't either, but the plane made good time." She stared sideways at Jake's outfit, grinned and said, "Who picked out your clothes for you, RuPaul?"

Before Jake could answer, Natasha Ferris walked over to them. She gave Jake a quick peck on the cheek and said, "You looked great out there."

"Uh, thanks Natasha." He put an arm around Maggie. "This is, Maggie Quinlan."

"Oh," Natasha said, extending her hand. "I'm Natasha Ferris, President of Sustennis Ecowear. We're thrilled to have Jake representing us." She handed Maggie a business card. "Text me with your sizes, I'll send some clothes for you."

"Oh," Maggie said. "Thank you."

Natasha glanced at her phone. "I have to run." She turned to Jake. "Good luck in your next match." Then to Maggie. "It was a pleasure meeting you."

Maggie smiled wryly at Jake. "You don't see me for a week and you go and get yourself another girlfriend."

"C'mon. She's no girlfriend. She's a sponsor."

"I saw the way she looked at you. She had love on her mind."

"Yeah. Love of the money she'll make thanks to me and Eugene."

"Speaking of that, you said you would never endorse a product, that it was dishonest."

"I still believe that. But I also believe in friendship."

He told her about Eugene's dream of opening a tennis academy in Croatia and how this would go a long way to help him do that.

"Are you sure it's not because she's a tall, gorgeous blonde?"

"Blondes never did it for me. I'm much more attracted to feisty redheads." He grabbed her and kissed her fiercely.

42

———

When they got back to the room, Jake said, "Did you have anything to eat today?"

"A bag of peanuts on the plane. I dumped my stuff in the room and took an Uber straight to the court."

"You must be hungry."

"I'm starving."

"Okay. I'm gonna take you to a special place."

"That's not necessary. I can just get a sandwich down in the coffee shop."

"No. You're in Cincinnati. You have to have the most Cincinnati-ish meal. And I guarantee it's something you've never eaten before."

Maggie rolled her eyes. "What?"

"Cincinnati Chili."

Maggie said, "I've had chili dozens of times."

"Never like this."

A five-minute Uber ride got them to their destination.

"This is it?" Maggie said incredulously. "I thought you were gonna take me to some fancy place."

"You can find fancy anywhere, you can only get Skyline Chili here."

A perky waitress was at their table a minute after they were seated.

Jake said, "Two three-ways, please."

She looked over at Maggie. "Something to drink?"

"Iced tea."

"Make it two."

"You got it."

After the waitress was gone, Maggie said, "What's a three-way?"

"It's a gigantic plate of spaghetti, covered with tons of chili and a whole bunch of shredded cheddar cheese on top."

Maggie grimaced.

"Just try it. It's one of those things that taste a lot better than it sounds. Before I ever ate a Reuben I thought it sounded disgusting. Corned beef, sauerkraut and Russian dressing, yuck!" He shuddered. "Now it's my favorite sandwich."

After Maggie had her first taste, Jake said, "Whaddaya think?"

"It's actually pretty good," she garbled through a mouthful of food.

To Jake's astonishment, she finished the entire plate.

When the waitress asked them if they wanted any dessert, Maggie said, "Are you kidding? I might not eat again for a week."

Back in their hotel room, Jake said, "So how'd it go with Kelleher?"

"Actually, pretty good. He even paid you a compliment."

"Really?"

"Uh huh. Mohammed Levi is gonna be doing a special concert in New York. He's calling it Unity Under the Unisphere. It's supposed to be the night of the U.S. Open Finals. He asked Kelleher to help him out with security."

"Security? Kelleher's a soldier, not a security guard."

"He's doing it more as a favor. Since that night in London they've kept in touch. He really likes Levi and wants to help him out if he can."

"Are we still talking about the same guy, the hard-ass, take no prisoners Jungle Jim Kelleher?"

"That's not even the wildest part. He said maybe he would ask you for some advice since you know the area and it's happening the same time as the Open."

"My God. I guess connecting with his long lost daughter has mellowed the old grizzly."

The next morning, Jake and Eugene were on Grandstand Court for their second doubles match. All 5,000 seats were filled. The Croats were back, shouting for Eugene when they weren't bellowing the Croatian National Anthem and waving a huge Croatian flag, three red, white and blue horizontal stripes with a red-and-white checkerboard shield in the center. There was also a smaller section of Serbians who came for Danilovic's match, which was up next. They booed Eugene every time he touched the ball but were drowned out by the cheers of the boisterous Croats.

Soon the Serbs and Croats were yelling and cursing at each other. When they started throwing things, it looked like an all-out brawl was imminent. That's when about a dozen security guards marched into the stands and the referee announced that they would all be expelled from the arena unless they settled down.

The fracas inspired Jake and Eugene and rattled their opponents. They won 6-2, 6-1 in a little over an hour.

After the match, Eugene went up into the stands and basked in the adulation of his compatriots. Jake toweled himself off and was about to go over the the players' row and give Maggie a quick kiss when the normally subdued Edgar

Schultz raced up to him, lifted him in a bear hug and kissed him on the forehead.

"Thank you. Thank you. Thank you."

A startled Jake said, "You're welcome, I guess. What'd I do?"

"You made history. We never sell out for a round-of-sixteen doubles match, not on Center Court and certainly not in the Grandstand. We're now sold out for every mens singles and doubles match here and Center Court. You also made me look like a genius."

"I don't know that we did anything special, but if it helps you out, I'm happy."

Jake patted Schultz on the back. The German gave him another hug and said, "Thank you again."

The next few days, Jake and Eugene were on fire. Jake was back to his championship form, and Eugene was playing the best tennis of his life. They made it to the finals on Sunday, where they were scheduled to play a rematch against Kull and Danilovic at noon. Jake was also slated to play Tommy Riemer in the singles final later that day.

Usually on finals day, Men's Singles is the headliner. Not on this day. When Jake picked up the *Cincinnati Enquirer* outside his hotel room door, the back page blared, 'WAR ON CENTER COURT.'

The article went on to say that this was more than a doubles match, that the pride and dignity of two countries were at stake. It talked about the war back in the 90's, the atrocities on both sides and how the bad blood has been passed on to succeeding generations. They interviewed leaders of the Serbian and Croatian communities from the area, as well as rabid fans from both sides. There was a full-page ad next to the article with a big color shot of Jake and Eugene in their new Sustennis tennis outfits.

The story about Jake's singles final against Tommy Riemer, which on any other occasion would dominate the back page, was buried between high school scores and horse-racing results.

Center Court was packed when Jake and Eugene entered to raucous applause. It looked like there were far more Croats than Serbs in the stands, which was confirmed by the boisterous boos, jeers, curses and catcalls that overpowered any cheers for Kull and Danilovic.

The beginning of the match was ballistic, with each player firing missiles on almost every point. The first set went to a tiebreaker. Jake and Eugene raced out to a big lead, then squandered two match points before Jake's service ace gave them the set.

The intensity level in set two was not quite as high, with the serving team winning every game until they were tied at 4-4. It looked like they were headed to another tiebreaker when Jake and Eugene broke Kull's serve. Now all Jake had to do was hold his serve and the championship would be theirs. Kull and Danilovic won the first two points. Then Jake hit two unreturnable serves, one for a clean ace. Jake missed his next first serve and Danilovic hammered his second serve return at Eugene's head. The crafty Croat deftly angled a sweet volley just beyond the Serb's reach.

Match point.

Jake hit a blistering serve into Kull's body. All the big Dane could do was loft a high, short lob that Eugene blasted into the second row.

Before the referee could announce the winner, Eugene threw his racquet high into the air and thrust his arms to the heavens.

Game. Set. Match. Championship.

The capacity crowd roared. It probably registered on the Richter scale.

A mass of frenzied fans, most wearing red and white checkerboard shirts, stormed the court. They surrounded

Eugene, hoisted him in the air and ran around the court, carrying him on their shoulders, belting out the Croatian national anthem.

It took an extra five minutes to disperse the mob and prepare the trophy presentation. After the obligatory sponsor speeches and kudos to the ground staff and referee, it was time for the winners to receive their checks and trophies, and make their speeches.

Eugene went first. Still beaming, he said, "My wedding, the birth of my daughters and today. The most best days of my life. Thank you everyone, especially my countrymen and thank you Jake Marks. I could have done none of this without you."

The announcer handed the microphone to Jake.

"Today Eugene carried an entire nation onto the court with him and led them to victory. I didn't have a whole country behind me, but I did have one very special person."

Jake put down his trophy, ran over to Maggie, kissed her and escorted her to Center Court as the crowd oohed and aahed and cheered.

Eugene hugged Jake, then grabbed his bag and headed to the Players Entrance, blowing kisses to the fans as he walked.

A minute later, a deafening explosion shook the arena. The stands erupted in cries and screams. People ran towards the exits in helter-skelter confusion, jostling and trampling each other. Security personnel tried to keep some semblance of order. Five people wound up in the E.R. Two sprained ankles, a broken arm, a concussion and a man whose heart attack turned out to be a panic attack.

The force of the blast staggered Jake and Maggie. Jake made sure that Maggie was okay then ran into the tunnel to check on Eugene. There wasn't much left to check. The only way Jake could be sure it was him was that an arm, dangling from the charred, bloody corpse, had his distinctive Croatian tattoo along with the names of his daughters.

Within minutes, police, firefighters and paramedics were on the scene. The EMTs offered to take Jake and Maggie to the hospital to be checked out, but they declined. A detective asked Jake if Eugene had any enemies. After Jake said none that he knew of, the detective pressed him about Eugene's fight with Danilovic. He asked if Eugene was in the Croatian military or had any previous encounters with the BIA, the Serbian Intelligence Agency. Jake answered that he didn't think so, but he couldn't be sure.

After a few more minutes of questioning, a policeman drove Jake and Maggie back to their hotel. Again Jake was surprised at how composed Maggie was. She was a little shaken, of course. Who wouldn't be after having been so close to the explosion and the grizzly death of someone she knew. But Jake believed most women would have been hysterical.

A couple of minutes after they got back, there was a knock at the door. It was Edgar Schultz, holding Jake's tennis bag. He looked like he aged ten years since the morning.

As soon as Jake opened the door, Schultz dropped the bag and enveloped him in a fierce bear hug.

"How could this have happened?" Schultz wailed. "I don't understand. Everyone loved Eugene. It doesn't make any sense."

"I know," Jake whispered. "It's horrible."

Schultz struggled to compose himself. "Of course, the Men's Final is cancelled. I don't know how we can even have a tournament next year." Tears streamed down his cheeks. "This is just awful. A nightmare." He looked down at Jake's tennis bag. "One of the grounds personnel brought this back. He thought there might be something in it you need."

Jake thanked him. "Are you going to be all right?"

"I have to be. I'm the one who has to clean up this mess."

He gave Jake another quick hug, shook his head sadly, then left.

Jake put his bag on the bed. He opened it, then he screamed, "Holy fucking shit!"

Maggie ran over. "What's wrong?"

"Look inside. See that necklace with the beads and the cross? That's Eugene's rosary. This is his bag. He grabbed mine by mistake. That bomb was meant for me."

FOURTH SET

43

Kelleher walked up Madison Avenue in a misty drizzle. It was close to midnight and the street was almost empty. He turned on 88th Street and walked east toward Park. The chrome and glass Millennium Spire stood like a gaudy rhinestone obelisk in the middle of the staid, tree-lined block, towering over the venerable brownstones and townhouses on either side of it. It was Goldbarr's middle finger to Manhattan's well-to-do elite, who always treated him like a party crasher.

A woman in a Burberry raincoat, holding a Gucci umbrella in one hand and a Louis Vuitton dog leash in the other, was whining at her snotty little French bulldog, "C'mon Sydney, piddle already. I'm getting drenched out here."

The dog, who was wearing her own Burberry slicker, gave her master a look that said, 'I'll piddle when I'm good and ready.'

When Kelleher got to the gold plated entrance, Herman, the gargantuan doorman, was blocking the entrance.

Kelleher said, "Remember me? I need to see Goldbarr."

Herman eyed him skeptically. He took out his visitors cheat

sheet and looked it up and down, moving his lips as he read. He glared at Kelleher and snarled, "No appointment."

"C'mon buddy, this is important. Goldbarr's gonna want to see me. He'll be pissed off when he finds out you didn't let me in."

Herman scowled. "No visitors without appointment. Now get the hell outta here before I mess you up."

"Gee, Herman. I thought we were pals."

"Fuck off."

"All right, I'm leaving. No hard feelings." Kelleher extended his right hand.

Herman looked confused, unsure whether to shake Kelleher's hand or to slap it away. In a flash, Kelleher grabbed his arm and yanked the big doorman towards him. With his other hand he plunged the razor-sharp electrodes of a military grade stun gun into the giant's neck, sending 150 million volts of electricity coursing through his body. The huge doorman's eyes bulged. He shook uncontrollably and collapsed to the floor.

While Herman was writhing on Goldbarr's gold-plated threshold, Kelleher jabbed a hypodermic needle filled with a triple dose of the powerful sedative midazolam into his shoulder. After waiting for a half-minute while it took, he pulled Herman's body inside the lobby, zip-tied his hands and feet, covered his mouth with duct tape, dragged him across the marble tiled floor and stuffed him into a utility closet.

He walked to the end car of the elevator bank, which was separated from the other cars with red velvet ropes on gold stanchions. A sign on a gold plated display stand in front of the elevator door read 'Goldbarr Express. Authorized Guests and Personnel Only.' He took it to the 26th floor. The thick glass doors had 'Goldbarr Enterprises' stenciled in huge gold leaf lettering across them. Kelleher opened the door to reveal a mocha skinned beauty with the face of an angel and the body of a centerfold sitting behind a glass-topped desk.

"Can I help you?" she said.

"Yeah. I need to see Goldbarr."

She smiled. "I'm really sorry, sir. He's in a meeting at the moment. It may go on for some time. Is there anything I can do for you?"

Kelleher imagined several things she could do for him, none of which pertained to the issue at hand. He lifted his shirt flap to reveal the Glock in his waistband.

In a pleasant voice he said, "It's really important that I see him now."

"Of course, sir. Through the glass doors. His office is to the right."

"Why don't you show me so I don't make a mistake."

She smiled. "My pleasure, sir."

Her black, knee-length dress clung in all the right places. She glided to the door in her five-inch stiletto pumps as if they were ballet slippers.

When they got to the corner office, she opened the door to a room the size of a middle school gymnasium. The walls were covered with paintings, photos and magazine and newspaper covers in gold frames. They were all of one subject, Ronald Goldbarr. The man, himself, was sitting at a conference table talking to an olive skinned guy in his late thirties. He had a full beard and long black hair tied in a bun on top. He wore black jeans and a khaki shirt, as opposed to Goldbarr, who always wore a navy blue suit and red tie that hung far below his belt.

The table was strewn with maps and photos.

Goldbarr glared angrily as the door opened. He began to yell, "Melissa, I told you I didn't want to be dist..." Then he saw Kelleher walk in behind her.

"What the hell are you doing here?"

"Guess."

Goldbarr turned to Melissa. "Wait outside with Mr. Bagheri while I deal with Colonel Kelleher. It shouldn't take too long.

And call downstairs. Ask Herman why Mr. Kelleher wasn't announced."

Bagheri walked out with the statuesque Melissa, who, in her heels, was a head taller than him. Kelleher walked over to the conference table. He picked up one of the photos.

"What is this, the Unisphere?"

"Yeah, so what?"

"What do you care about the Unisphere?"

"Not that it's any of your business, but I'm thinking of bidding on the TV rights to the U.S. Open Tennis Tournament for next year." Goldbarr looked up at him. "Are you here to inquire about my business plans or did you just come here to gloat?"

"Gloat? What are you talking about?"

"Thanks to you and Marks, I'm out of business."

"Bullshit! I just saw you doing business."

"I'm still running Goldbarr Enterprises. Millennium's finished."

"You're lying. You love doing all this political intrigue shit. Sitting here plotting to take over the world like some crazy James Bond villain."

"I did love it. Except I'm no villain. I was trying to save this country."

"So why stop?"

"You took out my two top men. Glynn and Stryker ran the whole tactical side of my operation. I know business. I know the media. I can sell anything. And I know the right people. The problem is I don't know shit about recruiting and super-vising military personnel. And I'm too old to learn. If I was forty I'd start over. But not now."

"There are plenty of men out there like Glynn and Stryker. I worked with some of them. Any one of them could do the job."

"I'm not talking about skills, knowledge or experience. Glynn and Stryker would walk through fire for me. They gave their lives for me. You can't buy that kind of loyalty. The guys you're talking about are hired guns. How do I know they wouldn't sell me out to the highest bidder?" Goldbarr shook his head. "That's it. You won. I'm finished."

"If you're finished, who did this?"

Kelleher took a folded newspaper clipping out of his pocket and handed it to Goldbarr. He read it and scowled at Kelleher.

"Some European tennis player gets blown away. What does that have to do with me?"

"He was Jake Marks's playing partner."

Goldbarr smirked. "Too bad it wasn't Marks."

"It shoulda been. The bomb was in Marks's bag. The other guy picked it up by mistake. If that didn't happen, that bomb would have killed Marks and anyone near him."

"I had nothing to do with that but if you find him, thank him for me."

"Don't fuck with me. If it wasn't you, who was it?"

"I have no idea, but next time I hope he doesn't miss."

Kelleher glowered at Goldbarr. "My daughter was standing next to Marks when that bomb went off. She was also in the Brooklyn Botanical Gardens the other day with Marks when someone started shooting at them. Tell me that wasn't one of your men."

"I'm glad your daughter's okay. I really am. But if you really want to protect her, keep her away from Marks. He's the one you should be threatening, not me. You can't really think he gives a shit about your daughter. He hooked up with her because he knew that you were after him after he shot your wife."

"He didn't kill Brigid. I saw the official police ballistics report."

"Reports can be forged. Police can be bribed. I know. I've done it myself."

Kelleher leaned over the table and glared at Goldbarr. "I'll deal with Marks later, but right now I'm talking to you. You got a daughter too." He reached into a pocket and took out two photos and placed them on the table like cards in a poker game. They were recent shots of Goldbarr's young daughter, Eliana, one at a horse show, another of her playing tennis at his club. "If anything happens to Maggie, you'll know exactly how I feel, because your little girl will be dead the next day. And unlike your bozos, I won't miss."

Goldbarr trembled. His swagger was gone and he looked shaken. He slumped down in his chair. It was said that his daughter was the only person in the world that he actually cared about, which didn't say much for his wife and two grown sons.

"All right, here's the truth," he said, his voice now soft and quavery. "The Botanical Gardens incident was a total fuck-up. One of the men on Stryker's team thought that by killing Marks he would prove to me that he could take his spot. I didn't know about it until after it happened. After that I ordered everyone to stand down. That's the truth."

"What was the bomb in Cincinnati, another fuck-up?"

"I told you I had nothing to do with that. I don't know who it was, but it wasn't me or anyone connected to me. I swear."

"Then you better hope that whoever it was won't try again. 'Cause if anything happens to Maggie, if she gets into a car crash or gets mugged, if she trips on the street or suddenly gets sick with some strange disease, I'm blaming you and coming after your daughter."

Kelleher marched out of the office.

44

———

Along with his elite athleticism, his uncanny concentration and his lightning reflexes, Jake's ability to adjust calmly to whatever was happening at the moment, even in the most stressful situations, was what made him who he is, a top-five tennis pro and one of the world's most feared assassins. Whether it was match point in a Grand Slam or the middle of a firefight with terrorists, he stayed cool. But as he walked up the steps to Maggie's brownstone, his heart was racing and his hands were clammy. He was going to tell her that he was ending their relationship. It wasn't that he didn't love her. He did, more than he ever believed he could love anyone. That's why he decided that he couldn't keep putting her life in jeopardy. Three times she was almost killed because of him. In London, at the Botanical Garden and in Cincinnati. He wouldn't risk a fourth.

She opened the door, gave him a big smile and kissed him lightly.

"You're my second surprise visitor today."

Kelleher was sitting on the living room sofa. He shot Jake a contemptuous look. Then he turned to Maggie. "I had a long talk with Goldbarr the other day."

Maggie said, "Really? About what?"

"About him trying to kill you. It won't happen again."

"How can you be sure?"

"I showed him a couple of recent pictures of his fourteen-year-old daughter. I told him if anything happened to you, I wouldn't be the only one mourning a daughter."

"What did he say?"

"He said he had nothing to do with what happened at the Botanical Gardens or Cincinnati." He cocked his head at Jake. "Then he said he's closing down the Millennium operation."

Jake said, "He's lying. Goldbarr's a narcissistic, sociopathic megalomaniac. He's obsessed with power, attention and adulation. The Millennium Society gives him that. It also positions him for the presidential run he's been dreaming about. He would never give that up."

"Maybe not. But he said that with Glynn and Stryker dead he has no more enforcement unit."

"Bullshit! They have dozens of men in their files, ex-military, FBI, CIA. Any one of them could do the job."

"That might be true except for one thing. Goldbarr's a major paranoiac. He thinks everyone is out to screw him. The only man he really trusts is his doorman-bodyguard Herman, who has the body of a whale and the brain of a guppy. Not the guy you want to run your military operation."

Jake said, "The sniper at the Botanical Gardens was one of Stryker's men. I've seen them together."

"You're right. Goldbarr admitted it. But he said the guy went rogue."

Jake said, "No way. Nobody made a move without orders from Glynn or Stryker."

"Glynn and Stryker are dead. Goldbarr said the asshole who shot at you was looking to take over Stryker's team. He figured that shooting you would be his way in."

"What about Cincinnati? Was that another rogue operation?"

"Goldbarr swears he had nothing to do with that."

"You believe him?"

"I don't believe anybody. But I gotta ask, why would he lie about Cincinnati and own up about the Botanical Gardens?"

"Because no one would believe two loose cannons."

Kelleher said, "Maybe. Who else besides Goldbarr knows you're the Lone Ranger?"

"No one."

Kelleher said, "Are you sure you were the target, not your Croatian pal?"

"The bomb was in my bag. Eugene picked it up by mistake. That should have been me and Maggie splattered all over the locker room."

"If nobody but Goldbarr and us knows you're the Lone Ranger, and Goldbarr's telling the truth, then the target was Jake Marks, the tennis player. Who hates you enough to want you dead?"

"I can't think of anyone."

Maggie said, "I can. That little shit Riemer."

Jake said, "Riemer's crazy, that's for sure. And vicious. I just don't think he's a murderer."

"He hired those guys who jumped you and Bunny?"

"He paid them to beat me up, not kill me. And even if he could figure out a way to make a bomb, which I doubt, how would he get it to Cincinnati? The TSA frowns on people putting explosives in their luggage."

"Maybe he hired somebody else to do it."

"And if he did, how did he plant it in my bag that was locked in my room? There were cameras all over the place. One focused right outside my door. I looked at the footage. Nobody was near there but you and me."

Maggie shrugged. "Well, somebody put that bomb in your bag."

"Yeah, that's the problem. I've been racking my brain to try to figure that out."

Kelleher's craggy face creased in thought. "Let's leave that alone for a minute. There's something else I wanted to ask you. You ever hear of a guy named Bagheri?"

"Parviz Bagheri?"

"All I heard was Bagheri. Late thirties. Long hair. Wears it in a bun on top of his head."

"Yeah, that's him. What about him?"

"He was with Goldbarr when I went up there. They were looking at maps and pictures. One was of the Unisphere."

"If it's Parviz Bagheri, that's not a good thing."

"So who is he? Goldbarr said they were talking about TV rights to the tournament."

Jake stiffened. "They weren't talking about TV. More like TNT."

"What are you talking about?"

"Bagheri's a bomb maker. One of the best. They call him the Master Blaster. He's half-Iranian and half-Danish. His grandfather was a minister for the Shah. The family escaped to Denmark when the Ayatollah came to power. Bagheri has a degree in Civil Engineering from Cambridge and spent two years in the Danish Army as an explosive ordinance specialist. Since then he's sold his services to the highest bidder. He won't even talk to you for less than a million dollars. He's done jobs for the Saudis, Israel and Yemen that I know of. His home base is Copenhagen."

Kelleher said, "How do you know so much about him?"

"Glynn gave me his dossier. He never said if he wanted us to work together or if he was a target. But whatever it was, it fell through."

Maggie jumped up and said, "That has to be it! If Goldbarr didn't hire him, Riemer did."

Jake looked skeptical. "There's no way Riemer would know how to contact Bagheri. But there's something else. The Cincinnati bomb isn't Bagheri's style. The police report said it was a pipe bomb with an old fashioned pressure fuze, hidden under a towel at the bottom of my bag. It was amateurish, homemade, like whoever built it got the plans off YouTube. Bagheri's a pro. He's meticulous. He uses state-of-the-art equipment, radio controlled detonators."

Maggie said, "Maybe he made the bomb that way to throw us off the scent. And now he's gonna blow up the Unisphere."

Kelleher stood with a smirk, arms folded. "Are you two just about done?"

They both turned and stared at Kelleher.

"We don't know anything about the guy I saw. It might not even be the same Bagheri as the one you're talking about. And if it is, I'll check him out." He pointed at Jake. "You have a big tennis tournament to prepare for." He looked over at Maggie. "And you're supposed to be training him. You two do what you're supposed to be doing. Don't worry about Goldbarr."

Maggie said, "That's easy for you to say. Goldbarr's not trying to kill you."

"Are you kidding? He wants me dead more than either of you. But as long as he knows that if anything happens to any of us, his daughter's dead too, we're safe." He stood and headed for the door. "I gotta go."

As soon as he was gone, Maggie looked over at Jake. "You agree with him?"

"About what?"

"That we don't have to worry about Goldbarr."

He shrugged.

"Well, I don't buy it for a minute. And I'm not gonna sit

around like a duck in a shooting gallery waiting for him to try again."

"What are you gonna do?"

"I dunno. By the way, didn't you want to talk to me about something?"

"Nah. It wasn't really that important."

45

———

Parviz Bagheri stood in front of a 75-inch TV monitor holding what looked like an oversized lunchbox made of blue Lego blocks with an antenna sticking out of the top. He opened it to reveal a bunch of dials, switches, push-buttons and a small LED screen about the size of an index card.

"This is the Blast-con 3, one of the most advanced explosive detonation systems on the market. It can ignite up to eight explosions either simultaneously or in sequence," he said, sounding more like the assistant engineering professor he once was than the man responsible for numerous deadly explosions on four continents.

Bagheri had been talking for less than two minutes and Goldbarr was already bored.

"Yeah, yeah, fine," Goldbarr said. "I don't need a sales pitch. If you say that thing will do the job that's good enough for me. What else ya got?"

Bagheri put the blue box on a table next to the screen and grabbed an iPad out of his leather messenger bag. He touched it and an overhead shot of the Unisphere filled the screen behind him. "Built of 350 tons of hardened steel, the Unisphere is as tall as a 15-story building. This is where the concert will take place."

He took a laser pointer out of the bag and aimed it at the fountain in front of the Unisphere.

"The stage will be erected here, over the fountain, which will be drained." As he spoke, computer generated renditions of the structures he talked about appeared on the screen. "Two speakers will be placed on either side of the stage. Two-tiers of VIP seats will face the stage. Everyone else who attends will be on the grass or the pavement surrounding the Unisphere. The concert will start after the conclusion of the U.S. Open Finals."

"I coulda got all that from the newspaper," Goldbarr barked. "Tell me about the bombs."

Bagheri's face flashed anger for a second, then he turned and took what looked like a large clay brick out of his bag.

"This is C-4. A few sticks of these is what Al Qaeda used to put a big hole in the U.S.S. Cole and kill 17 American sailors."

He slammed the brick on the table.

Goldbarr threw his hands over his eyes and shrieked.

Bagheri smirked. "As you can see, it's perfectly safe. Without a detonator, C-4 is nothing but a large piece of modeling clay. And like clay, it can be molded into any shape."

Goldbarr glared daggers at him. He didn't appreciate being made a fool of, even if there was no one else in the room to witness it.

Bagheri put the brick on the table and took out what looked like the barrel of a king-size ballpoint pen with a wire sticking out of the tip. He held it up in front of him.

"This is the detonator. Insert it into that harmless lump and it becomes a powerful explosive. As I said, the blue box can trigger as many as eight of these at once from 500 yards away."

"Great," Goldbarr said, still seething. "Can it blow up the Unisphere?"

"I'm not sure what you mean. It can certainly damage it."

Goldbarr banged his fist on the desk. "That's not good enough. TV cameras from all over the world will be covering this. There will even be a blimp from the tennis match. I want this to be the most tremendous video footage in history. Ten times better than the planes crashing into the twin towers or when the Hindenburg blew up. I want viewers to see their world exploding in a massive fireball of death and destruction. People running for their lives. All of it because of the stupid, inept and corrupt traitors who are running this country into the ground.

"Double up the explosive on the Unisphere. Cover the damn thing with it if that's what it takes. I want that big ball to blast into a million pieces. Then I want you to put charges under the stage and the VIP seats. Enough to blow them all away."

Bagheri's face froze in horror. "Do you know what you're saying? I thought you wanted an explosion at the Unisphere to make a point. Maybe with a couple of random casualties. You never mentioned anything about killing all those influential people. This isn't what we talked about. Sorry, I can't do that."

Goldbarr turned crimson and screamed, "When did you grow a fucking conscience? You've killed plenty with your bombs."

"This is different. This will be the crime of the century. The FBI, the CIA, Interpol and more will be investigating this. Sooner or later they'll be knocking at my door."

"All right, listen. After you're done setting everything up, give me the blue gizmo. I'll trigger it. You'll be off the hook."

"I'll still be an accessory."

Goldbarr smiled and nodded. "I get it, you want more money. Fifty million will buy you plastic surgery, a new identity and a new life anywhere in the world."

Bagheri was about to respond when the door flew open and

Maggie stormed into the office shrieking, "You bastard! You killed my mother. Now you're trying to kill me and Jake."

A clearly shaken Melissa ran into the office behind her.

"I'm so sorry, Mr. G. I couldn't stop her."

"Get Herman up here," he shouted. "Now!"

As Melissa scurried back to her office, he turned to Maggie. "You don't know what you're talking about, Ms. Quinlan."

Maggie stopped short. "You know who I am?"

"Of course I know you. I also know that it was your boyfriend Marks who killed your mother, not me or anyone associated with me."

"That's a lie."

"I'll tell you what else I know. I know you're trespassing. You broke into my office and threatened me. I could have you arrested, but I won't do that. Just get the hell out of here and I'll forget the whole thing. You can tell Marks that he has nothing to worry about from me."

"So you admit that it was your men who tried to kill us."

"I don't admit anything."

She looked over at Bagheri, who was standing in front of the monitor, dumbstruck.

"Who's he?" She pointed at him. "Another one of your hitmen?" Bagheri jerked back.

Melissa ran back into the office, trailed by Herman.

Goldbarr turned to the huge Samoan. "Herman, this woman is trespassing. Escort her out of the building."

Herman still had a bandage on his neck where Kelleher tasered him. He took a few lumbering steps towards Maggie. She jumped back and yelled, "Don't you touch me, you big gorilla." She reached into the bag that was slung across her shoulder.

Herman jumped back.

Maggie pulled out her phone.

"What the hell are you doing?" Goldbarr yelled.

"I'm making a video," she yelled. "If he touches me this will go viral. Then everyone will know what a bastard you are."

"Put that phone away right now or I'll have Herman take it away."

Herman lunged at her but she quickly scooted away from him, her world-class gymnastics training on full display.

"Keep your disgusting hands off me!" she cried.

Goldbarr yelled, "All right. You made your point. Now get the hell out right now or I will have you arrested."

She glared at him as she backed toward the door, her phone still in video mode. "All right, I'm going. Just keep him and all your other goons away from me and Jake."

She stormed out of the office, slamming the door behind her.

A contrite Melissa said, "I'm so sorry sir. I didn't know what to do. She came off the elevator and ran past me before I could stop her."

"Don't worry honey, it wasn't your fault. Take the rest of the day off."

He turned to Herman. "You stay."

He looked over at Bagheri who seemed shaken by what just happened. "Where were we? Oh yeah, you were getting squeamish about the job. Will fifty million dollars ease your worries?"

Bagheri said, "Seventy-five."

"Sixty."

"Sixty-five."

Goldbarr thought for a moment. "Okay, you got a deal. And just to make sure nothing happens to you between now and then, I'm assigning my best man to be your bodyguard."

"I don't think that's a good idea. "

"You don't have a choice. I got 65 million dollars invested in you now. I need to make sure my investment is protected."

"I still have several things I need to take care of before I can start. We don't have much time and he might scare my contacts."

"Don't worry, you won't even know he's there." He looked over at Herman and gestured at Bagheri. "I want you to make sure nothing happens to Mr. Bagheri, but don't get in his way. Is that clear?"

"Yes, sir."

"All right, Bagheri. I'm sure you have a lot to do. You can get started now."

The bombmaker looked over at Herman. "What about him?"

"Don't worry about him. Just do what you do."

Bagheri turned off the monitor and gathered up his show-and-tell items. He left without another word.

Herman started to follow when Goldbarr beckoned him over to his desk.

"Don't let him out of your sight for the next two weeks," he whispered. "I don't trust him. He does anything suspicious, let me know right away. On the day of the Unisphere concert, as soon as you see him hand me that blue case, he's all yours."

A sinister grin creased Herman's face. "Okay, boss."

46

Jake sat on a bench beside the net with a towel draped over his head. His face gleamed with sweat. A tennis ball launcher and a hopper filled with balls were next to him. He had just finished a two-and-a-half hour workout at the Vanderbilt Tennis Club. His body was exhausted, but his mind was racing. He wasn't thinking about the Open, which was less than two weeks away. He wasn't thinking about Bagheri and what he and Goldbarr were planning. All he could think about was Maggie.

Where was she? Was she all right? Why didn't she tell him where she was going or what she was doing? Was she having second thoughts about their relationship? Was he even capable of having a relationship?

Stop it! he screamed silently at himself. One of the things he loved about Maggie was her toughness and independence. She didn't need to report all her movements to him. When he sees her she'll tell him where she was, and if she doesn't, that's okay too. But suppose she doesn't come back? Maybe whoever has been targeting him will go after her.

You're doing it again.

He took a gulp of his homemade sports drink: sugar, salt

and lemon juice, a half-cup of orange juice and a quart of water.

"Hey."Maggie walked over to him.

He took the towel off his head. "Hi."

See. All that worrying was stupid.

"Guess where I've just been," she said, sporting a self-satisfied grin.

"I have no idea. Where?"

"Goldbarr's penthouse."

The worry was back. "What! Why? What happened? Did one of his goons grab you off the street? I'll kill him. I swear I'll kill him."

She grinned. "Calm down. It's nothing like that. I went up there on my own."

She sat down next to him.

"Why would you do that?"

"I told him to stop trying to kill us."

Jake's mouth gaped open in disbelief. After several seconds he gathered himself.

"Could you start from the beginning?"

"My mother always said that the best way to meet a problem is head-on. I don't know about you, but I think that people shooting as us and trying to blow us up is a problem. And since Goldbarr is probably the one behind it, I told him to stop."

Jake shook his head in disbelief. "Let's say Goldbarr is the one behind these attacks, and I'm not sure that he is, at least not all of them, do you really think that all you have to do is ask him to stop and that'll be it?"

"It sure beats the hell out of waiting for the next time."

"What did he say?"

"He denied it, of course."

"Then what happened?"

"He called that great big brontosaurus of a doorman to come up to his office and throw me out."

"Herman?"

"Yeah. What's his story? He seems a little stunad, as my Italian friends from the old neighborhood used to say."

"He's Goldbarr's personal enforcer, bodyguard and leg-breaker. He's Samoan. His real name is something like Here-manulu. He came to the U.S. to play football for Penn State. Halfway through his sophomore season he was off the team. There was never an official explanation, but the rumor was he raped a girl at a party and almost killed her. Joe Paterno, the Penn State coach, was able to make the charges disappear. But that was the end of Herman's football career."

"He raped and almost killed a girl and the only thing that happened was he got kicked off the team? That's so messed up. What about the police? What about the girl's family?"

"At that time Paterno was the most powerful person in Pennsylvania. As far as the girl's family, I bet they got paid a lot of money to keep quiet."

"Okay, I get it. Herman's a scary piece of work and college sports are evil and corrupt. But where does Goldbarr come in?"

"Penn State games were on Goldbarr's sports network. He spent a lot of time hanging out with the team. It's one of the ways he promoted his phony macho image. For some reason he took a liking to Herman. After he got thrown off the team, Gold-barr hired him to be on his network's wrestling show. That didn't work out either. Herman couldn't get it into his head that the fights were fake. He wound up injuring a couple of other wrestlers. That's when Goldbarr hired him to be his Luca Brasi."

"He seems even dumber than Luca."

"You know who Luca Brasi is?"

Maggie smiled. "Are you kidding, I love the Godfather."

Jake thought about how little he really knew about Maggie.

He didn't know what movies she liked, what kind of music she listened to, things that lovers know about each other. But the one thing he did know was that he was crazy about her.

"Did Herman hurt you?"

"No, he never touched me. He probably took it easy because he didn't want to scare the other guy."

"What other guy?"

"I think it was that bomber guy."

"Bagheri?"

"Yeah, I think so. He had a hair bun and olive skin. He was in the middle of some kind of presentation when I barged in. I guess they didn't have time to take it down."

"Presentation? What did it look like? Can you remember anything about it?"

"There was a big TV screen with a picture of the Unisphere on it and a table with some weird looking stuff."

"Weird stuff? Can you be a little more specific?"

She smiled. "I can do better than that. I can show you a video."

"Whoa. Really? I can't believe that Goldbarr let you shoot a video of what he was doing."

"No, of course not. I pulled out my phone and yelled that I was gonna record Herman manhandling me. That freaked Goldbarr out. Beating up women wouldn't be good for his image. Before I put it away, I shot as much as I could." She handed Jake her phone. "Here, take a look."

He ran the video a few times, pausing once or twice.

"It's a little blurry, but what's on the screen looks like the site plan for Mohammed Levi's concert."

"What about the stuff on the table?"

"I'm no expert, but it could be detonation equipment. It'll be easy to verify that."

A look of horror contorted her face.

"Oh my God, he really is going to set off a bomb at the concert. We have to do something!"

47

Kelleher couldn't remember the last time he was in Times Square, but it was a long time ago. This Broadway didn't look anything like the Broadway he remembered. Gone were the strip joints, peep shows, porno movies and sex shops. No more creeps standing in dingy doorways yelling at hicks to fork out ten bucks to see some strung-out hag fingering herself in a dark room. The hookers, pimps and junkies hanging out on the corners have all been exiled. Times Square used to be New York at it rawest. But that's what New York is supposed to be. This was pimped-out New York. Pre-fab glitz and glamour that was all flash and no guts.

The Hard Rock Hotel was the cream of the crap. Towering over 48th and Seventh, it was an acid-fueled rock and roll nightmare. It was the last place he'd expect to be meeting with Mohammed Levi, especially in the Rock Star penthouse suite.

"What the hell are you doing in a place like this?" Kelleher said as he sat stiffly in the plush blue armchair looking out at the Manhattan skyline. "I had you pegged as a man of the people."

Levi smiled. "They made me an offer I couldn't refuse. Free

rooms for me and my crew for as long as we're in New York. I guess having musicians stay here is good for their image."

Kelleher smirked. "Yeah, I guess."

He paced around the room. He had been in dark caves with wet gunk dripping on him, narrow tunnels where rats nipped at his feet and musty chambers that stank of fear, sweat and death, and he'd been unfazed. Here in the cheesy opulence of the newly Disneyfied Times Square he was squirmy.

"Speaking of offers, I'm gonna have to turn yours down."

"Is the money not enough? I can get more."

Kelleher shook his head. "Naw, it has nothing to do with money."

"Is our anti-war message bad for business? After all, you are a soldier for hire."

Kelleher smiled. "Are you kidding? Real soldiers hate war. We've seen the damage, death and destruction up close. I've comforted kids who lost their legs before they lost their virginity. Clueless douchebag politicians are the war lovers. The only battles they've ever seen are the ones starring John Wayne."

"So what is it?"

"I'm almost sixty years old. I've been a soldier for forty-odd years and I've been lucky enough to survive in close to one piece. But I'm not the man I was."

"I'm forty and I'm not the man I was either."

"Yeah, but when you hit a sour note or forget a lyric, the show goes on. If I screw up, people die."

Levi nodded, knowingly. "I understand. I'll tell you what. Be my guest at the concert. Stay backstage with me, not as a bodyguard or security, just a friend. After all, if it wasn't for you, there would be no concert. Probably be no Levi."

"Just as a friend, nothing else?"

"Nothing else."

"Okay, yeah. I think I'd like that ."

"Good. Now how about a drink? Beer? Wine? Whiskey? This fancy room comes with a top shelf minibar."

"I'll take a Bud if they have it."

"You're a cheap date."

His phone buzzed as Levi was walking to the minibar. It was Maggie.

"We need to see you now. It's urgent. Are you home?"

"No, I'm with Mohammed Levi at the Hard Rock Hotel on 48th & Seventh."

"Even better. This involves him too. We're coming over."

"Wait, where are you? What's going on? Who's we?"

"Me and Jake."

"Can't it wait? I'm not gonna be here that long."

"We're not far. Don't leave. We'll be there in ten minutes." She hung up.

Levi walked over with two bottles of Budweiser.

"Is everything all right? You look a little disturbed."

"That was my daughter. She's coming over here. She said it's something that involves you."

"Really? What?"

Kelleher shrugged. "She didn't say."

"Then I guess we should wait for her and find out."

Fifteen minutes later there was a knock at the door.

Levi opened it and saw Jake standing next to Maggie.

"You're Jake Marks the tennis player."

Jake smiled. "And you're Mohammed Levi, the performer and peace activist."

"Guilty as charged." He turned to Maggie. "It's a pleasure to meet you, Ms. Kelleher."

"It's Quinlan. But please call me Maggie," she said.

"Please come in," Levi said with a sweeping hand gesture. He turned to Kelleher. "You never mentioned that your daughter was coming here with Jake Marks."

"I didn't think it was a big deal."

"Are you kidding? Jake Marks is a very big deal. He's the best American tennis player since Andy Roddick."

He guided Jake and Maggie to sit on one of the two large cream colored leather sofas. Levi went to the red leather chair opposite them. "Please, Jake. May I call you Jake?"

"Of course."

"I would be honored if you and Maggie would be my guests at my concert."

"I would love to. Except if I'm in the finals of the Open. It's the same night."

"No worries. I'm not planning to start the concert until the finals are over. That way everyone watching the match can walk over if they want. But not everyone will have VIP backstage passes. Actually, just you three."

Maggie said, "Wow! Really?"

Kelleher, who had parked himself on the arm of the other sofa, said to Maggie, "Okay, what's so important?"

"I was up in Goldbarr's office this morning."

Kelleher's annoyed scowl morphed into shocked surprise.

"What?! What the hell for?"

"It doesn't matter what for. What matters is I saw that bomber guy there with him. They were looking at pictures of the Unisphere. It looked like it was set up for a concert."

"How do you know that's what it was? It could be something that has nothing to do with the concert."

"Maybe. That's why I took a video."

She thrust her phone at Kelleher. He grabbed it and watched the shaky video.

Levi said, "Well? Is it?"

"Maybe. Take a look." He handed him the phone.

"That's the plans for our concert, no doubt. I don't know how he could have got a hold of these. I just got them the other day, myself."

Jake said, "Goldbarr's got connections everywhere. Could

be someone in the mayor's office, one of the senator's aides, anybody."

Levi said, "How do you know so much about Goldbarr?"

"It's a long story."

Levi kept watching. When he got to the red case, he paused the video and showed it to Kelleher.

"What the hell is this?"

"Looks like a remote blast initiator."

"Really? Looks more like some kind of high tech cellphone."

"Works on a similar wavelength except this one is keyed to a detonator that's connected to plastic explosives."

Maggie said, "Thank God you know about this stuff. You do know how to stop it don't you?"

Before Kelleher could answer, Levi said, "Colonel Kelleher won't be part of my security team. But don't worry. My men are very well trained. They'll know how to deal with this."

Maggie looked quizzically at her father. "What happened, Kelleher? You told me you were going to help Mr. Levi with security."

"He has a great team. He doesn't need me. Besides, I'll be backstage just in case."

Jake said, "Is there anything I can do for you, Mr. Levi?"

"My friends call me Mo. And what you can do for me is win the U.S. Open. Then, if you could say something about the concert and maybe mention our anti-war message when you accept your trophy, that would help a lot. People all around the world will be watching that match. Anything you say would have more impact that 100 concerts."

Jake smiled. "I'll tell you what. If I win, I won't just mention the concert. I'll dedicate my victory to you and the peace you've been fighting for."

Levi brought his hands together as if in prayer.

"That would be a Godsend."
"With you and God rooting for me, how can I lose?"

48

———————

Jake was spread-eagle across the service line in Center Court at Arthur Ashe Stadium, lying in a bloodred puddle, turning the blue court a dark aubergine. Three jagged black holes pierced the logo on his green and blue Sustennis shirt, oozing a crimson trickle. Maggie knelt beside him holding his wrist, feeling for a pulse that wasn't there. She screamed for someone, any one to help, but no one came.

Then she woke up. She bolted upright, covered with sweat. The nightmare had been so real. She glanced over at the clock radio on the night table next to her. Ten am. She never slept that late, but she didn't fall asleep until after three.

Still freaked out from her dream, she threw the covers off, jumped up and yelled, "Jake, Jake where are you?!"

No answer.

She ran into the living room of Jake's Waldorf Towers condo and there he was, sitting on the couch, caressing his racquet, Wagner's 'Ride of the Valkyries' blasting through his iPhone AirPods.

Calming down, she walked over and plopped down next to him.

"Oh, hi," he said much too loudly. Then he muted his phone and in a normal voice said, "Are you okay? You look all out of sorts."

"I had this terrible nightmare. Somebody shot you in the middle of a match. You were lying on Center Court covered in blood. Then when I woke up and you weren't here I got a little panicky."

"I couldn't sleep. Pre-match nerves, I guess."

"Yeah, me too. But that doesn't explain the way you've been acting the last couple of weeks."

"What do you mean?"

"I don't know, distant, aloof. Like you wished I wasn't around. Maybe that's what my dream was about. Not that you're dead but that maybe something died in our relationship."

He turned to her. "C'mon, Maggie, that's not fair. You know how much this tournament means to me. For the last two weeks all I've been doing is practicing, playing and recovering. And in between, I've gotten nothing but shit from everyone. The tennis press have been on my case about dropping out of Wimbledon. That asshole Pirelli keeps bothering me to come on his podcast and badmouthing me every time I say no. Even the players turned on me. They treat me like what happened to Eugene was my fault. I thought you were the one person who understood what I was going through."

"You've been under stress since we met. As soon as we got to London it was one thing after another. That first day when you were attacked at the gym, the woman who was stabbed in the park, Glynn taking me hostage. You weren't like this then."

"I guess it all finally got to me. I've never been afraid for myself, but lately everyone I care about has either been killed or crippled."

"Yet here you are, in the finals of the U.S. Open."

"Yeah, it's weird. For some strange reason it hasn't affected my game. In fact, I'm playing the best tennis of my life. I guess

I'm taking out my frustrations on whoever's on the other side of the net. All I can say is I'm sorry if I've been treating you unfairly. Just hang in there with me for one more day. Starting tomorrow, win or lose, things will be different, I promise."

"What about today?"

"This is my chance to shut Riemer up once and for all. I want to get there early, get some practice time in. Then I'll need to be alone to clear my head. You're welcome to come with me, but I won't be very good company. It'll probably be better for you to go with Kelleher, hang out backstage with him and Levi, then come to the stadium to watch my match."

Maggie pondered for a few seconds, then said, "Yeah, that's what I'll do."

49

Goldbarr stared blankly at the cluster of color coded dials, knobs and switches in vivid red, blue, yellow and green, surrounding the LED screen. After a few seconds, his bewildered expression morphed into an angry scowl. He glared at Bagheri.

"What the hell am I supposed to do with this thing!?"

Bagheri had gone over the Blast-con 3 detonation procedure at least twice. He wrote the steps down and taped them to the front of the case. He couldn't believe that the person on the other side of the desk was one of the most influential men on the planet. Media mogul, corporate titan and the frontrunner in multiple polls to be the next president of the United States. Ye, as far as he could discern, the man was an idiot. Trying mightily to keep the derision out of his voice, he said, "It's the exact same device I showed you before."

"You held it up from across the room, but you never really let me look at it. Now that I'm seeing it up close, it looks like the goddamn control panel of a jumbo jet. How the hell am I supposed to do anything with that?"

"You said you wanted the gold standard. This is it."

"And you said I'd be able to operate it, no problem. I don't even know which end is up on this thing."

"It's really not that complex. There are only two controls you have to be concerned about." He pointed to a yellow toggle switch on the upper right-hand side of the panel. "This is the on-off switch. Flip it up to power up the device." Then he touched a red button just above the center screen. "And this is the Blast Initiator. Press it down and hold it for three full seconds to set off the charges, which are set to detonate simultaneously, as you instructed."

"What about all those other doodads and gizmos?"

"Don't worry about them. They're for use in different environments and situations."

"So I just turn it on and press the red button. That's it?"

Bagheri nodded. "Just make sure to keep it down for at least three seconds."

"What else do I need to know?"

"You need to be within 1,000 yards of the charges."

"Yeah, no problem. Anything else?"

"No."

"Good." Goldbarr thrust out his hand. "That's it. You're done. You can be a thousand miles away by the time the shit hits the fan."

"Yes. Now about my fee."

"Oh, of course. How much was it again, 50 million?"

"It was 65 million."

Goldbarr stared hard at the little bombmaker.

"That was when you were going to be involved from beginning to end. Since I'm doing the important part and you'll be gone, I think 50 is more than fair, don't you?" He smiled malevolently then glanced over at Herman.

The gargantuan Samoan walked over and stood behind Bagheri.

Bagheri was pissed at himself. He should have known that

Goldbarr would try to nickel-and-dime him. That was his reputation. For a short second he thought he might try to bargain, but with Herman's fetid breath on his neck, all he wanted to do was get away from these two horrible people. And 50 million dollars was still enough to establish a new identity, move to a place where no one knows him and no one can ever find him, and live like a king. Also, he'd never have to deal with egotistical assholes like Goldbarr ever again.

"All right." He handed Goldbarr a slip of paper. "If you could transfer the money to this account at the Nevis Trust Company."

"Nevis, huh?"

"Yes. Is that a problem?"

"No, that's fine. The banks there have a very good reputation. Very discrete. Very trustworthy. It's just that I've never dealt with them before."

There was a knock at the door.

"Come," Goldbarr bellowed.

Melissa, his assistant, walked in. "There are two FBI agents outside who say they want to see you immediately. What should I tell them?"

"Give me two minutes." He turned to Bagheri. "I think we're done here. Go out the back way and take the service elevator. You don't want to be here when the FBI comes in. Herman will go with you to make sure you don't get lost."

Bagheri said, "What about my fee?"

"Don't worry. I'm doing it right now. By the time you get downstairs the transaction should be completed. You can check your phone to make sure the money's there."

"Thank you." Bagheri stood and headed for the back door with Herman trailing behind him. When Bagheri was out the door, Herman turned back to Goldbarr who ran his finger across his throat.

Herman replied with a nod and a sinister smile and closed the door behind him.

As soon as they were gone, Goldbarr raced around the office inspecting the desk, the floor, the chairs and anything else that Bagheri might have touched. He even Lysoled the air to mask any residual body odor he or Herman might have left. Satisfied that there were no traces of them, he shouted into the intercom, "Okay Melissa, send them in."

A few seconds later, she ushered in a black man around forty and a woman about ten years younger. He was what Goldbarr thought an FBI agent should be. Tough but professional. Around six feet tall with broad shoulders and thick arms. Maybe played some football. He wore a navy blue blazer with a powder blue shirt open at the neck, gray slacks and black loafers. His thinning black hair was cut short, as was his goatee.

The woman looked more like a runway model or maybe an Olympic pole vaulter. Long and lean, she had olive skin and straight black hair that was cut blunt. Her gray pantsuit was belted around the waist. She wore a black shirt under it. She moved like a panther, lithely but with purpose.

Goldbarr stood. "Thank you for coming on such short notice." He extended his hand.

The older agent shook it. "No problem. I'm Special Agent Murphy and this is Special Agent Davi. How can we help you?"

Goldbarr smiled at the young woman. "Davi, is that Israeli? I have many Israeli friends."

"I'm American," she said stonily.

"I meant your nationality," he said, taken a little aback at her tone. "Where did your ancestors come from?"

"My grandparents were originally from Pakistan."

"Oh." He turned back to Murphy.

The agent said, "Your message indicated that you had some business you needed to discuss with us."

He looked from one to the other. "You know my news network, GoldenNews?"

"Yes," Murphy said.

"We have some really good investigative reporters. The best in the business." He paused for a response but none was coming. "We ran a feature on the sudden emergence of Mohammed Levi and one of the things we uncovered, besides his close ties with the Palestinians, was that most of his security team are current or former members of Hezbollah. Being that I know that the government considers Hezbollah a terrorist organization, I thought I should bring it to your attention."

Murphy nodded. "Thank you. We'll have some people look into that. Is that all?"

"No, that's just the appetizer. I could have phoned that information in. The real news I have for you will blow your mind."

Both agents eyes him skeptically. Goldbarr had a reputation for extreme exaggeration.

Murphy said, "Yes?"

"In their reporting, they came across a connection between Levi and the tennis player, Jake Marks."

"Okay?"

"I don't know if you follow tennis, but Marks disappears for weeks at a time, sometimes longer. He's very secretive about it. There were several rumors about what he does on those mysterious absences but no one knew for sure. Until now." Again Goldbarr waited for some kind of response but both agents were stonefaced. "We found out where he goes. I know you'll find this hard to believe, but Jake Marks, the tennis player, is also the notorious terrorist assassin known as the Lone Ranger."

That got their attention.

Both agents sat up in their chairs.

There were a few seconds of silence, then Murphy said, "That's a pretty strong accusation."

Agent Davi said, "Jake Marks is a well-known, world class professional athlete. One of the best American male tennis players of the last decade. I find it very hard to believe that someone of his stature has a part-time job as a global hitman."

Goldbarr nodded. "I felt the same way. I follow tennis and have met Marks a few times. I didn't think there was any way that could be true. I demanded rock solid proof. Then my reporter showed me this."

He had a laptop on his desk. He pressed a key then turned it to the agents. After a few seconds, a video close-up of Jake sitting on the bench at the Vanderbilt Tennis Center took up the entire screen. Glynn's voice, off-camera, said, "Listen, this guy needs to be eliminated, but it's a tricky operation. It needs the special talents of the Lone Ranger. Are you in or not?"

"When does this need to happen?"

"Soon, in the next two weeks."

"I'll be in London preparing for Wimbledon."

"I know. He'll be there at the same time. It's a perfect setup."

"Give me the packet."

Goldbarr closed the laptop.

Murphy said, "Where did you get this?"

"I honestly don't know. My reporter refused to divulge his source, even to me. I guess he knew what kind of a patriot I was and that I'd give the name to you in a heartbeat if I had it."

Agent Davi couldn't help but smirk.

Murphy said, "Play it one more time."

Goldbarr did.

After watching it again, Murphy said, "We'll have to verify that this is legitimate. Nowadays it's very easy to do fake videos."

"My guys checked it out and said it was the real thing. You do what you have to do but if I were you, I'd do it soon. After today, it could be a lot more difficult. Marks is playing tonight at the stadium in Flushing. Levi is giving a concert at the Unisphere, which is right next door."

"Yeah, we know all about that. Lots of important people are gonna be there. We'll have a presence."

"Good. If you get the okay, you'll have the men already there." He glanced over at Davi and said, "And women too, of course."

Murphy said, "We'll see. Can we take that laptop?"

"Sure." Goldbarr handed it to the agent.

"Thank you. We'll check this out right away."

"Always happy to help the FBI. Who knows, maybe one day I'll be your boss."

"Yes, sir. Thanks again."

Agent Davi nodded and followed Murphy out of the office.

As soon as they left, Herman came through the rear door.

"Did you hear most of that?"

Herman nodded. "Yuh."

"Any trouble with Bagheri?"

Herman shook his head.

"Where is he?"

"In the incinerator."

50

―――――

Kelleher never understood why people love going to concerts. It's noisy. It's crowded. It's loud. Most of the time the music, if you can hear it at all, isn't close to what you'd hear on a record (or CD, or MP3 or whatever the hell people listen to these days). And those big, outdoor bashes are the worst. Besides all the crap that goes with any concert, at an outdoor concert you have to deal with the weather and annoying bugs and birds shitting on your head. He'd seen the Woodstock movie and he thought it looked a lot like torture. Yet here he was, getting ready to go to what they're calling New York's biggest outdoor concert event since Simon and Garfunkel in Central Park. And that was more than forty years ago. He knew Levi thought he was doing him a big favor, giving him backstage passes and all that, but what was he supposed to do while Levi and his band were performing onstage, stand around with his thumb up his ass? He was thinking about whether to call Levi and tell him that he couldn't make it when his doorbell rang.

Who the fuck could it be? He wasn't expecting anybody. Why didn't the doorman let him know he had a visitor? Maybe the doorman had no choice. Maybe he's tied up in a closet like he did to Herman. And Vinnie was no Herman. He was short and skinny, walked with a limp and was well into his seventies.

Kelleher got his gun. He crept soundlessly to the door, yanked it open, and jumped immediately into a shooters stance.

Maggie threw her hands in the air as she backed up. "What the hell!"

Kelleher put the gun down at his side. "Maggie, what are you doing here?"

Still shaken, she said, "Should I not have come?"

"No, no, I'm always happy to see you. I'm just surprised. You always call before you come over."

"I did this time too, but no one answered. To tell you the truth, I was a little worried."

He put his hand into his pocket where he keeps his phone. It came out empty.

"Oh," he said sheepishly. "I must have put it down somewhere."

He walked back in. Maggie followed him.

She sat on a couch with big, puffy, blood red cushions that engulfed her like a big bowl of chocolate pudding. He plopped down in a lime green chair opposite her. The place was furnished sometime in the eighties. The previous owners sold all of it to Kelleher for a thousand dollars. The deal worked for everyone. They didn't want it. And as far as Kelleher was concerned, furniture was furniture.

"I thought you were going to the tennis match with Marks," he said.

"I thought so too. He doesn't play until around four o'clock, but he wanted to go there now. He said he needs to prepare physically and mentally for the match and he couldn't do it if I was with him. I didn't feel like wandering around the grounds by myself with nothing to do for six hours, so I figured I'd go with you. That's okay, isn't it?"

"Of course." After a few seconds he said, "Is everything good with you and Marks?"

"Yeah, fine," she said half-heartedly.

"You sure?"

"Really, everything's good."

Kelleher was still trying to figure out how to be a father to a grown-up daughter who never knew he existed until a couple of months ago. There were a lot of things he wanted to say to her, but he didn't want to say anything to upset her. He wasn't a guy who ever watched his words and always said what was on his mind, but this felt different. He liked having her in his life and didn't want to lose that, but he thought that what he was about to say needed to be said.

"I know I don't have a right to interfere with your life, but I do know something about guys who come home from the battlefield to try to live a normal life. It's really tough. We don't make good husbands. Or fathers. Your mother knew that. We loved each other, that's for sure, but she never believed that I could be the father you needed. I was scarred, physically and emotionally.

"Jake's the same. Except his battlefield was anywhere that Goldbarr sent him. And there was never a cease fire. He never knew when his cover might be blown, so he could never really relax. And on top of that, he was a world class tennis pro and had to deal with everything that comes with it. Living that kind of double life has got to screw up your brain, like that serial killer on the west coast who was a church deacon during the day and spent his nights murdering and torturing young girls."

Maggie jumped up. "Jake's no serial killer. He's a gentleman. Kind and considerate. Goldbarr and his people brainwashed him. They convinced him he was a special operative for the DIA. That he was a patriot doing vital work for the country. That he would get a medal if it wasn't so top secret. It wasn't until Stryker shot my mother that he realized that Goldbarr was a lying psychopath. He told them he was done. That he wouldn't do it anymore. Then they tried to kill him and use me as bait. If it weren't for you, we'd both be dead."

"You're proving my point. Anyone going through that would get messed up." He looked at her tenderly. "Listen, I don't give a shit about Jake Marks. But I care about you. And when Marks's problem becomes your problem, then it's also my problem."

"Okay, thank you. But I'm a big girl and I can take care of myself."

"All right. I said my piece. C'mon, let's go to to the concert. My car's out in front."

Maggie looked surprised. "I didn't know you had a car."

"I don't have much use for her here in the city, but it's over thirty years old and I've grown attached to her."

As they walked out of the building, Kelleher turned to the doorman. "Thanks for keeping an eye on it, Vinnie."

He smiled and saluted. "No problem, Colonel."

The car was parked in front of the building. It was a jungle beast of a car. More muscular than a Jeep, but not as bulky and unwieldy as a Hummer. The black exterior was polished to a high sheen. Imposing black bars shielded the front light and grill. The thick, nubby tires looked like they could roll over anything.

"What kind of car is that?" Maggie said, openmouthed.

"It's a Land Rover."

"Land Rovers are expensive SUV's. This looks more like a Jeep on steroids."

"This car was around before Land Rovers became status symbols for rich lawyers and bankers who want the world to think they're badass. It was my vehicle in Rwanda when I was there. It got me out of a few dicey situations and I sorta became attached to it, so I had it shipped over here."

"Are you sure this car is thirty years old? It looks brand new."

"I keep it uptown in a garage that specializes in British cars, mostly fancy Jaguars and Rolls Royces. I didn't know what they would say when I brought this baby in. But they were thrilled. They saw it as a challenge when I asked them if they could fix it up. They couldn't wait to start working on it. It was caked with jungle crap, riddled with bullets, leaking oil and blowing smoke when I brought it in. They made it look like new, inside and out. I don't use it a lot, but when I need it, they drive it down here. I told them I could go to their garage in Washington Heights and get it myself, but I think they get a kick out of driving it."

"That must have cost you a fortune. You must really love that car."

"That old girl was much more reliable than most of the men I've worked with. She's worth every penny. Besides, what else am I gonna spend my money on?"

Maggie looked around at the tacky furniture and scowled. "I can think of a few things."

He smiled. "Yeah, I bet you can. Let's go get a bite."

"They have food at the Unisphere?"

"I don't know what kind of food they have there, but I bet it cost a bundle and tastes like crap."

"The food is actually pretty good, but it is super expensive."

"I know a great diner that's on the way."

"Sounds good."

51

Jake was watching the Men's Wheelchair Finals at Louis Armstrong Stadium. He had never seen a wheelchair match and didn't know much about it, but he figured it would be a good distraction. Since he left the house a couple of hours earlier, his mind swirled with anxiety. The last thing he needed at that moment was a panic attack. He was stressing about his upcoming match with Riemer, about Goldbarr's bomb threat and about his relationship with Maggie.

He willed himself to wash the negativity out of his brain. As he watched the chairbound players whirl around the court hitting savage forehands, crisp backhands and monster smashes, he was impressed and amazed. These guys weren't 'special' athletes or disabled athletes, they were athletes. Period. They had every reason to give up on life and wallow in self-pity. Instead here they were, oozing sweat, confidence and joy, reveling in the cheers and applause of the sparse crowd, made up mostly of their friends and family, and other disabled kids and their caregivers, who came to see their heroes and dream that one day they might be out there.

At that moment, Jay realized he had no right to feel sorry

for himself. He was making a lot of money playing a game he loved. And he was with a great woman, if he hasn't already screwed that up. Sure he had baggage. Maybe more than most. He was still on Goldbarr's hit list. Riemer's thugs might still be after him. And somebody planted a bomb in his bag and will probably try again. Eugene was dead and Bunny was in the hospital, all because of him. This was his first Open without them, and he missed them. For the last few years they played an integral part of his daily routine here.

Bunny always drove him to the stadium. They would stop at the Starlite Diner on Queens Boulevard for breakfast. Jake would have his usual pre-match meal, a Greek yogurt smoothie with blueberries, walnuts, raisins and granola and a large orange juice. Bunny had tea and an English muffin, which he sneered at because he considered it neither English nor a muffin.

When he arrived at the Tennis Center he'd meet Eugene at the practice courts and they'd warm up. Afterwards, they'd talk about that day's matches and pump each other up. He never realized the difference his two friends made in his attitude and his preparation. It was a miracle that he was able to get through to the finals without them. He realized that it was his hatred for Riemer and the chance to crush him in front of thousands of people in the arena and millions on TV that propelled him.

Jake stayed until the end of the wheelchair match. He left feeling a lot better. He wished he could start his match immediately, but he still had hours to kill. He was taking a leisurely stroll around the grounds when he was surrounded by reporters who pummeled him with questions. About his supposed mental illness. About his lifelong feud with Riemer. About the fight at the Ball and Glove.

Jake threw up his hands and yelled, "All right, all right. You know I'm always happy to talk about tennis with you guys, but I've avoided all that other stuff because it has nothing to do with the game and I hoped you'd get tired of harping on it, but that hasn't happened. So I'm gonna talk about it now and that's it. Here goes."

He took a deep breath. "Along with about 40 million other Americans I suffer from panic disorder and have had panic attacks since I was a teenager. I don't take anti-anxiety meds because of how they affect my stamina and concentration. I try to control it naturally. Most of the time I can. My absences from the tour happen when I can't.

"About Tommy Riemer, I've known him since juniors. He was prone to temper tantrums even then. I thought that he'd eventually grow out of it, but it only got worse. The one and only time we faced each other as amateurs was the last straw. It seemed like every other point he'd fly into a rage and scream at me, his coach, random spectators, the pigeons flying overhead. After he slammed a ball at me when I wasn't looking, I walked off the court, even though I was way ahead. It was either that or punch him in the mouth.

"I managed to avoid him until earlier this year at Madison Square Garden. I'd been gone from the tour for awhile. I was out of shape and out of practice and played my worst match ever. When he attacked me on the Taz Pirelli Show I had no choice but to defend myself. As some of you may know, I've always been a big advocate of cross-training. Lately, I've been doing a lot of gymnastics work for balance and flexibility. I've also incorporated martial arts workouts into my regimen. You saw the results of that training at the Ball and Glove."

The reporters threw some follow-up questions at Jake. After a few more minutes, he told them the interview was over.

52

Kelleher hadn't been to Flushing Meadows in over thirty years. He had gone to a couple of Mets games at the old Shea Stadium before they tore it down, but that was in the eighties when Darryl Strawberry was belting tape-measure moon shots and Dwight Gooden was mowing down batters with 98 mph heat. He had a hazy memory of his parents taking him to the World's Fair back in 1964, but the only things he remembered from that visit were seeing a touch-tone phone for the first time and sitting in the first-ever Ford Mustang and, of course, the Unisphere.

Now more than 50 years later, the Mustang and the Unisphere are the only remnants of the fair that are still around. The Mustang's been through a lot of changes, some good, some not so good, but the Unisphere is exactly the same as when Kelleher first saw it. A massive globe that sits on three steel fingers that rise up out of a fountain.

For the concert, they drained the fountain, covered it with reinforced plywood and erected the stage on top. They set up a big tent backstage to store the instruments, electronics and everything else necessary to put on a major outdoor concert.

Two huge loudspeakers, each the size of a cargo container standing on end, were on either side of the stage.

Because it was an official New York City landmark, they needed a special permit to cover the Unisphere in lights, which were programmed to strobe during the concert and flash the words ONE WORLD, PEACE ROCKS and STOP WAR. What wasn't on the permit were the words FUCK WAR, which was secretly programmed into the computer.

As Kelleher and Maggie walked toward the Unisphere, almost every tree and lightpole had a poster of Mohammed Levi smiling fiercely. Both his arms were raised triumphantly in the air. The index and middle fingers of his right hand were extended to form the peace sign. On his left hand, only the middle finger was raised. A Star of David intertwined with a Crescent Moon floated over his head like a halo.

Emblazoned across the bottom of the poster in huge type and bold red ink was:

GIVE PEACE A CHANCE. GIVE WAR THE FINGER.
Free Concert and Rally to End War and Death in Israel,
Palestine and the World
STARRING MOHAMMED LEVI
Sunday After the U.S. Open Finals

Kelleher was surprised that they were able to walk right onto the stage without anyone from Levi's security team checking their credentials. They walked backstage and saw Levi on the phone screaming at whoever was on the other end. As soon as he saw them he ended the call and ran over to them.

"Thank God you're here. I don't know what I was going to do."

Kelleher said, "What's going on?"

"They took away my whole security team."

"Who? Who took your team?"

"ICE."

"Are you sure? Did you check their credentials?"

"Of course. But I still didn't believe it, so I called the New York field office. That's who I was talking to just now."

"What did they tell you?"

"They said they had credible information, and they had to check it out."

"Credible information, my ass. This has Goldbarr's stench all over it. Tell me exactly what happened."

"My guys had just started searching the area when they discovered a bomb. Then two federal agents showed up with a warrant that said my entire security team was on a terrorist watch list and they had to bring them in. What should we do?"

Kelleher put a hand on Levi's shoulder and spoke softly, "Nothing's gonna happen until the concert starts. That gives us plenty of time."

"What makes you so sure?"

"Goldbarr's a showman. He won't make his move until he thinks he has his maximum audience."

Levi took a deep breath, then said, "But what about the bombs? We don't know how many there are or where."

Kelleher said, "First things first. Where did they find the first one?"

Levi pointed to one of the giant loudspeakers at the side of the stage.

"There. A glob that looked like a big batch of Silly Putty was attached to the inside."

"Did it have a detonator attached to it?"

Levi nodded. "Yes."

"Okay. What did they do with it after they found it?"

"They left the stuff where it was. They said without the detonator it's harmless."

"Your guys knew what they were doing. Where's the detonator now?"

Levi pointed to a garbage can near the stage. "They threw it in there."

"First thing we gotta do is see what we're dealing with."

Maggie, who was standing quietly behind Kelleher, said. "I'll get it. What does it look like?"

"It'll be about a six-inch long cylinder, like a long lipstick case. There should be a wire coming out of it."

She ran to the garbage can and rummaged through it. Since it was still early, there were only a few soda cans and candy wrappers to sift through. She found the detonator, held it up and shouted, "Is this it?"

Kelleher said, "Yeah. Bring it over."

He held the thin cylinder close to his eyes and twirled it around.

"Okay. This is good."

Levi said, "What's good? We don't know how many bombs they planted or where they are."

"We don't need to know. This is a cell phone activated detonator. All we have to do is block it."

"How?"

"I have a jammer that'll do it."

"Do you have it with you?"

Kelleher shook his head. "No. I gotta go get it."

Maggie said, "Do you want me to come with you?"

"No. I need you here to be my eyes and ears. Look out for anything that doesn't seem right and call me. If you see Goldbarr or his stooge Herman, don't approach them. If you can, follow them and let me know where they are."

"Okay."

Levi said, "What should I do?"

"Don't do anything. Just get ready for your show like you would normally do. Goldbarr might be watching. We don't want him or any of his men to know that we know what's going on."

53

The guy behind the desk at the storage place looked like he'd be better suited guarding murderers and rapists at a maximum security prison instead of stuff that people couldn't fit in their closet. His shaved head was the color and consistency of mahogany. His arms were bigger than most people's thighs. His powder blue polo shirt stretched tightly across his shoulders. The logo on his shirt read, 'The Storage Vault.' His hard eyes and taut scowl was the only expression most people ever saw. When Kelleher walked in he looked up, and though he didn't exactly smile, the scowl softened a bit.

"Hey Colonel, it's been a minute. You doin' okay?"

"Not bad, Duke, you?"

"Yeah, good. What's this I hear about you retiring?"

"That was the plan. So far it hasn't worked out that way. That's why I'm here. Need to grab a few toys from my locker for a little job I'm doing."

"Got it." He pressed a buzzer under his desk and the steel bars behind him, which once guarded the vault of a now defunct bank, swung open. Kelleher walked through, then up a flight of stairs to a large space with row after row of corrugated steel doors. Kelleher stopped at the third door in the second row. He punched in the six-digit electronic combination and lifted the door. The room was the size of a small bathroom, eight feet long and six feet wide. On one side were stacks of wooden crates containing materiel that he accumulated over the years. In one box was an M-72 shoulder mounted rocket-propelled missile launcher, in another an M32 Multi-Shot Grenade Launcher. Other boxes contained ammunition, grenades, kevlar vests, maglights, batons, brass knuckles and night vision goggles. Small arms weapons were mounted on the back wall. Assault rifles, sniper rifles, submachine guns, shotguns and a half dozen combat knives. He grabbed a Sig Sauer P239 sub compact pistol and an ankle holster, along with a six-inch combat knife. He strapped the holster onto his lower leg and taped the knife to his forearm. He was already wearing his Glock 17 in a shoulder holster.

In another corner of the storage unit was what looked like a cross between a carry-on suitcase and a portable loudspeaker. It had wheels and a telescoping handle, plus knobs, dials and sliders. Scarred with dents, scratches, gashes and couple of bullet holes, it looked like it had been through a war. That's because it had been through three wars. The Sri Lanka Civil War, the Kosovo conflict and the Libya uprising. It was the world's most powerful signal jammer, armor plated and battle tested. It was rated to stop every cell, radio and satellite signal for a radius of more than a half-mile. It would be like throwing a huge electronic net over the Unisphere, the Tennis Center and everything around and in between. It would disable every device that sends or receives electromagnetic waves (which is what all cell phones, GPS and other wireless systems use), making it impossible for Bagheri, Goldbarr or anyone else to trigger the detonator. And if the detonator can't be triggered, the C-4 explosives, no matter where Bagheri stashed them, become as harmless as the Silly Putty they look like. Kelleher grabbed a smaller black case that housed the battery pack and antennas, and put it on top of the first one. Before he yanked down the door he stopped to make sure he had everything he needed.

It took him ten minutes to get from the Union Square storage facility to the entrance of the Midtown Tunnel. He checked his watch, 1:30. Traffic was moving pretty well. Five minutes to get through the tunnel. Maybe another twenty to get back to the Unisphere. With luck, he should be there around two, plenty of time to set up the jammer and still give Maggie enough time to watch Jake's match.

Unfortunately, Kelleher's luck was bad. Very bad. Halfway through the mile-long tunnel, a panel truck in the left lane hit the rear fender of a school bus in the right lane, inadvertently performing what the cops call a PIT maneuver, sending the bus and thirty screaming second- and third-graders skidding and spinning across both lanes, sideswiping a Toyota Prius before it skidded to a stop.

Brakes squealed, horns blared, a few bumpers nudged as traffic came to a screeching halt.

Kelleher pounded both fists on the steering wheel and screamed "Shit! Fuck! Sonuvabitch!" at the windshield. He was boxed in like the middle square of a Rubik's Cube. There were cars in front of him, in back of him and on his left. On his right was the tiled wall of the tunnel.

When the Men in Black were stuck in the same tunnel, Tommy Lee Jones told Will Smith to push the red button and their Crown Vic sprouted wings and a jet engine and they drove on the ceiling and zipped right through. But Kelleher's Land Rover didn't have that red button so he was at the mercy of the Sunday Service Crew of the Metropolitan Transit

Authority, which means he wasn't going anywhere anytime soon.

He tried to call Maggie but his phone was dead, or at least out of commission.

54

―――――――

In his early years at the Open, Jake had discovered some hidden spots at the periphery of the Tennis Center, away from the crowds and reporters, where he could be alone with his thoughts and mentally prepare for his match. When he cracked the top ten it was a lot harder to find anyplace for alone time. Now that his feud with Riemer had become big news, there was nowhere on the grounds to hide.

One of his other discoveries during his early wanderings was a pedestrian bridge that led from the back of Louis Armstrong Stadium over the Grand Central Parkway to the Queens Zoo, where there were no ardent fans or obnoxious hacks and flacks. Using all his evasive skills, he managed to get over the bridge and into the zoo without being recognized.

He spent the next couple of hours wandering around the cages, commiserating with the birds, bears and bisons and thinking about anything but his upcoming match. Mostly about Maggie and how he had been taking her for granted. And how lucky he was to have her in his life. And that if he screwed this relationship up he'd be kicking himself for a long time.

Back at Arthur Ashe Stadium, he headed to the players' lounge on the second floor. A mashup of an upscale sports bar, a five-star hotel lobby and a millionaire's man cave, the vast room had clusters of comfortable chairs and couches, walls of wide-screen TV's, even a foosball table. During most of the two-week tournament it was crowded with players, their loved ones, friends, coaches, agents and reporters. Now, almost all the players had gone home or to their next event, and the tennis press was down at Center Court covering the women's doubles final, so Jake had the room mostly to himself.

He sat down on an oversized chair, propped his legs up on an ottoman and tried to relax. He checked his phone. No message from Maggie. She was probably still pissed off at him. He called her.

As soon as she answered he said, "I'm sorry if I've been acting like a self-centered jerk lately."

"That's okay. I forgot what it's like when you're competing at a major event. I was the same way before the Olympic trials."

That went better than I expected, he thought. "Are you backstage with Kelleher?"

"I'm backstage, but Kelleher's not here."

"Really? What happened? I thought you two were coming here together."

"We did, but he had to go back."

"Back? Where? Why? What happened?"

"They took away all of Levi's security team."

"What do you mean? Who took them?"

"ICE. The agents said they were on some kind of terrorist watch list."

"That's bullshit. I'm sure they were all vetted before they entered the country."

"It doesn't matter. They're gone. Kelleher thinks Goldbarr's behind it. Levi's men had already found one bomb. They were looking for more when the agents took them away."

"Where the hell is Kelleher now? He should be trying to find the rest of the bombs."

"He said he needed some equipment that he had stashed in a locker somewhere near his condo in Gramercy Park."

"How long has he been gone?"

"It's been over two hours. He should have been back by now."

"Did you call him?"

"Yeah. A few times. It went straight to voicemail."

"That's not good. I'm coming over there."

"Absolutely not!" she yelled. "Your match starts in a little while."

"The match won't mean anything if thousands of people get blown away."

"Don't worry. Kelleher will be here. You just concentrate on beating Riemer. I'll call or text you with any news."

"Okay, but remember, once I'm on court no phones are allowed, not even during warmup. I could lose points or even be disqualified."

"What if you kept it in your bag and checked it at the changeover?"

"No. They don't want players getting any coaching instructions."

"All right. Don't worry. We'll handle it. Go kick the crap out of Riemer. Love you."

Jake's brain went into panic overdrive. Don't worry? How could he not worry? Who knows how many bombs they planted? Or where? There might be a blob of C-4 right here under the stands. Thousands of people could be killed. And thousands more at the Unisphere. Should he call off the match? Try to have the stadium evacuated? What about the concert? No, it's impossible. What would he say, that Ronald Goldbarr's a homicidal psychopath who's planning to kill thousands of people tonight? Jake's the one they'd lock up, not Goldbarr.

If he wasn't going to help Maggie, he figured he'd do some warmup exercises to help clear his head. He started with some stretches, then did some jumping jacks to get his heart rate up. He was in the middle of his second set of leg lunges when Riemer strode into the lounge followed by a gaggle of reporters. Jake walked to the other side of the room and sat on a chair facing the window, hoping Riemer hadn't noticed him.

No luck. Riemer swaggered over, followed by his press posse.

"Whatsa matter, you chickenshit cocksucker? You afraid to look me in the eye?"

A dozen phones snapped photos, others started recording or began scribbling.

Jake stood and faced his longtime enemy, hands at his sides. He abruptly lifted his right hand. Riemer immediately shuddered and jerked backward. Jake then ran his fingers through his hair and winked at the reporters.

"No, I'm not afraid of you. But it sure looks like you're afraid of something. Don't worry, the only beating I'm gonna lay on you today will be on Center Court."

"You sucker-punched me, you fucking sonuvabitch. You could never take me in a fair fight."

"If you really want to fight fair, why'd you pay those goons to take me out?"

"You're crazy," Riemer screamed. "I don't know what the hell you're talking about."

"Don't lie, Tommy. One of them ratted you out. They put my friend Bunny in the hospital. Cracked a few ribs, but that turned out to be a lucky break. The doctors found an aneurysm on his chest x-ray, scheduled him for surgery and saved his life. So I guess I really should thank you."

"Fuck you Marks. I'm gonna kick your ass on the court, then I'm gonna kick your ass on the street." He stormed out of the lounge.

FIFTH SET

55

Barney Bobbins' Finals Preview

Fasten your seatbelts, fuzzy ball fanatics.

It's not often that dreams come true, but in a few short minutes the matchup that tennis fans have been dreaming about will begin. The pugnacious, pugilistic Tommy Riemer versus his arch enemy, Jake Marks, the Nureyev of the net. Speaking of pugilism, this will be the classic brawler versus boxer confrontation. Riemer's bludgeoning baseline blasts versus the shotmaking majesty and surgical precision of Marks's all-court brilliance.

The seething hate simmering between these two is palpable. They've been taking verbal jabs at each other for many years with ever increasing vitriol. But a few weeks ago, those jabs evolved from verbal to violent. I'm sure most of you have seen the footage of the confrontation at the Ball and Glove sports bar, but suffice to say that Marks more than made up for the drubbing he received from Riemer at Madison Square Garden earlier this year, literally kicking Riemer's behind out of the bar.

This mythical matchup was very close to being quashed on a number of occasions throughout the fortnight. Riemer was hardly in jeopardy until he entered semifinal round, winning all his preceding contests in straight sets. Of course he still had his dustups with officials and his gang of grizzly followers disrupted play a number of times, but that is to be expected anytime time the Screamer takes the court. His semifinal with fourth seed Carlton Chu, the pride of Taipei, is where things really got out of hand.

Deadlocked at a set apiece with each player breaking serve just once, Riemer was serving at five-six to take the contest into a tiebreaker. Ahead 40-15, he served a wide angle slice for a clean ace but was called for a foot-fault, at which point the boisterous brat from Bay Ridge lost his mind. Cursing at the top of his lungs, stomping around the court like the Mad Bull of the Pampas and bashing his racquet into court hard enough to dent the deco-turf and turn his Babolat into bubble gum. Hideki Fukiama, the chair umpire, assessed him a point penalty for verbal and racquet abuse. This only served to heighten Riemer's rage. He accused Fukiama of cheating for his fellow Commie Chink, notwithstanding the fact that the umpire is of Japanese descent and grew up in Miami, and Chu is from anti-Communist Taiwan. For his bigoted outburst he was given a game penalty, which cost him the third set and a warning that another such display would result in his forfeiture of the match.

Riemer then stormed to the locker room for his allotted bathroom break. When he returned five minutes later, he had not only changed his clothes, he changed his demeanor. He reentered the court calm, composed and laser-focused. Chu, on the other hand, seemed unnerved by the altercation and hiatus, spending the time seated on his chair, fiddling with his racquet and exchanging puzzled looks with his team.

Riemer immediately broke the world number four at love, then proceeded to ride roughshod over him, prevailing 6-2, 6-3 in the next two sets to win the match. He refused to shake hands with either Chu or Fukiama. When asked, in the post-game interview, if he thought Chu was affected by all the hubbub, he smirked, placed his fingers at the corners of his eyes in a crass racist gesture and replied, 'Confucius say, 'You cheat, you get beat.' which got him another warning from the tournament referee.

For Marks, of course, it wasn't his decorum that was the issue, it was his play. His usual on-court elegance looked shopworn after his year-long absence from Grand Slam competition. His first match, facing a qualifier, went to four sets. In the second contest, it looked for all the world that Marks would face an early exit, falling behind two sets to love and looking thoroughly outclassed by the 44th ranked Danish baseliner, Lasse Karlsen. Then, suddenly, as if emerging from a trance, he found his former championship form. With effortless power, pinpoint precision and balletic movement, he dominated the next three sets, winning at three, four and two.

His next three matches were immaculate, never losing serve and facing only two break points. In his semifinal, he faced world number two, Manny Reyes, the Chilean Cheetah. There wasn't much to choose between these two grandmasters. After two sets, both ending in tiebreakers, they were tied at one each. Set three looked like it was headed for another deadlock when Reyes strained his hamstring after sliding awkwardly at the end of a full-out sprint to the backhand alley. He gamely finished the set but grimaced after every shot and could barely walk, much less run. With tears cascading down his cheek, he informed the Chair that he couldn't continue. Marks immediately ran over and embraced his worthy opponent and insisted on helping him to the locker room.

Which brings us to this afternoon's championship. Both players appear to be in top form. If Riemer wins, he will vault from his number six ranking to number two. For Marks, who at one time was one of the masters of the tennis universe, but due to injuries and unrevealed personal issues, left the tour for an extended period of time, plunging his ranking into the triple digits, a victory today would silence his critics, squelch the myriad rumors of the reasons for his mysterious disappearances and place him back at the top tier of the tennis firmament.

56

The area around the Unisphere was usually one of the quieter spots in Flushing Meadows Park, but not today. Today it was a mashup of a county fair, an anti-war demonstration and a Grateful Dead pre-show freakfest. The air was fragrant with the commingled aromas of hundreds of food carts offering pretzels, hot dogs, falafels, shish kabobs, Jamaican beef patties, egg rolls, pralines, doughnuts, ice cream, beer, coffee, soda, still and sparkling water of various flavors, mangoes, peaches, brownies and six different varieties of chocolate chip cookies.

Vendors worked the crowd, selling everything from FUCK WAR t-shirts to fake Rolexes and comic book versions of the Koran and the Old and New Testaments. Policemen on foot, bicycle and horseback mingled with Boomers, Millennials and Gen X, Y and Z-ers. Young and old anti-war activists were holding signs, wearing buttons and handing out flyers about peace initiatives in the Middle East, South Asia, Eastern Europe and Sub-Saharan Africa. Hippies, hipsters, beatniks, goths and freaks imbibed, inhaled or ingested a pharmacological cornucopia.

Young Arabs and Israelis stood near the front of the stage,

talking, laughing, holding hands. It was a scene that would make their parents and grandparents blanch. Wannabe influencers from dozens of social media sites and podcasts wandered through the crowd, searching for someone other than each other to talk to.

Meanwhile, Maggie was on anxiety overload. She checked her phone for about the hundredth time. No calls. No texts. No Kelleher. It was less than a half-hour drive back to Gramercy Park. It should have taken him less than an hour to get whatever he needed and drive back. He's been gone for more than three hours. Something's definitely wrong. Either Goldbarr's men have him or he's laying unconscious in a hospital bed somewhere or he's dead. If it was anything else, he would have called.

She felt helpless and inept standing all alone backstage doing nothing while hundreds of people could be blown to bits any minute. Maybe she should she search the bombs herself. But even if she found one, she didn't know how to disarm it. She tried to think of what else she could do but came up empty.

Her phone rang. She didn't recognize the number.

"Hello?" she said warily.

"It's Kelleher."

"Oh my God, are you all right?" she shrieked. "I've been worried sick. What happened? I thought you were dead."

"I'm fine."

"Where are you now?"

"I'm in the Midtown Tunnel. There was a huge accident and nobody's moving. I tried to call a half-dozen times but I couldn't get any service."

"How are you calling now?"

"I was sitting in my car trying to figure out what the hell to do when I looked around and saw people in other cars talking on their phones. Turns out some phones work in the tunnel, just not the piece of crap I got. I gave some guy twenty bucks to borrow his phone for five minutes."

"When do you think you'll get here?"

"Hard to say. There are cops and EMTs running around trying to figure out what to do."

Maggie looked around at all the people on the grounds.

"It's already very crowded here. Suppose Goldbarr triggers the bombs before you can set up the jammer."

"Not gonna happen. Goldbarr's a showman and an egotist. Everything he does is about getting himself in the spotlight. Right now every camera is covering your boyfriend's tennis match. When it's over, they'll move over to the concert. That's when he'll strike."

"What do you want me to do?"

"Tell Marks to stall the match. Nothing's gonna happen while he's playing."

"Stall the match? How?"

"He's the hotshot tennis pro. He'll figure it out."

"But..."

"Something's going on here. I gotta go."

"Stall the match!? It's not a freaking video game. You can't just hit pause at the U.S. Open finals," she yelled at the phone after Kelleher hung up.

She tried calling Jake but it went straight to voicemail.

"FUCK!" she screamed.

She glared at the phone in her hand like it was blame. She tossed it on the table in frustration and began pacing back and forth.

"I can't just stand here going crazy," she said out loud, even though there was nobody else there. Then she ran out the back of the tent and headed toward the Tennis Center, hoping she could somehow get to Jake before he started his match. She didn't know if she could reach him in time or if he could stall the match if she did, but she had to try.

The concourse between the Unisphere and Arthur Ashe Stadium was only a couple of blocks long. When she got to the main entrance, she realized that she left her phone and her handbag in the backstage tent. Her Friends Box pass was in the bag, along with her license and wallet. She didn't have time to run back and get it. Her only hope was to try to talk her way in.

The guy at the entrance stood ramrod straight with his arms at his side and a stern look on his face. All he needed was a big fuzzy hat and he could be one of the guards at Buckingham Palace.

"Ticket please."

"I'm Maggie Quinlan, Jake Marks's trainer," she said as ingratiatingly as possible. "I've been here for every match. I'm sure you've seen me here before. Can you believe it, I left my bag in the car and my Friends Box pass was in it."

He smirked. "Sorry."

"You don't understand," she said emphatically. "It's really important that I speak to Jake before the match starts. It's a matter of life and death. I'm not exaggerating."

He shook his head and stood silently in front of her.

"This is ridiculous," she screamed. "Who the hell do you think you are, you arrogant sonuvabitch!"

A small crowd began to gather to see what all the commotion was about.

Finally a stocky woman in her thirties walked over. She wore a blue uniform. STADIUM SECURITY was stitched above her left shirt pocket. A name tag over the right pocket said PILKINGTON.

She stared at the guard. "What's going on here?"

"She says she's Jake Marks's trainer, but she doesn't have a ticket."

Maggie strained to read the name tag. "Don't you remember me, Ms. Pilkington? Maggie Quinlan. Could you tell this bozo to let me through? It's really, really important."

The woman looked her over, nodded and said, "It's alright, I've seen her here before. She's in Marks's party."

The guard smirked and stepped aside as Maggie ran past him. She got to the Friends Box just as Jake was walking out of the tunnel. She started jumping up and down, waving her hands and yelling Jake's name as loud as she could. Unfortunately, 24,000 tennis fans were standing, cheering, clapping and yelling too.

Jake's pre-match routine was to close his eyes, put a towel over his head and visualize how he wanted to play the first few points. Miraculously, he cut short his meditation, looked up at his box and saw Maggie. She motioned frantically, waving her hands for him to come over, but he just smiled at her, waved back and blew her a kiss.

"Ughhh!" she screamed.

She decided to try one last desperate attempt. She ran down to the barrier, climbed over and jumped onto the court with several ushers chasing her. She ran over to a startled Jake who was grabbing a racquet from his bag. She threw her arms around hm and whispered, "Kelleher's stuck in traffic. You have to stall. Bombs are still loaded. When he disables them, I'll let you know."

Bewildered, Jake said, "What? When?"

Before she could explain, a burly policewoman, with shoulders a linebacker would be proud of and heavily inked arms from her thick wrists to her formidable biceps, rushed over, grabbed Maggie's arm and dragged her off the court and into the tunnel. The crowd applauded. Maggie didn't know if they were cheering her or the lady cop.

When they came to the exit, the policewoman said, "You're a little too old for that kind of nonsense, lady. We expect crap like that from some teenager who had a little too much beer, not from a grown woman."

"I know. I'm really sorry, officer. But I can explain. I'm Jake's fiancé. I give him a good luck kiss before every match. It's our tradition. But I got here late. I couldn't risk him having bad luck in the biggest match of his life."

"I don't care who you are or what your tradition is. It was a stupid and dangerous thing to do. We won't press charges this time. But if you do it again, you're going to jail."

Maggie said, "Thank you officer, Believe me, it'll never happen again."

57

———

"Fuck! Shit!" Maggie screamed. "Kelleher, where the hell are you?"

Levi smiled and said, "Don't worry. He'll be here soon. And as for the match, there's still plenty of time for Jake to come back and win."

Maggie shook her head in frustration. "Not if he keeps playing like this."

She and Levi were backstage watching Jake's match on a laptop.

The image on the screen cut from center court to the two men in the booth calling the match.

"Three sets have been played," Barney Bobbins said. "Riemer leads Marks two sets to one." They cut to the scoreboard. 3-6, 7-6, 6-4. "Not quite the fireworks we expected, but a surprisingly riveting contest all the same. What say you, G.B.?"

"I don't know how many tennis fans remember the famous Rumble in the Jungle between Muhammad Ali and George Foreman back in the seventies, but it sure looks like Marks took a page out of the Greatest's playbook, using the rope-a-dope to throw off Riemer's rhythm and timing."

Gil Bradford was a former top ten player who was acknowledged to be one of the best tennis analysts in the business. His colorful banter blended well with Bobbins' erudite commentary.

"Marks's M.O. had always been to win points with his supersonic serve, viper volley or fearsome forehand. Not today. Standing way back behind the baseline he's daring Riemer to hit it by him, taunting him like a matador toying with an enraged bull. Marks twisted the dagger by milking every second on the serve clock, dawdling on the changeovers and calling for the trainer to examine his wrist for an injury that no one saw happen. All this bigtime infuriated Tommy Tantrum, who plays every match like his shorts are on fire."

"It looked to all the world like Marks's unorthodox strategy was working to perfection when he took the first set 6-3," Bobbins said. "But Riemer emerged for the second set with a new game plan, summoning up patience and discipline that I didn't think he possessed. He curtailed his own pace, throwing in an assortment of moonballs and dropshots at Marks and wound up beating him at his own game, winning the second set in a tiebreaker and breaking serve after a half-dozen deuces at the end of the third for a two sets to one lead. I don't know how much longer Marks can keep up his slogging strategy."

"You're right Cal. Marks hasn't been back on the tour for that long and he hasn't gone past three sets against a top pro in over a year. Right now, things look pretty bleak for Gentleman Jake."

"Is anybody here?" Kelleher's voice boomed from outside the tent.

Maggie and Levi ran out onto the stage where Kelleher was standing with the jammer.

"Jesus," she said. "I was beginning to worry that you'd never get here."

Levi said, "What happened?"

"A truck hit a school bus in the middle of the Midtown Tunnel. Knocked it spread-eagle across both lanes. There were about twenty-five kids in it and each one had to be examined by paramedics before they could even start to figure out how to get the bus out. First, the police had to clear a path so the ambulance could get in. A few of the kids had to go to the hospital, so they had to call more ambulances. Then they had to figure out a way to turn the bus around before the tow trucks could start to hook them up. When we finally got out of the tunnel, the L.I.E. was stop and go for miles."

Levi said, "The important thing is you're here now." He pointed to the jammer. "Is the thing that stops the bombs inside that suitcase?"

"The suitcase is the jammer." Kelleher opened the case. "It's good for over a half-mile in every direction. It covers every frequency Goldbarr might try. I've used it in Eastern Europe, the Middle East and South America. It's never failed. Once I turn this badass baby on, every mobile phone, satellite phone, remote control, walkie talkie, TV, radio or baby monitor will be useless."

Maggie said, "Are you sure it will work? When was the last time you used it?"

"It'll work. I'd bet my life on it"

"You're betting all our lives on it."

"It'll only take me a few minutes to set it up. Then you can test it yourself."

"How?"

"You got a phone. Try to make a call or send a text."

It didn't take Kelleher long to have the jammer up and running backstage.

"Okay, it's on."

When Maggie checked her screen it read 'No Service.' Then, as she looked around, people all over the the park were staring quizzically at their phones.

"I guess it works," she said.

After a few seconds, a look of horror spread across her face.

"Oh my God, Jake's match," she cried.

Kelleher said, "What about it?"

"He's been stalling. And he's losing. I gotta go tell him he can play all out."

Kelleher shook his head "Bad idea. It's too dangerous. Goldbarr's stooge Herman knows what you look like. I'm sure he's lurking here someplace. If he sees you walking around, he'd liable to do anything. One swat from him will put you in the hospital."

"You don't get a vote. We worked too hard to blow it now because I couldn't get a message to him."

"How are you supposed to do that? You can't use your phone and you told me they threw you out."

"I don't know. I'll think of something."

"I still don't like it."

"Too bad."

She ran out of the tent and headed back towards Arthur Ashe Stadium.

58

———————

Hundreds of fans were crowded in front of the Stadium entrance, looking up at a gigantic video screen that was livestreaming the finals. Riemer was leading 2-1 in the fourth set with Jake serving at 5-30. Maggie pushed and squeezed through the throng, generating more than a few dirty looks and one elbow in the ribs. When she finally got to the front, she froze. Standing at the entrance, arms crossed in front of her, glaring stonily at the crowd, was the policewoman who dragged her out of the stadium, looking surlier than ever, like nurse Ratched's meaner, uglier, musclebound sister.

Maggie had two choices. She could try to talk the bitchcop from hell into letting her through, which had about as much chance as talking the Pope into becoming Jewish. Or she could find some other way into the stadium. Going back to the Unisphere would mean handing that asshole Riemer the U.S. Open finals trophy on a platter. That wasn't an option.

With the main entrance blocked, she started walking around the stadium looking for another way in. She found a couple of emergency exit doors but when she tried them, they were locked.

She was at the far end of the stadium when she saw that the loading dock back there was still in use. A parade of maintenance workers were carting big black garbage bags out of the stadium on heavy-duty trollies. She approached a guy who was heaving bags into a dumpster as sweat poured down his face.

"Excuse me," she said as she thrust her phone at his face. "I'm Betsy Houlihan. I'm a reporter at *Tennis Journal*. I'm doing a story about the real unsung heroes of the Open. The hard-working people in the trenches who make this tournament the great event that it is. The ushers, the vendors, the maintenance staff. I know you people are on a tight schedule, but would you mind talking to me for a few minutes?"

"Sorry, lady, I ain't got the time. You wanna talk to somebody, try my chief."

It was the answer she was hoping for.

"Your supervisor? Do you think he'd talk to me?"

He shrugged.

"Where is he?"

He motioned at the open door. "In there."

"Thanks," she yelled as she headed inside.

She ran down a long, dingy corridor until she found the service elevator. She took it to the Courtside level and ran toward the VIP entrance. Now all she had to do is figure out how to get a message to Jake. She went to the Friends Box gate hoping the guards and ushers there now hadn't witnessed her getting thrown out. No such luck. As soon as she walked in, the guard moved in front of her and said, "Sorry, miss."

She checked the scoreboard. Jake was losing 3-2, down a break. She wasn't sure he could turn it around and get to a fifth set even if she could somehow find a way to talk to him.

Back in the corridor she saw two policemen walking towards her. She didn't know if they were summoned to escort her out of the building and she didn't want to find out. Before they could reach her, she ducked into the ladies' room.

A girl, about sixteen, stood in front of the mirror, brushing her hair. She was wearing the distinctive blue, green and orange uniform of the U.S. Open ball crew.

"Hi there," Maggie said. "You're a ball girl, right?"

She turned and smiled. "Yes."

"I think I've seen you this week. I'm Maggie Quinlan, Jake Marks's trainer. I've been in the Friend's Box for all his matches." She frowned. "Except today."

"I know. I saw what happened at the beginning of the match. I thought it was pretty cool what you did."

"Really? Thanks. I just wanted to give him an extra kiss for luck, but I think it rattled him, seeing me get thrown out like that. I've been watching the match from outside the stadium on the big screen and he looks like he's off his game."

"Yeah, I noticed that too."

"Will you be back on the court?"

"Uh huh. I'll go back out on the next changeover."

"I wonder if you can do me a huge favor if it won't get you into trouble."

"Sure, if I can."

Maggie took a pen and a piece of paper and wrote, 'All good. Play your A-game and kick Riemer's ass. M.'

She handed the note to the ball girl. "If you could find some way to get this to Jake, I'd really appreciate it. And I'm sure he would too."

The girl folded the note and stuck it in her waistband. "I'll try." Then she blushed a little. "We're not supposed to play favorites, but I'm rooting for Jake, too."

"Thank you so much. What's your name?"

"Jessie, Jessie Laskey."

"Jessie, you're a lifesaver." Maggie gave her a quick hug.

She went back outside and joined the mob watching the match on the giant screen. The players changed sides at 4-3. All Riemer had to do was hold his serve two more times and he'd be the U.S. Open champion. Jake sat dejectedly as a ball girl brought him a fresh towel. Was it Jessie? Did she give him the note along with the towel? No way to tell.

Jake draped the towel over his head. When he emerged, his body language had done a one-eighty. He jumped up, grabbed his racquet and sprinted to the baseline to receive serve, a huge smile on his face.

Jake's A-game was back. Hitting impossible angles, attacking the net, mixing feathery slices and deft dropshots with forceful topspin drives. Riemer seemed flummoxed at Jake's sudden change of tactics and lost his serve at love. Though the set was tied at four apiece, all the momentum was now on Jake's side. He held serve easily and broke Riemer again to win 6-4. The match was now dead even at two sets apiece. The winner of the next set would be the U.S. Open champion.

With the break between sets, the crowd outside began to disperse. To get food, take a bathroom break or just to stretch their legs.

Maggie felt the tensions of the past few months waft away from her body as she started walking back to the Unisphere. The bombs were neutralized. Goldbarr would be exposed for the madman that he is. Jake was on his way to winning the Open.

Then she felt someone grab her arm and yank it behind her back, sending stabbing pain shivering through her shoulder.

Maggie turned and stared up at Herman's grotesque glare.

59

It wasn't the most important day in Becky Johnson's life. That was the day her husband Sam asked her to marry him. But it was definitely the most important day of her career. She'd been the Artistic Director of the Big Apple Parks Summer Concert Series for less than two months and suddenly she was responsible for the biggest concert event in a New York City park since Simon and Garfunkle's epic performance on the green lawn at Central Park in the early eighties.

And it was all going wrong.

It started with federal agents swooping in and arresting Mohammed Levi's entire security team and all his roadies. After that, things went smoothly for awhile. The vendors all showed up on time. The park never looked better. The grass was mowed. The trees were trimmed. And all the trash was gone. The temperature was in the low 70's and the humidity was bearable, which is as good as it gets in late summer in New York City. There was already a huge crowd and everyone seemed to be enjoying themselves, even though the concert wouldn't start for several hours.

Then, out of the blue, every phone, laptop and tablet went dead. Worse yet, it happened while she was on the phone with Matt Van Vyck, the chair of the NYC Parks Foundation, the parent organization of the Summer Concert Series. Also her boss. The boss who went out on a huge limb to hire her for this job. She was his executive assistant for three years. When the position for Concert Director opened up, she begged him to give her a chance. It was her dream job. She was a theater major at Barnard College with a minor in business. There were a few candidates with more impressive resumes, but she had worked closely with the previous director. Matt told her she had the hands-on experience and know-how to do the job and to navigate the New York City municipal bureaucracy. He was confident that she'd be terrific. And until today, she was. She had put together two concerts in Prospect Park in Brooklyn, a reggae performance and a do-wop revue that went without a hitch. But those were small shows with local artists. Today's performance was a major event with an international superstar and extensive media coverage.

It was also the first one Matt would be attending, along with the parks commissioner, the mayor, both New York senators and dozens of other bigwigs. A major screwup would probably cost her her job and maybe his too. That's why when every phone suddenly went dark and everyone around her began staring blankly at their devices, she stormed up to the stage in a panic.

Levi smiled amiably. "Ms. Johnson, how nice to see you again. How are you on this fine day?"

"I was great until about ten minutes ago when my phone, and everyone else's, went dead. What's going on?"

"I'm sorry," he said sheepishly, "I should have told you. It was on my list but with all the preparations and the loss of my security team and most of my tech crew, it somehow slipped through the cracks."

"I understand. But what about the phones?"

"Someone had figured out how to hack into our sound system and broadcast ear-splitting feedback through our speakers. We don't know if it's done by those who don't like our message of peace or some kids simply out to create mischief. We thought it might be some of those ransom thieves, but no one has asked for money so far. For smaller shows we go on unplugged. But for this kind of performance, where loudspeakers are a must, we use a signal jammer. It's very effective in stopping these sonic attacks. Unfortunately, it also disables mobile phone and some other transmissions. I know it's inconvenient, but I promise you, it's much better than subjecting all these people to a series of horrendous squeals and screeches."

"I see," she said, the tension oozing out of her body. "I just wish I knew about this before. We could have put something in the program about turning off phones."

"All I can say is mea culpa. You don't think it will ruin the concert, do you?"

"No, of course not. We don't want people on their phones during the concert anyway. And their cameras will still work, right."

"Absolutely."

"Do you think you can make an announcement to let everyone know what's happening?"

"Yes, of course."

"Okay. No harm done. I have to go give my boss an update. Good luck with the show."

She put out her hand for Levi to shake but he gave her a hug instead. She hurried off the stage.

Kelleher, who was standing off to the side, walked over to Levi. "That was a pretty good bullshit story."

Levi grinned. "When you're on the watchlist of the Palestinian Security Service, the Mossad, the CIA, the Russians and the Iranians, you have to be able to make up a good bullshit story at a moment's notice or else you wind up behind bars. Or dead."

60

"You're hurting my arm," Maggie said through gritted teeth.

Herman snarled. "Scream and I break it."

It took all of her willpower not to wince or gasp or cry. She didn't want to give him the satisfaction.

"What do you want?"

"Goldbarr wants you."

"Why?"

"Shut up," he said and jerked her arm hard as he started dragging her back toward the Unisphere.

She didn't allow herself to yelp, even though the pain in her shoulder was like an electric charge.

"All right, I'll go with you. Just ease up, please."

He loosened his grip slightly.

"Thanks."

They walked towards the Unisphere, but they didn't go straight. After only a few yards, they veered left onto a circular path. There were people all around, sitting on lawn chairs and lying on blankets. Some were even perched on tree branches.

They stopped in front of a bronze statue of a muscle bound adonis holding a warped pole with stars spiraling around it.

"What's with the statue? I thought we were going to see Goldbarr." Maggie said.

Herman didn't answer. He tightened his grip and dragged her over to an old guy sitting on one of the park benches opposite the cosmic pole vaulter. He looked like a hippie Rip Van Winkle who went to sleep in the sixties and just woke up. He had beads hanging from his turkey neck with a wig of long greasy black hair, a psychedelic headband and a long, fake black beard. He wore a purple dashiki with matching bell bottoms and Birkenstocks with black socks.

As they got closer to him, Maggie realized that underneath the ridiculous regalia was Ronald Goldbarr. She didn't know if it was fear, stress or a sudden bout of manic hysteria, but she began laughing hysterically.

"I'm sorry to tell you this, Mr. Goldbarr, but you're about fifty years too late for Woodstock."

Goldbarr's face contorted with rage. He stood almost nose-to-nose with her and bellowed, "How dare you laugh at me, you little cunt. Nobody laughs at Goldbarr."

Herman clamped his paw around her arm. "Do you want me to shut her up for good?"

"She's been nothing but fucking trouble. I was gonna wait until she got hers onstage with Levi and Kelleher, but I changed my mind. Yeah. Find someplace quiet and do it. Once the bombs go off, nobody will notice one extra body."

Before Herman could drag her away, she yelled, "How do you know we didn't find all the bombs and disable them?"

"Nice try, bitch. I know where they're located. I've been monitoring them all day." He held up a pair of binoculars. "No one's been anywhere near them except for the one that Levi's men found before I had them arrested."

"Your bombs are useless. We disabled them."

"I gotta give you credit, you don't give up. I like feisty

women, but I don't like pains in the ass. And you're a huge one." He turned to Herman. "Get rid of her."

Maggie yelled, "I'm not bluffing. Kelleher set up a phone jammer. Your phone won't work, and without it, you can't detonate the bombs. Don't believe me? Try it."

Goldbarr stared at his phone. The screen read: 'No Service." He banged on the keys but nothing happened. He restarted it. Same result. He let out a loud, guttural growl and said, "Bring the little bitch back here. Get some of those zip ties out of the bag." He gestured towards a tote bag with some kind of Mexican design on the ground near him. "Tie her to the end of the bench. If she tries to yell or scream, belt her. We'll wait until the concert is about to start, then we'll pay Kelleher a visit. We'll see how much he really loves his newfound daughter."

61

———

The chair umpire shouted, "New balls, please."

Jessie Laskey ran out onto the court and handed Jake three bright yellow tennis balls and whispered, "Good luck."

Riemer was ahead 5-4 in the fifth set. Jake had to hold his serve to stay in the match. He looked across the net at Riemer, whose narrow pig eyes looked even smaller. His ever-present sneer was, if possible, even more obnoxious.

Jake bounced the ball a few times, tossed it high in the air, then blasted it out of the sky for an ace down the middle that caught Riemer so flatfooted he didn't even move his racquet.

The crowd cheered. The umpire called, "Mr. Marks leads 15-love."

Jake pumped his fist in the air and moved over to the ad court. He hit another blistering serve that caught the center line. Riemer was able to get his racquet on it but hit it weakly into the middle of the net. Thirty-love.

Jake sliced his next serve wide to Riemer's forehand. He lunged for it and flicked a crosscourt return that looked like it would find an opening. Jake sprinted forward. When he saw the ball angling for the sideline, he abruptly changed directions, executed a split that James Brown would have been proud of, and scooped the ball over the net for a half-volley drop-shot winner.

Now it was Riemer's turn to be frustrated. He screamed an undecipherable expletive and slammed his racquet into the ground. The chair umpire calmly said, "Penalty point, Mr. Riemer, abuse of equipment. Game to Mr. Marks. The score is Five-all."

"What!" Riemer screamed. "This is the fifth set of the U.S. Open finals. You can't do that."

"You were warned, Mr. Riemer, more than once. Another outburst like that will cost you a game."

Riemer snarled and stormed back to the service line. Still seething, he slammed his first serve six inches long. He short-armed the second ball into the net for a double-fault and fell behind Love-15.

The rest of that game seesawed back and forth until, after two advantages for Riemer, it was ad-out. Jake was a point away from a service break and a chance to serve for the championship. Riemer hit a hard slice that bore into Jake's body. He managed to pirouette out of the way and block the ball back, imparting heavy sidespin, which produced a dying quail of a return that barely made it over the net. All Riemer could do was push a soft, high-arcing floater. Jake sprinted forward. He was only five feet from his hated rival. Each player glared into the other's eyes. As the ball reached shoulder level, Jake faked a crosscourt volley. Riemer darted to his right. Jake stepped back, let the ball bounce then stroked it into the open court. Riemer contorted trying to change direction, lost his footing and fell onto the court.

Wild applause poured out for Jake along with a smattering of derisive jeers for Riemer. Someone in the upper seats shouted, "Get up, ya little prick." The stadium cheered.

"Quiet please," the umpire called out as the players toweled off and switched ends. "Mr. Marks to serve. He leads the fifth set six games to five."

All Jake had to do was win four more points and he would be the U.S. Open champion. The match was closing in on five hours. He was running on fumes and adrenaline. Riemer, though more match tested, also seemed to be tiring. He went for broke on every shot and although he hit a couple of amazing winners, he made several unforced errors.

The chair umpire announced, "Mr. Marks leads 40-30."

The crowd, which had been raucous throughout the match, was eerily quiet, waiting for Jake to win the point, the game and the Championship.

He took two deep breaths, bounced the ball five times and served wide, flat, and hard to Riemer's backhand. Jake streaked to the net, anticipating a down-the-line return, but Riemer hit it crosscourt. Jake changed direction in mid-stride and dove headlong at the ball angling away from him. His arm fully extended, he managed to flick a weak volley that plinked off the top of his racquet and somehow cleared the net as he hit the ground hard, landing on his wrist, the same wrist he sprained in London. A shiver of pain shot up his arm.

Riemer, at full gallop, reached the ball at his shoetops and whipped a deep crosscourt forehand towards the baseline. From Jake's angle, it was impossible to tell if it was in or out.

"Out," the lineswoman cried as her arm shot towards the back of the court.

Thank God it's over, Jake said in a silent prayer. His wrist was swelling and the pain was excruciating. He thought it might be broken. He wasn't sure he could hold a racquet, much less continue playing.

Riemer ran at the umpire's chair, his arms flailing wildly. "Challenge!" he screamed. "That ball wasn't even close to being out."

"Mr. Riemer challenges the call," the umpire said calmly.

All eyes shifted to the giant video display on the scoreboard. A graphic materialized on the screen with the words "Official Review" outlined in white inside a black rectangular box at the top. A yellow facsimile of a tennis ball entered the picture, arcing in slow-motion towards the white baseline etched on the green background. It left a pixilated vapor trail in its wake as the oval silhouette barely but definitively touched the line. A blue rectangle at the bottom of the screen announced, "Call: In."

Riemer grinned, pumped his fist in triumph and strutted back to the baseline.

"Deuce," the umpire announced.

Jake's wrist throbbed as he tried to serve. He lobbed the ball a foot over the service line, grimacing in pain on the follow-through.

Sensing the kill, Riemer took two steps inside the baseline to receive the second ball, daring Jake to hit it past him. His eyes were wide with anticipation, his lips curled in the ever-present snarl.

Instead of serving, Jake put his racquet down and jogged over to the umpire's chair. "I need an injury timeout," he said, holding his wrist.

"Injury timeout, Mr. Marks," the umpire announced. Both players went to their seats. Two minutes later the trainer came jogging out with her medical bag.

She sprayed his wrist with lidocaine, numbing it, then taped it tightly. Jake took a big gulp of his energy drink, washing down six pain pills.

About ten feet away, on the other side of the net post, Riemer was spewing a steady stream of invective just out of the umpire's earshot.

"You're not hurt, you fucking faggot. You're just afraid to lose. You gonna quit on me again, you chicken-shit scumbag?"

Three minutes later, his wrist heavily bandaged, Jake walked back to the service line.

He decided to try to end the point quickly and used his first-serve motion and blasted a hard, flat serve that hit the tape, then trickled back down on his side of the net like a tear on a spurned lover's cheek.

He hit his next serve at half-speed and backpedaled to receive the return, hoping for an unforced error. Seeing his hobbled foe well back behind the baseline, Riemer hit a feathery drop shot. Jake's competitive fire overcame his pain. He charged forward, stretched, and pushed a floater that bounced on the service line. Conceding the point, Jake dropped his hands and his racquet to his side and stood at the net as Riemer closed in for the easy put-away. Instead of stroking the ball into the wide open court, Riemer slammed it at Jake's head. Jake reacted just quickly enough to take a glancing blow to his cheek.

The stadium resounded with a loud chorus of boos, jeers and catcalls.

"Quiet please," the umpire admonished. "The score of the fifth set is six-six. There will be a seven-point tiebreaker. Mr. Riemer to serve first."

After ten minutes, which included a couple of injury time-outs and visits from the trainer, Riemer was ahead 6-0, a point away from victory. Jake would need to win eight points in a row to win the match, a huge task anytime, but after more than four grueling hours of high intensity tennis and a bum wrist, it was near impossible. But Jake faced impossible odds before and beat them.

As they passed each other to change ends, Riemer spat in Jake's face. Either the umpire didn't see it or he was too shocked to do anything, because there was no response from the chair.

Jake tensed, balled his fists and was about to jump Riemer when from inside his head his coach's voice shouted, "Stop!

That's what he wants. Channel your anger to your game." Jake stood motionless for several seconds, shaking with rage. He took several deep breaths, grabbed a towel off his chair, wiped his face and walked deliberately to the other end of the court. Riemer stood a couple of feet inside the baseline hoping to swat an emphatic winner to end the match with a flourish. The combination of rage, adrenaline and painkillers eased the pain in Jake's wrist just enough. He reared back and slammed a 142 mile-an-hour serve that nearly knocked the racquet out of Riemer's hand.

The umpire announced, "Serve to Mr. Riemer, he leads six to one."

Riemer leered across the net at Jake, slowly shaking his head. He sliced a serve to Jake's forehand and followed it leisurely into net. Jake rifled a bullet down the line that Riemer waved at helplessly. After missing long on his next serve, Riemer spun his second ball to Jake's backhand, which he ripped crosscourt for an easy winner.

"Mr. Marks to serve. Mr. Riemer leads six to three."

Jake powered a hard serve into Riemer's body and punched the weak return into the open court to win another point.

Six-four.

Jake's next serve skidded as it clipped the center line bouncing harmlessly off the side of Riemer's racquet.

"The score is six-five, Mr. Riemer's service."

The sneer was gone, a wide-eyed gaze of panic in its place. Losing the U.S. Open final after leading 6-0 in a fifth set tiebreak would be a stain that could never be erased. He would be branded as the ultimate choker.

Jake bounced on his toes waiting to return serve. Riemer hit it as hard as he could, hoping to end the match with one final swing. It sailed long by several inches. Trying to catch Jake before he was ready, Riemer immediately began his service motion, but the ball caromed off the tape and landed just outside the service box for a double-fault.

"The score is six-six, Mr. Riemer still serving. Change ends, please," the umpire announced.

There was no salivary salutation from Riemer this time as he shuffled to the other side of the court.

Spooked by his previous double-fault, Riemer hit a three-quarter-speed kick serve high to Jake's backhand. Jake's cross-court blast sent Riemer scurrying far into the alley to make a weak return which Jake put away. He was now a point away from the title.

"Mr. Marks to serve. He leads seven-six."

Jake bounced the ball four times, two inside the baseline, two outside. He glanced up at Riemer, who was hopping all over the court, trying not to give him a target. Jake uncorked a hard, twisting serve that bore into Riemer's body, handcuffing him. As Jake closed in on the net, Riemer's only play was to try to lob it over his head. He hit it high but short. As Jake positioned himself under the ball, it looked like a big yellow balloon floating down in slow motion. Suddenly it morphed into Riemer's face, then Stryker's, then Goldbarr's. Jake leaped in the air and smashed it as hard as he could, bellowing an ear-splitting scream. The ball slammed into the tape on top of the net with the sound of a bullwhip crack. It balanced itself at the edge of the tape, undecided about which way to fall. Riemer, who had been backpedaling furiously in anticipation of the smash, slammed on the brakes and charged full speed towards the net. As the ball toppled over on his side, he dove for it, desperately trying to get one last swipe. The ball dribbled impotently off his outstretched racquet frame. Jake thrust his arms in the air in triumph while Riemer lay prostrate on the other side of the net, his head inches from Jake's feet, his arms outstretched at his sides like a fallen Jesus.

Hundreds of cameras clicked. It was the picture that

adorned the sports pages of most of the world's major newspapers the next day, as well as the covers of *Tennis* magazine and *Sports Illustrated*.

"Game, set, match, and U.S. Open Championship to Mr. Jake Marks," the umpire's voice boomed through the loudspeakers. Arthur Ashe Stadium erupted in thunderous applause. Jake turned, pressed his palms together and bowed to the four corners of the stadium. As he looked up, he saw two men standing guard at every exit out of the stadium, including the tunnel to the Players' dressing room. They wore black vests with "FBI" emblazoned across the front in large white block letters. And they were all staring at him. Of course, when you just won the U.S. Open, all eyes in the stadium are on you. But these weren't the worshipful gazes of adoring fans, they were the icy glares of hunters stalking their prey. He imagined that they planned to wait until the presentation was over, then quietly take him into custody.

Riemer, true to his boorish reputation, went straight to his bench without acknowledging Jake, the umpire or the fans. He draped a towel over his head, which did little to muffle his steady stream of bellowed profanities.

Riemer's Rowdies had pushed their way down from the top of the stadium to the front row and were chucking empty cans, plastic bottles and various other projectiles onto the court. Security guards and New York City police converged on the black-clad punks.

The ground crew was setting up a platform on center court where the upcoming awards ceremony would happen. Oblivious to the chaos in the stands and the debris around them, they finished in a few minutes.

Barney Bobbins, who would be emceeing the presentation, ushered Jake and Riemer onto the platform next to a trio of tennis bigwigs, the tournament director, the chair of the tennis association and the CEO of Chase Bank, a major sponsor of the tournament. The sterling silver trophies for the winner and runner-up, which looked like a big serving platter and a jumbo soup tureen, were on a small blue table at the front of the platform.

While the tournament director was at the microphone, thanking the officials, the ball boys and ball girls, the sponsors, the players and the wonderful New York tennis fans, Jake leaned over and whispered in Riemer's ear. "Who's the faggot now, faggot? Now everyone in the world knows you're a punk-ass piece of shit choke artist."

"Shut up, you son of a bitch," Riemer hissed. "Shut up or I'll shove that fucking trophy up your ass."

"Try and make me shut up you gutless prick. I kicked your ass on local TV, if you want me to do it again for the whole world to see, take your shot."

"I'll kill you, you fucking bastard!" Riemer screamed.

He leaped at Jake, knocking over the trophies and the table they was sitting on. The tennis dignitaries scurried off the platform as both men wrestled around on the floor, then toppled onto the court below.

Riemer took a wild swing which Jake easily blocked. Then, protecting his wrist, he slammed Riemer's head with a vicious elbow strike. With blood streaming from his mouth, Riemer glowered at Jake and rasped, "I shoulda told those guys to kill you when I had the chance."

Jake, enraged, delivered a knee to his hated rival's groin, then followed it with a ferocious head-butt. Riemer collapsed, unconscious, to the ground.

Riemer's Rowdies swarmed the court to defend their hero. Security guards and police rushed to confront them. Ushers, ball boys, reporters, food vendors and fans stampeded for the exits.

Center court was enveloped in a full scale riot with dozens of combatants punching, pinching, kicking, gouging, biting and ripping clothes off each other in an insane frenzy. Cameras, racquets, phones, stanchions and anything grabbable became weapons. The FBI agents abandoned their posts and ran to Center Court to help try to restore order.

The ground was littered with U.S. Open programs, posters and magazines, as well as hats and jackets lost in the melee. Jake grabbed an Event Staff vest, a Mets baseball cap and a pair of sunglasses off the floor and managed to weave his way through the brawling mob to an unguarded exit.

62

———————

This is Barney Bobbins, tennis analyst turned war correspondent, reporting from the wreckage of center court at Arthur Ashe, now Arthur's Ashes, Stadium. Jake Marks's stunning comeback from a 0-6 deficit in the final set tiebreaker to win his first U.S. Open Championship, a feat that would be headline news on any normal day, is relegated to an afterthought.

The tragic, shameful and horrific riot that took place here an hour ago has thankfully come to an end. But the stain on American tennis that it left in its wake may never be eradicated. A dozen people have been taken to the hospital, including Tommy Riemer, the culprit who initiated this monumental free-for-all. Many more, including yours truly, sustained minor cuts, bruises and other assorted injuries. But everyone who was present here today and the millions of tennis lovers worldwide who witnessed this reprehensible event will be scarred by what they saw. It was an abomination!

Of course, this glorious sport will go on. Blame will be adjudicated, penalties and punishments will be administered and changes will be instituted.

There are still many questions yet to be answered. Why were Riemer's hooligans allowed on the court? What did Jake Marks say to

Tommy Riemer that caused him to explode? Why were a cadre of FBI agents patrolling the stadium grounds? And the most vexing of all. Where is Jake Marks? He has been neither seen nor heard from since the melee, almost as if he vanished into thin air in the midst of the maelstrom.

63

———————

The blare of sirens reverberated over the Unisphere.

"What the hell is going on over there?" an agitated Mohammed Levi said to Kelleher, who was standing at the rear of the stage watching Levi and his band try to rehearse.

Kelleher shrugged.

"Could they have set off a bomb?"

Kelleher shook his head. "Something's happening, but it's not a bomb. We would have heard the explosion."

"I hate not knowing. Can't you turn off that jammer for just a few minutes? Goldbarr or whoever planted those bombs won't know. It won't take long to check the phone."

"Don't you think I'm dying to know? Maggie's somewhere over there. I don't know if she's safe. I don't know where Goldbarr is or what he's doing. And until I do, I don't want to risk him triggering the bombs and killing hundreds of people. Do you?"

"No, I guess not," Levi said sheepishly. "But I'm going crazy, not knowing when we can start the show or even if we can. I need to do something. We can't even rehearse now with all this noise. I'm going to see our audio man. We have fifty speakers all around the park."

He walked through the flap to the backstage tent. Kelleher followed. Harold Raines, a tall, husky black man who bore a passing resemblance to Clarance Clemons, Bruce Springsteen's legendary horn player, was the only one back there. He was standing in front of a huge console that looked like a combination of a fancy electric organ, an x-ray machine and the controls of the Starship Enterprise, with dials, buttons, knobs, sliders and screens.

"Everything good, Harold?"

"Couldn't be better," he said in a British accent.

"Just be sure to be careful with the faders. Remember in Queensland, when we were in a big park like this, you pushed them to the max and we got that godawful 130 decibel feedback. Here we have twice as many speakers. Don't want to deafen our fans. It's bad for business."

"Not to worry," Raines said.

Kelleher glanced over at the jammer tucked away in a corner. All the indicator lights were green.

He turned to Levi. "You hear that?"

"What? I don't hear anything."

"That's right. It's quiet. Whatever all that commotion was about, it's over."

"It's not over yet," Goldbarr bellowed as he walked into the tent. "But it will be soon."

Kelleher grabbed his gun and leveled it at Goldbarr. Before he could say anything, Herman lumbered in, dragging Maggie with him. He had his huge gun pressed against her side.

Goldbarr sneered at Kelleher. "Put that down or my man Herman will blow your daughter's brains all over this tent."

Kelleher knelt down and gently placed the gun on the ground.

"While you're down there, take off the one by your ankle and put it next to the other one."

Kelleher did as he was told.

Goldbarr pointed to the mixing console. "Is that the the signal jammer?"

Kelleher hesitated for a second, then said, "Yeah."

"Turn it off."

"Don't do it," Maggie screamed. "He's gonna kill us all anyway."

Kelleher didn't move. "She has a point. Once I power down, what's to stop you from killing us? Unless you have a death wish, you won't detonate the bombs until you're out of range. You'd have to kill me to make sure I don't turn it back on."

"Maybe I'll have Herman shoot you now and turn it off myself."

Kelleher smirked. "Look at this thing. It's a complicated piece of high tech equipment. You can't just turn it on and off like a radio. That cannon that Herman has, it's a Glock 40. It sounds like a bomb blast when it goes off. You shoot us and the cops'll be here before you're close to figuring out how to shut it down."

Goldbarr thought for a few seconds. "You're right. So here's what's gonna happen. Herman is gonna break every one of your precious daughter's fingers. Then her arms. And he'll keep going until every bone in her pretty little body is broken. Or she can die quickly and painlessly."

Kelleher shook his head slowly.

Goldbarr looked over at Herman. "Give me the gun. I'll keep him covered while you get to work on the girl."

Herman handed the gun to Goldbarr, who said, "Last chance, Kelleher. Shut it down or Maggie will suffer."

"All right, you win. Tell your pet gorilla to lay off."

Kelleher walked over to the mixing console. He grabbed hold of the controls and pushed them all the way up. An ear-splitting squeal reverberated through the tent. Everyone instinctively covered their ears, including Herman, who let go of Maggie.

"Everyone get the hell out of here," Kelleher screamed.

Maggie, Raines and Levi ran out of the tent.

Herman, mad with rage, charged at Kelleher. Kelleher grabbed the knife taped to his arm and, like a matador, stepped away and gashed the razor sharp blade deep into Herman's side. The huge man-ape, blood oozing from under his ribs, grabbed Kelleher by the throat and squeezed. A gasping Kelleher plunged the knife into Herman's neck. Herman let go and staggered to the ground as blood gushed from his severed carotid artery.

A flustered, quivering Goldbarr fired wildly at Kelleher, putting a hole in the back of the tent. As Kelleher dove to grab his pistol, Goldbarr ran out, clutching the big Glock with both hands. Kelleher checked Herman for a pulse. Nothing.

64

An hour later, New York's two United States senators, the mayor, the police commissioner, the Queens borough president, the head of the New York FBI Office and Mohammed Levi huddled at the front of the stage. Standing just below, chewing nervously on a thumbnail, was Becky Johnson, straining to hear what was being said.

Levi faced the assembled politicians. "There are still thousands of people out there who've been waiting a long time. If you send them home now, they'll be very unhappy."

Nobody said anything for several seconds. The mayor glared at the police commissioner, who cleared his throat and said, "I'm sorry, Mr. Levi, but I think we have to cancel the concert. We already found three bombs, suppose there are more. I can't take that responsibility."

"I can." New York's junior senator stepped forward. "There are no more bombs. The bomb squad, along with explosive sniffing dogs, have combed every inch of this place. This is a peace demonstration as well as a performance. If you cancel now, you're doing exactly what the bastards who planted those bombs want. Let us have our concert."

The mayor scowled and said, "If we allow this to continue and something bad happens, it's on you."

She nodded. "That's fine."

A few minutes later, Mohammed Levi grabbed the microphone and said, "The authorities wanted to cancel." There was a collective groan followed by a chorus of boos. "But the Senator here," he gestured towards her, "wouldn't let them." A great cheer echoed through the audience. "For those of you who don't know, there was a bomb planted here tonight," a smattering of gasps punctuated the crowd's raucous murmur. "It has been disarmed and we are all safe, thanks to the brave men, women and canines of the New York City Bomb Squad. And especially to the man standing beside me. We all owe Jim Kelleher more than our thanks, we owe him our lives."

Levi put his arm around Kelleher.

Everyone stood and cheered. Kelleher waved awkwardly to the crowd.

Levi gestured at the dignitaries at the back of the stage.

"The people here with me tonight: the mayor, both New York senators, a few congressmen and other politicians, they'll be happy to tell you why they're so passionate about working for peace in the Middle East and everywhere else." Levi paused. "They're all full of shit." Thirty thousand people laughed, then cheered. "It's the politicians who created this mess. And if we ever want to have real peace, we have to throw the politicians out. All of them. Israeli, Palestinian, American, Arab, European, Muslim, Christian, Jew. All of them!"

"I have Palestinian blood and Israeli blood. It's the same blood," he yelled into the mic. "The Palestinian people and Israeli people both have dreams for their children: health, happiness, opportunity, freedom. They're the same dreams. Palestinians and Israelis come from the same place, eat the same foods, even worship the same God, the God of Abraham. Yet, thanks to the politicians, they hate each other. And trust me, the mullahs, the rabbis and the priests are all politicians, and nothing but politicians. At one time, in the very distant past, they dedicated themselves to serving God. Now all they care about is preserving their own power.

"We must stop the religion of holy hatred. Mohammed, Moses and Jesus would throw up if they saw the horrors perpetrated in their name. And these horrors will continue unless we make them stop. Not by force, but by friendship. Not with hatred, but with humanity. Not with bullets and bombs, but with kindness, forgiveness and understanding. We really can defeat the politicians. And we can conquer war. We can kick war in the ass and send it running back into its hole like the rat it is. War lives on fear, hate, and mistrust. On bigotry, jealousy and an endless cycle of grievance and retribution. If we take those away, war will choke on its own bile and die. Let's give peace a chance and give war the finger."

He thrust both middle fingers into the air and screamed, "Fuck War."

The audience broke into frenzied applause, as Levi yelled "Fuck War" into the mic over and over. A few people took up the chant, then more and more joined and soon thousands of people were shouting "Fuck War" over and over and over. Up on the Unisphere, FUCK WAR in pulsating halogen lights emblazoned the night sky.

While the crowd was in a frenzy of anti-war primal screaming, no one noticed an overage hippie walking furtively towards the stage. It was Ronald Goldbarr. He had Herman's gun and he was pointing it at Levi.

Startled, the singer backed away. Still holding the mic, he said, "Who are you, and what do you want?"

The crowd hushed.

Goldbarr grabbed the wig off his head and hurled it at Levi.

"You know damn well who I am. And what I want is to tell these people the truth about you."

"You want to tell the truth? That would be a first." Levi paused for a few seconds. "For those of you who don't recognize him, this man is Ronald Goldbarr, hate-based media mogul, fascist power broker and a declared candidate for President of the United States."

He turned to Goldbarr. "All right. Let's hear your version of the truth. If you even know what the truth is. You've been lying for years. About your wealth. About your past. About the size of the crowds you draw. Now, here's the crowd of your dreams."

Goldbarr lumbered onto the stage. He glared at the half-dozen policemen who surrounded the stage. "Back off or I'll shoot this sonuvabitch right now."

They looked over at the police commissioner, who nodded. They lowered their guns and stepped back.

Levi handed Goldbarr the microphone and walked over to where Kelleher was standing.

"All right, Mr. Goldbarr, say what you came here to say."

Goldbarr clutched the mic in one hand while the gun dangled at his side in the other. He tried to look calm, but his eyes betrayed the inner psycho. His hand shook with rage.

"This man, Levi, is a terrorist and a criminal. He's an agent of Iran, China, Isis and Al Qaeda. He wants to destroy America and impose worldwide Sharia law. And all of you are complicit in his treachery."

The audience greeted this pronouncement with an ear-splitting array of catcalls, jeers and boos.

"Look at you. Drug addicts, drunkards and degenerates. Spoiled weaklings. Brain-dead idiots who can't see your world crumbling all around you. Giving you morons the vote was the first step towards America's destruction. Democracy, puh." He made a loud spitting noise. "Democracy is government of the stupid, by the stupid, for the stupid."

Levi said, "Thank you, Mr. Goldbarr, for that very enlightening discussion of your world view. Hitler, Stalin and

Mussolini would all be proud. Now, you've said your piece. Put down your weapon and leave us in peace."

Goldbarr screamed, "I won't let a punk like you destroy everything I've worked to build."

Holding the mic in one hand, he leveled the gun at Levi with the other.

65

———

Goldbarr's arm wobbled as he fired the heavy gun, sending his first shot harmlessly into the air.

He threw the microphone to the floor in frustration, steadied the gun with both hands and walked toward Levi until he was just a few steps away. Just as Goldbarr fired, Kelleher pushed Levi aside, knocking him to the floor. The bullet burned itself into Kelleher's side.

Goldbarr stood over Levi, who said, "You don't have to do this."

Goldbarr's face contorted with rage. "Oh yes, I do. I'll see you in hell, you sonuvabitch."

Before he could squeeze the trigger, a shot rang out. Goldbarr's eye morphed into a bloody hole, contorting his face into a grotesque death mask as he crumpled to the ground like an unstrung marionette.

A tall figure in a hoodie and sweatpants, wearing dark glasses, a baseball cap and a red bandana across his face stood at the other end of the stage holding a pistol. As the police charged the stage, he fired two shots over their heads and ran into the backstage tent.

The crowd went into hysterics. Gasping, crying, praying, screaming, hugging total strangers, then running helter-skelter in every direction.

Most of the police officers checked on Levi, Goldbarr and Kelleher. A couple chased after the shooter. Within two minutes, paramedics were on the scene. They walked Kelleher, who refused a stretcher or a wheelchair, to a waiting ambulance. They examined Levi, who was sore from being thrown to the ground but had no other injuries, and verified that Goldbarr was dead.

Fifteen minutes later, after a quick meeting with the mayor and police commissioner, Levi announced that the concert was cancelled. There were loud groans from the diehards who remained.

The stage, now a crime scene, was crowded with law enforcement types. Detectives interviewed Maggie, Levi, his bandmates and crew. Officers fanned out across the park to get statements from potential witnesses. Crime scene investigators collected evidence, fingerprints and blood spatter. The chief medical examiner arrived in a big white van. He performed a quick examination, then had his technicians take Goldbarr's body back to his office.

The fact that the police commissioner and the mayor were sitting in the front row observing everything they did jacked up everyone's tension.

After being interviewed by a New York City detective, Maggie was approached by a woman, around thirty, with long, silky black hair wearing a charcoal gray business suit. Her light brown skin was flawless and her makeup was perfect. She introduced herself as FBI Special Agent Anika Halder.

"I don't understand," Maggie said. "I've already spoken to the detectives about what happened."

"I'm here to talk to you about your relationship with Jake Marks."

Maggie bristled. "What has that got to do with anything?"

Agent Halder checked her notes. "You're his fitness trainer, is that correct?"

"Yes."

"And you're also romantically involved with him."

Maggie scowled at the agent. "I'm not answering any more questions until you tell me why my love life is any business of the FBI."

"We received credible evidence that Jake Marks is the terrorist known as the Lone Ranger."

"You are out of your mind!" Maggie screamed. "If you know who I am, then you know that my mother was killed by the Lone Ranger. Do you think I'd be with the person who murdered her?"

"You have no knowledge of Marks being involved in any sort of terrorist activity?"

"No, of course not. Jake's a world-class tennis pro. The U.S. Open champion. He's also a gentleman. I can't believe you're wasting your time trying to connect him with the Long Ranger. Maybe if you people did your job my mother would still be alive."

Two plainclothes police approached, escorting a prisoner in handcuffs. His head was down. A gray hoodie obscured his face.

"We got him, ma'am," one of them said. "He was by the tennis stadium."

Jake shrugged off the hoodie. "Maggie!" he cried.

She ran to him. "My God. I've been so worried about you. Are you okay?"

"I'm fine. What about you?"

Before she could answer, agent Halder said, "Jake Marks, we have reason to believe..."

"Stop!" came a shout from offstage.

A tall and slender woman in a gray suit and white shirt

walked briskly toward them. It was Cassandra Curtis, the FBI special agent in charge of the Joint Terrorism Task Force. She looked more like a news anchor or corporate CFO than the highest-ranking African-American woman in the history of the FBI New York Field Office.

"Mr. Marks," she said, "you are free to go after you've been debriefed. And on a personal note, let me congratulate you on winning the U.S. Open Championship." She extended her hand.

He tentatively shook it and mumbled, "Thank you."

Agent Halder looked dumbfounded at her boss. "But Ma'am, I don't understand. We had specific instructions..."

"I just received superseding instructions. Our agents found the man who shot Ronald Goldbarr hiding back there." She pointed to the backstage tent. "He was killed in a firefight. He was tentatively identified as the Lone Ranger. His body is already on its way to the Medical Examiner's office. The associate director and the police commissioner feel that there's no need to cause Mr. Marks and his thousands of fans any more unnecessary angst or embarrassment. Ronald Goldbarr was the Lone Ranger's final victim, and the world is well rid of both of them." She turned to Jake. Her expression was stern, but her eye had an ever-so-slight twinkle. "Wouldn't you agree, Mr. Marks?"

Jake stared at her in stunned disbelief. "Uh...yes, of course. Absolutely."

Maggie ran over and threw her arms around him. "Thank God you're all right." She turned to Agent Curtis. "Can we go home now?"

"I'm sorry. Mr. Marks still needs to come with us."

A mob of reporters appeared near the stage shouting questions at Jake and the agents.

Curtis turned to the reporters and yelled above the din. "Please people." They quieted a little. "There's still more police business to be attended to. Afterwards, there will be a press conference at One Police Plaza."

The reporters quickly scattered.

Jake turned to Agent Curtis. "Does Maggie need to come downtown too?"

"No. We already have her statement."

"Maggie, why don't you go home."

"No. I want to be with you."

"It's really not necessary. I have no idea how long this will take. It could be several more hours." He glanced over at Curtis, who was noncommittal. Then back to Maggie. "If you're there with me, it'll be one more thing for me to worry about. You going home and getting some rest would be the best thing for both of us."

"You really want me to go?"

He nodded.

"Okay." She started walking off the stage.

"I love you," Jake said to her back.

66

———————

One Police Plaza, a big, ugly box of a building, was the command center of the New York City Police Department. Located in New York's Civic Center, which in addition to being the headquarters of America's largest police force, was home to half-a-dozen federal and local courthouses, the Southern District U.S. Attorney's headquarters, a federal prison and more lawyers per square foot than anywhere else on earth.

Jake made the half-hour drive from Flushing Meadows in a black Ford Explorer with a couple of detectives he hadn't seen before. One sat in the back seat next to him. The other drove.

"What's going on?" he asked.

The detective sitting next to him shrugged. "Don't know."

He was a husky, fortyish Hispanic guy, dressed in what they call business casual, a blue polo shirt, tan pants and and blue running shoes. His thinning hair was jet black.

The driver, a couple of years younger, and a couple of pounds lighter, said, "They told us to take you downtown and make sure you were comfortable. You comfortable?"

"I'm fine."

"Good."

That was it. Nobody said anything else for the rest of the ride.

When they arrived, a gaggle of reporters was waiting at the front entrance, shouting questions at Jake as he exited the car. A tall, slender African American woman flashed a wallet at him with her credentials.

"Mr. Marks, come with me."

As she hustled him into the building, she shouted at the reporters, "Go to Bloomberg Hall on the first floor. You'll have all your questions answered shortly."

As the door shut behind them, she turned to Jake.

"I'm Michaela Malone, public affairs officer for the Joint Counterterrorism Task Force."

She extended her hand.

He grasped it and said, "Can you tell me what's going on?"

"Not here."

She took him to a room on the fourth floor. It was furnished like a lounge in a boutique hotel with a wood floor, a round cherrywood table with four chairs around it and colorful paintings of New York street scenes on the walls.

Jake looked around the room. There were no mirrors. No cameras or mics that he could see. Of course they might be hidden, but why would the police need to hide recording devices in an interrogation room?

"Would you like something to eat or drink?" Malone said.

Jake hadn't eaten since breakfast, but his appetite was shot.

"Just some water."

"Sure. I'll be right back."

Two minutes later, she returned with a large bottle of Evian and some plastic drinking glasses. Cassandra Curtis walked in behind her. She sat down facing Jake. Malone sat next to her.

He said, "Are all your interrogation rooms this fancy?"

Malone said, "This isn't an interrogation room. It's the Public Affairs conference room. In about ten minutes, we'll go down to the auditorium. The mayor will address the media. The press will probably want to talk to you, too."

"I don't understand. There's a press room at Arthur Ashe. Why couldn't we do it there?"

Malone looked over at Curtis, who said, "This isn't about the U.S. Open. This is about the bomb threat at the concert and the deaths of Goldbarr and the Lone Ranger."

Jake didn't know what Maggie, Levi or Kelleher told the investigators and he didn't want to contradict anything they might have said, so he stayed silent.

"We've had our eye on Ronald Goldbarr for a long time," Curtis said. "We know he's behind several murders of prominent political figures, as well as other seditious acts."

"If you knew all this, why didn't you arrest him?"

"Knowing and proving are two different things. He's a celebrity and a politician who is very popular with a certain segment of the population. He's also very cagy about making sure that there's no direct link between him and any of the incidents that we know he's responsible for.

"Before we arrest him, our case would have to be air tight and even then, many people wouldn't believe it. His getting shot on national TV saved us a lot of trouble. We want to stay ahead of the situation before the social media conspiracy machine has a chance to set the agenda."

"Okay, but what does that have to do with me?"

"We also know that the Lone Ranger was working for Goldbarr. We looked at several possible suspects. One was Mohammed Levi."

"That's crazy. He spent his whole life fighting for peace."

"The perfect cover. He traveled all around the world and had access to places most other people don't. And who'd suspect a peace activist of being an assassin?"

Jake shook his head. "I still don't think Levi could be the Lone Ranger."

"Neither do we. He was in Israel when a confirmed Lone Ranger hit happened in Mexico. We do have one very strong candidate."

"Really? Who?"

She leaned forward.

"I'm looking at him."

67

Jake recoiled as if Agent Curtis just kicked him in the nuts. His brain and stomach were both convulsing. His mouth gaped open, but no words came out.

She put her phone on the table and tapped it.

A voice recorder played:

Mr. Goldbarr.

You've got some fucking nerve calling here after the way you screwed up today.

Don't worry. This is the last time you'll hear from me. The Lone Ranger has fired his last silver bullet.

What? What are you saying?

I'm done. I won't do this anymore.

What the hell are you talking about?!

We were supposed to be the good guys, fighting for freedom. What did you call it, a public-private partnership, doing the dirty work that has to be done that the feds can't or won't do? Now I realize it was all bullshit.

Calm down. If you're upset about that Quinlan bitch, don't be. I'm glad you killed her, even though it was a mistake. She was a loudmouth, left-wing, anti-American pain in the ass.

I didn't kill her. I fired four times and they all hit Townsend.

Curtis stopped the recording and looked at Jake with a self-satisfied grin.

"Does that voice admitting to killing Russell Townsend sound familiar?"

Jake slumped in his chair. "Are you going to arrest me?"

"For what? We never got around to doing a voice print analysis and now there's no need to waste our time on it. The Lone Ranger's dead. His body's on a slab in the medical examiner's office."

"I don't understand."

Curtis turned to Malone. "Can you get us some more water. I'm suddenly feeling parched."

"Yes, ma'am."

After she left, Curtis looked intently at Jake.

"What you are about to hear was never said. Understood?"

He nodded.

"A huge number of people around the country idolized Ronald Goldbarr, worshipped him like some modern day Jesus. Another large group are big fans of Jake Marks. And I'm sure that group will get a lot bigger now that you've won the U.S. Open. It seems very clear to us that whoever the Lone Ranger was, he wasn't some blood-thirsty terrorist, he was a patriotic American convinced he was working on behalf of the U.S. Government and when he realized he wasn't, he quit.

"Proving that whoever was the Lone Ranger is guilty of murder would be difficult under those circumstances. Proving one of America's most popular athletes is guilty would be much harder. And it would significantly undermine the credibility of the Justice Department and many others in Washington. Do you understand what I'm saying?"

"Yes. I think so."

"Do you have any questions?"

"Just one. The dead guy backstage weighed well over 300

pounds. The guy who shot Goldbarr was half that size. Suppose someone checks?"

"There are a lot of stiffs in the coroner's office. I'm sure we could find one that fits the general description. And, every once in awhile, a body mistakenly gets cremated prematurely. Anything else?"

"I don't think so."

Curtis hit a few keys on her phone and Michaela Malone came back into the room and sat down next to her.

Curtis said, "There are a lot of unanswered questions about what happened at the U.S. Open Finals awards ceremony and where you disappeared to. We think it best that you answer those questions here and now and put an end to the speculation that's already spreading on social media. Let's start with the riot at Arthur Ashe. How did that happen?"

If Jake's brain was spinning before, it was now in a cyclonic vortex. He fought to clear his head and remain in the moment. He took a deep breath.

"I was sitting at the podium waiting for the awards presentation to begin. I looked over at Riemer and flashed on the way he's been badmouthing me. I don't usually trash talk, but I couldn't help myself. I said, 'Who's the loser now?' He went berserk. He started screaming curses and then he attacked me. Next thing I knew, all hell broke loose. A couple of dozen of his crazy, drunken hooligan fans stormed the court. They were yelling, 'Get Marks.' I was afraid for my life. I really thought those maniacs were gonna kill me. Then other people joined in. Cops, officials, security guards, fans. People were screaming, thrashing around, hitting each other. It was a barroom brawl on steroids. In the confusion, I was able to get Riemer off me and crawl away. I grabbed a baseball cap and a hoodie that were laying on the ground. I used them as a half-assed disguise and managed to sneak away. I headed for the exit and kept going. I didn't know where to go or what to do. I had just played the most important match of my life and then gotten into the middle of a crazy free-for-all. I was exhausted, dehydrated and aching all over. I wandered around aimlessly on the streets outside the Tennis Center. I'm not sure how long, I was in a daze. Then I saw a church. I went inside. I don't even know what kind of church it was, but I said a little 'Thank you' prayer for finding a place where I could sit, recover and collect my thoughts. I stayed there for awhile. When I started to feel like myself again, I headed back to the stadium."

"Why did you go back there?"

"All my stuff was still in my locker. My wallet, my phone, my clothes. I had no money and no idea what happened after I left. I got my stuff and was walking out of the stadium when those agents grabbed me and dragged me over to the Unisphere."

Curtis nodded. "Good. Tell it just like that. I especially like the church bit."

Malone stood, glancing at her watch. "Time to go. The press conference starts in a few minutes."

They took an elevator to the first floor. Bloomberg Hall was the size of a high school auditorium. There was a stage in front and facing it were fifteen rows of seats in three sections. The center rows were filled with reporters from the *New York Times*, *Washington Post*, the major network and cable TV stations, and the New York City tabloids. Also sportscasters and commentators from ESPN, Fox Sports, *Sports Illustrated* and other tennis magazines, blogs, newsletters and podcasts.

Standing in the aisles near the stage were cameramen and videographers, jostling each other for position. Scattered in the rear seats and the side sections were people that Jake recognized from the tennis world. Agents, coaches, sponsors and some diehard fans. Natasha Ferris was among them. When their eyes met, she gave him a thumbs-up.

The mayor stood in front of a microphone in the center of the stage. On either side of him were the NYPD Deputy

Commissioner of Counterterrorism and Cassandra Curtis representing the FBI. Standing in back of them were a half-dozen law enforcement and tennis officials.

Malone positioned Jake next to Agent Curtis. Then she walked up to the microphone. She stood silently for a few seconds while the buzz of the crowd quieted down.

"Thank you all for your patience. It's been a very long, eventful and some would say crazy day."

Then she introduced everyone onstage, said that there would be some brief remarks by the mayor and then the floor would be open for questions.

The mayor said he was proud of the way the NYPD and FBI worked together to prevent a disaster that could have been another 911. He praised the bomb squad and all the officers who kept what could have been an extremely volatile and dangerous situation under control. Then he said that the FBI and NYPD were investigating the circumstances that led to Ronald Goldbarr's death, and he would say more about that when he had all the facts.

Malone stepped forward.

"For those of you who don't know her, Cassandra Curtis is the FBI Special Agent in Charge of the Joint Terrorism Task Force. She will answer any questions about the thwarted terrorist attack and the shooting of Ronald Goldbarr."

Curtis took the mic. She pointed to a woman in the front row.

"Molly Schultz, *New York Times*. Do we know who planted the bombs?"

"Our examination of the bombs that we recovered has just begun. But we have a good idea about who the bombmaker is. I won't mention his name until we are sure."

"Elizabeth Kordiss, *New York Post*. Ms. Curtis, can you confirm that the person who shot Ronald Goldbarr was the Lone Ranger and is he still at large?"

"We have forensic verification that the shooter was in fact the Lone Ranger. I can also report that after a confrontation with our agents, he was shot and killed."

Another reporter shouted, "Who was he?"

"We haven't established his identity as of yet. We're in the process of doing fingerprint and DNA analysis in coordination with our friends at Interpol and other law enforcement agencies. As soon as we have a positive I.D. we'll announce it. What I can say is that all the rumors about the Lone Ranger's identity were wrong." She pointed to a woman in the second row. "Next question."

"Roberta Wong, *CNN*. Why did Ronald Goldbarr want to kill Mohammed Levi?"

"We were wondering about that, too. A preliminary report from the medical examiner indicates that Mr. Goldbarr had a large brain tumor. These tumors have been known to produce hallucinations and psychotic episodes."

Before Malone could call on anyone else, Taz Pirelli stood and shouted. "Hey Jake Marks. What the heck happened at the awards ceremony and what happened to you afterwards?"

Jake glanced over at Curtis, who nodded. He stepped up to the mic and told the same story he told Malone and Curtis, leaving out the part about being taken into custody by the FBI.

A reporter from *World Tennis* asked, "Did you ever get your trophy?"

"Not yet."

Somebody else shouted, "What about your check?"

Jake smiled and said, "Not so far, but I'm sure the U.S. Open is good for it."

Michaela Malone walked up to the mic and stood in front of Jake. "That's all for now. We'll have an update in a day or two."

She led him off the stage as everyone in the audience slowly headed for the exit.

"You were good out there. Very believable."

Jake said, "What happens now?"

"You're free to go."

"Really? That's it?"

"Yes, that's it. And congratulations on your amazing comeback."

"Oh...thanks."

She grinned. "And also on winning the U.S. Open."

68

Jake walked out of One Police Plaza to find a few reporters waiting for him.

"Why did Riemer attack you?"

"Should he be banned from the tour?"

"Why does he hate you so much?"

"What's next for you?"

Jake raised both arms. "Okay, okay. I'll give you a couple of minutes. I don't know about you guys, but I've had a very long day and I really need to get some rest."

"About Riemer. I truly think he's ill and needs psychiatric help. And I really hope he gets it. He's a very gifted player and still young. I don't know why he hates me other than we're both from New York and our paths crossed a lot. I'm a little older than him and was always a level ahead. Maybe he wanted me to be a mentor but I had my own issues back then. To tell you the truth, I was sort of a jerk myself and I probably didn't treat him right. I imagine he felt rejected by someone he looked up to, so whatever respect or admiration he had for me turned to hate and resentment.

"About what's next for me, I'm thinking of taking some time

away from the tour. Winning the Open was my life's dream. Now that I've accomplished that..." He shrugged. "I don't know." He started walking down the block. The reporters followed.

"What does that mean?"

"Will you play next year?"

"Are you quitting tennis?"

Jake turned to them. "That's all I have for now. I truthfully don't have any idea about what my future plans will be. After I've digested everything and figure out what's next, you guys will be the first to know."

This time, when he walked away, no one followed. He sat down on a bench across the street, trying to process everything that had happened. He was U.S. Open champion. Goldbarr was dead. The FBI knew he was the Lone Ranger but it didn't seem to matter. He should be feeling great, but all he felt was empty. A familiar voice startled him.

"Jake, Jake."

Natasha Ferris jogged towards him.

"Jake, we have to talk. It's important."

"Uh, hi Natasha."

"I heard what you said about maybe leaving the tour."

"I don't think I said that. I said I wanted to take some time off."

"You can't do that. You just won the Open. This is the most crucial time in the history of Sustennis. We're developing our entire new marketing campaign around you. If it's successful, it could put us up there with the giants, like Nike, Fila, Lacoste. If you leave the tour, our brand will be forever linked with a quitter. That's something we probably won't survive. If it's money, we'll rewrite your contract. We'll give you a percentage of the profits. Anything you want."

"I'm so tired I can hardly think. I promise I'll talk to you soon. Right now, I'm going home and then to bed."

"You don't have a car here. How are you getting home?"

"I'll get an Uber."

She looked at her watch. "I'll tell you what, my car's in the garage across the street. Let me drive you. It'll be quicker than waiting for an Uber at this time of night and we can talk on the way."

Jake thought for a moment. "Okay. Why not?"

The garage was nestled between a high rise office building and a juvenile correctional center. It had three levels and rooftop parking. There was no attendant. You took a ticket from a vending machine on the way in and paid at a kiosk on the way out. Once you paid, the barrier arm would lift and let you through.

During the week, every one of the five hundred parking slots was filled. But late Sunday night it was empty, except for a few cars on each level.

Natasha said, "My car's on the roof. Let's take the elevator."

Jake wondered why she would go all the way up to the roof when there were tons of empty spaces as soon as you drove in.

Natasha's red BMW convertible was the only car up there and it was parked all the way in the back.

When they got to it, she said, "Stay there. I want to show you some new designs. I'm sure you'll be blown away."

Jake sighed. "Can't we do this another time?"

"Just a few more seconds."

She opened the passenger door and rummaged around inside. When she emerged from the car, a blue and green t-shirt was draped over her arm.

"It looks exactly the same as the old t-shirt. What's so different?"

"This." She lifted the shirt to reveal a gun. And it was pointed at Jake's chest.

He jumped back, threw his hands in the air.

"Whoa! What the hell are you doing?"

She glared at him. "You killed my father."

"That's crazy. I don't even know your father."

"My father was Richard Morrison."

Jake was stunned. No one knew about Morrison. Not even Goldbarr. It was the one assassination he did on his own, not as the Lone Ranger. How could she know about that? And what else did she know?

"I don't know who you really are, but I know you're not Morrison's daughter. He never had children."

"I was his love child. My mother was twenty-two. He was forty-eight. They met in L.A. He was married and living in New York. But he didn't abandon us. Every time he was on the west coast, he would come see us. And he supported us. He bought us our house, sent my mother money and made sure I got the best of everything. After I graduated from college, he gave me a job as his executive assistant. I was with him at the airport that morning. I saw you go into the plane with him."

"I read about the day Morrison's plane crashed. The guy with him wore a motorcycle helmet with a visor. No one could see his face. And, if I remember correctly, he went down with Morrison."

"They never found a second body. The man I saw that morning was your height, your build and had your voice. But I wasn't sure until I saw the scar on your neck. I saw it that night at the airport and I got a good up-close look at it when I measured you in the hotel room. It's the same scar."

Jake instinctively rubbed his scar. He remembered the day he got it. A couple of inches lower and it would have severed his carotid artery.

"I'm not the only person with a scar like that."

"My father kept a list of people who might want to do him harm and the reason why."

"I bet it was pretty long. Morrison caused a lot of pain for a lot of people. Any one of them would have a reason to kill him."

"Your name was near the top. He said you believed he killed your grandfather. That's why I approached you in Cincinnati. Then, when I saw the scar, I knew for sure."

If the situation wasn't so dire, Jake might be amused at the irony. With the FBI, CIA, Interpol, mob hitmen, terrorist assassins and Goldbarr's henchmen all trying to kill him, he would be done in by a sportswear manufacturer.

"So it was you who put that bomb in my bag. Now it all makes sense. I couldn't figure out how anyone could get into my room without it showing up on the video. But you didn't have to go into my room. You put the bomb in the bottom of the bag, piled all the clothes on top of it and sent it to me." He nodded in approval. "Very clever."

A car alarm went off, probably some eager young lawyer working late Sunday night to impress his boss. Natasha flinched. That split-second was all Jake needed to snatch her gun away from her.

She went pale and trembled as Jake leveled the gun at her.

Part of him wanted to pull the trigger. She killed his friend. She nearly killed him and Maggie. She should pay for what she did. But that would make him the same as Glynn and Stryker.

"Oh God, now you're gonna kill me, too."

Jake shook his head. "I'm not the monster you think I am. I did kill Morrison, but only after he admitted murdering my grandfather. You killed Eugene. He was a good man with a young family. He didn't deserve to die like that."

Tears streamed from her eyes. "It was an accident. I never meant for anything to happen to Eugene. I really liked him. I cried my eyes out when I found out he took the wrong bag. That bomb was for you."

She put her hands over her eyes. Her whole body quaked. "Get it over with."

"I'm not gonna shoot you. I can even understand how you feel. Morrison was a cruel, heartless son of a bitch, but he was good to you and you loved him. Eugene was one of my closest friends. Accident or not, you killed him and, unlike your father, he didn't deserve to die. I'd say that makes us even. But just in case." He took his phone out of his pocket. "I have you on tape admitting to planting the bomb that killed Eugene. If anything suspicious happens to me or anyone I care about, this goes to the police."

"You mean you're really not gonna kill me?"

Jake shook his head. "The only thing I'm gonna kill is our business relationship. As of this moment, I'm officially severing my marketing agreement with Sustennis. Now get the hell out of here before I change my mind."

TIEBREAKER

69

———

An Uber dropped Jake off in front of Maggie's brownstone a little after one a.m. It was the only house on the block with lights blazing. As Jake walked up the front steps, Maggie came out to greet him.

"What are you doing up?" Jake said. "I thought you'd be fast asleep."

"How could I sleep? Kelleher's in the hospital with a bullet in his gut. When I called, all they would tell me is he's in surgery. You get carted away by the FBI. I didn't know if they were going to lock you up, send you to Guantanamo or what." She ran to Jake and wrapped him in a fierce bear hug. "I'm just so happy you're here. Are you okay?"

"I'm fine. No wait. I'm better than fine. I'm free."

"I don't understand."

He told her what happened at police headquarters.

Maggie looked bewildered. "They know that you're the Lone Ranger and they're letting you go? I mean, that's great, but it doesn't make sense."

"I know. I thought it was crazy too. But I wasn't going to argue."

"No, of course not."

"But that's not all. I found out who put the bomb in my tennis bag."

"Who?"

"Natasha Ferris."

"What? The tall blonde slut? I thought she was trying to get into your pants. Why would she want you dead? Didn't she just sign you to a big sponsorship deal?"

"It's a long story."

"Give me the Reader's Digest version."

"Did I ever tell you about Richard Morrison?"

She thought for a second. "The sleazy corporate fixer? Maybe. You told me he had something to do with your grandfather, right?"

"They were bitter enemies, also first cousins. Danny was a labor lawyer, one of the best. Morrison was the ultimate corporate shark. They had plenty of legal battles. But it went deeper than that. Danny blamed Morrison for my father's death. Both my parents, actually."

"What? How?"

"That's an even longer story. The short version is that when my father graduated from law school, my grandfather was hoping that he would come work with him. Instead, Morrison recruited him into his firm and trained him to be a ruthless legal predator, just like he was. The kind of lawyer Danny hated."

"I still don't get it. How did that kill him?"

"Like Morrison, my father ruined a lot of lives. One of his victims walked into his office one day and shot him, then killed himself. My mother was eight months pregnant with me at the time. She was driving when she heard the news of my father's murder on the radio. She fainted, lost control of the car and crashed into a pole. They were able to save me, but she didn't make it. I was an orphan before I was born. Danny raised me as if I was his son, not his grandson."

"That's the most awful story I've ever heard. But how does it connect with Natasha Ferris?"

"She was Morrison's love child. He was crazy about her, saw her every chance he could. And she loved hm. She's convinced I murdered him."

"I read something about Morrison's death. I thought it was a plane crash. And from what I know about Morrison, a lot of people had a reason to kill him. Why would she think it's you?"

"Because she saw me."

Maggie's mouth gaped open. "Oh my God! How?"

"She was with Morrison at the airport that day."

"She witnessed you killing him?"

"No. She saw me get into the plane with him."

"Why didn't she tell the police at the time?"

"She didn't know it was me."

"I can't believe you killed a man in cold blood. Even an evil man like Morrison."

"It wasn't cold blood. It was justice. Morrison murdered Danny. I couldn't let him get away with it."

"How can you be sure it was him?"

"Right before Danny died, he told me Morrison killed him."

"I swore to him that I would make Morrison pay. It was the last thing I ever said to him. And when I told Morrison what Danny said, he admitted it."

"He confessed? To you? Why would he do that?"

"Morrison was a pilot. He was at the airport about to fly to Washington for some sort of meeting. I made him get into the plane with me and forced him to take off. I told him I knew he murdered Danny. At first he denied it. Then I told him what Danny said and he admitted it."

"Really?"

"Why would he admit to killing your grandfather?"

"Because he was a cruel sonuvabitch. Once we were in the air, he thought he had the upper hand. He said if I shot him, the plane would crash and we would both die. Then he taunted me. He said there was nothing I could do about it. That I was going to be arrested as soon as we landed and no district attorney would believe anything I said. And I realized he was right. So I convicted him then and there. Then I put a bullet in his heart, if he even had one."

"You don't know how to fly a plane. How did you survive?"

"I can't fly a plane, but I've jumped out of plenty of them. I put the plane on autopilot and parachuted out. It crashed in the Atlantic Ocean."

She composed herself, then said, "I see. How did Natasha Ferris know it was you?"

"You know that scar on my neck that you think is so cute? She saw it that day. Then she saw it again when she fitted me for the tennis clothes I was supposed to sponsor."

He told Maggie about the confrontation in the parking garage.

"How do you know she won't try it again?"

"I have her on my phone saying she put the bomb in my bag. That it was supposed to be me, not Eugene who was killed. I'll make some copies. One to my lawyer, one for you and one that I'll keep in my safe deposit box. She knows that if anything happens to me or anyone I care about, the tape will go to the police."

"Do you really think we're safe?"

"Yeah, I do. Goldbarr's dead, Ferris won't try anything and Riemer knows we're onto him. I think we're in the clear."

"What are you gonna do now?"

"Right now I'm gonna take a shower. Then get some sleep if I can. After that, I don't know." He shrugged.

Maggie said, "Go take your shower."

When Jake came out of the shower, Maggie was asleep in the bedroom. Still wired, he sat on the couch and checked his phone. Both his voicemail and text inboxes were full. Before he got through the first text, his eyes got heavy, he laid his head back and conked out.

70

Maggie tapped Jake lightly on the shoulder until he turned over and half opened his eyes.

"Your fans are outside calling for you."

"Wha...what?"

"For the past hour, people have been gathering. They want to see their new hero."

"What's going on?"

"Go outside and see."

He quickly threw on a t-shirt and shorts and walked out the front door.

Standing at the bottom of the stoop were about fifty people of all ages. Men, women, teenagers and grade-schoolers. Most of them wore tennis clothing. A few held signs that said 'Congratulations Jake,' 'You did it!' 'PSTA Loves Jake Marks.' As soon as they saw him, they began to cheer.

Jake waved his hands in the air.

"Thank you all so much," he shouted. "You guys are what make all this worthwhile."

A ten-year-old kid ran up the brownstone front steps

holding an oversized tennis ball. He handed Jake a Sharpie. As Jake signed the ball, others started running up.

Jake shouted, "Hold on! Someone could get hurt this way. If you all get back on the sidewalk and form a line, I'll sign whatever you want."

Still holding the Sharpie, he turned to the first kid. "Can I borrow this?"

"Yes, sir."

For the next fifteen minutes Jake autographed balls, bags, racquets and random pieces of paper. One girl asked him to sign the back of her hand. She told him she was going to have his autograph made into a tattoo.

When he was finished, he walked up the steps and waved to the crowd one more time. Maggie was waiting for him inside wearing a sardonic grin.

"How does it feel to be the new king of tennis? At least as far as Park Slope is concerned."

"I don't know. Scary, exhilarating, confusing."

"It's worse than that."

"What do you mean?"

"When I was at Phillipi's gym training for the Olympics, he brought in a couple of former gold medalists to talk to us about how your life is never the same after you win a gold medal. You get inundated with requests for interviews, appearances, appointments. Everyone from the President of the United States to the president of your hometown PTA wants to give you an award or a proclamation."

"Wow. All I ever thought about, dreamed about, was winning the Open. I never thought about what happens after."

"You better start thinking about it now, because your situation will probably be even more intense. There are plenty of American gold medalists. No American has won the U.S. Open since Andy Roddick. That's a long drought."

"Yeah, it's starting already. My voicemails and texts are maxed out."

"Well, good luck. I gotta go."

"Wait. Where are you going?"

"I'm going to see Kelleher. He's out of surgery."

"Do you want me to come with you?"

She shook her head. "I have a feeling that you're gonna be pretty busy for awhile. You better stay here and figure out how to manage your newfound fame and glory."

"Tell Kelleher I hope he's feeling better."

"Sure." She gave him a peck on the forehead and was out the door.

Jake scrolled through hundreds of messages from sports reporters, news reporters, bloggers, podcasters, well-wishers, fans and haters. *Sports Illustrated*, the *Sporting News*, *World Tennis Magazine* and all the New York newspapers wanted to interview him. ESPN, FOX Sports, the Today Show, Good Morning America, The Tonight Show and Saturday Night Live wanted to book him.

He stared at his phone like it was a live grenade. This was scarier than any tennis match or Lone Ranger assignment. He was trained for those. Right now, he felt totally overmatched.

He had never had an agent or manager. He never felt he needed them. He had Alex and his grandfather, and when they were gone he handled things himself. It would have been awkward explaining the random absences that happened when he was on a Lone Ranger assignment.

As he scanned his texts, he was getting more and more flustered. Then he came across a message from Andy Whetstone. Jake met Andy when they were on the Challenger tour together. The two young Americans bonded while playing in godforsaken places like Kigali, Rwanda; Bengaluru, India and Manama, Bahrain. Not blessed with a lot of power, Andy made up for it by being smart, tenacious, lightning quick and never giving up on a point. He always managed to wrong-foot his opponent with a variety of spins, slices, dropshots and lobs. After he quit the tour, his savvy and tenacity made him an outstanding sports agent, his clientele consisted of mostly tennis players.

Unlike other agents' messages, which bragged about their client lists, marketing and promotional connections and the huge earnings they generated for the athletes on their roster, Andy's text was short and to the point. 'Call me if you need help.'

Jake called. A half-hour later he was in Andy's office. After the obligatory congratulations and man hugs, Andy got to work, setting up radio interviews with sports talk programs, bloggers and podcasters, arranging appearances on the major morning and late night shows and scheduling meetings with writers from *Sports Illustrated, ESPN Magazine, World Tennis,* the *New York Times, New York* magazine and others.

After that was done, Andy put Jake through a mock interview. He didn't hold back. He grilled him about his fight with Riemer, his unexplained absences, his relationship with Maggie, the rumors of his mental illness and his mysterious disappearance after the finals. When Jake got defensive, Andy pressed harder.

"Do we really have to go through all this now?" Jake said, "I'm still recovering."

"You wouldn't go into a match without practice. This is the same thing. Reporters are relentless. You don't want to talk to them without being prepared. Even with all this, there are gonna be some questions that we didn't anticipate, and you'll have to wing it with those."

"We never talked about money. I never had an agent. I don't know how this works."

"Right now we're in the middle of the storm. We'll have plenty of time to deal with all that once the skies clear."

The next few days were a blur. The more interviews Jake gave, the more people came out of the woodwork asking for just a few minutes of his time. But it was never just a few minutes. And it wasn't just reporters. Charitable organizations from the Boys Club to the Sierra Club asked for his endorsement. Civic groups from the Park Slope Tennis Association to the Jewish American War Veterans wanted to make him their man of the year. There were also interview requests from the west coast, Europe and Australia, which had to be done either early in the morning or late at night because of the time difference.

When Maggie told him this would happen, he thought she was exaggerating. But it was even worse than she said. He called her to tell her how right she was and also that he'd be staying in the city for a few days because his schedule started at six a.m. and ended after midnight.

The media marathon lasted a couple of weeks, almost as long as a grand slam, except there were no days off in between. When Jake finally trudged up the steps of Maggie's brownstone, he was mentally fatigued and emotionally spent.

Maggie greeted him with a hug. "Are you okay?"

"I'm alright. A little tired. Andy said most of the craziness is over until the Australian Open. Melbourne is really cool. You'll love it."

She gazed at Jake with sad, soulful eyes. "We need to talk."

"Sure. About what?"

"Us."

"Oh?"

"I've been doing a lot of thinking while you were gone. Remember that first day at the Vanderbilt Tennis Club. That girl was wearing a t-shirt. The front said, 'Never love a tennis player' and on the back was, 'Cause in tennis love means nothing.'"

"That's just a joke."

"I know. But there's a saying, 'Many a truth is said in jest.' I think it works for this."

"What are you saying? That you don't love me?"

"I do love you. And I believe that you love me."

"So what's the problem?"

"The problem is you love tennis more."

"You're wrong. I'll give up tennis right now if that's what it takes for us to be together."

Maggie shook her head. "You're a tennis player. It's in your blood. You've been doing it since you were four years old. If you stopped playing tennis, you wouldn't be the same person I fell in love with."

"What happens now?"

"I'm not sure. We'll always be in each other's lives. It's just that my life is here, coaching gymnastics, teaching phys ed, hanging out with the other teachers. Yours is all over the world. When you first asked me to come with you to England, it sounded unbelievably exciting compared to my boring life. Now I realize I like my boring life. The excitement in London almost got us both killed."

"That's not fair. That was Goldbarr, Stryker and Glynn. They're all dead. And so is the Long Ranger."

"Yes, but what about Riemer and that crazy Ferris woman. They both tried to kill you and they're still around."

"I took care of that. Neither one of them is a threat anymore."

"Even if that's true, you're still the first American U.S. Open champion since forever. It's what you always dreamed of and that's great. But it's your dream, not mine."

"So this is it? We're breaking up?"

"That sounds so final. Let's just say we're taking a break."

"Okay, let's say that." Jake kissed Maggie on the forehead, then walked slowly out the door. He didn't turn around. If he did he would have seen Maggie standing on the top stoop with tears streaming down her cheeks.

He walked down the block to Prospect Park, sat on a bench and watched some kids kick a soccer ball. He looked up to see a tall guy walking toward him, clean shaven, short hair, late twenties or early thirties. He wore khakis and an untucked, button-down blue shirt. He flashed an FBI badge.

"Jake Marks?"

"I thought I was done with you guys."

"Please come with me."

He stood and walked resolutely with the agent to a black Ford Expedition. The agent opened the back door and motioned for him to get in. Cassandra Curtis was sitting in the back seat.

"Hello Mr. Marks. How have you been?"

"I'm okay," he said warily. "I gotta say, I'm surprised to see you. You told me that as far as the FBI was concerned, the Long Ranger is dead."

"I'm not here about the Lone Ranger. This is about Jake Marks."

"Oh?"

Jake thought maybe Natasha Ferris told the FBI about Richard Morrison. But the FBI didn't investigate murders, that would be the NYPD.

"My superiors think that someone with your unique skill set might be of value to the bureau from time to time."

"You want me to work for the FBI?"

"No. We'd just like you to be on call for those occasions when we might need to utilize your special abilities on an ad hoc basis."

"And if I say no?"

"The Lone Ranger file is inactive. It isn't closed."

"I understand. Okay Agent Curtis, I guess I'll be seeing you."

"Yes, I believe you will."

www.ingramcontent.com/pod-product-compliance
Lightning Source LLC
Chambersburg PA
CBHW070207310726
48976CB00001B/240

* 9 7 9 8 9 9 0 7 6 1 5 5 1 *